The Captivation

Captain Alexei had barely touched the Princess
Katya and he was hard. How the hell was any
man supposed to resist the liquid heat in
those eyes or the way her nipples hardened at
the briefest touch? He had to slake his lusts
on the nearest available woman. Svetlana
would do. For the time being. After that he
was determined to have Katya. He would
make sure that she was not to leave the
encampment - under any circumstances.

By the same author:

The Captivation
Natasha Rostova

BLACK LACE

Black Lace books contain sexual fantasies.
In real life, always practise safe sex.

This edition published in 2007 by
Black Lace
Thames Wharf Studios
Rainville Rd
London W6 9HA

Originally published 1998

Distributed in the USA by Holtzbrinck Publishers, LLC, 175 Fifth Avenue,
New York, NY 10010, USA

A catalogue record for this book is available from the British Library.

www.black-lace-books.com

ISBN 978 0 352 33234 9 [UK]
ISBN 978 0 352 34148 8 [USA]

Typeset by SetSystems Ltd, Saffron Walden, Essex
Printed and bound in the UK by CPI Bookmarque, Croydon, CR0 4TD

The paper used in this book is a natural, recyclable product made
from wood grown in sustainable forests. The manufacturing process
conforms to the regulations of the country of origin.

Chapter One

Katya Leskovna looked out of the window at the frozen Russian night, her hands embedded deeply in the pockets of her night-robe. Her black hair spilled around her shoulders, capturing and holding the dim light from the lamps and the fire. She looked at the clock on the wall as she moved closer to the flames that twisted and danced in the large, stone fireplace. She lowered herself into the comfort of a plush chair and let the heat from the fire caress her bare feet.

Pulling up her robe and nightshift, she exposed her slender legs to the heat and rested her head against the back of the chair. Her eyelids drifted closed as warmth slid up her calves and banished the chill from her bones. She was half-asleep when she heard the click of the door opening.

Katya didn't open her eyes, but her blood warmed with anticipation as footsteps came rustling towards her through the Oriental carpet. A hand, callused from a soldier's work, brushed against her forehead and through her thick hair.

With slow deliberation the hand reached down to caress her neck, resting briefly against the pulse thudding underneath her creamy skin. Long fingers slid

1

down to tug at the belt of her night-robe and then began undoing the buttons of her nightshift with a swiftness that made Katya's breathing grow shallow. Then two hands began to push aside the folds of her nightshift to expose the white mounds of her breasts. Her nipples hardened into tight peaks as a rush of cool air wafted through the room, and she gasped at the sudden sensation of warm, male lips closing around the tip of her breast.

His hands continued to work the buttons of her nightshift until it had been unbuttoned completely, and then the halves of her gown fell open to reveal her nakedness. Her pale skin glowed in the firelight; the dark curls between her legs a striking contrast to the whiteness of her limbs. The rose tips of her breasts jutted forward as if silently asking for a touch. The man's lips laved her breast with an adoration made all the sweeter by Katya's self-imposed lack of sight. He traced her other nipple with his finger, sending shafts of warmth quivering through her. Heat pressed against Katya's skin from inside, and she lifted her shoulders to slip off the heavy dressing gown.

She edged her hips forward in invitation. The man's hands obligingly moved down to caress her thighs, creating a warm friction that flowed upward to her sex. Katya parted her lips to draw in a breath, while her head remained against the back of the chair. She wanted to ask him to kiss her, but it somehow seemed as if words would break the sensual spell in which she was wrapped. Instead, she flicked her tongue out of her mouth and drew it across the sensual fullness of her lower lip; the signal was evident. Katya felt the man's hands clutch at her hips as he lifted himself up to kiss her. His mouth covered hers. Katya let out a low moan of approval as his tongue delved into the deep recesses of her mouth. His lips stroked hers slowly as his tongue caressed her warm cavern, and Katya's limbs loosened and relaxed in response to his sensual ministrations.

His hands moved back down to her knees and gently parted her legs until she felt the muscular strength of his hips insinuated between her thighs. She tightened her muscles around his hips as he continued to move his lips over hers with an aching slowness that heightened all of her senses. She wanted desperately to reach up and bury her hands in his thick, dark hair and hold him against her, but she forced herself to clutch the arms of the chair, her arousal building with her refusal to reach for him. He moved closer between her legs and Katya pushed herself towards him until her sex encountered the roughness of his trousers.

The fact that he was still clothed caused a shiver of disappointment to race through her, but that was quickly replaced by a jolt of awareness as she felt the hard ridge of his erection through his trousers. The sensation of the rough material against her bare sex was surprisingly exciting. Katya squirmed against him, rubbing her moist labia on his bulge as if he could penetrate her through the cloth. His low chuckle was part amusement, part frustration, but he didn't make a move to release his engorged flesh.

Coils of pleasure began to wind through Katya's lower body and she ground herself against him with renewed need. He gripped her hips in his strong hands, forcing their bodies together in even more intimate contact. Gasping, Katya plunged her tongue into his mouth as she writhed on the evident strength of his arousal.

Excitement expanded along every nerve, and a light sheen of sweat covered her body as her skin was heated from the flames of the fire and from the burning within. His erection grew even harder. Katya squirmed against him with the single-minded desperation of a release. Her groan of pleasure was lost in the hot depths of his mouth as her orgasm rocked through her, waves of sensation flooding her body from the sensitive nub of her clitoris.

Her body sagged against the chair, her head falling back as he continued to explore her mouth with his tongue. Sensations radiated along Katya's nerves, and her sex felt achingly empty. His hands slipped away from her. She heard the distinctive sounds of his shirt and trousers being unbuttoned, the rasping of leather as he removed his belt, the shuffling noise of him sliding material over his shoulders and hips. His shirt and trousers fell to the carpet with a whispered softness.

Awash in sensual anticipation, Katya had to force herself not to open her eyes to take in the glorious sight of his muscular physique and his strong, erect cock. Still in her haze of darkness, the reddish glow from the fire flickering behind her closed eyelids, she fumbled in front of her, silently asking him to help her. He didn't. He edged himself between her legs again, but let her hand reach out to try and find his arousal.

Her fingertips encountered the hard planes of his abdomen, and she trailed them down through the dusting of hair that arrowed to his groin. Her breathing grew ragged as she stroked her fingers through the crisp, dark hairs to find the base of his manhood. With the same kind of slow deliberation he had used on her, she curved her fingers around his shaft. His sharp intake of breath made her smile. He throbbed with blood, his skin velvety soft over the hardness, and Katya tightened her hand as she stroked him. She knew well what his cock looked like, the hard knob bulging and darkened to a deep purplish colour. She rubbed her fingers slowly over his glans, feeling the dampness of his arousal wet her fingertips. Her own sex responded with a surge of moisture and swelled in readiness for his delicious penetration.

Katya's chest heaved with excitement, and her hands trembled as she spread her legs further apart. She edged her hips forward until she had nearly pushed her bare bottom over the end of the chair cushion, and then his hands slid underneath her to hold her in place. With his fingers digging into the resilient flesh of her buttocks, he pulled her towards him as he pushed forward. His cock

4

edged between her wet labia and into the tight passage of her vagina. Katya gasped as her body stretched to accommodate his thickness, but she accepted him easily and willingly. He pulsated inside her with an intensity that resounded in Katya's psyche. She lifted her hips towards him in a movement that was both a plea and an invitation. He responded by easing out of her and thrusting forward again, increasing the pace of his rhythm until he was pounding into her with a force that made Katya moan with pleasure.

His mouth brushed against her neck and she fought again the urge to bury her hands in his clean-smelling hair. She gripped the arms of the chair as tension built in her sex. Pressure curled around her loins, making her clitoris ache for a touch to soothe the pleasurable pain. She drew in a sharp breath when his hands suddenly clutched her around the waist, hauling her off the chair in one, powerful movement. He went back on his heels, and she wrapped her legs instinctively around his hips as she sank down fully on to his erection. Her arms went around his strong shoulders and they both stopped to momentarily savour the feeling of his deep submersion in her tense channel.

Katya arched her back as her breasts brushed against his chest, and the friction of his chest hair rubbed deliciously against her taut nipples. In their sitting position, she controlled the movements of their union. She moved slowly up his shaft, adoring the sensation of sliding along his hardness, before sinking back down. His arms held her around the waist; he began to lick and nibble at the soft skin of her shoulders and neck while she rode him with an increasingly agitated rhythm. Katya kept her eyes tightly closed as she drove herself up and down on him; their chests heaved as their ragged breathing and heat merged in a perspiration that made their skin shine in the firelight.

Katya felt another orgasm begin to ripple through her and let out a strangled cry. She thrust her body down on to him almost frantically as warm rivers of sensation vibrated through her veins, accompanied by a rush of moisture between her legs that flowed down to bathe the rigid stalk of flesh on which she was riding. His cock trembled inside her on the verge of his own release and a final squeeze of Katya's inner muscles sent him over the edge. A hoarse groan emerged from his throat as his body exploded inside her, hot splashes of seed dampening the very juncture of their union. His entire body shook, sending shivers anew along Katya's nerves.

She clutched his shoulders tightly as the sensations drained from their bodies with luscious ease. After a long minute, Katya slowly pulled back and opened her eyes to gaze at him.

Nicholas looked at her with dark eyes filled with satisfaction, the strong, handsome planes of his face glistening with a fine sheen of sweat. Katya smiled and bent her head to kiss his sensual mouth lingeringly as she caressed his masculine features with her fingertips.

'I've missed you,' she murmured, her voice throaty.

'I love you.' He stroked his tongue along her lower lip as they unwillingly detached themselves from each other.

Nicholas leant against the chair, pulling Katya into the v of his legs. Her back relaxed against his muscular chest as they let the heat bathe their already-warm skin. Katya sighed with contentment, rubbing her palms over his legs, tracing his muscles with her fingers.

'How long are you staying?' she asked.

'Only until the day after tomorrow. Unfortunately.' He nuzzled her hair with his lips.

'What has been happening?' Katya asked, sensing the sudden tension that vibrated through him.

'It's not a good situation,' Nicholas murmured. 'The Bolsheviks, workers, and even the Duma are all saying the Tsar should abdicate.'

Katya shivered, reaching out to take his arms and wrap them around her body. She felt him tighten them, his forearms tucked securely underneath her breasts.

'If he abdicates the Bolsheviks are going to use it as an opportunity to increase the momentum of the revolution,' Katya said.

Nicholas had never lied to her, and he wasn't about to start now. 'Yes,' he said.

'What about Uncle Vladimir?'

'There have been threats,' Nicholas admitted.

Katya bit her lip as she stared into the leaping flames of the fireplace. Her uncle was a Tsarist minister, one of the rich princes of the Russian monarchy now the targets of angry people determined to regain land and democracy. Katya had come to stay in her uncle's country villa only three years before and had lived there during the atrocities of war and the brutal attacks of German armies throughout Russia.

Katya turned her head to look at Nicholas. 'Everyone around here is nervous,' she said. 'The servants, my cousins. Some of the French and British servants have left already. My aunt thinks that more are planning to leave.'

'What about you?' Nicholas asked.

He was one of the Tsar's army officers, a man sworn to fight against the waves of rebellious mobs threatening the monarchy. There was little that Nicholas Fedorov feared but any danger to the woman in his arms was something that alarmed him.

'Aunt Tatiana won't leave the villa,' Katya said. 'She refuses. Uncle Vladimir has left to fight on the Crimean steppe, but Tatiana insists no one will harm her because she is royalty.'

Nicholas groaned as he rubbed his jaw against her silky hair. 'She's wrong. They not only want the Tsar's abdication, but many of them want the fortunes of the royalty.'

'Do you think he will abdicate?' The thought made

7

Katya nervous. None of them knew what would happen if the Tsar abdicated the throne.

'We'll soon find out.' He bent his head to press his lips against her neck. 'I should go. I don't want anyone to find me here.'

Katya reluctantly pulled the folds of her nightshift closed as she eased her sated body away from him. She sank back on to the chair as she watched him dress, her gaze roaming over his muscular soldier's body with admiration and renewed longing.

She had met Nicholas when he attended a dinner party given by her aunt and the two of them hadn't been able to take their eyes off each other for the entire evening. He danced with her as much as protocol would allow and she had felt, even then, the sparks of awareness flaming the air between them. They had gone out to the terrace late that evening for heated kisses and caresses, but hadn't become lovers until two weeks later.

Nicholas knelt before the chair to press his lips against hers, cupping her face in his hands. 'I wish I could stay the entire night with you.'

Katya smiled at the thought of having him wrapped around her while they slept. 'I wish you could, too.'

'I'll try and see you again soon,' Nicholas said. 'I think they're going to send me to Petrograd for a couple of days because of the unrest there, but I shouldn't be gone long.'

His dark eyes were tinged with worry. 'I want you to be careful. I wish your aunt would take you somewhere safe. One of the soldiers will warn you if anything is about to happen.'

Katya wrapped her arms around his neck and hugged him hard. 'I'll be fine. You be careful, too. I've heard they're rioting in Petrograd.'

Nicholas kissed her again and picked up his greatcoat as he walked out of the room. Katya sighed when he was gone and drew her knees to her chest as she curled back into the chair.

She didn't know what they were going to do if they were forced to leave the villa.

Katya found her aunt the following morning sitting in the dining room with her two daughters. Tatiana was a tall, noble woman with delicate, symmetrical features and blonde hair that she wore swept up into a fancy knot. She had been one of the Tsarina's first maids of honour, a distinction of which she was extremely proud. Her daughters, Sofia and Ana, had inherited their mother's fragile, blonde regality. They were eating soft-boiled eggs and toast, and one of their remaining servants poured them fresh tea from the samovar.

Although Katya never ceased to be grateful to her relatives for taking her in after her father died, she had felt out of place ever since she arrived. Her dark beauty contrasted sharply with her cousins's blonde delicacy, and her free-spirited nature seemed at odds with their conservative approach to life. Katya got along very well with Ana, who was only ten, but Sofia was both older and more judgemental. And Katya always felt as if Sofia and Tatiana disapproved of her, particularly since Tatiana had made certain that Katya would bear a royal title.

Although, Katya admitted to herself, sometimes they had good reason to disapprove. She thought of Nicholas and smiled to herself as a renewed rush of longing swept over her.

'Katya, we have been talking about what we might have to do if we must leave the villa,' Tatiana said, frowning at Katya's late appearance at the breakfast table.

Katya slipped into her chair, giving the servant a grateful smile for having brought her food out already. 'Have you?'

'Those villains want our money,' Tatiana said, her voice trembling with an echo of outrage. 'Our fortune and our jewels.'

'Perhaps we could go to our home in Paris,' Ana suggested.

'They would look for us there,' Katya said.

Sofia shot Katya a withering look. 'They don't want us dead, Katya.'

'Yes, they do,' Katya replied quietly.

The three others stared at her, for she had just voiced their greatest fear.

Tatiana patted her lips with a napkin and cleared her throat. 'Katya, that is nonsense. My husband has assured me that we have nothing to fear from a group of peasants. And, as the Tsarina said, it is the aristocrats and not the masses who have been leading lives that may contribute to the downfall of the royalty.'

'The "masses" are rioting in Petrograd,' Katya pointed out, wondering if her aunt was in denial due to her age or her standing.

Sofia glared at her. 'Where are you getting this information, Katya? Not from a certain soldier?'

Katya nearly choked on her egg as she looked up at her cousin. She had been certain no one knew about her relationship with Nicholas.

A knowing smile curved Sofia's lips as she saw her barb had hit its mark. 'Where has he been lately, Katya?'

'Who?'

Sofia laughed. 'Don't act so innocent, Katya. Everyone knows you're far from it.'

Tatiana's lips thinned into a tight line as she looked at her niece. 'I will not tolerate lewd behaviour under my roof, Katya.'

Katya tried to look suitably chastised. 'I know, Aunt.'

'I think he's very handsome,' Ana put in.

Katya gave her younger cousin a quick smile of thanks.

'He is far below your social standing,' Sofia said pointedly.

'He's the only one who knows what is really going on in the country,' Katya retorted. 'He knows we're probably going to have to leave and that we have nowhere to go.'

'We will not leave until there is reason to do so,' Tatiana said with finality.

Thankfully, Tatiana did not press the issue of Nicholas Fedorov. After breakfast, Katya hurried outside so Sofia wouldn't pester her. She went past the well-manicured gardens to the stables at the far end of the grounds. The entire villa was eerie in its stillness. Katya remembered the days when it teemed with people. Uncle Vladimir was an affable, friendly man who had opened his home to friends with a wave of his arm and a broad grin. Tatiana and Vladimir had parties almost every weekend and the villa had a constant air of liveliness and energy about it.

Not anymore. Only a few servants remained, and Katya made certain that the numerous horses continued to be taken care of.

She wrapped her cloak around her, enjoying the sharp, cold air. Winter was lingering on – the sky still a threatening grey overhead in spite of the melting snow. Katya went to the stable where one of the hands helped saddle her favourite horse.

Katya adored horse riding, even though her aunt and her cousins admonished her for not riding side-saddle like a lady. But then they were always admonishing her for her bold and sometimes reckless confidence.

She tucked her skirts underneath her and swung her leg over the saddle so she could grip the horse with her thigh muscles and gallop until she felt like she was flying. She cantered over the frosty ground, guiding the horse towards the soldiers' quarters on the perimeter of the estate. Reining in the horse, she peered across the garden towards the quarters. It would have been wholly inappropriate to go there and ask for Nicholas so Katya waited patiently until his tall figure emerged from the front door and headed towards the stables.

Katya's horse snorted as if he wanted to alert Nicholas

to their presence. Nicholas looked up and changed his course, a smile of welcome lighting up his face.

'I hoped to see you today,' he said, when he approached, 'but I thought you would be busy with your aunt and cousins.'

Katya smiled and bent to kiss him, nibbling gently at his lower lip. 'They know about you.'

'Do they?' He didn't seem concerned.

Katya nodded. 'I think they also know there's nothing they can do. You're far too valuable to them.' She grinned. 'And to me.'

Nicholas glanced back at the quarters before he grasped the saddle and swung himself up behind her. He reached around her and took the reins, then pressed a kiss against the back of her neck and urged the horse on with a movement of his thighs.

His body felt strong and good so close to hers, and Katya wiggled her hips mischievously against his groin. Nicholas let out a murmur of approval that made Katya smile. She felt the growing hardness of his erection through the cloth of her skirt and his trousers; it sent a thrill through her that he was aroused so swiftly. He guided the horse towards a secluded area of the garden. Katya grasped the horse's mane to slide off, but Nicholas's hands slipped to her hips and held her in place.

Katya turned to look at him. 'What?'

'Don't move.' He grasped the thick cloth of her skirt in his hands and began to pull it up over her legs.

Katya squirmed. 'Nicholas, there's a blanket in the saddlebag.'

'I know.' He slipped his hands underneath her buttocks, gently squeezing her before continuing to pull up her skirt and petticoats.

With a start, Katya realised that he was going to take her here on the horse. Her entire body awakened with excitement at the thought, a shiver of apprehension and longing running through her body and centring on the throbbing cavern of her sex. Nicholas tugged at the drawstring of her drawers as his own breathing increased in pace. With a slow kind of impatience, he pushed her gently forward until she was leaning over the horse's neck. Then he pulled her drawers over her hips, baring her to the freezing air.

Katya drew in a sharp breath at the delicious sensation of cold air on her bare flesh. She pushed herself up further to allow him complete access to her most private areas.

'God, Katya, you're so lovely.' Nicholas's voice was hoarse as he stroked his hands over the smooth globes of her bottom. He trailed one finger along the shadowy cleft between her buttocks, causing Katya's heart to pulse wildly in her chest.

She gripped the horse's mane as her body began to tremble. Nicholas's finger slid down slowly, tracing the puckered ring of her anus before moving into her labia. He let out a husky laugh of pleasure when he encountered her hot dampness.

'I see why you enjoy horse riding like a man,' he murmured.

Katya squirmed against him, silently asking for the penetration of his finger. Her sex throbbed with need, creating a wash of sensations down through her legs. A familiar tightness began to curl in the pit of her stomach, heightened by the unexpected sensation of sitting on a horse. The powerful animal shifted underneath them, then stilled at a movement of Nicholas's legs.

Katya arched her back when Nicholas slipped a finger into her. His other fingers began to swirl around her clitoris, and the burn of arousal increased the pressure in her loins. Katya sighed with voluptuous pleasure, her thighs straining with the tension of gripping the horse's flanks. Nicholas moved his finger in and out of her, stroking her inner walls with a light touch that ignited flames in her blood. Her eyelids drifted closed as she succumbed to his touch.

'Nicholas,' she whispered.

The husky note of need in her voice made him stop what he was doing and reach for his belt buckle. With quick agility, he stripped off his belt and unbuttoned his trousers just enough to free his manhood from its confinement. Katya gasped when he stroked the hard, hot knob against the cleft of her buttocks, teasing her gently as he moved it down to the moist folds of her sex. With a slowness that made Katya want to grind herself against him in frustration, Nicholas rubbed the head of his erection through her labia. Then, with the same ease, he began to push himself gently into the taut channel of her vagina.

Katya moaned softly, letting her body go limp over the horse's neck. Nicholas held her in place with his strong hands gripping her hips as he eased into her until his cock was fully embedded in her warmth. He pulsed against the walls of her vagina, sending delicious heat into the veins and nerves already stimulated with need. Katya realised quickly that she was the one in a position to move, and she began to lift and lower her hips. Nicholas let out a ragged sigh as she enclosed him again and again, as the intermittent sensation of her heat and the cold air drove him slowly to an explosive release.

Katya reached behind her to try and touch him, but the awkwardness of her position made it difficult. Nicholas took her hand and wrapped it around the base of his cock as it slipped in and out of her. He felt hot and wet underneath her hand, and a shiver went through Katya at the tangible knowledge of his excitement. His entire shaft moved like hot wax in her, and she adored the delicious, contrasting sensation of freezing air against her bare flesh. She felt utterly filled, her body tightening around his cock as she squirmed wantonly against the leather saddle until flames burst inside her and shuddered along her nerves. A cry broke from her throat, and she writhed on him until the sensations ebbed. A fresh rush of heat sparked through her when she felt Nicholas expanding inside her, and then his own shout was

14

followed by warm spurts of seed that made them both groan with rapture.

Nicholas bent over her, his lips cold against the back of her neck. Katya shivered with delight as she felt the lessening of his tumescence inside her. She relished the sensation of making love with Nicholas so surreptitiously.

'Oh, Nicholas,' she sighed.

She reached back to find his hand and linked her fingers through his. They had been lovers throughout the long years of war, as Katya resisted her aunt's efforts to marry her off to one of the eligible men of royalty who frequented the social milieu. She wanted no one but Nicholas.

'Promise me something,' Nicholas murmured, his warm breath brushing her skin.

'Of course.'

'You'll marry me when the revolution is suppressed,' Nicholas said, his voice throaty with the easing of passion and the emotion of love.

Katya squeezed his fingers tightly between hers as an unexpected lump formed in her throat.

'Of course,' she whispered.

Neither one of them voiced the fear that the revolution had a good chance of succeeding.

Chapter Two

*T*he resounding clatter of horses' hooves woke Katya from a sound sleep. She sat up in bed, shaking the threads of a dream from her mind as she heard the shouts coming from outside. Grabbing her night-robe, she climbed out of bed and hurried to the window.

A group of men galloped up the road to the front drive of the house. Their powerful, muscular horses looked like demons carrying riders from hell as they careened up the pathway, their horse-flesh glistening with sweat. Several of the men held flaming torches, sparks flying behind them. The eerie glow of the fire glinted sharply against the melting snow.

An arrow of alarm pierced through Katya. She didn't hear the bedroom door open, but suddenly felt Ana's hand on her arm. She turned to look at her cousin, whose blue eyes were wide with fear.

'Katya, what is it? Is it the Bolsheviks?'

'I don't know.' Katya took off her night-robe and wrapped it around her shivering, younger cousin. 'Quickly, get into my bed. I'm going to find out what's happening.'

'No!' said Ana, horrified, and she gripped Katya's hand. 'What if – oh, God, you can't go down there.'

'If anything happens, you run out the back.'

Katya pulled her hand from Ana's and pushed her gently towards the warm bed. She ran to her closet, grabbed a cloak and, shoving her arms into the sleeves, hurried out the door.

The polished marble floor was freezing underneath her bare feet, but Katya barely felt the cold. She padded down the long hallway to the front entrance. A loud, banging noise echoed through the entire house. With a start, Katya realised that the men were pounding at the front door in an effort to break the heavy locks and bolts.

Her heart leapt into her throat, and she ducked into the shadows of the balcony overlooking the entrance. She had no idea what she would do if it was a Bolshevik mob or of how she could warn Tatiana and her cousins. If they heard the noise, perhaps they would realise what was happening and try to escape from the back of the house. Katya sent up a silent prayer for them.

She pressed her hand against her chest when the final lock splintered and broke, the noise cracking the air. Her heart pounded so hard she could hear it inside her head. Fear bit into her nerves when the door crashed open and half a dozen men stormed inside.

'Nicholas!' With a cry of relief, Katya saw him come through the door, his boots ringing against the floor as he headed for the stairs.

Startled, he looked up in surprise. Katya ran down the stairs to him, and he caught her up in his arms, holding her tight against his chest. He felt so strong and familiar that Katya almost burst into tears with relief.

'Katya, you have to leave,' Nicholas said roughly, as other soldiers rushed past to warn the other members of the household. 'They're on their way. There are rumours that the Tsar and his family have already been arrested.'

'What?' Stunned, she pulled back to look at him.

'They're going to ransack the entire villa and take whoever is here hostage,' Nicholas said, setting her back gently on the floor. He looked haggard and exhausted with dark circles under his eyes and a haunted expression. 'You have to leave now.'

'My cousins –'

'Come on. Everyone needs to leave. How many servants are left?'

'Six, I think. Maybe more.' She hurried upstairs beside him, her heart thudding – both with fear over the impending raid and with relief that Nicholas was here.

They went into Katya's bedchamber, where Ana, her face pale with anxiety was still sitting in bed. She gripped the bedcovers fearfully in her hands when she saw the tall figure, obscured by shadows, that followed her cousin into the room.

'It's all right.' Katya ran to the young girl and hugged her. 'Come, Ana, Nicholas is here to help us.'

'Ana, you're going on a journey,' Nicholas said. 'It's a bit of a secret, so you won't be able to take all of your belongings.'

'Go and take Nicholas to your room,' Katya said gently, trying to keep her voice from shaking. 'He'll help you pack your things. All right?'

Ana nodded, her thin frame trembling. Nicholas held out his hand, and Ana slipped her small fingers into his as she climbed out of bed.

Nicholas looked at Katya. 'I'll come back.'

She nodded, forcing herself to think clearly as she watched them hurry out of the room. She ran to her closet and pulled out a valise, then rummaged in the back to find her oldest sets of clothes. She hurried to pack plenty of warm travelling dresses, boots and stockings, but paused when Tatiana entered the room.

'How dare they do this?' she snapped. 'Take your jewels, Katya. They will not get the Leskov jewels.'

Katya stared at her aunt. 'Aunt Tatiana, they're too heavy. Please, we only need clothes and some money. We can't –'

'Take whatever jewels you can,' Tatiana ordered before she turned and stalked out of the room.

Katya fumbled through her chest of drawers for her more precious jewels, including an emerald necklace and several ruby and diamond broaches. She avoided the heavier jewellery, and put the velvet-covered boxes in the bottom of her valise.

'Are you all right?' Nicholas strode back into the room. 'I've helped Ana pack her clothes, but her mother is insisting that she take her jewels.'

In spite of everything, Katya smiled ruefully. 'Yes, she has a bee in her bonnet about the jewels.'

'Come here.' Nicholas crossed the room to her and pulled her into his arms. 'Katya, you're not going to be able to stay with your aunt and cousins. The Bolsheviks know that four women are here and they'll be looking for you. You'll need to split up into two groups.'

Katya nodded against the front of his uniform, wanting to sink into the warm sensation of his body. 'Ana will want to stay with her mother. I can go with Sofia.'

'Try and get to Turkey,' Nicholas murmured. 'Istanbul. You should be able to get a cargo ship to cross the Black Sea. From there, try and get passage to London.'

He pulled back to look at her and rested his palm against the side of her face.

'I can't go with you,' he said hoarsely. 'It's too risky. They're looking for Tsarist soldiers. If they discover I've deserted, we'll be caught before we even get to Kostov. I don't know if I'm going to see you again.'

'I know,' Katya whispered, pain filling her heart at the thought. A glimmer of tears shone in her dark eyes. 'What are you going to do?'

'I'm going to Petrograd to fight the revolt,' Nicholas said. 'We'll stay here and try and fend off the Bolsheviks before we leave.'

He bent his head to kiss her long and hard, a desperate kiss of farewell that sent fevered blood rushing through Katya's veins.

'I'll find you,' Nicholas said, 'If I get out of this alive. I'll search everywhere if I have to.'

'Come to Istanbul first, then London,' Katya murmured. She swallowed hard past the lump in her throat as she gazed at the strong planes of his face and memorised every detail. The thought of never seeing him again broke her heart. 'I'll be waiting for you. I love you.'

'I love you.' Nicholas pulled away from her reluctantly. A brief smile lit in his eyes as he glanced down at her attire. 'As much as I adore you when you're naked, you'll have to change for travelling.'

Katya realised that she was still wearing her cloak and nightshift. She hurried back to her closet and found a travelling dress.

'Katya, did you pack old clothes?' Nicholas asked as he pulled the clothes out of her valise. 'Don't wear anything that will give you away.'

'I packed the things I brought from Tobolsk.' Katya changed quickly into a ragged but warm blue dress she had brought from the village and a pair of woollen stockings.

When she emerged, Nicholas was stomping on her empty valise with his heavy boot so it wouldn't look so elegant. They repackaged her clothes in the now-tattered valise and latched it up.

'I feel like I'm in the middle of a nightmare,' Katya murmured.

Nicholas gripped her tightly in his arms again before they left. 'You're going to be fine. You're the strongest woman I know.' He let her go and picked up her valise. 'We have to hurry. I told one of the men to bring a motor car around to the back. It will take you to the train station, but you have to be careful. No one can know that you are royalty.'

Katya took one last look at her bedchamber before following Nicholas out of the room.

Katya and Sofia stood shivering on the desolate expanse of the station platform. The morning sun barely crept over the edge of the horizon, shedding a weak, reddish light on to the remnants of melting snow. Several soldiers had passed and looked at them suspiciously, but had so far left them alone.

'Where is the train?' Sofia tugged her fur hat further over her ears and looked impatiently at the ribbon of railroad track. 'God's blood! It's no wonder people can't get out of the country.'

Katya kept silent and let her cousin fume. They had said goodbye to Tatiana and Ana five hours ago and had managed to purchase train tickets to the next town. They were all shaken and scared. Katya felt great sympathy for Sofia, who didn't know if she would ever see her mother and sister again.

She squeezed Sofia's arm and prayed for the train to arrive soon. A soldier at the end of the platform was giving them strange glances, which didn't really surprise Katya. She had rubbed some dirt on her cloak so it would look worn, but Sofia had refused to sully herself. As a result, she looked both regal and lovely in her fur-lined cloak and hat. It was a dangerous combination, and Katya made a mental note to try again to convince Sofia of the necessity for artifice.

She didn't say anything now, however, knowing that Sofia's irritated demeanour was hiding fear and growing despair.

'Here it comes.' Katya nodded at the glorious sight of a curl of smoke rising in the distance.

She glanced nervously at the soldier, who had started towards them. Katya squeezed Sofia's arm again in silent warning and then winced at the sound of her cousin's gasp.

'Are you both travelling alone?' The soldier stopped next to them, his blue eyes piercing. A thick, black moustache snaked across his upper lip, giving him a faintly shady appearance.

'Yes,' Katya replied, her voice cool and steady. 'All of our papers are in order. This is my cousin from England.

21

She doesn't speak Russian,' she added quickly, fearing Sofia would say something that might give them away.

She took their papers out of her cloak pocket. Nicholas had shown the foresight to obtain forged papers, which he'd given to her as they got into the motor car.

The soldier unfolded the sheets of paper and scanned the writing. Katya held her breath, praying they would fool him.

The train was getting closer.

Katya held out her hand impatiently. 'I trust you realise everything is in order,' she said crisply. 'Our train is arriving.'

The soldier glanced at Sofia. 'What's your name?'

'Her name is Sofia,' Katya said, grateful that Sofia kept silent. 'As I said, she doesn't speak Russian. She's visiting from England. It says that on her papers.'

The train's whistle blasted through the cold air as the huge engine chugged up the tracks and came to a halt alongside the platform.

The soldier folded up the papers, his blue eyes still suspicious. 'Be careful,' he said. 'The country is in turmoil.'

'Thank you.' Katya took the papers from him and shoved them back into her pocket so he wouldn't see her hand trembling.

She bent to pick up her valise, nudging Sofia subtly with her elbow. Her cousin started towards the train.

'That was close,' Katya sighed, as she followed Sofia on to the train. 'I think we should find alternative transportation to Kostov. I'm worried that they'll look for us in train stations when they discover we're gone.'

They hurried to settle in the crowded train car. A rush of cigarette smoke, a cacophony of voices and the ringing of vodka bottles wafted towards them. Families and soldiers sat in the numerous seats, the women's heads covered with scarves and the men stern and bearded. Children sat on the floor, gripping wood-carved toys, their dark eyes wide and innocent. Overstuffed suitcases and valises filled every available space.

Katya and Sofia squeezed into two seats near the back; Katya sat next to the window. The train lurched forward and began rumbling along the track. An hour passed as Sofia fell into a restless sleep and Katya sat thinking about her aunt, young cousin, and lover. She hoped with everything she had in her soul that they would all be safe. And she prayed she would see them again.

Tears stung the backs of her eyes as she thought of how the very fabric of Russia was being torn apart by war and rebellion. The casualties of the strife were the very people and traditions that made the country so vibrant and beloved. And now they sought to kill each other. Please, she thought, please let this all be over with soon.

Her gaze settled on a young man who sat alone in a chair diagonal to her. Blond hair fell over his forehead, his sharp profile etched with lines of stress and fatigue. His eyes looked too old for his age; his slender frame was encased in a tattered, Bolshevik uniform covered with numerous patches and uneven stitches. Despite the raggedness of his clothing, his worn shoes were polished to a shine, every buckle and button of his uniform was in place, and his hat rested carefully on his lap.

A Bolshevik. One who wouldn't hesitate to lay siege to any royal residence in the country. One who polished his shoes and mended his own uniform.

Katya's heart ached. He should be in university, courting young women, planning for his future rather than sitting on a train that would take him to God knew what other battle.

He lifted his gaze. His green eyes met hers.

Katya gave him a tentative, sad smile. She wondered if he even knew what he was fighting for.

'What is your name?' she asked softly.

'Dimitri.'

'Where are you going?'

'Novocharkassk. A band of rebels has been forcing their way through a Bolshevik stronghold.'

'And where are you coming from?'

'Moscow.'

'You have family there?'

His jaw tightened as he looked away. 'No longer. The Tsarist pigs killed them all.'

Katya's heart constricted. 'I'm sorry,' she whispered.

'We will have revenge,' Dimitri said, his voice hardening with resolution. 'We'll kill them all if we have to, starting with the Tsar himself.'

Katya swallowed, trying to force away the lump in her throat, the painful tears stinging her eyes. 'You think that will solve everything?'

Dimitri shot her a glare, his green eyes hostile. 'Of course it will. The royalty is the cause of all problems in this country. Bolshevik ideals will drag us out of this mess and give real Russians, the ones who work in factories and fields, what they deserve.'

'But killing –'

'They killed my family,' Dimitri snapped, his hands clenching on top of his hat. 'Every last one of them. The only reason I survived was because I was at a recruitment meeting. I'll be damned if I'll let their deaths go unavenged.'

He stood, his knuckles white as he turned away from her, but not before Katya caught a glimpse of despair in his eyes. Heart aching, she followed him into the compartment between the train cars. She reached out and put her hand on his arm when he went to go into the next car to get away. The door clicked shut behind her, leaving them trapped in between the train cars, the vibrations rattling under their feet.

'Dimitri, wait. I'm sorry. I'm sorry for what happened to you and your family. No one should have to go through that.' Least of all someone like you, she thought to herself.

Anguish lit in his eyes as he stopped and glared at her. 'You know nothing about it.'

Bolshevik, she thought.

'No. No, I don't.' She couldn't even imagine what it would be like if everyone she loved and cared about was killed.

Her hand tightened on Dimitri's arm. 'I'm sorry,' she said again, aware that the words were painfully inadequate.

The muscles of his arm didn't relax under the pressure of her hand, but he didn't try and pull away from her. They looked at each other for a moment. Katya had a sudden urge to erase the haunted look from the depths of his sea-green eyes. She reached up with her other hand and rested her palm against the side of his face.

Bolshevik.

'I'm sad because you're so young,' she murmured. 'No one deserves what's happening in this country. You shouldn't be thinking about battle and war.'

'Well, I am.' His voice was hard with defiance.

Although Katya knew he would deny it, the young man's desperate loneliness glittered in his eyes. She rubbed her fingertips over his cheekbone and down to his lips, sliding the pad of her thumb along his lower lip.

Bolshevik.

She didn't take her hand away from his jaw even as he stepped forward, his body so close that she backed up against the wall of the train. Some long-extinguished fire stirred in the depths of Dimitri's eyes as he looked at her. Vibrations hummed through the metal wall and into her bones.

'You shouldn't . . .' Her voice faltered.

'No? Then what should I be thinking about?'

Without warning, he turned his head. His lips brushed against her fingers. His tongue flicked out, stroking her forefinger in an oddly tender and erotic gesture.

'What should I be thinking about?' he asked again, his breath hot against her fingertips.

25

Katya shook her head, unable to think past the idea that they were two lonely people travelling in the midst of a war-torn land. A country they both loved, a country that would never be the same again.

Bolshevik, she told herself again.

Dimitri's hands came up to rest on either side of her head, pinning her between his body and the wall. His lower body pressed against her. Heat seeped through layers of clothing, making her draw in a breath, heightening her senses and awareness of him.

She stared at a polished button on his uniform, at a mended tear in the fabric, imagining him fumbling with a needle and thread to create uneven stitches that might come apart at the slightest tug.

'Is this what I should be thinking about?' He bent his head close to her ear, his breath stirring the tendrils of her hair escaping from her chignon.

A shiver slipped down her spine and desire prickled her skin.

Man, she resolved.

Katya's eyes drifted closed as she felt Dimitri's palm come between them to rest on her abdomen. When she didn't protest, his hand slid upward to her breast, cupping it through her travelling dress. Her heart hammered as he slowly pushed his knee between her thighs, lifting her skirts at the same time, spreading her legs apart. Katya's eyes flew open as she felt his hard length pressing against her skin, surprised at the swiftness of his arousal.

A hint of a smile twitched at the corner of Dimitri's mouth. 'I'm thinking more pleasurable thoughts now,' he assured her.

Katya smiled. 'I'm glad.'

His fingers slid underneath her drawers, finding the core of her femininity: warm and fluid with heat. Katya inhaled sharply as she let herself open to his seeking penetration. His forefinger slid gently through the folds of her labia. Pleasure tightened in her belly, pleasure and the illicit thrill of intimacy with a stranger in a public place.

Dimitri's lips moved along her jawline to her cheek, his whiskers scraping against her skin. But when he moved to kiss her lips, Katya jerked her head away instinctively.

'No,' she said hoarsely, not meeting his green-eyed gaze.

He didn't question her protest; nor did he try and override it. As if to make up for her refusal, Katya put her hand on the front of his trousers, tracing her fingers along the hard length of his erection. Her forehead sank against his shoulder, and the pulse in her neck beat unceasingly against his lips. Heat rose off her skin, making her clothes feel heavy and cumbersome. Her mind spun with the sensation of his strong chest pressing against her, his hand cupping her, and she began to struggle with the buttons of his trousers. Fumbling suddenly in haste, she undid four buttons and reached into the opening to find the hot skin of his sex.

A groan vibrated from Dimitri's chest when she took him in her hand. A fleeting query raced through Katya's mind as she wondered when he had last been with a woman, but a flood of stimulation drove the thought from her mind. She wrapped her hand around the thickness of his cock, her fingertips tracing fine veins pulsing with blood.

'Oh –' Katya bit down on the rough material of Dimitri's coat when his fingers slipped further into her, manipulating her inner folds with a gentle expertise that had her melting in his arms.

Her head fell back against the metal wall of the train car. Rhythmic vibrations, the slow, steady undulating of the train wheels, shook against her back and made her entire body tremble. Dimitri rubbed and squeezed her secret folds, caressing the tight nub of her arousal with the heel of his hand. Katya moaned, clenching her inner muscles around him as he began to draw his fingers slowly back and forth.

A frenzied energy washed over them both. Katya's nipples were so hard they hurt against the pressure of her corset, but the sensation of being restrained made her feel the freedom of her bared sex all the more exquisitely. She hooked a leg around Dimitri's thigh to steady herself when the pressure mounted to intense dimensions, her hand working the length of his cock with a desire to pleasure him as much as he was pleasuring her.

Dimitri put his hand on her lower back to steady her when an explosion of rapture shuddered along her nerves, causing her to cry out. His ragged breathing increased in pace before a moan broke from his throat as he reached the peak of his own release. Katya gripped on to the front of his coat as the final waves shook them both. Her body went limp, still standing only by the support of the wall and Dimitri's weight.

His forehead pressed against hers, his warm breath like a kiss on her skin. Forever passed before they finally moved, parting with the reluctant knowledge of reality.

Katya straightened her skirts, lifting her gaze to his. The ache returned to nudge at her heart, reminding her of Dimitri's probable fate.

'Be careful,' she whispered.

Without thinking, she closed her eyes and reached up to press a kiss against his lips. Then she turned and fled back to the safety of the train car.

Sofia was still asleep when Katya returned. Alone in a crowd, Katya curled up next to the window and watched the passing scenery. She dozed off, her dreams filtering back and forth between memories of happier times at the Leskov estate and nightmarish images of their country's deterioration.

The rattle of the train jolted her out of her restless sleep. A porter shuffled through the car with a brass samovar and gave people cups of tea. The train clattered along, blurring the view into streams of cold hills and trees. The train stopped several times for refuelling, and Katya hurried out to the various station platforms to purchase *piroshki* for her and Sofia. Weariness crept into Katya's bones. Their old life at the palatial estate suddenly seemed very far away. Hours and hours passed before they finally pulled into Novocharkassk train station. It felt as if they had been travelling for weeks.

'What are we supposed to do now?' Sofia's face looked white and pinched, as if her skin hadn't been exposed to the sun – to light – for weeks.

'Let's find a place to get some food and sleep for a few hours,' Katya suggested, reaching out to squeeze her cousin's hand in reassurance. 'Then we can try and find a ride to Kostov.'

They picked up their belongings and pushed through the crowd to leave the train. Katya looked around for Dimitri, but saw no sign of the young Bolshevik.

The two cousins walked across the platform to the steps descending to waiting carriages. The horses shuffled and stamped, their breath creating puffs of white smoke in the freezing air.

Sofia and Katya looked at each other.

'We shouldn't take a carriage,' Sofia said, before Katya could voice the same thought.

Katya nodded and hurried inside to ask the ticket salesman how far it was into town. She received directions and went back out to Sofia.

'He said it wasn't far,' Katya said. 'There's a pathway through the woods we can take.'

Summoning their reserves of energy, they started walking through the woods. The carriage drivers called for them to take a carriage, but neither woman turned around.

'Are you all right?' Katya glanced at her cousin as they walked through a clearing. She had grown up in a village, and she had always enjoyed walking, exercise, and labour. Sofia, on the other hand, didn't have the same constitution.

'I'm exhausted,' Sofia said, her delicate features strained with both fatigue and shock. 'All I want right now is a hot meal and a soft bed.'

Katya glanced up at the sudden burst of noise that sliced through the silence. Male laughter resounded through the trees, sending a mild shiver down Katya's spine.

'What's that?' Sofia asked.

'I don't know. Hurry.' She gripped Sofia's hand to quicken her pace along the pathway.

'Katya, don't run!' Sofia stumbled behind her.

Another burst of laughter cut through the air, closing in on them. Katya's hand tightened on Sofia's as several men emerged into the clearing.

They wore tattered Bolshevik uniforms and cracked, worn shoes. Shadows of whiskers marred their faces, and lines of blood shot through their eyes. Several of them held half-empty bottles of vodka and rifles. Their gazes widened when they saw the two women.

Katya instinctively pulled Sofia behind her as her heart thudded with fear.

'Well, look what we found.' One of the men approached them, staggering slightly.

'Katya . . .' Sofia's voice shook.

Katya glowered at the man, drawing herself up with regality. 'Let us pass.'

'Where are you going?'

'To Novocharkassk. Let us pass.'

The man's bloodshot eyes raked over her dirty coat, then moved past her to look at Sofia. His expression suddenly gleamed with interest as he took in Sofia's refined elegance.

Katya's gut tightened with apprehension. She moved in front of Sofia to block her from the man's view.

'Who are you?' he asked.

'We're going to visit my mother in Kiev,' Katya

snapped, her dark eyes flashing with sudden anger at the interrogation. 'Let us pass.'

She eased Sofia to the side, only to discover that the other men had blocked their path. Her breathing grew shallow as fear tightened her nerves. She knew she had no choice.

In one quick movement, she yanked hard on Sofia's hand and darted towards an opening between the men. Sofia gasped, nearly slipping on the frozen mud as they ran frantically for safety.

'No!' Katya screamed in outrage when a large hand suddenly grabbed her around the waist, making her jerk to a skidding halt.

Her mind spinning out of control, she released Sofia's hand and shoved her cousin forward. 'Sofia, run!' she shouted.

Sofia ran. For all her lack of athleticism, she darted between the drunken men and ran with all her might, pausing only once to look back fearfully at Katya imprisoned by the man's grip.

'Run!' Katya yelled again.

Two of the men shouted and ran after Sofia, but alcohol had dulled their movements and they only made it halfway down the pathway before a racing Sofia was out of their line of sight.

Katya sagged in relief, even as the man's arm tightened around her and she felt his stale breath on her ear. His stench permeated the air.

She glared at him, struggling angrily against his strength. 'Let me go!'

'Not on your life, witch,' he muttered.

'She's getting help,' Katya snapped. 'They'll be here any minute!'

'Not before we're done with you.' His big hand crawled underneath her cloak to grab at her breast.

A feeling of nausea rose in Katya as she heard the laughter of the other men.

31

'Which should we do first?' one of the men asked. 'Have her or kill her?'

His words pierced her like needles, creating a renewed rush of terror and strength. She flailed at her captor with her heels, but another man grabbed her by the ankles. With a start of shock, she realised that the man holding her had a knife. Sliding the blade under her cloak, he slashed at her dress. The ripping material sounded hideous. Pain cut through Katya's entire body when the blade of his knife sunk into her flesh and the wetness of blood swelled.

Katya fought back a fresh wave of horror when she felt his grimy hand on her bare skin. She blocked out the pain and kicked furiously at the man holding her ankles. She could hear a distant sound of horses' hooves.

Katya was so engrossed in her struggle and so afraid that she didn't realise the man's hold on her had slackened. Adrenaline burst through her as she yanked her feet away and pulled herself out of the man's grip. Breathing hard, she staggered away and nearly collided with a huge, black stallion. She gasped in shock as her eyes flew up to the man in the saddle and she saw the powerful figure looming over them like an avenging angel.

He glowered down at the drunken Bolsheviks as if they were rats. He wore a grey, Cossack captain's uniform, and the men behind him all wore Cossack uniforms of varied ranks. They were each on horseback, their big, intimidating physiques having the desired effect on the drunken men.

Katya stumbled backward at the sight of them, her lips parting in surprise as she clutched her cloak around her.

The captain pointed a sabre at the man who had been holding Katya captive. 'You drunken fools,' he spat. 'You are a disgrace, you bastards.'

'This isn't your business,' the Bolshevik growled.

Katya winced when the Cossack pressed the tip of the

sabre against the man's neck. One of the other Cossacks suddenly fired a gun into the air. The sound shattered the air.

'Back off!' the captain snarled, his hard features twisting into an expression of disgust.

The Bolsheviks knew they were outnumbered, and began slowly to disperse, yelling obscenities in their drunken outrage.

Katya drew in a shaky breath, trying to collect her thoughts. Her heart continued to hammer violently against her chest as she fought the tremors wracking her body. She looked around for Sofia, but her cousin was nowhere to be seen.

The captain slid his sabre back in its sheath and glared at Katya. Then, so suddenly she didn't realise what was happening, he reached down, grabbed her around the waist, and hauled her up on to his mount.

'Sit,' he ordered, pulling one of her legs over the saddle so she sat astride the horse in front of him.

With that, he kicked the stallion's flanks and galloped out of the clearing. They rode for a good five minutes before Katya finally came to her senses. The gash on her chest throbbed, and she felt blood trickling down her breast. Taking a deep breath, she tried valiantly to ignore the pain as she turned to look at the Cossack captain.

'Wh–'

'Be quiet,' he snapped.

Katya glowered at him, but closed her mouth for the time being. This man had saved her life.

She reached down to grip the horse's mane, trying to stop shaking. The captain's arms reached around her to hold on to the reins. His muscled thighs hugged her hips. He controlled the powerful stallion with minute shifts of his legs, moving with the animal as if they were one being.

Katya had no idea where he was taking her, but soon realised they were not heading towards the town. She shivered and tucked her arms underneath her cloak.

33

As far as she knew, Cossacks were loyal to the monarchy. Their love of freedom and land meant that they should be natural allies of the Tsar and royalty. Everything they stood for was anti-Communist. She didn't have anything to fear from Cossack soldiers.

Did she?

Chapter Three

Katya lost track of how long they rode. Exhaustion crept up on her after the adrenaline from her struggle began to drain away. She had scarcely slept for at least two days and it seemed as if her entire world had been turned upside down in the blink of an eye.

And now she had no idea where this intimidating Cossack was taking her.

Shivering, she closed her eyes and let her body relax slightly against his chest. He didn't react, and she relaxed a little more. His body felt warm. She could feel the strength of his chest even through his greatcoat. Katya was so tired that she almost dozed off despite the discomfort of riding, her mind shifting hazily between reality and the safety of her thoughts.

The stallion came to a halt so quickly that Katya's eyes flew open. She stared in shock at the sight in front of her as she tried to piece together her thoughts. They had arrived at a large estate with a stately mansion sitting in the middle of the grounds. From a distance it looked like a grand manor, but, upon closer view, it was in serious disrepair. Huge, iron gates opened to let the group of cavalrymen in. The gardens were unkempt and ragged, with burned ashes from fires scattered on the lawns.

Tents and campfires dotted the grounds, and dozens of Cossack soldiers milled about. Rotting boards covered several of the manor's windows, and dried leaves dusted the driveway and the steps. Grassy slopes extended far into the distance of the vast grounds, so far that their boundaries were invisible.

As they rode through the gates, Katya noticed several women walking around the encampment. Most of the soldiers lifted a hand in respectful greeting as the group passed on the way to the manor.

Katya was shell-shocked. She barely felt the captain vault off the horse behind her, but she was acutely conscious of the sudden loss of warmth. She shivered, wrapping her arms around herself.

The captain reached up and grasped her waist to swing her to the ground. Katya's entire body was stiff from the long ride, and she curled her hand around his hard forearm to steady herself.

'Where are we?' she asked, her voice hoarse from exhaustion and nerves.

'This is the Cossack encampment for the Revolutionary Army,' he said, his dark eyes raking dispassionately over her. He wrapped his hand around her wrist to lead her up the steps into the house. His tight grip felt as if it could cut off her circulation.

'What's the Revolutionary Army?' asked Katya.

'We're allied with the Bolsheviks against the Tsar,' he said.

Katya's heart plummeted. She could never let them know she was royalty. The discovery made her feel sick and frightened.

'What in the hell were you doing out there alone?' the captain snapped.

Her gaze went to him in surprise. 'I wasn't alone. My cousin was with me.'

He frowned. 'Your cousin?'

'Yes. Sofia. Didn't she tell you I was in trouble?'

'No. We were returning from the steppe when we heard you.'

Katya stared at him. Her legs suddenly felt weak. 'Then you don't know where she is?'

He released her arm as they stepped through the carved, ornate doors. 'No. I don't.'

Tears sprang into Katya's eyes, but she blinked them away. If she couldn't find Sofia then she was on her own. Completely.

She took a deep breath, wincing as the movement hurt her chest. Through her haze of confusion, she looked around the house. It would have been beautiful in its heyday, but it now bore the after-effects of years of war and the start of a revolution.

A large, grand staircase led to the upper floors, but the Aubusson carpet was dirty and worn bare in places. Rock crystal chandeliers hung from the ceiling, covered in dust and cobwebs. Cold, late-winter air swept through the expansive rooms, ruffling dried leaves and dirt on the dull, marble floors. The remaining furniture was shabby and torn. Stains marred the numerous oil paintings and brocaded wallpaper. The Karelian birchwood panelling of the drawing room bore scars and dents, apparently from battles. Candles and portable lanterns lit the rooms, and Katya suspected that the electricity had been turned off long ago. What was once an estate of a wealthy nobility was now a haven for renegade soldiers and other dissidents of the monarchy.

Katya was too tired to feel any anger over what was happening to their beloved Russia. She only wanted to stay alive.

'Why did you bring me here?' she asked wearily.

The Cossack crossed his arms over his broad chest as he looked at her. 'Who are you?'

'Katya Petrovna,' she said, using the last name Nicholas had put on her forged papers. 'I'm originally from Tobolsk, but I was travelling to Kiev to visit my mother.'

'With your cousin?'

'Yes.' The thought of Sofia brought fresh tears to Katya's eyes. She swiped at them impatiently. 'Now I don't know where she is.'

He was silent for a minute. 'Come with me.'

He turned and headed up the stairs. Katya looked after him for a minute before she realised she had no choice. She followed him up the stairs.

His boots rang against the dingy marble as he strode through a long, barren hallway to a pair of oak doors. He pushed the doors open to reveal a neglected bedchamber housing shabby chairs with pockets of stuffing, a rug rolled against the wall, scarred tables, and a torn, ragged bed canopy.

Katya stopped in the doorway uncertainly. The captain gestured towards the bed.

'You can sleep there for the night,' he said.

'Who are you?' A rush of confused anger tightened her words.

He barely glanced at her as he began tossing some wood into the fireplace. The logs cracked and splintered. 'Captain Alexei Rostovich.'

'I don't want to stay here, Captian Rostovich.'

'I don't care what you want.' He grabbed a box of matches from the mantle and struck one of them before tossing it into the fireplace. 'You're in Don Cossack territory. This is where all of the Tsarist armies will come in the hope that the Cossacks are allies.'

'Why aren't you?'

'Some are,' Alexei said. He picked up an iron poker and stabbed at the fire until the flames caught. 'The Revolutionary Army isn't.'

Katya leant her shoulder heavily against the doorway as she looked at him. The increasing flames threw shadows into the room, sculpting his tall frame in an almost diabolical glow. His features were hard and unforgiving, his black hair shredded into luminous strands. Black eyebrows arched over a pair of dark eyes that seemed to hold a million, fathomless secrets.

'Take off your cloak,' Alexei said. 'The room will be warm soon.'

Katya remembered her wound, and she clutched her cloak more securely around her. 'I'd prefer to keep it on.'

He frowned at her reluctance. 'I'm not about to pick up where those men left off, if that's what you're worried about.'

Katya glared at him. 'That wasn't what I meant to imply.'

A faint smile curved his lips. 'Then take off your cloak.'

His words held just the hint of a challenge. Katya was never one to back away from a challenge.

Her gaze fastened on his. She reached up to unclasp the cloak and let it fall over her shoulders. Cold air hit the bared skin of her chest, exposing the gentle swell of her breast where the Bolshevik's knife had ripped through the fabric.

The captain's gaze slipped down to her chest, but fixed on the raw cut slashing through Katya's white skin in a diagonal from her collarbone almost to her armpit. Blood had dried on her skin and stained the material of her dress.

Anger darkened Alexei's expression. 'Why in the hell didn't you tell me you were hurt?'

'You didn't exactly give me an opportunity.' Katya felt the pain of the wound with a sudden, renewed force.

'You foolish woman.' He stalked across the room and grabbed her arm, hauling her towards the bed. 'Get into bed.'

'Don't touch me!' Katya yanked her arm away from him.

She was intensely relieved when he released her arm and strode out of the room, shutting the doors behind him.

Katya retrieved her cloak from the floor and hurried to the bed. All she wanted to do now was sleep this nightmare off. In the morning, she would leave this dilapidated place and try to find Sofia. She climbed underneath the tattered blankets and put her cloak over them to provide more warmth.

Her head jerked up at the sound of the doors opening again. The captain walked back into the room, holding a bowl of steaming water and a cloth.

'Sit up,' he ordered. 'If you don't clean your wound, it might get infected.'

Katya reached out to take the bowl. 'I can do it, thank you.'

'Don't be foolish.' He sat down on the side of the bed. 'Rest assured that I can resist your feminine charms. I've seen plenty of others.'

Katya flushed. 'Not like mine,' she shot back before she could stop herself.

Alexei stared at her for a minute before he threw back his head and laughed. He had a nice laugh, warm and rich, and it sent a rush of pleasure through Katya.

'I'll take your word for that,' Alexei said, still grinning as he dipped the cloth into the bowl.

He reached out to tug the blankets down. He pulled apart the slashed halves of her dress, and his mouth tightened as he examined the wound.

'It's not deep,' he said. 'It could have been much worse.'

With a surprisingly gentle touch, he washed the wound and cleaned the dried blood with the cloth. Katya caught her breath when his warm fingers brushed against her bare skin. The motion was impersonal and accidental, but her spine tingled with awareness.

The captain reached into his pocket and pulled out a thick piece of gauze, a tube of medication and some tape. Katya tried not to feel anything when he began stroking medication into the cut, but it was impossible. It was impossible not to feel the heat of his touch, to be aware of the rhythm of his breathing and the slight crease of concentration between his eyebrows.

When his wrist brushed the curve of her breast,

Katya's nipple tightened in response, budding up against him. Alexei's hand froze as his dark gaze lifted to hers.

Katya was grateful for the dim light as she felt her face flush again. She had no explanation or excuse for her instinctive reaction to him and she didn't want him to know that she was embarrassed. She met his gaze steadily while her blood warmed.

The captain didn't say a word. In a movement so quick Katya almost missed it, he pressed his fingertips against her hard peak before his hand dropped away. Then he was again impersonal and clinical as he ripped off a piece of gauze and taped it against the cut.

'You should change it tomorrow,' he said.

Katya nodded, her chest tight with a mixture of desire and confusion. She was more disturbed by the brief intimacy than she would ever let him see.

Alexei gathered up the bowl and cloth and strode to the door. He didn't turn to look at her again. The door closed with the hard ring of finality.

Alexei had to force himself not to slam the door. He stood in the hallway, furious with himself for being even the slightest bit aroused. As it was, 'slightest bit' didn't qualify at the moment. His cock was half-hard already, and he'd barely touched her. Barely touched her, he thought. But how in the hell was any man supposed to resist the liquid heat in those dark eyes of hers, or the smoothness of her pale skin, or the way her nipple had hardened at the briefest touch?

He did not like the feeling of lacking control.

With a scowl of irritation etched on his features, Alexei nearly threw the bowl on to a table before he stalked up the stairs to the next floor. He pushed open the double doors of another bedchamber, feeling his blood start to flare with the firestorm that had been kindled only fleetingly in the downstairs chamber.

The pretty, blonde woman sitting by the fireplace

looked up sharply when she heard his abrupt entrance, but her body relaxed when she saw him.

'Alexei, I –'

'Come here.' He crossed the room to her, clutching her shoulders as he lifted her out of the chair.

Svetlana's soft gasp was lost in the pressure of his mouth. Unprepared for the sudden onslaught, she grasped his shoulders to regain her balance. Alexei reached down to grip her soft buttocks through the material of her night-robe, pulling her against him.

His sex hardened further in response to her softness and began to strain against the front of his trousers. He gripped the material of her gown in his fists and slowly drew it up her legs until the fleshy globes of her bottom were bared to his touch. He dug his fingers into her skin as he ground his pelvis against her, his need suddenly intense with urgency. Slipping his fingers into the cleft of her bottom, he felt her shiver against him. Her head fell back to allow him deeper access to the recesses of her mouth. Alexei responded by driving his tongue past her lips with a force that made her gasp.

She pulled away from him slightly, her cheeks flushed and her eyes stunned as she saw the raw hunger etched on his face. 'Alexei, what's come over you?'

'Kiss me back,' he growled, bending his head to bite at the yielding skin of her neck.

Svetlana sucked in a breath of pleasure as his mouth sparked a glow inside her. Her eyes brightened with growing excitement. Still, her response was restrained when he plundered her mouth again. She let him kiss her, but her lips moved against his almost cautiously, as if she were afraid of what she was feeling.

It was not the kind of response Alexei usually experienced with women, but his blood burned and his cock began to pulse with the need for release. He slid his finger between Svetlana's buttocks, pausing at the puckered opening of her anus. Tracing his finger around it, he heard her catch her breath.

'Oh!' exclaimed Svetlana as her face flamed with embarrassment. Her entire body went limp against him as he probed her dark cavern with his finger. 'Oh, Alexei.'

Alexei's jaw clenched as the taut ring of muscles enclosed his digit, and a rush of moisture from Svetlana's sex dampened the tips of his other fingers. His arm gripped her around the waist, holding her against him, and he pressed his knee between her thighs. Slowly, he edged his finger back and forth in her aperture, eliciting low moans from Svetlana's throat. He slid his other fingers into the wetness of her sex and stroked the soft folds of her labia, coaxing passion out of her.

Her arms snaked around his neck, silently urging the delicious invasion of her secret depths. Alexei smiled grimly when Svetlana murmured a protest as he removed his finger from the snug channel. He gripped her waist, pushing her down on to his thigh. The warmth of her sex fairly burned through the cloth of his trousers as she straddled him. Alexei pulled up her gown until her bared vulva pressed against him. His fingers dug into her hips.

'Move,' he hissed.

Svetlana's eyelids flew open in shock. 'Alexei –'

'Move,' he said again, this time with greater demand in his tone.

She hesitated, but then began to move. With tentative twists of her hips, she rubbed her sex against his thigh.

The sensation of her hotness seeping through the material sent another shaft of urgency twining through Alexei's nerves, and his prick bulged against the front of his trousers. Svetlana's gyrations began to increase in pace, and her head fell back, exposing the tanned column of her throat. With an impatient movement, Alexei untied her robe and pushed it off her shoulders, then grasped the cotton of her nightshift and wrenched it away.

The sight of her plump nakedness sent a rush of blood

straight to his groin. Her large breasts dangled enticingly in front of him, swaying with the movement of her body, their nipples hardened to tight peaks. Svetlana closed her eyes, her excitement mounting and her chest heaving as she continued to writhe against his hard thigh.

Whimpers began to spill from her throat, escalating in intensity as her hips pumped up and down. Alexei watched her until he knew she was nearing the explosion of pleasure and then pulled his thigh out from between her legs so quickly that Svetlana almost fell. His grip around her waist prevented her from stumbling, but her eyes were glazed with need as she looked up at him.

'Please,' she whispered, every one of her sensibilities telling her that such wanton behaviour was indecent.

Her acknowledgement of need inflamed him. Alexei bent his head to grind his mouth against hers again. He slid his hands down to her thighs and gripped her flesh as he picked her up. Svetlana's legs wrapped around him almost hesitantly and she gasped as she felt the hardness of his erection. In three, long strides, Alexei crossed the room to the window. He put Svetlana on the window ledge. She squirmed at the sensation of the cold wood against her bare bottom.

'Alexei, shouldn't we –' Her blue eyes swept past him to the bed.

Alexei ignored her as he slid his hands underneath her thighs, spreading her legs apart and exposing her moist, open labia. With his forefinger, he slowly traced the damp folds. Svetlana opened her mouth and shivered, her eyelids finally drifting closed as she leant her head against the window and succumbed to pleasure.

Alexei pushed his finger into her tight passage. His cock leapt in response to the wet, enclosed softness capturing his finger, and he reached down with his other hand to undo the buttons of his trousers. He was rock hard and aching. His freed cock pulsed with blood and heat and he grasped the base in his hand to guide it to her vagina. Svetlana wiggled her hips towards him, but didn't move beyond that as he slipped inside her.

He plunged into her with one thrust. His body was acutely aware of the gripping sensation of her tightness as she sheathed his cock, but his mind felt somehow distant as he began to drive into her. He looked down at her face: her eyes were closed and her lips half-parted as he withdrew and pushed into her. They had been lovers countless times before, but Alexei knew that Svetlana was constantly battling her conscience when it came to feeling her own pleasure.

He drove into her, gyrating his hips, plunging into her with heavy, intense thrusts. Sliding his hands underneath her thighs, he pushed her legs even further apart to enter her to the hilt. He reached down and pressed his fingers against the swollen nub blossoming forth from beneath its protective hood. Svetlana gasped, her body tightening with tension as he rubbed her sensitive flesh.

'Come,' Alexei murmured, his breathing ragged as he watched her hover on the edge. 'Spend all over my hand.'

Svetlana's entire body quivered as he continued to thrust into her and manipulate the core of her sex. He bent his head to capture one of her protruding nipples between his teeth, tugging at it with a force that drove Svetlana over the edge.

A squeal broke involuntarily from her throat. She reached up to cling on to his shoulders as her body shook and shuddered. Alexei withdrew his fingers from her sex and rubbed them over her other nipple until it shone with her moisture. Amused at her surprised gasp, he lowered his head to her dampened nipple and rolled his tongue around it, sucking off the unique taste of her secretions.

The taste of her jolted through him. He plunged his cock into her again with renewed vigour, thrusting until his body exploded with pleasure. As his climax shuddered through him, he gritted his teeth, refusing to yield completely to the sensations, retaining control.

'Oh, Alexei.' Svetlana lifted her face to him.

Alexei lowered his head to kiss her, but he was already pulling away and hitching up his trousers.

'What if someone saw us?' Svetlana asked. She looked nervously out the window at the lanterns and fires dotting the camp through the darkness. She closed her legs, her face flushing anew at the memory of her response.

'Then they must have enjoyed themselves.'

'When did you return?' Svetlana slid off of the ledge on to trembling legs. She moved quickly away from the window as her cautious gaze went to the inscrutable man in front of her.

'A couple of hours ago.' Alexei finished buttoning his trousers and reached out to brush his hand through her blonde hair. 'I have work to do. I'll see you later.'

Svetlana watched him leave. Her love for him knew no bounds, but she knew quite well that he was always holding something back from her. From everyone.

It was in his blood, she thought. The craving for freedom ran deep in a Cossack man's blood, and Alexei's self-control meant that his mind and his soul would always be fiercely independent.

She frowned. She was beginning to dislike that fact. Although that didn't mean she couldn't try and change it. Suddenly conscious of her nakedness, she hurried to retrieve her nightshift from the floor where Alexei had tossed it.

Alexei strode down the hallway, his lust sated and his mind on the news from Moscow that Tsarist armies were nearing Cossack territory. They would find allies in Don Cossack lands, but not in the Revolutionary Army. Not in him.

He went downstairs and into the drawing room, which had been converted into a workroom. Low, wooden tables were covered with maps and battle plans, and several soldiers sat examining them from the flickering light of candles and lanterns. Crumpled papers and journals were scattered over the floor, along with cigarette butts, bottles of vodka, and pencil stubs.

One of the young soldiers, Ivan, looked at Alexei when he walked into the room.

'Sir, one of our regiments has been fighting down near Kiev,' Ivan said. 'They might have some prisoners.'

'Send word that they should be taken to the camp in Novgorod,' Alexei replied.

He sat down in front of one of the maps, his forehead creasing with irritation. He hadn't liked having to threaten Bolsheviks, with whom they were supposed to be allied, and he detested the thought that some of their men weren't even bothering to fight. Just as he detested the thought that most of the Cossacks weren't willing to take up arms against the monarchy.

'Ivan,' he said sharply.

The young man glanced up. 'Sir?'

'Send two men back to Novocharkassk and tell them to look for a woman named Sofia Petrovna.' Alexei reached into his pocket and pulled out the papers he had taken from Katya. 'Here are her papers. See if you can find her.'

'Yes, sir,' said Ivan, as he took the papers. 'We've already retrieved Katya Petrovna's valise.'

Eager to gain the captain's approval, he hurried out to the entry hallway and returned with Katya's tattered valise in his hand.

Alexei looked at the valise. The sight of it brought back an image of Katya's furious, fearful expression as the drunken men mauled her and tore at her clothes. His hand clenched into a fist.

'Bring it here,' he ordered.

Ivan brought him the valise and put it on the table. Alexei hesitated only briefly before he unlatched it and began to rummage through the contents. His hands sank

47

through layers of rough, cloth skirts, dresses and softer cotton blouses. He frowned slightly when he discovered some lace and silk petticoats, feeling a rush of blood to his groin as he thought of how Katya would look in them.

Ruthlessly shoving away the thought, he continued through the contents until his hand hit a velvet-covered box. He pushed aside the other clothes and removed the box from the bottom of the valise.

'What's that?' Ivan reached out to touch the soft velvet.

A sickening feeling of disgust began to coil in Alexei's gut. He flicked open the gold latch to reveal a shimmering necklace of diamonds and emeralds. The jewels glistened in the dim light, glowing from their very core as the light sank into them.

Ivan's eyes widened in awe. 'Good Lord,' he breathed.

Alexei jabbed a finger at the bottom of the necklace, where a gold plaque bore the unmistakable symbol of a royal coat-of-arms. Embedded in the small sheet of precious metal was a lion encircled by two intertwined snakes. 'Find out which family this belongs to.'

'Are there more?' Ivan said and glanced towards the valise again.

Alexei snapped the box closed and shoved it back into the valise. 'Send out word that Katya Petrovna is not to leave the premises. Under any circumstances.'

Chapter Four

Katya awoke with the sensation of having had an extremely vivid, intense dream. One look at the bedraggled canopy of the bed told her it had been anything but a dream.

She groaned softly and rolled over to bury her face in the pillow. Not only was she in Cossack territory, but she was also in a Cossack camp. An anti-monarchist, Cossack camp.

'You must be wanting a bath, dear.'

Katya lifted her head at the sound of another woman's voice. She looked uncomprehendingly at the robust, older woman who was pulling back the shabby curtains. The room had been straightened, the faded rug rolled out, and the scarred tables dusted.

'Who are you?' Katya asked.

'My name is Eliza,' said the woman. 'I heard you arrived last night.'

'I didn't exactly arrive,' Katya muttered. 'I was brought here.'

'Yes, well, we could use your help,' Eliza replied.

Katya looked at her suspiciously. 'Is that why he brought me here?'

Eliza pulled open another curtain, sending a billowing

cloud of dust through the room. 'The captain does what he can. A couple of the servants are bringing some water up for you.'

'Servants?' asked Katya. She was so confused she no longer knew what to think. 'What, exactly, is this place?'

'It used to belong to Alexei's parents,' Eliza explained. 'Then, when the Tsar started to appropriate Cossack territory, they rebelled against him in order to keep their land. A battle nearly tore the place apart, but they managed to hold on to it. When they died, Alexei took over. He turned the estate into the headquarters for the Revolutionary Army when the war started. It's been that ever since.'

'So, the entire army lives here?'

'Not really. Most of the regiments are out fighting. All of the servants stayed on, mostly for lack of anywhere else to go. We still try and keep things running, although we're so busy with the soldiers that housekeeping has gone by the wayside.' She chuckled and picked up Katya's valise, which was near the door. 'Come with me. I'll show you where you can have your bath.'

Katya realised that she felt intensely grimy after the nightmarish events of yesterday. She climbed out of bed, pulling her cloak around her shoulders to ward off the cold. She followed Eliza out of the room and down the hallway to the bathchamber, almost groaning with relief at the sight of a marble bathtub filled with steaming water.

'Come down to the kitchens when you're done,' Eliza said. 'I'll get you something to eat.'

Katya smiled and thanked the older woman for her kindness. She felt as if it had been ages since someone was kind to her.

Eliza left Katya alone and closed the door behind her. After locking the door, Katya stripped off her clothes. She sank into the bathtub with a sigh of relief as swirls of steam rose around her and the hot water covered her like a lover. She carefully removed the bandage covering

50

her cut, remembering again the way her body had reacted to one touch of the captain's fingers. She shivered suddenly, in spite of the near-scalding water, probing carefully at her wound. It no longer hurt and appeared to have started healing a little.

Katya leant her head against the marble and closed her eyes, letting the water relax her limbs and the steam clear her thoughts. She would simply have to go to the captain and tell him she had no intention of staying there. And then she would return to Novocharkassk and try to find Sofia, or go directly to Kiev in the hope that Sofia had somehow managed to arrive there.

Her eyes flew open at the sudden click of the lock. The door burst open to reveal the powerful figure of the Cossack captain.

Katya gasped as her hands moved to cover her nakedness. 'What are you doing here? Get out!'

He slammed the door and strode into the room, his expression as dark as midnight, his black hair falling over his forehead. 'The monarchy has been deposed, Princess Leskovna. We no longer take orders from you.'

Katya stared at him in shock as his words sunk into her. He knew. She was so stunned she didn't know how to react. 'W-what are you talking about?' she stammered.

He tossed something towards her. The object fell into the water with a splash. Katya forgot her attempt to conceal her nudity from his prying gaze and picked it up. It was her ruby and gold ring. 'You went through my valise,' she accused.

'Damn right I did.' He walked to the tub until he was towering over her, his hands planted on his hips. 'Rest assured, Princess, that you are not going to leave the premises until I figure out what to do with you.'

'You can't keep me here against my will!'

'Indeed I can,' Alexei replied. 'You can consider yourself a prisoner of the Revolutionary Army.'

Katya swallowed hard as a spark of fear twisted

through her gut. This was exactly what they had all dreaded.

She glared at Alexei. 'What do you have to gain by keeping me here?'

'Much more than I have to lose, evidently.' He made his meaning obvious by letting his gaze travel slowly down her naked figure submerged underneath the steaming water.

Part of Katya felt intensely vulnerable and wanted to shield herself from his hot gaze. Another part of her defied his insinuation. He might have the power to keep her here, but that didn't mean she would cower before him. She met his gaze challengingly as she lifted her arms and rested them along the sides of the tub, leaving her nakedness revealed.

If he was surprised by her actions, he didn't show it. A hint of a smile touched his mouth as he sat down on the edge of the tub.

'Well,' he murmured, 'it appears as if royalty does not go hand in hand with prudishness.'

'Or dread,' Katya shot back. 'If you expect me to be afraid of you, then you're going to be disappointed.'

'Oh, I don't anticipate being disappointed,' Alexei replied softly. He reached out and took the ring from her.

'You want me to be your whore, is that it?'

Alexei turned the ring around in his fingers, as if he were examining its quality. 'No. I don't think whores usually enjoy what they do. I have a feeling you are quite different.'

He sunk his hand into the water, brushing his fingers gently over the swell of her breast before finding the soft peak of her nipple. With a touch that sent a shudder of pleasure through her, he pulled and tugged at her nipple until it budded into a tight knot. He took the ring and hung it on her hard nipple, pressing the gold circle lightly against her as if he wanted to draw attention to her arousal, then moved to her other breast. He rubbed

52

the pad of his forefinger in concentric circles around her rosy areola until he reached the hardening peak. Katya nearly gasped when he took her nipple between his thumb and forefinger, squeezing and pulling at it so lightly that showers of delicate sparks rained down the length of her spine.

Katya didn't move as the captain's fingers trailed down between her breasts. Her nerves flared with awareness, but she refused to let him know he was affecting her. He moved his hand to her abdomen, barely touching her skin with his fingertips, and then he reached the soaked curls shielding her most private areas. His eyes still watching hers, he skimmed his fingers over her mons before slipping them between her thighs.

Katya snapped her legs together so quickly that Alexei's eyebrows lifted in surprise. She clenched her muscles, trapping his hand between her thighs and daring him to try and arouse her.

Alexei laughed softly, flashing even, white teeth. 'Princess, you don't have to do that to keep my hand there. I'm more than happy to touch you voluntarily.'

Katya was glad the steam and hot water had already flushed her skin because her body stirred like a live coal. Her eyes hardened. 'Surely you're not the kind of man who finds it arousing to take a woman against her will.'

Alexei chuckled again. 'Oh, no. But I have the distinct feeling that will not be the case with you.'

As if to prove his point, he began to run his finger slowly up and down the plump lips of her sex. The tight constriction of her thighs trapped his hand, hindering the erotic gesture, but his touch was so light and teasing that Katya felt her muscles turning to water. Alexei couldn't ease a finger into her sex since she kept herself clamped against him, but the movement of his fingertip over her outer labia was excruciatingly exciting.

She continued to hold his gaze as they challenged each other in a silent battle of wills. She wanted to look down at his trousers and gauge the extent of his arousal, but she refused to look away from the deep fathoms of his eyes. Her thigh muscles fought against the sensations he was evoking in her loins, and her self-imposed tension, combined with Alexei's relentless touch, created a spiral of agitation in her like none she had ever experienced before.

She parted her lips to draw in a breath, seeing the unmistakable gleam in the captain's eyes as he recognised her slipping control. He twisted his hand, the strength of his forearm overpowering the muscles of her thighs, as he created just enough yield to slip his forefinger into the delicate pleats of her labia.

Katya gasped at the sensation of his strong finger probing into her, and her muscles relaxed slightly to give him easier access. She struggled to clench them again, but the hot water of her bath and the sensuality of the man sitting next to her fought ruthlessly against her efforts. Much to her annoyance, her body began unwillingly to surrender to him.

Alexei stroked his finger up one of the crevices created by the folds of her labia, swirling around her swollen clitoris before stroking down the other side. Katya couldn't bring herself to let her legs loosen completely, but her muscles barely gripped his hand as his touch licked flames of heat through her entire body. Her sex betrayed her growing desire, as she knew the captain could distinctly feel the viscous fluids coating her secret flesh.

As she watched him, she was gratified to note that he was not entirely immune to the evidence of her excitement. The dark pupils of his eyes dilated, and Katya didn't doubt that there was a significant bulge in his trousers. Her body twitched when his finger slipped down further. He paused, circling his finger around her vaginal opening with a laziness that made Katya grit her teeth in frustration.

'Let it go, Princess,' Alexei taunted softly.

Her dark eyes flashed at him, even though they both

knew who had the upper hand. Alexei eased the tip of his finger into her. Katya's heart began to pulse wildly in her chest as she fought the urge to squirm against him in a plea for deeper penetration. She wanted to rest her head against the dewy marble and let her body accept the expertise of his touch, but she would not relent easily.

Alexei's thumb began to revolve around her sexual bud as he submerged his finger deeper into her. Katya's muscles slackened, and her hand clenched into a fist. With his other hand, Alexei began to pluck and pull at her achingly tight nipples. The double assault was more than she could bear, as every nerve ending seemed to centre on the conduct of heat from her nipples to her sex. Her breath caught on a gasp, and she tore her eyes away from his when the first shudders rippled through her body.

Triumph flashed in Alexei's dark eyes as Katya's entire body tightened and shook with the release of tension.

Alexei chuckled. 'No,' he murmured, 'definitely not against your will.'

Katya's face flushed a deep red. How could she react to him like that?

'Get out,' she said bitterly, even as her sex continued to throb against his fingers. 'I won't be your whore.'

To her shock, the captain bent his head to kiss her, running his tongue gently over the inside of her lower lip. Another rush of warmth spilled through her.

'No,' he agreed huskily. 'You won't be my whore. But, you will beg me to be your lover.'

She yanked her head away from him furiously. 'Never.'

Alexei laughed. He curled one hand around her wet hair, forcing her head to turn back to him. She thought he was going to kiss her again, but he captured her lower lip between his white teeth, biting down with a force that was both a warning and a punishment.

Katya gasped at the pain and tried to pull away, but

his grip on her hair was inexorable. His dark eyes bore into hers as if he were daring her to contradict him.

'Don't fight me, Katya,' he said, his voice low and inflexible. 'You will not win. And I promise you that your situation could be far worse.'

'That's why you brought me here, isn't it?' Katya snapped. 'You wanted me to be a servant and, probably, a whore for your soldiers.'

'I could never ask a princess to lower herself like that,' Alexei replied. 'Calling yourself a prisoner is far more acceptable.'

'Get out!' she cried.

He stood, but not before reaching down into the water and rubbing his finger slowly across her taut nipple. 'You can be as defiant as you like, Princess, but your body will always give you away.'

He turned and strode out of the room.

Katya let out her breath in a long, shuddering sigh when the door closed behind him. She sank down into the water until it reached her chin and let her eyelids drift closed. The Cossack captain disturbed her as no man ever had before. It terrified her to think that his words might very well be true.

The manor was always cold. The captain didn't force Katya to stay in her bedchamber, and she took advantage of the chance to roam around the estate. She discovered quickly the reasons for his leniency. The estate was filled with Cossack soldiers who had been given clear instruction that she was not to leave. The perimeter of the grounds was obstructed by a huge, wrought-iron gate, and soldiers guarded the various entrances in the event of an attack.

It was her prison. Although spring broke through the chill of winter, the vastness of the manor harboured the cold and Katya was forced to wear her cloak constantly. Eliza informed her, with a sudden severity, that she was to help out in the kitchens. Alexei had told everyone she was a prisoner, and no one appeared to find it necessary to treat her decently after that.

Not that it mattered. Katya had worked while growing up in the Siberian village of Tobolsk and she wasn't afraid of labour. And she tried to look on the bright side: the kitchens were the only part of the manor that remained warm.

She refused to succumb to the fear of what might happen to her. Thoughts of Sofia, Ana, Tatiana, and Nicholas seared her through the heart every time she surrendered to them; so she tried, valiantly, to lock the memories away and to concentrate on her own dilemma.

The kitchens were huge, lined with cooking stoves and fires. Long, scarred wooden tables held numerous pots and bowls, and bunches of herbs hung from the ceiling. Five servants spent the day cooking for the hundreds of soldiers and they put Katya to work cleaning up after themselves.

There was no running water so Katya had to pump water from the well out back to wash the pots and dishes. One day, after hauling in two buckets full, she huddled close to a stove and rolled up her sleeves as she got to work.

'Are you using hot water?' asked Sergei, one of the cooks, as he glowered down at her. A brawny, blond man, he would have been a soldier were it not for the fact that he was blind in one eye.

Katya looked up from the low stool on which she was sitting. 'No. I had to get water from the well.'

'Heat it up,' Sergei snapped. 'Wash in hot water, rinse in cold.'

Katya glared at his retreating back, but grasped one of the buckets of water and dragged it to the stove.

She heated up the water, casting the occasional glance at the various knives with which the cooks were chopping vegetables and meat. If she played her cards right, she might be able to steal one. At least then she wouldn't feel quite so defenceless.

The thought heartened her, and she resumed her task with a new enthusiasm. The piles of pots, pans, and dishes were endless. As soon as she finished one stack, another would invariably appear at her side. The soldiers seemed to be eating constantly and the sight of old food sticking to the plates made Katya feel nauseous. She plunged her hands into the hot water to start scrubbing another copper pot. The combination of work and the warmth from the stove made her perspire and she wiped a sheen of sweat from her forehead with the back of her hand.

She didn't fail to notice the somewhat hostile glances several women tossed in her direction, and she reluctantly assumed that they must somehow know about the captain's plans for her. Although there were a number of people at the camp, word would spread quickly in the close quarters.

When the water became too filthy for her to continue washing, she dragged one of the pails outside to empty and refill it. The freezing air felt blessedly cool against her heated skin. She tossed the water out near a pen holding a bunch of scraggy chickens and went to the water pump.

'Katya!'

Katya turned to find Eliza standing in the kitchen doorway.

'Bring some potatoes in from the storage shed,' Eliza ordered. 'It's down in the direction of the stables.'

Katya was glad for another task besides dishwashing. She put the pail down and started towards the storage shed.

Tents and campfires covered the immense grounds, and Katya realised that it wasn't easy to walk past men whose lives were characterised by violence and sexual hunger. She suddenly wished she had her cloak with her, as she had to endure more than one lecherous look or rude comment. Her perspiration and the steam from the hot water had caused her blouse to cling to her, outlining the curves of her breasts. The material felt clammy against her skin, and she fought the urge to cover herself, refusing to give them the satisfaction of knowing they had unnerved her.

A male body suddenly stepped into her path. Katya's head jerked up, her heart thudding with an abrupt image of the drunken Bolsheviks. He was an older man with a grizzled beard; his hair was streaked with grey, and deep grooves of age marked his face. Despite his years, he moved with the swiftness of youth, and his body looked taut and lean under his Cossack uniform.

'Let me pass,' Katya snapped.

He didn't step towards her, but his eyes fixed on her with an alarming intensity. 'You are the Tsarist, yes?'

She had never been called that before, but she supposed it was the truth. Highly conscious of the other soldiers watching them, Katya refused to back away. 'Why do you want to know?'

He looked at her as if he were willing her to understand something. 'My name is Lev,' he explained, his voice low. 'It would not be a good time for you to escape.'

Katya frowned. 'I'm aware of that.' Even if she did escape, which seemed impossible while the estate remained crawling with Cossack soldiers, she had no idea where she would go.

'However, fate always changes, does it not?' Lev asked.

Why was he talking in riddles? Katya wondered. 'Yes. I suppose it does.'

'Remember that then.'

Confused, Katya watched him turn and walk away from her. What was he trying to tell her? Could he help her escape? Did he know something she didn't?

She shook her head and continued on her way, ignoring the hungry eyes of the Cossack soldiers that seemed to burn through her clothing. She reached the storage shed with a rush of relief. She found an empty basket and filled it with potatoes before picking it up and heading back outside.

'What are you doing out here?'

Katya looked up at the sound of the captain's hard voice. He was standing a distance away from her, with his hands on his hips and his dark hair ruffled by the wind.

'Dancing the *mazurka*,' Katya replied dryly.

He didn't find her sarcasm amusing. 'You should be wearing your cloak.'

'I know. I was warm.'

Alexei's gaze travelled over her figure, lingering on the curves of her breasts displayed by the clinging material.

'I might also suggest that you don't display yourself with such wantonness,' he said coolly. 'Most of the soldiers have been without a woman for months. They would think nothing of taking one as lovely as you without hesitation.'

Katya's face flamed. She hitched the basket into her arms to cover her body. 'Thank you for the warning,' she bit out.

A faint smile touched his mouth. 'Now the thought of submitting to me doesn't seem so terrible, does it?'

'You're stronger than me,' Katya pointed out. 'We both know you can take me without my consent, so why don't you just get it over with?'

Alexei reached out and traced his finger slowly over the neckline of her blouse. His finger brushed against her skin with a light, tickling touch that reminded her of the way he had stroked her the other day.

'Because,' he said softly, 'I will have your consent. Come to my bedchamber at midnight tonight.'

Katya's heart leapt into her throat. To her shame, her body quickened with anticipation. She dropped her gaze so he wouldn't recognise the look in her eyes.

'I warn you,' Alexei said, 'I need only to say one word,

and my men will be more than delighted to share you amongst themselves.'

'If you're trying to frighten me into accepting this, then you are going to be disappointed,' Katya replied curtly, aware that she was skating on very thin ice.

Alexei chuckled. 'Then I shall expect you in my chambers, willing and without fear.'

'Why don't you stop playing games with me?' Katya snapped. 'We both know you want me to be your whore, to . . . to satisfy all your sick desires. Why not admit it?'

'Very well,' the captain replied smoothly. 'I want you to be my whore and to satisfy all my sick desires.' Cold amusement lit in his dark eyes. 'There. Does that make it easier, Princess?'

Katya stared at him as he walked away from her. Well, she thought, not exactly.

Chapter Five

*K*atya refused to knock on the captain's door as if she were requesting permission to enter. Instead, she turned the doorknob and let herself in, grateful for the rush of warm air that greeted her chilled bones.

Alexei didn't look up when she entered. He was sitting in a chair by the fire, his long legs stretched out in front of him, his expression somewhat brooding as he stared into the flames. He had taken off his captain's jerkin but still wore his white shirt and trousers.

Katya stopped, uncertainly, halfway into the room. 'Captain.'

He looked up, his dark eyes raking over her cloaked figure with the slow insolence she had come to expect from him. Even though the folds of her cloak concealed her figure, she felt as if he could somehow see through to her very core.

'Come here,' he said.

She walked towards him, stopping in front of the fire. She had just taken a bath, and her hair was still damp. She moved closer to the flames to gather the heat against her.

Alexei looked at her for such a long time that she began to get nervous. It was as if he were determining what he wanted to do with her.

Finally, he spoke. 'Take off your cloak and shoes.'

She reached up, unlatched her cloak and let it fall to the floor in voluminous folds. Her breathing grew slightly shallow, and an odd shiver began in her stomach. She wasn't particularly afraid but she suspected that the captain's appetites were as formidable as the man himself. She unlaced her boots and took them off.

'Now your blouse,' he ordered.

With a start, Katya realised that he wanted her to strip in front of him. Her hands shook as they went to the fastenings on her blouse. She slipped the buttons slowly out of the buttonholes. Her heart began to pulse with slow, heavy strokes, warming the blood in her veins. She let her blouse drop to the floor and reached for the buttons on her skirt. When it fell away, she stood before him in nothing but her petticoats and corset.

Alexei's dark gaze went to the swells of her breasts. Katya began to unlace her corset.

'Stop.' The command in his voice made her look up in surprise.

Alexei stood and approached her. He stopped right in front of her and reached out to pull at the laces himself. With quick movements, he unlaced her corset and drew it down over her shoulders.

Katya flushed at the exposure, even though he had seen her naked before. Somehow, though, this time it was different. This time, they both knew how it would end.

Alexei took her bare breasts in his hands and began slowly stroking his thumbs over her hard nipples. His touch sent quivers straight through her body to her sex. Katya wanted to press herself against him but forced herself to stand still. Her wound no longer required a bandage, but her skin bore a healing scar and Alexei touched the line with his finger. Katya thought she saw a flash of anger in the depths of his eyes, but it was gone so quickly that she wasn't certain she had seen it at all.

Alexei's hands slipped around her waist and undid the drawstring of her petticoats, letting them fall to the floor in a cloud of lace. His fingers slipped underneath the string of her drawers, and Katya had to fight her trembling reaction when he drew them over her hips.

To her surprise, he actually knelt down in front of her as he pulled the drawers over her thighs and calves. Katya put her hand on his shoulder to steady herself as she stepped out of them. Her skin heated when he looked at her, his darkened eyes the only evidence of his growing arousal. It gave Katya a momentary sense of power and control, but then the captain stood up. His height and the pure strength of him reminded her of their respective positions and of her vulnerability.

Alexei reached up to caress her breasts again, then put one, rough hand flat against her abdomen and slid it down to the juncture between her thighs. With a movement so quick that Katya didn't have time to react, he slipped his fingers through the springy, dark curls of her mons before delving them into the moist pleats of her labia.

Katya gasped at the sudden intrusion, and Alexei smiled when he realised she was already wet. Embarrassment flamed Katya's skin and she pulled herself away from him as her body started to shake.

'Oh, no, Princess,' Alexei said, his voice soft. 'You can't hide it. Come back here.'

Katya didn't move. She was suddenly afraid, although she didn't know if she was afraid of him, or of herself.

Alexei frowned darkly. 'Didn't you hear me?'

Katya's eyes flashed at him with rebellion, but she forced herself to approach him again. When his fingers found her sex again, she didn't flinch. She had no reason to be ashamed of her arousal. She met his gaze steadily and reached out to stroke her own fingers over his groin.

A hint of a triumphant smile curved her lips when she felt his growing hardness. Something resembling irritation crossed Alexei's hard features.

Katya knew then that this would be another battle.

She lifted her gaze to his, lightly squeezing his erection. 'You can't hide it either, Captain.'

In response, Alexei curled his hand around the length of her hair and tugged on it, forcing her to her knees on the soft carpet. It was a hideously subservient position and, for a moment, Katya's resolve faltered. Alexei held her with one hand as he began to unbutton his trousers with the other.

'Show me how much you want it,' he murmured.

His words took away most of Katya's advantage, and she glared at him resentfully. He might try and degrade her, but that didn't mean she had to let him. She straightened and reached out to work his buttons herself. She pulled his trousers down his muscular legs and drew in a breath at the sight of his manhood. He was almost fully erect, his cock projecting out towards her like a vigorous stalk from a nest of dark curls.

Katya swallowed hard at the sight of its long length and thickness, but she refused to let him see her trepidation. She moved towards him, grasping the base of his cock in her hand as she guided him to her lips. His hand tightened on her hair when her mouth enclosed the tip, and Katya read the gesture as a sign of his increasing need. She drew him slowly into the warm hollow of her mouth. He throbbed inside her, both soft and hard against the velvety surface of her tongue.

Slipping back, Katya stroked her tongue gently over the entire, pulsing surface of his cock, all the way down to the base. Then, she gripped him in her hand and took his testicles in her mouth one by one. She had never done this before, but she knew it worked when she heard his sharp intake of breath. A surge of satisfaction coursed through her. She began to stroke her hand up and down the entire length of his erection as her lips and tongue laved and caressed the twin sacs suspended tightly between his thighs.

Alexei tugged on her hair, not hard enough to be

painful but with enough force to make her stop what she was doing and look at him.

He pulled her head back. 'Take it in,' he said hoarsely.

Flushed with her own arousal, Katya slipped her lips over the hard knob of his cock, slackening her jaw as he slid over her tongue. She took him in as far as she could before he hit the back of her throat, nearly making her choke. Katya closed her eyes and breathed in through her nose, silently telling herself not to let him know that she couldn't do it. Then, he thrust forward suddenly, abruptly obstructing her breathing, and she gagged. She yanked herself away from him, gasping as tears of panic filled her eyes.

'You bastard.' She fell back on her heels, her chest heaving as she caught her breath.

Alexei's mouth curved into a slow smile. 'You'll learn, Princess.'

'That was downright cruel,' Katya snapped as panic metamorphosed into anger. A sudden thought occurred to her and she looked at him with a slight gleam in her eyes. 'Or was it proving to be too much for you, Captain? Don't tell me you couldn't just ask me to stop.'

'Rest assured my control is not quite so lacking,' Alexei replied. He reached up to undo the buttons of his shirt.

Katya's gaze travelled down to the hair-roughened skin that he exposed inch by inch. Her heart thudded painfully when he pulled his shirt off. His chest and shoulders were broad and muscular, all the more imposing with the imprint of numerous battle scars. With the eerie, reddish glow of the flames sliding over the surface of his skin, he looked like a dark, dangerous phantom.

He looked up and met her intrigued gaze. A flash of something she did not recognise appeared in the depths of his eyes.

'What's the matter, Princess?' he taunted, 'Don't tell me you're afraid of a few scars.'

Katya swallowed hard and shook her head. 'No,' she

murmured. She almost told him she thought he was beautiful, but she stopped the words just in time. She could never let him know that.

His eyes were still hard. 'Get up.'

Startled by the coldness of his words, Katya stood, steadying herself on the back of a chair.

Alexei approached her so rapidly that she didn't have a chance to back away. He grasped her shoulders and turned her around, bending her over the arm of the chair so her bottom was uplifted towards him.

Katya gasped, not prepared for her exposed position. 'Captain –'

'Be quiet,' he snapped.

Katya twisted angrily to glower at him. 'I will not be quiet,' she retorted. 'There is no reason for you to treat me like a –'

'Dammit, woman, do you want me to gag you again?' Alexei interrupted.

'Of course not, but you can't just . . . oh!' Her words stopped in her throat when she felt his inquisitive fingers prying into the folds of her sex.

He stepped between her legs, pushing them apart with his own as he spread her fully for his gaze and his touch. Katya's forehead sank into the plush velvet of the chair as she felt her entire body open up to him. A shiver of both alarm and arousal coursed through her as Alexei's fingers continued to stroke and squeeze the dewy lips of her labia. Her clitoris felt heavy and swollen, and Alexei's touch made it blossom out towards him with a painful ache that desperately needed relief. One of his fingers slipped up to the tight ring of her anus, and he probed at it gently as he leant over her, his muscular chest pressing against her back. He put his lips next to her ear.

'Has a man ever taken you here?' he whispered, pushing his finger gently into her.

Katya gasped in alarm. 'No! No, of course not.'

Alexei chuckled softly at her evident apprehension as

his finger was entrapped by the tight channel. 'No? What a shame.'

Katya squirmed underneath his weight.

'And don't think you're going to!' she snapped.

Alexei laughed again, but he withdrew his finger and resumed his stroking of her vulva. Then he levered himself off her and grasped her waist as he lifted her from the chair.

With a sudden gentleness that surprised her, he lowered her to the carpet in front of the fire. She wanted to ask him to kiss her but she couldn't bring herself to ask for anything. Instead, she closed her eyes when his lips enclosed one of the hard peaks of her breast. His tongue rasped against the taut surface, heating her skin until a light glaze of sweat broke out on her forehead. She lifted her hand to stroke it through his thick hair, but stopped the gesture of fleeting tenderness.

Alexei moved his mouth to her other breast as he edged between her legs. Katya's entire body throbbed with fervent need for him, and she betrayed her desire by spreading her legs apart to allow him easier access. The triumph that flashed in his eyes inflamed her and she silently vowed he would break first. At the moment, however, all she wanted was to be filled by his hard stalk. Her breathing grew ragged as he lowered himself on to her and guided his erection directly to the opening of her body. Katya tensed in anticipation. Her gaze went to his. She knew her face was flushed, her eyes heavy with need.

They stared at each other for a long minute. Shadows twisted across Alexei's hard features which glistened with a sheen of sweat. A pulse pounded in his jaw, but his eyes were hard as he looked down at her.

'Beg me,' Alexei whispered savagely.

'Never,' Katya gasped, even as her hips pushed against him in a silent plea.

The movement edged his cock further into her until the knob was enclosed in her heat, leaving the rest of her

68

channel burning for more. Alexei held himself off her body with his arms on either side of her head and she could practically feel the tension of his muscles. Their lower bodies were pressed so closely together that his heat flowed into her sex, making it surge with renewed excitement.

The captain's control seemed inexorable. The coil of tension around Katya's loins was so tight she thought it would break her apart unless she had the relief she so desperately craved. She closed her eyes, her entire being resisting the idea of pleading for anything, much less the penetration of her captor. Her chest heaved with ragged breaths and she writhed against him in another silent entreaty.

'What is it you want, Princess?' The derision behind the husky note in his voice made her cringe.

She turned her head away from him, her cheeks flushed from both embarrassment at his words and a need she could not deny. She pushed her hips towards him again, but he moved away until he slipped out of her completely, leaving her feeling totally bereft.

Katya groaned in frustration. 'You are such a bastard.'

Alexei put his lips against her ear, his breath brushing her skin with a hot shiver.

'Tell me what you want, Katya,' he murmured.

'I hate you,' she hissed.

'Do you?' His teeth bit gently at her ear, sending a quiver of pleasure through her, but still he did not move.

The struggle in her felt like an outright war. Katya squeezed her eyelids shut, hating him and hating herself for the words that broke involuntarily from her throat.

'Please,' she whispered, her voice so low that it was almost inaudible as her desperation overcame her resistance. 'Please, Alexei . . . I want you.'

Then, in one, swift movement, he surged into her with a force so powerful it shook her to the core. His hardness filled her completely, bumping against her cervix, and her body stretched beyond what she thought was possible.

Katya gasped at the suddenness of his submersion, even as her body welcomed and revelled in it. Her head fell back as he withdrew halfway and plunged into her again, as all of her thoughts and feelings focused on the delicious sensation of him thrusting in and out of her. Everything else seemed to disappear into oblivion as her body drove upward to match his rhythm, as she throbbed with warmth and heat from the friction of their union. Alexei bent his head to tug at her nipples with his teeth, augmenting the ache in her sex to unfathomable degrees.

His tongue rasped between her breasts, licking up a bead of sweat as the heat enveloped them both. He lowered his hands to cup them underneath her thighs, spreading her fully apart for his thrusts. Katya moaned with the rapture of it all. He slid so easily in and out of her, his pace increasing slowly as he pushed into her to the hilt before drawing back. She clenched her inner muscles around him, gripping him even as he withdrew, and increasing the strength of his immersion.

Katya's body was on fire. Moisture dripped from her sex, but the trickles felt like paths of flames. She felt wholly open to him, fully exposed, and her blood pounded ceaselessly in her head as she sank into the myriad sensations enclosing her. Alexei's ragged breathing was hot against her neck, and she closed her eyes as her hands came up to delve into his thick hair. She gripped his hair tightly as the spirals of pleasure wound inside her with a tension that kept her teetering on the edge of total bliss.

She almost sobbed with relief when Alexei's hand slipped down through the damp curls of her sex before finding the aching nub in which all of her tension was centred. He continued to thrust inside her as he rubbed his fingers around her clitoris before finally, finally, stroking it directly and sending her careening into rapture.

Katya let out a broken cry. Her body quivered and shook as waves of violent ecstasy and relief washed over her; she clutched on to his shoulders to try and keep herself steady as her world spun out of control. She heard his low murmurs in her ear, but her senses were swimming and she didn't know what he was saying. All she knew was that his cock felt like pliable iron inside her. Then his hoarse groan against her skin was followed by a shudder of pleasure through his body and splashes of molten seed rushed into her.

One final hard thrust jolted her to her very soul as Alexei's own pleasure peaked with a force that could only have come from him.

Katya drew in a ragged breath, her chest heaving and glistening with sweat as she tried to collect her senses. She fully expected to feel the weight of Alexei's body collapse on to hers, and she welcomed it with everything in her, but he pulled away from her so suddenly that she was shocked.

She lifted herself on to her elbows to look at him as he rolled away from her and on to his back. His eyelids drifted closed as he, too, tried to catch his breath. Katya gazed at him for a long minute, considering the austere planes and angles of his face that spoke of an unforgiving man. And then she remembered that she had capitulated to his harsh order, that she had broken first, and her face suddenly flushed with shame.

With a muffled groan, she rolled over and buried her face in her arms. For all her intentions he had still got everything out of her he wanted.

Katya edged herself closer to the fire. Her sated, exhausted body urged her into sleep, even as her mind continued to berate her for having surrendered.

Alexei opened his eyes when he heard Katya groan. He looked at her smooth, glowing back as her body shifted

71

into the rhythm of sleep. A rush of satisfaction went through him, even though he had come dangerously close to losing his own control.

He sat up and reached for Katya's cloak to cover her, but then he realised that he could gaze, unhindered, at her nakedness. He tossed the cloak aside, figuring she would be warm enough from the fire. Still naked himself, he sat in a chair and looked down at her. He did not like the fact that his self-discipline had almost collapsed at one touch of her lips on his prick.

Alexei frowned: the princess had hit a little too close to home when she realised the truth of his abrupt thrust into her mouth.

He reached out with his foot and brushed his toes lightly over her arm. Katya waved her hand over the disturbance but remained asleep. Alexei prodded her again. She reacted to the touch and rolled over, mumbling something unintelligible.

A slight smile curved Alexei's mouth as Katya's nudity became fully exposed to his gaze. She had small, high breasts, with rosy nipples, and pale, slender limbs that contrasted sharply with her dark hair. Her features were strong, her eyelashes casting shadows on her high cheekbones as she slept. Her gently rounded belly reminded him of the silken softness of her skin. The curls between her thighs were dark and lush, still damp from the evidence of their combined arousal.

Alexei felt his body stir with renewed stimulation. He ruthlessly fought back the urge to wake Katya up and take her again. And again. And again. He had always had a vigorous sexual appetite but he had never had such an urge for one woman. Katya was pretty enough, although not as beautiful as most women he had been with, and Alexei detested his inability to pinpoint the source of his craving for her. This was not a lust that could be satisfied with Svetlana or any of the other women at the encampment. That knowledge infuriated him.

As if she had read his thoughts, Katya stirred, her eyelashes fluttering. Her dark eyes moved to him sitting in the chair. She didn't try and hide her nakedness and simply lay there watching him as if she were trying to figure him out.

'You always get what you want, don't you?' she asked quietly.

'Absolutely.'

'Why are you fighting against the Tsar?'

'I come from a long line of rebellious Cossacks,' Alexei replied. 'And Tsars have appropriated our land from the days of Peter the Great. I have no intention of allowing that tradition to continue.'

'Because to you, land is freedom.'

'Yes. At any cost.'

Katya shivered suddenly and sat up, reaching for her cloak. A shadow passed across her face. 'How long are you going to keep me here?'

'I don't know.' He paused. 'I believe your cousin Sofia has arrived safely in Kostov.'

Katya's gaze flew to him in shock. 'What?'

'There's a record of her having purchased a ticket to Kostov. I sent a couple of men there to see if they could find her.'

He recognised the warring emotions in her expression.

'You're not ... you didn't send them to ...' Her voice trailed off, and she looked down at her hands.

Alexei shoved away the spark of sudden tenderness that flared inside him.

'No,' he said, keeping his voice neutral. 'They're not going to take her prisoner.'

Katya's body sagged slightly with relief. 'Thank you.'

His eyes slid over her cloaked figure, all the more enticing now he knew the delectable secrets hidden underneath.

'So, Princess,' he murmured. 'Are you going to tell me where you learnt all of your luscious, little techniques?'

73

Her skin flushed a deep red. An emotion flashed in her eyes that Alexei did not like.

'I don't think that's any of your business,' Katya replied, her voice chilly. 'You enjoyed it, didn't you?'

'And, yet, you're still strangely inexperienced, aren't you?' Alexei continued, as if she hadn't spoken. 'Interesting. I shall have to change that.'

Katya's flush deepened, and she reached for her clothes with shaking hands. 'I'm going back to my room.'

Alexei didn't try and stop her.

Svetlana emerged from the dusky shadows of the hallway. Her gaze narrowed as she watched Katya, covered by her cloak, leave Alexei's bedchamber. Svetlana knew Katya had been in there for several hours and now she was carrying her clothes.

A rush of jealousy nearly choked her. Word that the woman was royalty had spread like wildfire around the encampment. Svetlana had thought Alexei couldn't possibly be attracted to a member of a royal family, but it appeared she had been mistaken.

Svetlana frowned as she watched Katya. The pretty, dark-haired woman didn't have the delicacy one usually associated with royalty, but she walked with a self-assurance that spoke of a regal bearing. She had been forced to work hard this last week, but she did so without complaint and with a hint of a challenge, as if daring anyone to break her.

Svetlana's hand clenched into a fist as she thought of Alexei with another woman. Alexei belonged to *her*. It was as simple as that.

She hurried back to her own room. Her entire chest hurt with the pain of betrayal, and she fought image after image of Alexei and Katya entwined in lust. Tears stung the backs of her eyes. She gave Alexei everything he wanted. She always succumbed to him when he came to her and she always did whatever he asked her to without complaint or argument.

Svetlana paced back and forth in agitation. Alexei had sent out word that the young woman was a prisoner of the camp, which meant Katya was here to stay indefinitely. Svetlana didn't dare oppose Alexei's dictum but there had to be something she could do.

She stopped by the window, gnawing thoughtfully on her thumbnail, and stared out at the milling soldiers. It certainly wasn't as if Alexei was the only man in the encampment. Maybe, if he realised that she had her pick of men, he would get jealous enough to return to her. He had no future with some royal whore. When the revolution died down, Alexei would surely want to settle down with a wife. And she was the perfect woman for him. It was about time he realised that.

She hurried back out into the hallway and down to Alexei's bedchamber. She knocked tentatively and felt relieved when she heard his gruff order to enter.

Svetlana pushed open the door and stepped into the room. Alexei was sitting naked by the fire, his expression so austere that she almost couldn't approach him. He was no less formidable in his unselfconscious nudity; in fact, he seemed all the more imposing because of it.

He looked up and frowned. 'What do you want?'

'I just, er . . .' Svetlana began hesitantly. She closed the door behind her and padded across the room. 'I just wanted to be with you.'

Alexei didn't reply, but watched her approach him. This was an unprecedented move for her as she always waited for him to come to her. Svetlana remembered what he had just been doing with his whore and a shaft of jealous anger shuddered through her.

'Don't you want me?' Svetlana reached for the belt of her robe and pulled it open. She let her generous breasts fall forward and took pride in the fact that she was far more fully endowed than Alexei's whore.

Alexei's gaze slipped down to her cleavage, but he didn't make a move towards her. Svetlana hesitated, uncertain how to take the initiative. She was so used to

Alexei coming for her in a heated passion that she didn't know how to handle his apparent passivity. Alexei was never passive.

Svetlana knelt down in front of him, reaching out tentatively to rub her hand over his flaccid penis. His shaft stirred slightly at her touch and gave her the courage to stroke him with more force. She felt stunned when Alexei's hand suddenly reached down and clamped around her wrist.

'Leave, woman,' he said, shortly. 'I have no need of you.'

Svetlana stared at him in shock. 'W-what?'

Alexei pushed her hand away from him. 'Leave me alone. Go back to your own chambers. I do not appreciate you acting like a whore.'

Svetlana scrambled to her feet, fumbling to pull her gown together. 'Oh, but you like having her for a whore, do you?'

Alexei's eyes flashed with dangerous anger. 'Quiet.'

'You think you're the only man I want?' said Svetlana, as her voice grew higher with indignation. 'Is that what you think? For your information, I happen to have several lovers!'

'Then go to them to satisfy your desires.' He began to look faintly bored.

'You will grow tired of your royal whore, Alexei,' Svetlana snapped furiously. 'And then you will want me again because we both know she will never be able to give you everything you need!' She whirled around and stalked out of the room. Her entire body trembled with resentment, and the outright jealousy inside made her feel sick.

She stood in the hallway for a minute, her breath coming in rapid gasps as she tried to process the fact that Alexei had rejected her. She gathered her robe around her and stormed down the stairs. She would show him, she thought. He would regret rejecting her.

She pulled open the heavy, front doors and drew in a

sharp breath when the chilly air hit her. She steeled herself against the cold and descended the marble steps. The night was clear, and the light of the moon lit her pathway to the soldiers' tents.

Svetlana paused for only a minute, to allow her eyes to adjust to the light, before she walked purposefully towards a tent located just underneath the window of her bedchamber. She knew who slept in this tent; she had seen the young soldier watching her when she passed by and she had looked out her window more than once to find him staring up at her.

She didn't bother announcing her entrance. With a sharp movement, edged with the hurt of rejection, she flipped back the tent flap and went inside. The interior was warm from a small, gas lantern, and held a foot-locker, a small writing desk, and a cot. Ivan was lying on his side on the bed, facing away from her.

'Ivan,' she said.

Ivan gasped at the sudden voice and reached frantically for a blanket to cover himself.

Svetlana stood in the middle of the tent and put her hands on her hips; she realised with a start that she had interrupted Ivan while he was in the midst of pleasuring himself.

A smile quirked her mouth. This would prove easier than she had anticipated. 'Ivan, look at me.'

Ivan turned, his handsome face flushed as he tried to process the fact that she was in his tent. His gaze widened when he saw that she was only wearing her night-robe. 'Miss, I –'

'Hush.' Emboldened by the definitive knowledge that he would die before rejecting her, Svetlana unlaced the belt of her robe and let it fall open.

Ivan swallowed, his gaze fixed on her generous cleavage. Svetlana smiled. Yes, this would be easy.

She walked over to his cot, reaching out to curl her hand around the blanket. She yanked it off him, and Ivan grabbed for it in a panic.

Svetlana tossed the blanket on to the floor as her gaze swept over him. He wore a dark blue shirt and grey pants, which were pulled halfway down his legs. His thick cock was half-erect against the light brown hair of his pubis. Ivan's hand shot down to cover himself.

'Ivan,' Svetlana said and shook her head. 'Are you jerking your own flesh for pleasure?'

Ivan stared at her in shock. His face was flushed with embarrassment and he didn't seem able to say anything.

'A pity,' Svetlana clucked. 'If I had known you were forced to resort to such drastic measures I would have come down here sooner.'

She wrapped her hand around his wrist and moved his hand away from his groin. With approval, she saw that his erection was already growing. She reached down to touch the quivering flesh with her fingertips, feeling a surge of power at his reaction. He would never dare push her away.

'Miss,' Ivan gasped. 'I can't –'

Svetlana laughed throatily. 'Oh, but you can, Ivan. You most definitely can.'

She grasped his cock in her hand and began to stroke it slowly. Satisfaction filled her when he grew harder in her hand. Yes, he would want her; they would all want her. And then Alexei would know first hand the biting cut of jealousy.

'Miss, the captain –'

Svetlana chuckled. 'The captain doesn't own me, Ivan. And don't call me "miss." My name is Svetlana.'

She bent her head to kiss him, letting her long, blonde hair fall over his chest. Ivan looked so stunned that she chuckled again. She pressed her mouth against his, licking his lips with her tongue.

'Ivan, don't tell me you're a virgin,' she murmured.

'No, mi–' he stammered. 'Svetlana. But everyone knows the captain –'

'The captain has nothing to do with this,' Svetlana

retorted, irritably. 'Stop mentioning him. He doesn't have to know anything about this.'

Ivan's cock jerked against her fingers. She smiled, knowing she had him.

'You're quite well-endowed, aren't you?' she whispered against his lips. 'How old are you, Ivan?'

'Twenty-four.'

His eyes began to dilate with the stunned amazement of her appearance and what she was doing to him. Svetlana released his cock and shrugged off her dressing gown, watching him as she began to unbutton her nightshift. Ivan's lips parted as his breath whistled out in a gasp.

Svetlana let the nightshift fall to the floor and stood naked in front of him. She smiled triumphantly when his heated gaze fixed in awe on her full, voluptuous nudity: her large breasts with hard, reddened nipples, the curve of her hips and legs, the light curls between her thighs. She had never felt so totally confident of her own beauty.

Ivan's strong chest heaved with desire at the sight of her, his brown eyes smoky. Svetlana walked back to him and straddled his waist, letting her breasts dangle over him.

'So, Ivan,' she said softly, 'do you think about me when you stroke yourself?'

Ivan swallowed hard and nodded. He reached up tentatively to touch her breasts with shaking hands; his fingers rubbed her hard nipples. Svetlana leant far enough over him so that her breasts dangled above his mouth.

'Suck them,' she offered.

Ivan's lips instantly closed around one of the rosy peaks, sending a shot of pleasure travelling down towards her sex. Svetlana moaned and arched her back, loving the feeling of power she had over him. Her sex dampened with moisture and he hadn't even touched her there. She pulled back, running her hands over his chest, feeling his heart racing wildly underneath his skin. Yes, she was certain, he would die before rejecting her.

She rubbed her vulva against his abdomen. Reaching behind her, she grasped his sex again and began stroking him up and down until he started to pant and thrust his hips up to meet her movements.

Suddenly, he let out a hoarse cry, and his cock jerked violently as his seed splashed out on to his thighs and Svetlana's buttocks. She continued stroking him until the shudders had passed through his body. Then she gave him a reproving look.

'You shouldn't have done that yet, Ivan,' she chided.

His face flushed a deep red with shame, even as pleasure continued to pulse through him.

'I'm sorry,' he mumbled. 'It's just . . . you're so beautiful . . . I never thought . . .'

Svetlana moved up his body until her damp sex hovered over his mouth. She paused, enjoying the feeling of his hot breath against her intimate folds. Slowly, she lowered her hips until he could lap at her labia with his tongue. Warmth spread through her loins, radiating outward to her veins. For all his nervousness, Ivan's tongue and lips were surprisingly confident as he licked and sucked her until she felt her own excitement tightening around her. Her head fell back as her hips undulated with increasing frenzy. She writhed over him, gasping with need as the pressure mounted and finally burst through her with a rush of dampness. Her squeal of pleasure broke through the air, and Ivan continued his laving of her sex until she pulled away from him.

Ivan stared at her, his eyes so heavy with passion that he appeared dazed. With a sigh, Svetlana slid down his body until she was lying on top of him. She smiled lazily, bending her head to kiss him.

'Well, Ivan,' she murmured. 'I think you and I can have a very satisfying relationship.'

He muttered something through his daze, looking as if he couldn't quite believe what had just happened.

Svetlana giggled and leant her head against his chest. She reached down and rubbed her fingertips over Ivan's sex again. It jerked immediately at her touch and started to harden.

Svetlana smiled.

Chapter Six

Katya wiped her forehead with her sleeve as she reached for another potato. The starchy, dusty smell of them filled the air, and she had lost track of how many she had peeled. She continued to be grateful for the fact that she could sit by the warmth of the stove, but the work was monotonous and exhausting. Her hours at the encampment had fallen into an uneasy routine.

During the day she washed dishes and pots for most of the morning then took on whatever task the kitchen staff assigned her. Sergei, the main cook, seemed to take particular delight in sending her on repeated trips to the storage shed. Katya suffered from headaches and colds due to the constant difference of interior warmth and the freezing air outside. And, of course, there were the inevitable lewd looks and comments from the soldiers.

But Katya's nights were different. She suppressed a shiver of carnality. Her nights were filled with little sleep and pure pleasure as the captain made her feel things she hadn't known were possible. Most of the time he told her to come to his bedchamber at a certain hour, but some nights he came to her; always in the late, late hours. She heard him as she was drifting off to sleep. He entered her bedchamber, stripping off his clothes as he walked towards the bed. And then he was there with her, his palms sliding over her skin, his lips and tongue stroking her body, his fingers between her legs, his flesh firm and taut underneath her seeking hands.

She thought of nothing when he was urging her body towards an ultimate release; letting her mind be submerged in a fog of sensuality; allowing him to take her to shuddering havens of warmth and sensation. He wasn't a gentle man, his sexuality was as hard and domineering as his demeanour, but he filled her completely, satisfied her utterly, demanding her surrender to the erotic forces that swirled around them.

She had begun to wait for him, to expect him, to want him. The realisation was both thrilling and shameful. He was her captor, and yet her body awakened when she saw him; craved him when he walked into her bedchamber. She disliked intensely the knowledge that he had been right in his arrogant remark that she would beg him to be her lover. She had begged him. And she did so again, night after night when he whispered the command in a gravelly voice, his breath hot against her neck. And she knew she would continue to do so.

She tried not to think about Nicholas. She loved him with everything she had in her. Guilt clawed at her insides when she contemplated the idea that she was being unfaithful to him. Guilt over enjoying what Alexei did to her and what she did to him.

Biting her lower lip, she stared down at her work-roughened hands. There was nothing she could do about the captain wanting to bed her. But, she supposed that she might, at least out of respect for her and Nicholas's relationship, try not take such pleasure from it. And yet she knew such an attempt would be as impossible as draining the sea with a thimble.

A pot suddenly crashed to the floor from the stove and broke her out of her reminiscences. A river of soup spilt across the floor, causing a flurry of voices and activity. Katya sighed and returned her attention to yet another potato.

Despite her constant presence in the kitchens, she hadn't yet had an opportunity to steal one of the kitchen knives. Still, she kept an eye on the cooks in case they happened to leave one lying around. She looked down at the potato peeler in her hand and smiled without humour. Technically, she might still be royalty, but there wasn't very much about her that suggested she was anything more than a kitchen servant. And a captain's concubine.

She glanced up at the sound of Sergei's heavy foot-steps; the big man stopped near a pot full of peeled potatoes. Then he shocked her by reaching out and grabbing her breast, tweaking her nipple painfully between his fleshy fingers. Katya gasped in outrage and overturned her footstool as she leapt up. 'You keep your hands off me!' she screamed.

Sergei shot her a look. 'You're nothing but a wench here, woman,' he snapped.

'That doesn't mean you can put your hands on me!' Her entire body shook with fury.

Sergei looked at her, a gleam appearing in the depths of his eyes that created a quiver of anxiety in her gut.

'It means,' Sergei said, 'that I can put my hands on you wherever and whenever I want.' His gaze skimmed over her body. 'Word is out you're available to any soldier who has the urge.'

He picked up the pot and walked away, leaving Katya staring after him in shock. She fumbled to right the footstool and sank down on it. Despite the warmth of the stove, she was suddenly cold.

Surely he couldn't mean that. She remembered Alexei telling her that the soldiers hadn't had a woman in ages and she winced. She prayed that he couldn't have told them he was finished with her and was ready to turn her over to them.

Katya's entire being filled with revulsion at the

thought of being violated by any number of soldiers at the encampment. She glanced furtively towards the kitchen tables again. She had to get her hands on a knife. Without one, she was totally defenceless.

She picked up another potato and started peeling it, casting quick glances at the knives used by the cooks. After she had filled another pot, she picked it up and carried it to the one of the tables. She avoided Sergei and placed the pot next to one of the female cooks.

'Where do you want me to put these?' she asked.

'Over there.' The woman waved distractedly towards the stove.

Katya timed her next move carefully, her gaze on a knife that lay on the table nearby. She picked up the pot, bumping her elbow against a pile of carrots hovering near the edge of the table. The carrots fell to the floor with a dull clatter.

'Oh, you stupid girl!' said the cook, and glowered at Katya as she bent to retrieve a carrot near her feet.

Katya grabbed the knife and shoved it quickly into her pocket before dropping on to her knees to pick up the carrots. Apologies spilled from her lips in a torrent, but the cook was not appeased and told her to clean the carrots and retrieve another bushel from the storage shed.

Katya finished her tasks with a lighter heart when she realised that no one had seen her take the knife. The weight of it felt heavy and comforting against her thigh. As she walked down to the storage shed, she silently dared any of the soldiers to try and touch her. A knife in their gut would be her response.

'You are all right, my lady?' said a gruff voice.

Katya looked up in surprise. Lev, the older man who had spoken to her the first time she had gone to the shed, was standing off to the side of the pathway. His question surprised her. 'Yes. I'm fine.' she said, and looked at him curiously. 'Are you a soldier?'

His mouth turned up in a slight smile. 'Of a sort. I'm not your enemy, but the time is not yet right.'

With that, he crossed in front of her, his hand reaching out to slip something into her palm. Instinctively, Katya's fingers closed around the object. She opened her hand and looked in shock at the sight of a small, metal plate that bore the Tsar's symbol. Katya gasped softly, her heart thudding as she lifted her head to find Lev again. He was gone.

Katya put the metal plate in her pocket as she absorbed the implications of what had just happened. A Tsarist soldier right here in the midst of the anti-monarchist Cossacks! Lev had to be an infiltrator of some sort, which meant that he could surely help her escape. Her heart lifted as hope surged through her. She had an ally. She was not alone.

With a renewed burst of energy, she carted another load of carrots back up to the kitchen and resumed her potato peeling. She would have to be discreet, but somehow she would talk to Lev about how she might escape. She could only pray that it would happen soon.

Dusk settled into the sky, and Katya paused only to eat some bland potato soup. By the time she went upstairs, with a pail of hot water for a bath, she was sick to death of potatoes.

She went into her bedchamber, built a quick fire in the fireplace, and hid the Tsarist plaque under the rug in a corner of the room. She boiled a few buckets of water to fill the tub, before sinking into it with a sigh of bliss. The water eased some of the weariness in her bones, as she soaped her dusty skin with a bar of soap. She kept the stolen knife within reach and the mere sight of it comforted her.

After the water had cooled, Katya dried off and slipped on her nightshift and robe. She put the knife in the pocket of her robe in the event of an unpleasant encounter in the corridor. She went back to her bedchamber, glad she had already built a fire to keep the room warm. She pulled open the door and tossed her dirty clothes on the bed as she hurried to the fire.

She skidded to a halt at the sight of the captain warming himself. 'Oh,' she said, 'I didn't realise you were here.'

A corner of his mouth turned up slightly. 'Apparently not.' His gaze raked over her figure, and then he walked towards her. 'I hear you've been causing a few problems in the kitchen.'

'Have you?' Katya said, and thought of the knife in her pocket. A shiver ran through her. The captain had never come to her this early in the night, but now Katya regretted not having hid the weapon in her room. 'I didn't mean to.'

'I'm sure you didn't.' Alexei stopped in front of her and reached out to grasp the end of her belt. He wrapped it around his hand and tugged her towards him.

Katya's heart suddenly pounded hard as she realised that he was going to kiss her. He pulled her body against his. Katya winced inwardly when she felt the flat edge of the knife hit his thigh.

Alexei noticed it, too. He looked down at her for a minute, then eased his fingers into her pocket. His hand closed around the knife and he drew it out. Firelight glinted off the steely blade. Alexei gazed at the knife in his hand and then lifted his eyes to Katya. The look in them was as steely as the knife blade. His entire expression hardened.

Katya backed away from him in sudden fear. 'Captain, I –'

'Did you steal this?' His voice sounded like iron.

'I wasn't –'

'Did you steal this?' he repeated, coldly.

A spark of rebellion rose inside her; she lifted her head defiantly. 'Yes,' she replied. 'But I had good reason.'

'Good reason for stealing?' Ice blazed in his eyes as he walked towards her. 'Were you planning to use this on me?'

Katya couldn't reply past the tightness in her throat. He appeared more menacing than she had ever seen him before. Her legs hit the end of the bed, and she realised there was nowhere she could go. She reached out to grasp the bedpost.

'Were you?' Alexei repeated, his voice dangerously low.

'No,' Katya whispered. 'They ... I didn't want you to hand me over to your soldiers.'

A brief surprise flickered in his expression. 'Who said I was going to do that?'

Katya almost told him, but she knew Sergei would make her life miserable if he ever found out. 'I heard it somewhere.'

'You should have come to me first, Princess.' His gaze slipped down to her lips, his eyes glittering. 'None of this excuses the fact that you stole. I would hate to have to lock you up.'

Katya's mouth felt dry. 'You don't have to. I won't do it again.'

'Come down to the cellar in half an hour,' Alexei ordered. 'You'll find a shift in the *armoire* you can wear.'

He turned and left the room, his fist clenched around the handle of the knife. Katya sank down on to the bed. Her legs trembled at the thought of actually being locked up. What in the world was he going to do with her?

She sat there shaking until she realised that time had passed. Not wanting to enrage him further, she hurried to the *armoire* and found a simple, white, silk shift with long sleeves and a scooped neckline. The cool fabric felt delicious against her bare skin and fell to her ankles in gentle swirls. She slipped her robe over the shift and went out into the cold hallway. A shadow moved at one end, but Katya was too nervous to wonder what it was. She hurried downstairs and through the silent, empty kitchens, until she came to a wooden door leading to the cellars.

Cold, stone steps led down to the depths of the manor.

The cellars were freezing and filled with musty air that smelled like dust and wine. The first room used to be a wine cellar, and the huge racks still contained several, dusty bottles. Beyond that, two corridors led to rooms that now served as storage facilities for military equipment and ammunition. Heavy, wooden doors guarded the equipment, and the entire place was covered in eerie darkness.

Katya paused, shivering in the middle of the wine cellar, as she wondered where Alexei was. She silently prayed that he wouldn't leave her here. Surely she would freeze to death.

'Captain?' Her whisper sounded loud and abrupt against the frozen, stone walls of the cellar. She hugged her arms around herself, nervousness threading her insides.

The captain's tall figure detached itself from the shadows down one corridor.

'Come here,' he said, and his deep voice echoed against the stone walls.

Relief and fear battled inside her. She approached him hesitantly, her feet feeling like blocks of lead. She wanted to ask him not to leave her here, but she couldn't bring herself to plead with him. She followed him down the corridor to one of the storage rooms.

Alexei pulled a key from his pocket and unlocked the door. He stepped aside and Katya went into the room before him. The dim flickering of campfires glinted through a high, barred window, providing a low illumination of several wooden crates filled with weapons and equipment. Katya heard the door click shut behind her, and she whirled around in sudden fear that he had locked her in.

To her relief, Alexei was leaning against the door, his arms crossed against his chest.

'So, Princess,' he murmured, 'what kind of punishment do you think you deserve for stealing?'

Apprehension shuddered through her. 'I don't know,' she said.

He approached her and reached out to tug at her belt. He slipped the belt off and then pushed Katya's robe off her shoulders.

The cold air bit through the flimsy silk of her shift. Katya shivered, but didn't dare reach for her robe. Alexei's unyielding disapproval permeated the air and, for the first time, she felt as if she might truly have reason to fear him.

Alexei reached into his pocket and pulled out a strip of black silk. He stood in front of her and put the blindfold over her eyes. His hands were deft and sure as he smoothed the soft material and knotted it behind her head.

Katya's hand instinctively clutched the front of his shirt to steady herself when the blindfold blocked out the flickering, reddish light. Darkness now shrouded her world, and her heart began to pound with trepidation.

The loss of sight suddenly made her aware of her other senses. She smelt the faint scent of soap and smoke lingering on Alexei's skin, and heard the distant crackle of the campfires and the occasional rumble of a voice from outside.

Alexei bent his head close to her ear.

'Are you afraid?' he whispered. His breath was warm against her neck.

Katya's hand tightened on his shirt. 'Yes.'

'Good.' He took her earlobe between his teeth and nipped gently.

The warmth of his body heat radiated from him, and Katya fought the urge to sink against him and let him drive away the cold. Now, he was the only secure element in her world, and she almost panicked when she felt him withdrawing from her.

'Alexei –'

'Let go, Princess.' He reached down to disengage her hand from his shirt and moved away.

Katya fought to keep the unsteadiness at bay as she suddenly found herself alone. Agitation and fear coiled in the pit of her stomach as she realised that she was totally at his mercy. Her fingers itched to rip off the blindfold. Her heart pounded panicked blood through her body, but she didn't dare defy him again. Not now.

'Captain?'

'Princess.' His deep voice came from behind her.

Katya waited tensely, straining her ears for any sign of what he was going to do. His hands encircled her wrists, pulling them behind her back as he tied them together with the belt of her robe.

Katya had never felt so helpless. She nearly fainted when she heard the distinct sound of a sabre rasping out of its sheath.

'Alexei, please –'

His low chuckle echoed in her ears. 'Didn't I say you would beg me?'

'You never said I would have to beg you not to hurt me.' Her throat tightened.

'Is that what you think I'm going to do?'

'I don't know what to think.' Katya flinched when she felt the sharp tip of the sabre against the base of her throat. Her heart pounded wildly with terror, her entire body trembling.

'Don't move, Katya.' Alexei's voice was implacable.

She fought not to cringe, expecting to feel the blade slice through her skin at any second. The tip of the sabre slid slowly down her neck with enough pressure to leave a little indention in her skin, but not enough to hurt. Sweat broke out on her forehead despite the freezing air.

Alexei trailed the point down her chest to the scooped neckline of her shift and then, in a swift movement, sliced the sharp blade through the silky fabric.

Katya drew in an audible breath when she felt the cold air wash over her exposed breast. She stepped away until her back hit the stone wall. Her breath came in rapid gasps, and she knew then that there would be no escape.

The point touched her again. The blade trailed along her skin, over her breast, circling her nipple with a slowness that made her shake. Her nipples hardened in reaction to the cold and fear, even as she could not deny that there was something erotic in the sensation of the steel blade against her skin.

Alexei sliced the blade through her shift again until the folds of fabric fell apart to reveal her other breast. With slow movements that would have felt like caresses if he had been using his hands, he cut thin strips down her arms, across her abdomen, over her legs. Ribbons of silk were left clinging to her body. The point of the blade barely touched her. Then Alexei's hands grasped her shoulders and he pulled her away from the wall without a word; the sabre blade sliced the material with a whispered softness to expose her back and her bottom.

White silk fluttered around Katya's body like wisps of clouds, shifting with her rapid breaths. She listened tautly for Alexei's movements and heard, with relief, the sound of the sabre sliding back into the sheath. The cold air insinuated itself between the silk shreds, stirring the fabric against her naked skin. She wanted to say the captain's name again, if only to hear his deep voice responding to assure her he was still there, but the word stuck in her throat.

She started at the sensation of his hands on her shoulders again, as he turned her towards him. She began to tremble with the sudden, almost desperate urge to feel his arms go around her so her world would consist of more than fear, darkness, and shredded silk drifting around her body.

'Are you still afraid?' Alexei asked, softly.

Katya shuddered and swallowed hard. 'Should I be?'

Alexei didn't reply. His forefinger brushed against the trembling fullness of her lower lip and pushed slowly between her lips and into her mouth. Katya's lips closed around his finger as he slid it past her teeth until she felt him against her tongue. Instinctively knowing what he wanted, she caressed his finger with her tongue and sucked it with her lips. After a minute, Alexei pulled his finger out of her mouth.

He moved his rough hands down her shoulders and over her arms, gripped her and pulled her to him. Katya gasped at the sensation of his hardness as his groin pushed against her. An odd shiver spilled through her when she realised that he was aroused by what he was doing. By the fact that she was at his mercy.

'Am I going to have to keep you tied up now that I know you're a little thief?' Alexei whispered. He lowered his head, swirling his tongue around the shell of her ear.

Katya shook her head as her body swayed towards him. 'No . . .'

His hands slid to her hips, finding her skin underneath the shreds of silk. He stroked his hands around to her buttocks and slipped the tips of his fingers into her crevice.

Katya trembled at the unexpected caress. She felt totally powerless, unable to see, unable to touch him, unable to do anything but stand there and wait for him to tell her what to do. Her heart pulsed hard in her chest, sending a stream of warm blood through her veins. She brushed her hard nipples against the rough fabric of his shirt, hearing his low chuckle resound in her ears.

With the fingers of one hand embedded in the cleft of her bottom, Alexei lifted his other hand to squeeze the aching peak of her breast. Sparks flooded Katya's body from the sensitive nerves, and she couldn't suppress a low moan of approval. She pushed her lower body towards him, feeling his hard bulge press insistently against the soft flesh of her belly. Her sex responded uncontrollably, swelling and moistening with anticipation.

'Yes, Princess, I know what you want,' Alexei murmured.

Katya's insides tightened suddenly with alarm over what she was feeling and how he had managed to manipulate her. She was completely vulnerable, he was virtually sadistic, and yet she wanted him with a force that was almost overwhelming. Confusion and fear made her body tense despite the compelling power of the man before her.

As if he sensed her sudden anxiety, Alexei stroked his hands down her back and lowered his head to her neck again. 'You *are* afraid. Of me? Or of yourself?'

'Both.' Her voice was barely audible, even to her own ears.

She felt his smile against her skin.

'Fear is good,' he whispered. 'Right now, you can blame your desire on emotion, rather than your innately sexual nature. But one day, Katya, you will realise that the exploration of your sensuality requires honesty. Only then will you know what so many others have failed to discover.'

'What is that?' Apprehension glazed her words.

Alexei laughed softly. 'Oh, no. You'll make that discovery yourself.'

His callused hands slid over her buttocks, and his fingers dipped between her thighs, spreading them apart enough to test her wetness. Katya bit her lip, forcing back a moan as she alternated between need and shame.

'It's fascinating, isn't it?' Alexei continued. 'The discovery that fear and helplessness are so arousing?'

'How would you know?' Katya whispered hoarsely. 'I don't think you've ever been afraid or helpless in your entire life.'

'If I hadn't, then I wouldn't know how you feel right now, would I?' Alexei eased his hands more aggressively between her thighs, spreading her buttocks apart at the same time.

The cold air touched her inner folds and crevices with a shocking rush. His fingers grew more inquisitive, slipping into her with an ease that made her all the more aware of her arousal. Her shoulders ached from the strain of having her hands tied behind her back, and the ribbons of silk continued to shift against her naked skin. She had never been so utterly aware of her senses, of her body; or of the feeling of Alexei's rough shirt against her, his erection against her belly, his fingers inside her.

She waited tensely for him to order her to beg him for what she wanted, but he didn't. His fingers slipped out of her and moved to the belt binding her wrists together. Katya almost groaned with relief when she felt him start to untie the constraints. His hands encircled her wrists, massaging away the ache.

'Now, put your arms over your head,' he directed, softly.

'Please don't –'

'Katya.' The tone of his voice was like velvet over cold steel.

She lifted her arms, feeling her breasts rise and jut outward with the movement. Alexei put his hands on her hips and guided her backward until her back hit the smooth stone of the wall. In a quick movement, he tied her wrists together again and suspended them over what felt like a metal hook above her head.

'I don't like this,' Katya said, even though her body throbbed with both desire, and with anticipation over what he was going to do next. She took a deep breath, breathing in the scent of his skin and feeling little pulses of arousal travel down to her loins, settling in her damp sex.

'You will,' Alexei promised.

She felt his hands cover her breasts, stroking and squeezing them gently, her nipples like little pebbles against his palms. Her posture with her arms over her head made her breasts swell out towards his touch. Katya's lips parted on a moan of pleasure. The warmth of his body flowed into her, banishing the frigid air of the cellar. A trickle of viscous fluid ran down her inner thigh, making her want to squirm with need and press her thighs together to ease the growing ache.

Alexei's hands moved away from her, and she heard the rasping sound of him removing his belt. The sound assaulted her with the memory of the time she had made love with Nicholas in front of the fire; when she had forced herself to keep her eyes closed and take pleasure from the heightening of her other senses. Only then, there had been no fear, no coldness, no apprehension. Then, there had been love and warmth and pure, honest trust.

Tears filled Katya's eyes behind the smooth silk of her blindfold. Where was her beloved Nicholas now? Was he thinking about her? Was she betraying him by taking pleasure from another man? What kind of person was she to find a thrilling fascination in the illicit, dangerous actions of the Cossack captain, to be aroused so easily by his dominant, overbearing sexuality? Unbeknown to her, a tear slipped underneath the black silk and fell down her cheek.

A moment of silence filled the cold air. Then Alexei's warm tongue touched her cheek and licked away the salty tear. It was an oddly touching gesture coming from him and it alleviated some of her escalating pain. His fingers smoothed down her abdomen, through the dark curls between her thighs, and slipped between her legs to part them. He rubbed a strip of ripped silk into the moist pleats of her labia and the soft material felt delicious against her own silkiness.

Alexei moved his hands under her thighs, lifting and parting her legs with an ease that reminded Katya all too clearly of his physical and psychological power. Hooking her legs over his forearms, he lifted her off the ground until she was supported only by the strength of his arms.

Katya gasped, her fingers fumbling for the hook above her head so she could regain a sense of balance and control.

'Don't,' Alexei whispered, his breath hot against her lips. 'I won't let you go.'

Katya wondered if he meant his words to have a deeper meaning, or if she was only reading them that way. She squeezed her eyes shut behind the blindfold and let her hands go limp. Alexei's hands curved underneath her, holding her in place. A trembling urgency began in her lower belly and radiated to the ache at the centre of her being. She felt the heavy, hard knob of his cock press against her inner folds, spread like a fleshy oyster for his penetration. Exposed and feeling intensely vulnerable, Katya sank her teeth into her lower lip and tried not to betray her growing need. She had never felt like this before, immersed in the compelling eroticism of simultaneous helplessness and want. Her heart hammered in her chest, flaming her blood, and her mind fogged with the sensuality of cold air on her skin and the hot warmth of Alexei's muscular forearms, his hardness between her legs.

She waited tensely for him to say something; to order her to beg him. She would do it again, she knew she would; she would beg and plead for him to thrust into her and satisfy the painful ache of desire. But the order did not emerge from his lips. Instead, he pressed into her slowly, centimetre by hard centimetre, stretching her tight, slick passage to accommodate him.

Instinctively, Katya wrapped her legs around his hips to urge him closer. She felt the blood rushing through him, the dampness that trickled from the tip and mingled with her own fluids of arousal. Her chest heaved with deepening breaths, and she gasped when she felt Alexei's teeth close around one of her hard nipples. The sharp edge of his teeth sent a shot of pleasure through her entire body. Alexei's hips pushed forward further, easing his large stalk into her until he could go no further. Katya felt the movements of his chest as he exhaled deeply, his hot breath warming her taut peak.

She moaned. She tightened her legs around him,

relishing the sensation of his hard length throbbing inside her. Her inner muscles clenched around him and she pushed down so her swollen clitoris rubbed against him. The pressure built in her loins.

'Yes . . .' The word escaped her on a groan as he began to move, and she lost all sense of inhibition. Her head fell back against the wall, exposing the arched column of her throat to his seeking lips.

'Faster,' she gasped, squirming against him as her legs quivered with tension and her sex surged. 'Harder.'

He thrust into her with a quick movement, and Katya winced with a mixture of pleasure and discomfort when her body strained against his length. Then, he pulled out of her and thrust forward again, creating a slick, easy rhythm that made her soul burn. His strong arms held her easily, even as he increased the pace of his thrusts, and her body shook with the force of both his and her heated movements.

Pleasure shattered Katya, sparking through her body with bursts of glitter and sensation. She cried out in rapture and desperation, wanting to wrap her arms around Alexei and hold him to steady her spinning world, but his cock inside her and his hands digging into her buttocks were the only things that kept her rooted to physical reality. His grip tightened as his body tensed and his hot seed spurted out of him and flowed into her.

Katya drew in a sharp breath and discovered suddenly that she could raise her bound hands off the hook. Arching her body upward, she lifted her arms and draped them over Alexei's head and around his shoulders, letting herself collapse against him. Without thinking that she was clinging to her captor, she tightened her arms around him and buried her face in his neck. Her blindfold was wet with tears and perspiration, and she still felt him pulsing inside her.

Alexei didn't move. His hands still clutched her buttocks, but he eased her down the length of his slick, muscular body until her tied hands caught on the back of his neck. She wanted desperately to see him; she could sense his dark gaze burning into her and searing her with heat. The shredded silk of her shift clung damply to her body. The instant Alexei's body separated from Katya, the coldness of the frigid air quivered against her skin with the shock of remembrance.

Blindly, she stood on tiptoe and stretched to lift her arms back over his head, ashamed of the display of her growing obsession with him and what he could do to her. With her arms in front of her, she knew she could ease the blindfold away, but she didn't want to anger him any further.

Alexei didn't make a sound, but Katya knew the second he moved away. Then she heard the sounds of him dressing, the heavy stomp of his boots against the stone floor. She stood silently, her body continuing to pulse with lingering pleasure, waiting for him to say or do something.

Finally, he moved towards her again and his fingers began to untie the belt binding her hands. He untied the black silk of her blindfold. Katya blinked, opening her eyes slowly as they adjusted to the dim, reddish light. She wiped the dampness on her cheeks with the back of her hand and lifted her gaze to the captain.

He stood with his hands on his hips, looking down at her with inscrutable eyes. His expression was hard and rigid, crossed with shadows and flickering light from the campfires. There was nothing about him that suggested he had just engaged in an erotic encounter. Katya suddenly felt foolish and unguarded, embarrassed by her wanton display and the evidence that she had secretly thrilled in the things he did to her.

'You can leave in ten minutes,' he said. 'No sooner than that.'

With that, he turned and strode out of the room. Katya stared at his retreating back, wrapping her arms around herself as a blade of coldness sliced through her. She had no idea what time it was, nor how long it would be

before ten minutes passed. With Alexei gone, the coldness of the cellar was all the more acute. She grabbed
her discarded night-robe and wrapped it around her
body, curling up in a ball to stay warm. She began
shaking so hard that her teeth rattled, and a sudden rush
of anger swept through her over Alexei's order.

Katya stood and strode towards the door, fighting the
disgust and shame that rose in her like bile. She hurried
out of the cellar and up the stairs, nearly running
through the kitchens to avoid being seen by the servants
or the soldiers. Thankfully, she didn't encounter anyone
in the corridors, and she slammed her bedchamber door
with relief.

She removed the torn, silk shift and tossed it in a
corner, then washed herself as best she could with the
basin of water she kept by the bed. She didn't understand how it was possible to feel such an intense attraction and need for a man who was so forbidding and
austere. He kept her wavering between fear and desire
with an authority that made her wonder just how far she
might go for him. She had a feeling he could make her
do things she would never have imagined.

An hour later, Katya sat before the fire. Unable to sleep
or read, all she could do was think about what else
might happen to her in the encampment. She looked up
at the sound of a knock on the door. Her entire body felt
rather bruised from the captain's powerful lovemaking
and she didn't think she could take another occurrence.
To her relief, the door opened to reveal an attractive
woman with blonde hair and a sympathetic smile.

'Katya?' said the woman.

'Yes.'

'I brought you some tea.' The woman walked into the
room, pushing the door closed behind her. She carried a
tray with a cracked teapot and a filigree silver glass that
looked tarnished and old. 'I thought you might like
some.'

'Thank you. That's very kind of you.'

'My name is Svetlana.' Svetlana set the tray down and poured some tea into the glass. She handed it to Katya with a rueful smile. 'I, of all people, should know how demanding Alexei can be.'

Katya gave the other woman a startled look, then silently berated herself. Of course the captain would sleep with different women, she resolved. Why on earth would she imagine herself to be the only one? Still, she found the thought strangely unsettling.

'I'm terribly sorry this has happened to you.' Svetlana said.

Katya forced a smile. 'I suppose it could be worse.'

'It's really not so terrible around here. The soldiers are fighting for their freedom.'

'So are the Tsarist armies,' Katya pointed out.

'Yes, well, it's a good thing we women don't have to worry about that,' Svetlana continued soothingly. 'And don't worry, Katya. It won't be long before he tires of you.'

Katya read the subtext of the other woman's statement and, for some strange reason, it irritated her. 'Why do you say that?'

'Dozens of women have passed through his chamber,' Svetlana replied. 'Prisoners of war, you might say.'

Katya remembered Sergei's words telling of how Alexei gave women to his soldiers. 'What has happened to them?'

Svetlana shrugged. 'Some are still here. Some have . . . well, they couldn't take it.'

'And you?'

Svetlana laughed. 'I'm not a soldier's whore, Katya. I am going to be Alexei's wife.'

The cool confidence in the other woman's words seared Katya through the heart. And then she mentally chided herself for caring the slightest bit what Alexei did or didn't do with other women. 'How nice.'

'You and I will have to get together for a nice talk

sometime,' Svetlana said, as if they were at a weekend estate party rather than at war. 'I would love to hear about your life among the royals.'

Katya smiled politely, forcing away image after image of her aunt, her uncle, her cousins, and her Nicholas.

'Well, I can see you're rather tired,' Svetlana said. 'I'll say goodnight. Please let me know if there's anything I can do for you.'

'Thank you.' Katya said, and watched the other woman leave.

Svetlana smiled to herself as she closed the door of her bedchamber. As long as Katya Leskovna knew exactly where she stood in Alexei's eyes, her status as a whore shouldn't be a problem. Svetlana knew that word of her liaison with Ivan had started to spread. It was only a matter of time before Alexei heard of it. Then, he would certainly see how valuable she was to him and he would send the supercilious princess off to satisfy his soldiers.

It would not take long. From the looks of Katya's sated expression, flushed skin, and red marks on her neck, Svetlana figured that the other woman would last only about another week. Alexei did not like women who were obviously passionate or aggressive.

Maybe if Alexei thought that Katya was defying him, Svetlana considered, he would focus on making things miserable for her. Maybe he would lose interest in her sexually. If he punished her, then surely he wouldn't want her. Alexei wouldn't want a woman who didn't submit willingly to his orders. Surely he wouldn't.

That knowledge sparked a seed of an idea in Svetlana's mind. She hurried to pull on her cloak, then slipped through the shadows in the corridors and went outside. She walked to Ivan's tent, ignoring the knowing glances the soldiers tossed in her direction. They only wished they could have her as Alexei did. And, now, as Ivan did.

* * *

'Ivan,' she said, as she threw back the tent flap and strode inside.

Ivan's heartbeat quickened as he looked up from his desk at Svetlana. She was as beautiful as ever with her hair swirling around her shoulders. He still found it difficult to believe that she had actually come to him. He had been enraptured by her for months. At first, he had been so achingly attracted to her beauty that he'd hardly noticed anything else about her. But then, the more he watched her, the more he realised how hurt she always was by the way the captain treated her. And his anger towards the captain began to fuse with jealousy and a desire to rescue Svetlana from her blind love.

'You're early,' he said. He stood and approached her, bending to kiss her full lips.

Svetlana pulled her head back impatiently. 'I need your help, Ivan.'

'With what?' He cupped her breast in his hand and began to stroke her nipple to arousal.

'You know that woman who is Alexei's new whore?' Svetlana asked.

'You mean the royal woman?' he replied. 'Katya?'

'Yes. I want you to help me disgrace her in front of Alexei.'

Ivan lifted his head and frowned down at her. An uneasy feeling stirred in his gut. 'What are you talking about?'

As if wanting to alleviate his apprehension, Svetlana stroked her fingers over his groin. She massaged his soft bulge for a moment before the warmth of her fingers flowed through the fabric of his trousers. Ivan's breathing increased in pace.

'I think she is hurting Alexei,' Svetlana whispered, her blue eyes wide as she looked up into his face. 'I think he is obsessed with her and that she might create problems for the success of the army.'

'Why do you say that?' His cock began to expand under her touch. Part of him was irritated by his reaction to her, while the other part wanted nothing else than to sink into her softness.

'If he isn't paying attention to his work the entire army suffers,' Svetlana said, a glint of satisfaction sparkling in her eyes as she felt his growing hardness. 'You don't want that to happen, do you?'

Ivan knew the captain's possessiveness of Katya Leskovna stemmed from his desire to control everything around him, but it was also evident that he treated her far differently than he had ever treated Svetlana.

'If the captain is obsessed with anything, it's the army,' he said.

'I'm telling you, she's highly manipulative,' Svetlana persisted, looking somewhat annoyed that he hadn't agreed with her immediately. 'I simply want Alexei to know what kind of slut she really is. Perhaps that might take his mind off her and put it back on battle manoeuvres.'

Ivan almost smiled. 'I doubt anything can distract the captain from the army. Not even Katya Leskovna.'

'Well, she is,' Svetlana murmured. 'I think she's some sort of witch.'

'What do you want to do?'

Svetlana unbuttoned his trousers and slipped her hand into the opening, her fingers drifting casually across the hot, warm skin of his cock. 'You know the group of gypsies that travel around the area? Sometimes they're allowed into the perimeters of the estate to entertain the soldiers. I want Katya to be caught with one of them.'

Ivan felt a mild aversion to her idea. It wasn't like her. He knew Svetlana wasn't vindictive, and this desire to arouse Alexei's wrath against a prisoner seemed too spiteful for her. At the same time, a little thrill went through him at the knowledge that Svetlana wanted to infuriate the captain.

Her hand tightened around his cock. He exhaled sharply. The woman worked magic on him. 'Why one of the gypsies? Why not another soldier?'

'I think she should be with another woman,' Svetlana whispered.

Ivan's eyes flew open in surprise, and his cock hardened further at the thought. 'Another woman?'

Svetlana smiled and nodded. She slipped her fingers over the length of his cock, rubbing her thumb against the tip. 'Alexei will be furious. And a gypsy of all people: that's so low. So base. You'll help me, won't you, darling?'

Desire and her touch scorched away Ivan's unease. His mind swam with images of a naked Katya Leskovna with another woman, their bodies pressed together, white skin glowing with perspiration.

'Yes,' he gasped. 'Of course I will.'

Chapter Seven

*A*lexei marked a point on the map spread out on the table in front of him. The Tsarist White Armies were closing in on several areas of Cossack territory towards the south, and the Revolutionary Army troops had joined forces with several Bolshevik regiments to fight against them.

The pencil snapped suddenly in Alexei's hand from the force of his grip. He threw down the halves almost angrily. That was where he wanted to be, dammit. He wanted to be with the troops, fighting and making strategy on the battlefield, not sitting here mapping out manoeuvres on a piece of paper. How he craved the acrid smell of gunsmoke, the pounding of horses hooves, the sting of cold air, the rush of adrenaline like quicksilver through his veins . . .

He stood and grabbed a bottle of vodka from his desk, splashing some of the potent alcohol into a glass. Tilting his head back, he drained the glass in several swallows, trying to quench the burning, undying thirst for battle. He hated this, hated having to oversee the situation from headquarters, but the rational side of him knew that this was his only choice right now.

The situation did not look promising. He could do

more good for their cause by plotting strategies and letting others carry them out. He trusted no one else to assimilate all of the information pouring into the head-quarters. This dilapidated estate was the hub of their rebellion, and he had to be the one to ascertain what information was important and how to put it to use. However, that knowledge did not diminish his hunger to be on the battlefield. He was trapped here, his burning need for freedom suffocated under the dictates of war.

He threw the empty glass against the fireplace. The shattering sound rang through the room. An anxious knock sounded on the door and Ivan looked in.

'Captain, is everything all right?' he asked.

'Everything's fine,' Alexei snapped. 'Go away.'

'I just received word that one of the troops is bringing a group of Tsarist prisoners from the north,' Ivan said. 'About twenty-five of them. We're going to have to house them here until we can transport them to Novocharkassk.'

'Fine. Clear out the cellars. We'll put them there.' Alexei turned his attention back to the map, looking up in irritation when he realised that Ivan was still hovering nearby. 'What now?'

'I wanted to let you know that the gypsies have returned,' Ivan said. 'I let them into the estate. Some of the soldiers have been wanting entertainment.'

'Fine.'

Ivan turned to leave. Alexei's voice stopped him. 'Ivan, where is Katya Leskovna?'

'In the kitchens, where she usually is.'

'Send her in here.'

'Yes, Captain.' Ivan hurried out of the room.

Shortly afterward, there was a knock on the door. Katya walked in, her gaze sweeping the expanse of the library. She looked hot and tired; her hands reddened from washing dishes and her dress soiled with grease. Alexei noticed her eyes linger on the walls of books lining the room.

'You can borrow them, if you like.'

Katya turned to look at him. 'Oh. Thank you.' She hesitated. 'You wanted to see me, Captain?'

'Yes. Sit down.'

She sat down on one of the chairs in front of the desk. Alexei stood and walked to a cabinet near the fireplace. He removed a key from his pocket and unlocked the cabinet, taking out a small, oblong box. He opened the box to reveal a slender dagger with a silver handle. The blade was covered by a leather sheath.

'Keep this with you at all times,' he said, holding the dagger handle-first towards Katya. 'Do not hesitate to use it.'

Katya stared at the dagger, then looked up at him in shock. Alexei took her hand and placed the dagger in her palm.

'It has my initials carved on the handle,' he continued. He pointed to the Cyrillic letters inscribed on the silver handle. 'If you lose it, someone will know to return it to me. I trust, however, that you will not misplace it.'

Disbelief flashed in Katya's eyes. 'Why?'

'Despite your ideas, I have no intention of turning you over to my soldiers,' Alexei said, as his gaze lingered briefly on the gentle curve of her breasts underneath her bodice. Then, he added, 'not yet, anyhow. And it is necessary that you protect yourself.'

'And what makes you think I won't use it against you?' Katya asked, her voice hoarse.

'I suppose I don't know that,' Alexei replied, even though he knew quite well that she would not. 'Although I trust you will bear in mind that your situation here would be much worse should anything happen to me.'

Katya looked at the dagger, closing her fingers around the handle. 'Thank you.'

Alexei nodded shortly.

Katya went back to the kitchen, her heart hammering at the thought that he had actually consented to give her a weapon. She slipped the dagger into her pocket and returned to her position by the stove. The weight of the weapon felt comforting, although her confusion over Alexei's actions was increasing daily. He seemed alternately harsh and almost tender, but always painfully compelling and sexual. Katya's own admission of her attraction to him began to feel like an outright war.

She worked in the kitchens until late into the night. Weariness settled in her bones, but she forced herself to carry buckets of hot water up to her bathchamber so she could wash away the grime of labour.

After soaking in the bathtub, she slipped on her cotton nightshift and robe as she made her way back to her bedchamber. She had just climbed into bed when she heard a knock at the door.

'Come in,' she said reluctantly, knowing it could not be the captain. When he wanted her, he simply strode in.

The door opened, and Svetlana walked into the room.

'Oh, you're almost asleep,' she said in dismay.

'Yes, it's been a long day,' Katya replied.

'I was hoping you would come with me to the gypsy camp.'

'Gypsy camp?'

Svetlana nodded. 'Sometimes they're allowed within the perimeters of the estate if they're travelling around the area. They perform dances and theatre shows for the soldiers. I thought you might like to see them.'

'Thank you, but I'm very tired,' Katya said. 'Perhaps tomorrow?'

'They're leaving at dawn,' Svetlana said. 'Come with me, Katya. I hate walking through the camp alone, especially at night. Please. It gets so dreadfully boring around here, and the gypsies are in the area so rarely.'

Katya sighed. She didn't relish the idea of going out into the cold night, but so far Svetlana had been the only person who had been kind to her. Katya didn't trust Svetlana completely, although she didn't know why, but she was grateful for her amiability. Besides, it was late, and Alexei probably wouldn't come to her chamber tonight.

'Well, maybe for a little while,' she acquiesced.

Svetlana beamed. 'Wonderful! I'll get you some warm clothes.'

She hurried to the closet and pulled out a dark green, wool dress and a pair of stockings. She brought them back to Katya and waited while she dressed.

Katya sat on the edge of the bed and bent to slip the stockings over her legs.

'How many gypsies are there?' she asked, glancing up at Svetlana.

Surprise made her body tremble slightly, as she saw that the other woman was watching her with a wholly different expression. Katya realised that the scooped neckline of her shift had fallen forward with the movement of her body to expose the sway of her breasts, their peaks tautened by the cold air.

Svetlana was staring at her breasts.

Katya jerked upright, a flush creeping over her neck and cheeks. Never before had another woman looked at her like that.

'I'll meet you down in the foyer,' she suggested.

Svetlana lifted her gaze to meet Katya's. The blueness of her eyes had darkened further, and a small smile played about her lips.

'You haven't been with another woman, have you?' Svetlana asked.

Katya stared at her. 'No, of course not.'

'I didn't think so.' Svetlana held out the green dress. 'Hurry and get ready. We don't have much time.'

Katya hesitated, but took the dress and slipped it over her head, managing some quick manoeuvres to dress with a minimum of exposure. She pulled her stockings over her legs and bent to lace her boots. Svetlana gave her her cloak and the two women hurried soundlessly out into the corridor, and down the steps.

They passed several soldiers on the way, but the

soldiers paid little attention to them. The outside air had warmed with the advent of early summer, but a chill continued to linger like a curtain. Katya tugged her cloak more securely around her as she followed Svetlana through the camp. Gauzy smoke from the numerous fires hung in the air, along with the low sounds of the camp. Lanterns illuminated most of the tents, and the men were busy playing cards and drinking.

A tall, young soldier stepped suddenly out of the shadows. Katya came to a halt. She peered through the darkness and recognised the soldier as Ivan, one of Alexei's top men.

'Ivan!' Svetlana said in surprise. 'What are you doing here?'

'I overheard your plans to go to the gypsy camp,' Ivan replied. 'You must not go alone. You require an escort.'

'We require nothing of the kind,' Svetlana retorted.

'I will go with you,' Ivan said. 'The captain would not be pleased to hear that you went alone.'

Katya noticed Ivan and Svetlana exchange a particular look, but she figured their relationship was none of her business.

'Very well.' Svetlana reached back and took Katya's hand as they hurried through the camp to the perimeter of the estate with Ivan following them. A group of five gypsy wagons were arranged in a circle near the surrounding gate, and a large fire in the middle illuminated the half-dozen or so dark-haired men and women at one end of the camp.

A pretty woman with large, black eyes and long, flowing black hair that fell to her waist looked up and saw Svetlana and Katya approaching. She smiled with delight.

'You are Katya, yes?' she asked in a mellifluous voice, her Russian touched with the hint of a Ukrainian accent.

'Yes.' Katya was taken aback when the gypsy leant forward and kissed her full on the lips. The kiss was unexpected, although not entirely unpleasant. The woman's lips were large and soft, brushing Katya's with a tenderness that Alexei's kisses lacked.

'Come. I am Zora.' Zora smiled at Svetlana and Ivan. She curled her hand around Katya's, leading her to the centre of the camp.

Warmth from the fire reached out to caress Katya's cold skin. The other gypsies gave Svetlana, Ivan, and Katya curious glances, but then returned to their conversations and games.

Katya looked at Svetlana as they sat down on low, wooden footstools by the fire. 'I thought they performed theatre and dances,' she said.

Svetlana nodded, glancing at Ivan as he sat down next to her. 'They do. They might be finished for the evening. Most of the men and women have gone to sleep.'

'Oh.' Wondering why Svetlana had brought her here if the performances were over, Katya stood. 'In that case, I'll go back to the manor. I'm tired and –'

'Come, sit down.' Svetlana interrupted and reached up and tugged on Katya's arm. 'Zora is wonderful. You'll like her, and perhaps we can convince her to dance for us.'

Katya sat. Zora smiled at her and removed a leather flask from her pocket. She handed it to Katya.

'Drink,' she suggested. 'It will banish your fatigue and warm you.'

Katya tilted her head back and took a swallow. The liquid was thick and sweet, flowing effortlessly down her throat. It seemed to warm her blood almost instantly.

Zora handed the flask to Svetlana, who also drank.

'You would like me to dance for you, yes?' Zora asked, her dark eyes sparking mischievously as she looked from Katya to Svetlana.

'Yes,' Svetlana murmured.

Katya didn't notice the look exchanged by the other two women, and she reached for the flask again to consume more of the delicious, warming drink. She discovered that Zora was right: her weariness was replaced by a hum of energy flowing through her veins.

'Wait here.' Zora hurried towards one of the surrounding wagons.

Svetlana reached out to squeeze Katya's hand. 'I'm so glad you're here. Isn't Zora beautiful?'

Katya nodded, realising that Svetlana, too, was quite lovely. Firelight danced in her deep, blue eyes, and cast a glow of red over her delicate features. Katya stared at her for a minute, wondering suddenly what it would be like to kiss Svetlana as Zora had kissed her.

Disturbed and embarrassed by the thought, she ducked her head and took another drink from the flask. 'This is wonderful. What is it?'

'I have no idea.' Svetlana took the flask from Katya and swallowed some of the liquid, then passed it to Ivan.

Zora returned with bells around her ankles and a stringed instrument like a guitar, but smaller and with dangling bells. She smiled at Katya again and bent to kiss her on the lips. Katya wasn't disturbed by the kiss this time; in fact, she decided that she rather liked it.

She stared at Zora as the gypsy woman began to dance. Her long hair flew around her, and her brightly-coloured clothing shimmered and swayed in the firelight. The bells attached to her ankles and instrument rang cheerfully into the dark, cold night. The beat was a heady one, pulsing in Katya's veins as Zora began to simultaneously beat on the instrument and strum the tight strings. Her feet, clad only in a pair of thinly-strapped sandals, pranced lightly on the frozen ground as she twirled and whirled in front of them.

Katya found herself entranced by the sight of Zora dancing. Her gaze slipped down to the gypsy woman's breasts, which moved unhindered beneath the thin cotton of her bodice. Her breasts were large, her nipples tenting beneath the fabric and swaying with her rhythms. Katya's mouth went dry and she reached for the flask. She felt her body responding to Zora's sensuous movements.

The realisation didn't shock her as much as it should have. Katya's entire body felt warm, languid, and relaxed from the drink, and she parted her legs slightly to experience the rush of cold air that swept underneath her petticoats and cooled her heating sex.

Svetlana put her lips against Katya's ear. 'She's so beautiful.'

Katya nodded. Then Zora reached down, took both her hands and tugged Katya off the footstool.

'Come, Katya,' she said, her eyes sparkling. 'Dance with me.'

'No, I –' The words died in her throat when Zora put her arms around her waist and pulled her close. Katya felt Zora's breasts press against her own; the heat of Zora's body from her exertion seeped through their clothing.

Zora's hands slipped down to Katya's hips and drew her even closer. She began to gyrate her pelvis against Katya's with movements that created a swirl of warmth in her belly. She found herself captivated by the gypsy's heated sensuality and erotic movements, by the sound of bells ringing through the air. The drink had made her light-headed and loose, and she began to sway willingly and move wherever Zora wanted to take her.

None of the other people in the camp seemed to be paying attention to them, save for Ivan and Svetlana, who stared at them unceasingly. Katya caught a glimpse of Ivan's rather aroused look, and a little thrill shot through her at the thought that the young man liked watching her and Zora together.

Katya didn't protest when Zora leant towards her to kiss her again, slipping her tongue past Katya's lips and into her mouth. The other woman felt so different from men like Nicholas and Alexei. Zora was all softness and sweetness, her hot breath caressing Katya with a desire that Katya began to feel herself. She parted her lips

114

tentatively, allowing Zora deeper access into her mouth, and felt a rush of pleasure when Zora murmured her satisfaction.

'That's it,' Zora murmured, swirling her tongue around Katya's mouth, biting gently at her lower lip. 'Open for me.'

A part of Katya knew she should put a stop to this, but the rest of her refused. Zora kissed and caressed her with a tenderness Katya had been sorely missing, and she welcomed it now with the entire force of her being. She let her hands drift down the gypsy's body, hesitating at the swell of her breasts.

Zora threaded her hands through Katya's hair, bringing their lips and mouths into full, open contact as she simultaneously pushed her breasts into Katya's hands. Her hard nipples poked against the material, and Katya traced them almost wonderingly with her fingers. She had touched her own breasts, of course, but never those of another woman, and she was fascinated by the sensation of hardness and softness all at the same time.

The heat from the fire washed over her. She edged her hands into Zora's bodice, letting her fingers brush over the warm, slightly damp skin underneath. Her own clothing felt heavy and confining, weighing her down, and she suddenly longed to rid herself of it. She felt Zora's heart pounding against her fingers, her breathing rapid.

Suddenly, Zora stepped away from her. Her dark eyes gleamed with heat and need as she met Katya's gaze and reached for the laces of her own bodice. With slow, deliberate movements, she tugged open her bodice to expose her large, gleaming breasts, peaked with hard, dark nipples.

Katya drew in a breath, her eyes following Zora's movements as the gypsy pulled off her skirt and let it fall into a puddle around her feet. Her body was full and luscious, her long, shapely legs taut with muscle from dancing. Katya's gaze moved lower to the dark mat of pubic hair at the juncture of Zora's thighs. Her heart leapt when the firelight caught the glistening moisture between Zora's legs, and her own body responded with a surge of fluid.

'Your turn,' Zora whispered, huskily.

Katya lifted her gaze to meet Zora's, seeing the dark flame of passion burning in the depths of the gypsy's eyes. She felt as if she was no longer herself, as if she no longer had a history or an identity as she began to slowly remove her clothing, knowing all the while that she would make love with this dark, exotic woman.

Cold air wafted against her back, but the heat from the flames was strong and all-encompassing. Dimly, Katya remembered several other gypsies were still in the camp, that Svetlana and Ivan were seated close by, but she no longer cared. Nearly dizzy with attraction to Zora and the stimulation of a new, sensual experience, she let her petticoats fall to the ground and pulled down her stockings.

Zora's eyes drifted admiringly over Katya's body. 'You're so lovely.'

She moved forward and took Katya in her arms, bending her head to kiss the side of her neck. Katya shivered as her body made contact with Zora's nakedness, their breasts crushing against each other. The other woman felt so warm and soft that Katya almost melted into the embrace. She took Zora's earlobe between her lips and sucked on it gently as she let her hands drift experimentally over Zora's smooth back and down to her buttocks. She caressed the twin globes of flesh with her hands, then shocked herself by slipping her finger into the cleft between them. Zora murmured her approval and encouragement, which bolstered Katya's courage. She probed more deeply with her fingers, eliciting a moan of pleasure from the other woman.

'Oh, yes . . .' Zora moaned and pressed a series of kisses across Katya's chest, before moving slowly down to her breasts.

Katya gasped when Zora took one of her nipples between her teeth, swirling her tongue around the hard nub and sending a jolt of pleasure right to her groin. Her knees went weak as sensations swirled through her, mingling with the effects of the strange drink and making her head spin. Zora put her hands on Katya's hips and urged her to the ground. A blanket had been spread out in front of the fire, and Katya's legs parted involuntarily when she laid down on her back. Zora came down on top of her.

The feeling of having another woman on top of her was both thrilling and unnerving. Zora began to gyrate her hips again as she had when she was dancing. Her large breasts dangled over Katya's as she lifted her head to smile at her.

'It feels good, yes?' she asked.

'Yes,' Katya whispered, letting her body relax as she sank into the very different sensations created by the touch of another woman.

An image of the Cossack captain flashed briefly into her mind, but it did not disturb her. Instead, she almost laughed. Being here with Zora had nothing to do with Alexei and his overpowering sexuality. This was about Katya and her own sensual nature, about allowing herself to make love to another woman and regain a sense of autonomy over her own body. With that resolution, she lifted her arms and wrapped them around Zora's neck, pulling the gypsy down to kiss her.

Zora laughed with delight at Katya's sudden aggression. She kissed her willingly, opening her mouth over hers, their tongues dancing together. Katya parted her legs further, wrapping her calves around Zora's to allow their vulvas to come together.

Zora moaned. 'Oh, my love, how perfect you are.'

She lifted her head, kissing Katya lingeringly, and began to rub her hands over Katya's breasts, smoothing and plucking at her tight nipples until Katya thought she would melt with pleasure. Zora moved down, her long fingers seeking and stroking as she licked a path of fire from Katya's nipples and over her belly to her mons. Apprehension shot through Katya, but she pushed it ruthlessly aside and succumbed to the sensations. Zora stroked her tongue over the dark hairs of Katya's pubis until she reached her heavy, swollen sex.

Katya gasped at the first touch of Zora's lips on her vulva, her entire body jerking in reaction. Her loins ached with pressure, ribbons of need winding through her body. Zora's breath was hot on the secret folds of her labia, and perspiration broke out on Katya's forehead. She moaned, stretching her arms over her head in a posture of utter submission. The gypsy seemed to know exactly what would pleasure Katya the most, and her tongue darted into the tight passage of Katya's vagina with a swiftness both startling and hugely exciting.

Full of the other woman, Katya lost herself to pure feeling. Her eyelids drifted closed and moans of pleasure emerged from her throat as she pushed herself towards Zora, burning for the release of passion. Zora circled Katya's clitoris with her tongue, making Katya buck against her and cry out her name as the pressure mounted and the universe exploded around her in a hail of bright colours and flames.

Katya's body went limp, her legs falling to the sides as if her muscles had turned to water. She forced her eyes to open as Zora moved back up her body, her own expression filled with satisfaction. She lowered her head to press her moist lips against Katya's. A shudder of excitement went through Katya at the taste of herself on the other woman's lips. She grasped the gypsy's arms and shifted so Zora was now lying on her back.

Zora smiled, her eyes bright with anticipation as Katya settled herself between her legs, gazing almost in awe at the sight of another woman's spread labia. Her heart hammered almost painfully in her chest, hot blood running like liquid fire through her veins. She inhaled the musky, private scent of the other woman, and her body throbbed in response.

Tentatively at first, Katya touched the tip of her tongue to Zora's inner folds, tasting her experimentally. She tasted pungent and salty, unlike anything Katya had ever experienced before. At Zora's encouraging moan, she became bolder with her tongue. Zora moaned with ecstasy, her head thrashing from side to side as she pumped her lower body up towards Katya's mouth. Katya felt Zora's body tighten as an orgasm swept through her, her body shaking and convulsing.

A low moan emerged from beside them. Katya turned her head, remembering suddenly that Ivan and Svetlana had been watching the entire scene.

Svetlana watched Zora and Katya make love to each other, stunned by how aroused she felt. She had intended to hurry back to the manor with Ivan and find Alexei, but she had been so entranced by the scene unfolding before her that she hadn't been able to move.

Her breath had come in rapid gasps as she watched Zora's and Katya's bodies shudder with powerful orgasms. She sensed Ivan becoming equally aroused beside her. They had drunk deeply from the flask, and the warm liquid created a heady feeling in her veins.

Katya returned her attention to Zora as the gypsy grasped her arms to urge her over her body. Svetlana looked at Ivan, whose face was flushed with excitement, his eyes glazed as he watched the naked, writhing women. An erection pressed against the front of his trousers.

Svetlana leant over and nipped at his earlobe with her teeth.

'You had better be saving some for me,' she breathed.

Her body throbbed with arousal, her sex hot and fleshy between her legs. She stroked her fingers against herself through her skirt, suppressing a gasp as she watched Katya licking Zora's nipples. Moans and whimpers of encouragement filled the air as the two women became lost again to their carnal pleasure. Svetlana parted her lips, seized suddenly by a desire to have Katya squirming around on top of *her*, licking her with that pink tongue, kissing her with those full lips.

As if sensing Svetlana's urge, Zora looked up, and her dark, smoky eyes met Svetlana's. The gypsy smiled with languid desire, and stretched out a long, slender hand towards Svetlana.

Svetlana gasped. Never had she imagined, she couldn't possibly ... why, she had barely been able to bring herself to put the idea in Katya's mind or to look at Katya's breasts, let alone asked her if she had ever been with a woman.

But, now she couldn't take her eyes off them. She was transfixed by the sight of Katya's slender body covering Zora's fuller figure, their breasts pressing together, legs entwined, vulvas rubbing against each other. Suddenly, Ivan didn't seem nearly as appealing. Without looking at him, Svetlana stood.

As if she were in a dream, she walked towards the naked women and knelt beside them. She looked into Zora's dark eyes, somehow feeling as if she could discover the mysteries of her soul. Her lips parted in an involuntary invitation. Zora reached out and put her hand around the back of Svetlana's neck to pull her down. She kissed Svetlana deeply, winding her tongue around her mouth and causing the most exquisite sensations. Zora reached out to pluck at the laces of Svetlana's bodice, but urgency swept over Svetlana like a wave and she undid the laces herself.

She shed her clothing quickly, wanting nothing more than to rub her naked flesh against the other women. Katya shifted on Zora's body, moving to the side so Svetlana could ease in beside her. Zora smiled, lifting her hand to stroke it through Svetlana's hair as she settled into the crook of her arm.

Svetlana looked at Katya, whose dark eyes watched

her as if they shared a secret. She couldn't help herself from leaning over and kissing Katya, tasting Zora's secretions on her lips. This was so wholly unlike her that part of her was shocked, but Zora's fingers had drifted down to her sex and she gave up any inhibitions. She parted her legs, wondering at the intense sensation of Zora's long fingers seeking and spreading her very core. Moisture dampened Zora's fingers. The gypsy gave a husky laugh.

Katya sat back on her heels. Her small breasts, topped with taut, quivering nipples, looked so pretty in the firelight that Svetlana wanted to kiss them. Katya smiled at her; a slow, dreamy smile that made her all the more lovely.

'You are beautiful,' Katya whispered. She leant over as her tongue began to trace the shell of Svetlana's ear and her hand fondled one of her breasts. 'Exquisite. I've dreamed of making love to a woman like you.'

Pride fluttered in Svetlana's belly, and she suddenly wanted to please Katya as completely as she had ever pleased Alexei. Even more so.

She turned her head, reaching out to put her hand somewhere, anywhere, on Katya's body, to feel as if the other woman was actually real and tangible. Her hand found Katya's thigh, and she stroked upward until her fingers encountered the wiry hairs of her pubis. After hesitating for only a second, Svetlana slipped her fingers into Katya's sex and explored the moist, silky folds pulsing with heat. Her heart lurched as her mind spun with a ribbon of pleasures and sensations.

The three women made love for what seemed like hours. Pleasure ran together like streams of heat, orgasms pulsing through them endlessly, tongues and fingers seeking, stroking and exploring. Their bodies grew damp with perspiration; their nerves hummed with longing. Svetlana thought they attempted every position known to humankind; anything that would allow them access to each other's hidden secrets and would create the rainfall of desire.

When exhaustion and satiation finally took hold of them, they curled up on the blanket, Svetlana tucked warmly between Zora and Katya, and slept.

Svetlana woke when it was still dark, but the grey sky overhead had just begun to lighten. Her body shivered with cold, even though someone had put several blankets and cloaks over their sleeping bodies. The fire had died to bright, glowing embers.

Iciness clenched Svetlana's insides. She shifted slightly, her gaze going to the spot where Ivan had been last night. He lay asleep against a large crate. Remembering why this had all started, Svetlana felt shame wash over her.

The cold light of the pre-dawn hours wiped away the heated sensuality of the night. Sveltana eased herself carefully out of the warm cocoon created by Katya and Zora's bodies; the other women shifted and murmured in protest, but did not wake. Svetlana nudged Zora towards Katya. The gypsy moved instinctively towards the warmth of a naked body. Within seconds, Zora's arms were around Katya from behind, her breasts pressing against Katya's back. They continued to sleep.

Her heart pounding, Svetlana dressed as quickly and silently as possible. She tossed her cloak around her shoulders and bent to shake Ivan's shoulder. He stirred, while mumbling something in his sleep.

'Ivan, wake up,' Svetlana hissed. 'We must find Alexei.'

Ivan yawned, reached up to rub his eyes, and looked up uncomprehendingly. Then, it was as if memory hit him all at once: his eyes widened and he looked at Svetlana with a significant gleam.

'You,' he said hoarsely. 'And them.' His gaze went to Zora and Katya. Svetlana shook him again in frustration.

'Forget that,' she snapped in a low voice. 'It was a

mistake. I was drugged, do you hear me? There was something in that drink.'

Ivan stared at her. 'But, you –'

'Button your pants,' Svetlana whispered. 'We must find Alexei, or the entire plan will be ruined. And don't you dare breathe a word of this to anyone. If you do, I'll personally see to it that Alexei has you drawn and quartered.'

'What if they tell him?'

'Then I'll deny it,' she answered. 'And you will support me.'

Ivan fumbled to button his pants as he stood, and shook his head as though to clear his thoughts. Svetlana whirled around and hurried out of the gypsy encampment towards the manor.

The soldiers were just beginning to rouse, but Svetlana knew Alexei would already be at work in his study. She pulled open the front door and ordered Ivan to wait for her in the marbled foyer.

She raced upstairs and into her bedchamber. She tried as best as she could to wash the mingled scents of sex off her body, but she didn't want to waste time with a bath. The gypsies were supposed to leave around dawn, and there was little time left. She dressed in a heavy, clean gown and brushed her hair. She paused for a moment to look at herself in the mirror, stunned by the flushed, sated look on her face.

Hoping Alexei would attribute her expression to good health and not a heated liaison with two other women, Svetlana hurried back downstairs. Ivan was waiting in the foyer, his uniform rumpled, but his expression was clearer and his eyes sharp.

'Now,' Svetlana said. 'You will agree with everything I say.'

'You know, there was a time when I wouldn't have expected you to carry out something like this,' Ivan said.

She tossed him a stern look. 'What does that mean?'

'You're not a spiteful person,' Ivan replied. 'I know

that. I've seen you tend to wounded soldiers, work alongside the servants in the kitchens, clean up after men who are too sick to do it themselves.'

'Thank you for noticing my saintly qualities.'

'I'm serious,' Ivan persisted. 'What has Katya Leskovna ever done to you? And don't tell me this is for the captain's benefit. I agreed with you the other night because you had your hand wrapped around my prick.'

'Maybe I need to lead you around by it to get you to agree with me,' Svetlana retorted.

Something pained flashed deep in his eyes, but Svetlana was too preoccupied to worry about it.

'I know you need someone on your side,' Ivan said. 'I don't mind being that person. I just hope you don't make a habit of enacting vengeance.'

Svetlana made a noise of irritation and headed towards the library.

The library was the only room in the manor, besides his bedchamber, that belonged solely to Alexei. It was his office and his sanctuary; no one dared bother him there unless they had an item of the utmost importance.

Svetlana considered her dilemma to be on such a level. She knocked once and let herself in when she heard his hard voice. He was sitting at his desk, his attention focused on a collection of papers, several candles lit around him to banish the pre-dawn shadows.

He looked up when she and Ivan entered. 'What?' he demanded.

Svetlana quailed inwardly at the tone in his voice, but forced herself to approach him. 'Alexei, I'm so sorry to bother you . . .'

'What do you want?'

She stopped in front of the desk and fixed her blue-eyed gaze on his. 'Ivan has come to me with a matter you will find important.'

'Has he?' Alexei said, and shot Ivan a look.

'Yes, sir,' Ivan said.

'He didn't want to disturb you in case it wasn't

important,' Svetlana continued. 'I assured him that it was.'

'And what is the matter?'

'Ivan went to the gypsy performance at midnight,' Svetlana explained earnestly.

'And?' Alexei's voice was impatient.

'He saw that woman. The royal woman.'

'Katya?'

'Yes. Katya. She was with another woman.'

'What do I care about that?' Alexei turned his attention back to his papers, as if that were the end of the conversation.

'No,' Svetlana insisted, gathering her courage in both hands. 'You don't understand. She was *with* a gypsy woman, Alexei. Making love to her.'

Alexei looked up sharply and pinned a glare on Ivan. 'Is that true?'

'Yes, sir.' Ivan looked somewhat relieved, as if he had realised he wasn't exactly lying. 'I didn't know what your orders about such matters were. I believe she's still there.'

Alexei's mouth tightened. 'At the gypsy camp?' he asked.

Svetlana sensed a close victory.

'With a gypsy woman,' she said. 'Isn't that dreadful?'

Alexei frowned and pushed himself away from the desk. He stood and stalked out of the room, grabbing his greatcoat on the way out. Svetlana felt a little thrill go through her as she hurried after him with Ivan close behind.

They followed Alexei through the camp, rushing to keep up with his long strides. His greatcoat billowed behind him as he approached the gypsy camp, his boots crushing the frozen grass. The sun hadn't yet risen, but the lightening sky and the moonlight provided a milky illumination.

Alexei's only thought was one of anger. If Ivan's words were true, Alexei reasoned, then he would have to prove to Katya again just what it meant to be a prisoner. No movement or activity emerged yet from the wagons or the gypsies. Alexei strode into the centre of the camp, his gaze going immediately to the two sleeping bodies by the fire.

He quickly crushed the jolt of desire as he saw the form of the gypsy woman beneath the blankets with her arm around Katya's body. The two women were sleeping deeply; the gypsy's long, black hair streamed over Katya's neck and shoulders as she pressed against her back.

Alexei turned to Svetlana and Ivan. He did not like the triumphant expression on Svetlana's face, nor the rather heated one on Ivan's.

'Leave now,' he said shortly. 'I will deal with this.'

'But, Alexei,' Svetlana protested.

'Leave.' Alexei demanded. He shot Ivan a pointed, cold look that made the younger man wrap his hand around Svetlana's arm and take a step backward.

'Come along, Sv– miss. I'll see that you get safely back to the manor.'

Svetlana tried to protest again, but Ivan was stronger than she was and he pulled her away and back towards the manor.

Alexei stood for a minute with his gaze on the sleeping women. So, the princess dared to defy him like this, did she? Perhaps he had to show her again who was in charge here. Show her who dictated what she did.

He approached the women and moved around so he was standing in front of Katya. He looked down at her face, her features relaxed in sleep, her eyelashes creating long shadows on her cheekbones. Her lashes fluttered, and then her eyes opened and looked uncomprehendingly at the black boots in front of her. She focused on the boots, and then her gaze travelled up Alexei's legs and torso until they reached his face.

He was satisfied to note the flicker of fear that sparked in her dark eyes.

'Captain –' she said.

'Did you have a nice night, Princess?'

Katya clutched at the blankets as her face went white. 'I don't . . . I didn't . . .'

The gypsy stirred beside her, her eyes still closed as she pressed a series of languid kisses across Katya's shoulder.

Alexei fought back another wave of desire as the blanket slipped and he caught a glimpse of the gypsy's dark nipple. She continued sleepily kissing Katya, who seemed frozen with shock.

'I suppose my question was redundant,' Alexei mused. With the toe of his boot, he pushed aside the blanket that covered Katya's torso, exposing her bare skin to the early morning air. 'You appear to have been thoroughly enjoying yourself.'

The gypsy frowned, her eyes opening with reluctance at the sound of an intruding, male voice. She looked up at Alexei, her eyes dark with lingering passion. 'Ah, sir, you have a lovely woman here.'

'Apparently, so do you,' Alexei replied.

The gypsy laughed. 'My name is Zora. Katya and I are wonderful friends.'

She reached down and began to fondle one of Katya's breasts. Katya's pale skin flushed a deep red. Alexei pushed her blanket down further, feeling his prick start to grow heavy at the sight of her lush, dark pubic hair.

For once, Katya appeared to be speechless. She jerked away from Zora as if the other woman's touch was suddenly repulsive.

Alexei met the gypsy woman's dark eyes. 'It appears as if you enjoyed her last night, Katya,' he said, softly.

The gypsy's eyes laughed with acknowledgement. As if making a silent agreement with him, she reached again for Katya's breasts.

'Now, Katya, darling, you must appease your man for being unfaithful,' Zora murmured, as she captured Katya's earlobe between her lips.

'He's not my man,' Katya snapped, yanking her head away from Zora's lips. 'He's my captor.'

'Ah, then you truly must appease him,' Zora said. 'It will not do to anger one's captor.'

Anger flashed in Katya's expression. She grabbed for her clothing, but Alexei pushed it out of her reach with his foot.

'Give me my clothes,' Katya ordered. 'I want to go back to my room.'

'No,' Alexei replied. 'I think you have some appeasing to do.'

Zora's eyes twinkled as she looked up at him and she reached to still Katya's frantic hands. 'Come, Katya. Kiss me like you did last night.'

'No!'

'Then I will kiss you.' Zora pinned Katya's hands at her sides and bent over her, pressing her lips heatedly over hers. With her elbow, she eased the blanket off their naked bodies. Their skin glowed an eerie white in the strange, pre-dawn light.

Alexei felt his sex stiffen further as he looked down at their nakedness, but he didn't move. Zora held Katya still with the top half of her body, pushing her tongue into Katya's mouth. Katya fought, arms straining and hips bucking to gain release, but Zora would not let her go.

'I won't do this,' Katya gasped. 'Not with him here.'

'Oh, yes, you will,' Alexei said softly. 'Unless you would like me to think of some other punishment.' He knew she was remembering the night in the cellar because her expression darkened and her face flushed even deeper.

'I hate you,' she hissed.

'How enlightening.'

Zora laughed while her hand slid down Katya's abdomen to her sex. She slipped her fingers into Katya's labia and began to gently massage her.

128

'Stop,' Katya whispered, turning an imploring gaze on to the gypsy woman. 'Not with him . . .'

'Ah, darling, your sensuality is so beautiful,' Zora murmured. 'You have no need to be ashamed. Come, open for me.'

Zora's seeking fingers soon created enough tension for Katya's legs to part slightly, but Katya turned from Alexei and buried her face in Zora's neck. Zora smiled up at Alexei, her gaze moving down to the significant bulge in his crotch as her fingers continued to stroke Katya.

'Katya, look at me,' Alexei ordered sharply.

'No,' said Katya, in a muffled voice.

'Katya.'

At the tone in his voice, she tore her face away from the comfort of Zora's shoulder and gave Alexei a rebellious glare that still could not hide the growing need in her expression.

'On your knees,' Alexei said softly.

'No.'

'Oh, you are going to be difficult, aren't you?' Zora murmured. She sighed and detached herself from Katya. Her dark hair shifted around her naked body as she got to her knees and moved towards Alexei.

Alexei heard Katya draw in a breath, but he didn't spare her a glance. He kept his eyes on Zora as she came to him. Her heated gaze focused on the bulge in his trousers. She reached out, undid his belt and then pulled at the buttons of his trousers. Katya stared at them both in shock.

Zora eased her hand into Alexei's trousers and closed it around his stiffening member. She murmured a low sound of surprise and approval at the size of it, her dark eyes glinting with excitement as she drew his prick from his trousers and guided it into her waiting mouth.

Her hot, damp cavern closed around his flesh with an expertise that didn't surprise him. Slowly, she took him fully into her mouth, easing her lips over his shaft until she had taken him in completely. It was not an act Katya had been able to perform. Alexei sensed her watching them with a growing mixture of emotion.

His hands delved into Zora's long hair and his fingers dug into her scalp as she began to slide back slowly. The sensation of cold air on his wet shaft sent a jolt through him.

Zora reached down to unbuckle his boots and remove his trousers. She looked at Katya, who was sitting up, her cloak clutched to her chest, her stunned gaze on them.

'Come here, Katya,' Zora murmured.

Katya shook her head. Fear darkened her eyes suddenly. Alexei was once again struck by the sudden urge to protect her. At the same time he wanted to keep her on the edge, to make her wonder what would happen next, to make her wonder if she really did have cause to fear him.

Keeping people on the edge meant he would always have an advantage over them. And having an advantage meant he would always have freedom.

He moved away from Zora and approached Katya. He saw that she was trembling. He stopped to look down at her.

'You defied me, didn't you?' he asked.

Numbly, Katya nodded.

Alexei reached out and took the cloak away from her, tossing it to the side. Her naked body glowed milky white in the dimness. Alexei cupped both of her breasts in his hands, stroking his thumbs over the hard tips. Katya let out a ragged sigh as her body continued to tremble.

'Turn around, Princess,' Alexei murmured.

She shook her head again.

'Turn around. I know you're afraid.'

'I didn't mean . . .' The words seemed to stick in her throat, and she swallowed hard.

Zora hurried to Katya's side and put her hands on Katya's waist. 'Katya, my love, I am here with you.'

Katya's body relaxed slightly in Zora's presence, and she allowed the gypsy to turn her around.

Zora sensed what Alexei wanted. She eased Katya on to her hands and knees with her buttocks towards Alexei.

'Captain, I –' said Katya.

'Shh.' Zora put her lips against Katya's ear as her hand began to caress the globes of the princess's buttocks. 'You know you have done wrong. You know he must punish you.'

Alexei removed the glove from his right hand. The sight of Katya's full, white, trembling buttocks projecting towards him made him so hard it was almost painful. He met Zora's gaze again. The gypsy smiled.

In a quick movement, Alexei slapped his hand against Katya's bottom with a light, stinging blow. Katya cried out more from surprise than pain and Alexei rained several more slaps on to her buttocks until they glowed red. He noted with satisfaction that her sex had begun to dampen with arousal. He dipped his finger into her labia to test her wetness.

A strangled gasp emerged from Katya's throat; Alexei sensed that she was trying to fight her excitement. He felt the tension of her muscles as she tried to close her legs and hide herself from the overt exposure, but his strong hands slipped down to hold her apart. He nodded at Zora, who moved around willingly to lap at Katya's vulva.

'Oh.' Katya let out a low groan when she felt Zora's tongue working at her labia.

Alexei reached underneath her, finding the tight button of her clitoris. He placed his other hand flat on the small of Katya's back as he massaged and manipulated the nub of her pleasure. Katya's body tightened and then shook with convulsions as she climaxed with a cry. Zora winked at Alexei before moving aside.

Without a word, Alexei positioned himself at the tight channel of Katya's sex and plunged inside. Katya moaned, her body jerking forward as she received the full extent of his hardness. Zora laughed with delight as she reached underneath Katya to caress her breasts.

'Ah, it feels good, does it not?' she asked.

Katya groaned in response as Alexei pushed forward again. Sweat dampened his forehead, but he reigned in his control and refused to allow himself a release. Instead, he reached around again and brought Katya to another sharp orgasm, feeling her inner walls clench around him. He pushed into her until he was fully embedded in her damp, satiny warmth.

With a glint in her eye, Zora lay on her back and wiggled her body underneath Katya. Alexei felt Zora's tongue lick at him, then find Katya's engorged clitoris. Swirling her tongue around the little nub, Zora rubbed Katya's nipples with one hand until Alexei felt Katya's body stiffen and shudder yet again. He pumped his cock into her and imagined spurting out his seed on to the globes of her bottom. He refused to indulge in the fantasy and when he felt close to the edge he pulled out of her quickly.

Katya's breathing was unsteady. Her entire body trembled as she turned around without meeting Alexei's eyes. Zora's long, brown fingers slid down to push Katya's thighs apart. By now, all of the fight had gone out of Katya, and she succumbed to the pressure of the other woman's hands.

Zora shot Alexei another quick smile and climbed on top of Katya so their breasts were pressed together. Zora gave Katya a long, slow kiss, spreading her legs apart at the same time. Alexei found himself staring at the highly enticing sight of two vulvas, one atop the other, spread wide as if waiting for him to fill them. He knelt between their legs and slipped his cock into Zora's passage. She enclosed him easily, letting out a sigh of approval as he started to thrust inside her. Alexei reached down again to find Katya's damp sex, sliding his forefinger into her vagina as he worked her clitoris with his thumb. Within seconds she convulsed around his finger. Zora squirmed, easing her own tension by rubbing against Katya's mons, before her climax shook through her body.

Alexei pulled out of her, his cock slick and throbbing. Zora seemed to know what he wanted because she eased herself off Katya. Katya lay on the blankets, her chest heaving with passion. Alexei smiled grimly to himself. He bent to stroke his tongue over the wet cavern of her vulva, rasping over her clitoris. She cried out as her body shook, almost instantly, with another orgasm; then she went limp and her eyelids drifted closed.

'Open your eyes, Katya,' Zora whispered, a secret smile playing about her lips as she gazed at Alexei's erection.

Katya obeyed, her eyes filled with confusion and satiation.

Alexei stepped back and allowed Zora to move in front of him and take him in her mouth again. He was so close to the edge that it didn't take long before the movement of the gypsy's lips and tongue caused him to explode. He groaned as his seed shot out of him in copious jets. The gypsy's body shook with another small, intense climax as she swallowed all of him.

Katya stared at them in a stunned silence. She didn't move as Alexei stood, pulled on his trousers and hooked the belt around his waist. He sat down on a nearby footstool and buckled his boots.

'Get dressed, Katya. You have a long day of work ahead of you.'

She didn't move. Zora hurried over to pick up Katya's clothes. She brought them to her and murmured in soothing tones as she helped her dress.

'I do hope we will see each other again, my love,' Zora whispered, kissing Katya on the lips.

She smiled at Alexei and kissed him as well. 'Take care of her, Captain. She is a treasure.'

The sun just began to break over the horizon as Alexei wrapped his hand around Katya's arm and led her from the camp. She stumbled beside him, her legs shaky, her expression bewildered.

'Perhaps that will remind you again which one of us is in control here,' Alexei said coolly, sparing her a sideways glance. 'Do not defy me, Katya. I do not like it.'

Chapter Eight

Katya plunged her hands into a bucket of scalding hot water and began to wash another pot. Her hands were badly chapped, her fingernails torn and brittle, but she scrubbed furiously at the pot as if she were doing penance. She wiped at her forehead with her sleeve, hoping that she could somehow scour away the shame and embarrassment of dawn.

Her face flushed heatedly as she remembered how the captain had manipulated her again. His calculating coldness had brought on wave after wave of pleasure, until sensation streamed unendingly through her entire body; until she had craved him more than she had ever craved anything in her life. He had proven all too clearly that he had the power in their relationship, and she had trembled and shuddered under his cool expertise, as he had known she would.

Katya grabbed a pile of dirty plates and thrust them into the hot water. Her heart began to pound with the memory of Alexei's orchestration of her pleasure. And as much as she had enjoyed Zora's sensual company, Katya had been unable to prevent the shocking rush of jealousy when she had witnessed the gypsy woman kneeling before the captain and taking him fully into her mouth. And then, when Alexei had penetrated Zora rather than Katya . . .

Damn him, she thought. Katya's teeth sank painfully into her lower lip as she scrubbed at the plates. How could she possibly be jealous of her captor? How could she have wanted to plead for his attention, for his erotic ministrations?

She tasted blood as her teeth cut into her tender flesh. Tears swam before her eyes. She didn't want to feel anything for Alexei. It was too confusing, too painful. Her emotions battled between hatred for the man who was forcing her to stay here and a cutting attraction and need that could not be denied.

Katya's mind went back to the few hours before Alexei had shocked her with his sudden presence in the gypsy camp. Her liaison with Zora had been so lovely and tender, and her memory of their carnal encounter was now as soft-edged as a dream. And when Svetlana had joined in the eroticism . . .

Svetlana!

Katya's thoughts had been in such turmoil over the past few hours that she hadn't even thought of the blonde beauty. Now, with the clarity of daylight, Katya realised that Svetlana had escaped their warm, sapphic embrace during the night and that she must have been the one to tell the captain what had occurred.

Katya's hands stilled as a rush of anger swept through her. Svetlana had told her she was going to be Alexei's wife, so it was obvious that she had been threatened by Katya's presence and had wanted Alexei to degrade her in some fashion. Which meant that Svetlana's kindness had been both shrewd and false.

As she rinsed the dishes in cold water, Katya thought of telling Alexei that Svetlana had hardly been immune to the sensuality of making love to another woman, but she dismissed the idea. Telling Alexei would serve no purpose and might anger him further, since he would probably believe she was lying. Besides, Katya was not one for informing on others. She would have to find another way to get back at Svetlana.

Katya smiled slightly. She had a feeling it wouldn't be difficult, not if Svetlana's submission the night before was anything to judge by.

She tensed when Sergei appeared at her side. The cook glowered down at her.

'You're working very slowly today,' he said.

Katya looked pointedly at the pile of clean pots, pans, and dishes next to her chair. 'I've finished with those,' she said.

'I think you need to be punished,' Sergei said, a gleam appearing in his eye that Katya had seen before.

She was ready when he reached for her, leaping off her footstool in defence. Her hand disappeared into the pocket of her skirt, and she withdrew Alexei's dagger faster than Sergei could move. She slashed the blade across Sergei's hand, drawing a deep line of blood.

Sergei grunted in pain and swore, his eyes flashing angrily at her. 'You bitch.'

'Stay the hell away from me,' Katya snapped. 'You touch me again, and I'll drive this dagger into your heart.'

'Is there a problem here?'

Both Katya and Sergei looked up in surprise as the deep sound of Alexei's voice cut through the haze of fury. He stood in the doorway, his gaze fixed on Sergei, his hands resting on his hips in a deceptively casual stance.

Sergei dropped his hand and wrapped the edge of his white apron around the wound. 'No, sir.'

Alexei's eyes swept to Katya, who still clutched the dagger in her hand. 'Katya?'

'Sergei and I had a little misunderstanding,' Katya said coolly. 'But I think it's been settled now, hasn't it, Sergei?'

A heavy silence settled in the air as they waited for Sergei's response. Finally, he nodded.

'Good,' Alexei said. 'Katya, I believe Eliza could use your help with laundry. She's upstairs stripping the sheets.'

Katya slipped the knife back into her pocket, her gaze still on Sergei as she walked out of the room. A feeling of triumph washed over her. She knew Sergei would not bother her again.

She didn't meet Alexei's gaze as she went past him and hurried upstairs. As she started up to the third floor, her gaze swept over a soldier standing in the shadows. She recognised him instantly: Lev.

He stepped forward, inclining his head towards a closed door. And, without a word, he opened the door and stepped inside.

Katya hesitated. He meant for her to follow him, but she had no proof that he was who he claimed to be. What if he wasn't a Tsarist? What if he was just another Cossack who wanted to find out what the captain found so appealing about her?

But, then, what if Lev really was a Tsarist? He was her only hope, her only link with the outside world. Katya slipped her hand into her pocket, closing her fingers around the dagger. She glanced furtively down the corridor, then ducked into the room after Lev.

The door closed behind her. Startled, Katya looked up at Lev, whose palm rested flat against the door. Katya's hand tightened on the dagger.

'Who are you?' she asked. 'Tell me the truth, or I'll tell the captain you've been bothering me. He won't take kindly to that.'

A corner of Lev's mouth lifted into a smile.

'Don't tell me you're becoming attached to the Cossack,' he said. 'I would be disappointed in you. He leads one of the few anti-monarchist Cossack armies.'

'I know. You haven't answered my question.'

'I'm a soldier in the fifteenth regiment of the Tsar's Cossack army,' Lev explained. 'I joined the captain's Revolutionary Army under false pretences, as you've probably guessed. I relay information about the Revolutionary and Bolshevik tactics to the heads of allied armies.'

Katya was startled by the rush of indignation that swept through her on Alexei's behalf. She ignored it, reminding herself that Alexei had taken her captive. What an odd thought. Why did she even have to remind herself?

'You're a spy,' she said.

'Yes.'

'Can you help me escape?'

'Not yet. There will be a time soon.'

'When?'

'A regiment of the Tsarist Army knows about the Revolutionary Army,' Lev said. 'They also know other Cossack armies are reluctant to attack them due to Cossack ties. However, the Tsarist armies have no such dilemma. They are en route as we speak.'

Katya's eyes widened. 'Truly? They are entering Cossack territory?'

'They already have. Once they learn of this encampment, they will most certainly stage an attack. The fifteenth regiment knows that a member of royalty is a prisoner. They will look for you when they arrive.'

'When will this happen?'

'I don't know yet,' Lev said apologetically. 'The situation changes every hour. The Tsar and his family are imprisoned at Tsarkoe Selo, and we can only hope the Russian people call for his return to the throne. If not . . .' His voice trailed off.

They both fell silent for a moment.

'Why can't I try and leave now?' Katya asked.

'Should you escape now, my lady, the captain will tear this place apart looking for the person who assisted you. I cannot risk that, not now. This is a crucial time, and we mustn't raise the slightest suspicion. I will find a way to tell you in advance, when I receive word of the impending plans.'

Katya put her hand on his arm. 'Thank you,' she said. 'Your presence here comforts me greatly.'

Lev gave her a slight smile and patted her hand. 'Leave now. And do not look at me or approach me if you see me. I will come to you.'

He nudged her towards the door. Katya slipped back into the corridor and hurried up to the third floor. Her entire soul filled with hope and gratefulness. She wasn't going to waste away here at the mercy of the Cossack captain and his army. The Tsarists would come. Someday soon, she would be free once again. All she had to do was bide her time.

She found Eliza in one of the bedrooms, giving the older woman a bright smile that seemed to startle her. Then she spent the rest of the day helping with the laundry.

That night, Katya took a bath and went into her bedchamber. She would not be able to leave the encampment for quite a while if Lev's words were anything to judge by. And she still had a plan of revenge to enact.

She slipped on her nightshift and wrapped her dressing gown around her body before she hurried out to the corridor. Emboldened by the memory of how Svetlana had betrayed her, Katya went up the thinly carpeted staircase to the next floor. Katya had stripped the sheets from Svetlana's bed that afternoon and so knew which room was Svetlana's bedchamber.

Without knocking, Katya opened the heavy, carved door and stepped into the room. Svetlana was sitting in a large, plush chair by the fire, sipping on a glass of tea. She wore her night-robe, and her long, blonde hair shimmered in the firelight.

Katya closed the door behind her with an audible click.

Svetlana looked up in surprise. Her blue eyes widened at the sight of Katya. 'What are you doing here?'

'I know it was you,' Katya said softly. 'I know you told Alexei where to find me this morning.'

Svetlana's mouth tightened. 'I did nothing of the kind, you little whore.'

'Oh, I'm a whore now, am I?' Katya asked. 'You didn't seem to think so when you were writhing around naked with me.'

Svetlana flushed deeply. 'I was drugged,' she said. 'That drink had something in it.'

'Don't make excuses,' Katya snapped. 'You know you wanted it.'

'I did not!'

'Didn't you?' Katya walked across the carpet to Svetlana. She reached out and ran her hand slowly through Svetlana's hair, watching the flickering light spill through the strands.

Svetlana jerked her head away as if she had been burned. She leapt off the chair and clutched a pillow in front of her like a shield. 'Get out of here.'

'You don't want me to go.' Katya felt the heady adrenaline of power as she watched Svetlana tremble slightly. Her sex dampened with anticipation.

'Yes, I do. I'll tell Alexei you were here.'

'No, you won't.' Katya had no doubt of her words. She crossed the room until she was standing directly in front of Svetlana. Slowly, she lifted her hands and undid the belt that laced Svetlana's night-robe together. She let the gown fall open and reached to cup Svetlana's breast through the cotton of her nightshift.

Svetlana's body twitched in response and she tried to step away. 'Don't touch me.'

'You know you want me again.' Katya saw how Svetlana's eyes had darkened to a deep blue; how her chest had started to rise with increasing breaths. Katya traced her finger around the other woman's nipple, watching it pucker and harden beneath her fingers. She lifted her hand and aroused Svetlana's left nipple.

'And you know you betrayed me,' Katya murmured. 'Don't you?'

Svetlana's lips parted. 'I didn't –'

141

'It was all a set up,' Katya continued. 'Only, you weren't there when the captain arrived, were you? He found the little scenario to be highly arousing.' Her gaze dropped to Svetlana's lips. 'He fucked us both beautifully,' she whispered. 'I'm sorry you weren't there to see it. Or to join in.'

Svetlana gasped, and her colour rose. 'Y-you're lying . . .'

'Oh, no.' Katya shook her head. 'You know Alexei. He's very sexual. He would never miss an opportunity like the one you presented to him.' She leant closer and brushed Svetlana's mouth with her own. 'His cock stays hard forever, doesn't it? I lost track of the number of times I came.'

She smiled in satisfaction as Svetlana's entire body trembled. Knowing she had the other woman under her spell, Katya flicked her tongue out of her mouth and licked Svetlana's lips. Then, she used the element of surprise and plunged her tongue into Svetlana's mouth as far as she could, tasting the hot sweetness.

Svetlana made a muffled sound that could have been a groan of pleasure or a protest, but she didn't try to move away. Katya's hands slid down to Svetlana's hips, moulding her soft curves to her palms, feeling the heat of her through the cotton of her gown. She continued kissing Svetlana deeply as she reached up to undo the buttons, sliding her tongue around her teeth and lips, feeling Svetlana start to respond.

'Don't move,' Katya whispered. She pushed Svetlana's gown off her shoulders, leaving the other woman standing naked in front of her. She looked with admiration at Svetlana's lush curves and heavy breasts, her nipples aroused to taut peaks. 'Tonight, you are going to do everything I say. Promise.'

She bent her head and took one of Svetlana's nipples in her mouth, swirling her tongue around the hardness. Svetlana gasped and arched her back, almost in offering.

'Promise,' Katya murmured again, injecting a warning note into her voice. 'You will obey me.'

Her body warmed with desire and the dizzying sensation of power. Already, she felt somewhat vindicated for the betrayal, heady with the feeling of sexual domination. She could now well understand why it was such a part of the captain's nature.

Svetlana knew she was on the edge of danger. Humiliation washed over her, even as she knew she would capitulate before this woman who held such a sexual sway over her. The sensation of Katya's lips on her nipple was driving her mad with desire, raining fire along her nerves.

'Yes,' Svetlana moaned. 'I promise. Everything you say.'

Katya smiled. She reached up to play with Svetlana's other nipple as she laved her with her tongue. 'And you're going to tell me what you want.'

'Yes.'

Katya stepped back, her gaze raking over Svetlana's body and stopping at the juncture of her thighs.

'Touch yourself there,' Katya instructed.

Svetlana balked, her face paling. 'No.'

Katya frowned. 'Am I going to have to punish you?'

Svetlana's breathing quickened, her breasts rising and falling with every breath. The idea of failing Katya was as distressing as the knowledge that Katya could very easily tell Alexei what she had figured out. With slow, embarrassed movements, she slid her hand down her belly and over her mons before she reached her vulva. Her eyes drifted closed as she touched her sex. Dampness glistened on her fingertips.

'Go lie down on the bed,' Katya said. 'And spread your legs.'

Svetlana flushed, her pretty features colouring with embarrassment. And yet, she made her way over to the bed and lay down, pride glowing in her belly at the way

Katya looked at her with a lusty expression. She made a move to open her legs, but an image of herself, of what she was doing, flashed in her mind. She closed her eyes.

'Please, I –'

'Do it,' Katya said sharply.

Trembling, Svetlana spread her legs, exposing her damp labia to Katya's heated gaze. She slipped her long fingers back into the soft folds as her head fell back against the pillows. Her eyes closed again as she traced her labia with her fingers, unable to prevent the waves of pleasure caused by her own touch. The bed dipped slightly as Katya climbed on to it.

'Open your eyes,' Katya whispered. 'Look at me.'

Svetlana's eyelids lifted slowly as she prayed that she would see approval in Katya's expression. Katya undid her dressing gown, letting it fall to the floor. She unfastened the buttons of her nightshift and slipped it off her shoulders as Svetlana's eyes travelled hungrily over her breasts crowned by rosy nipples that stood out like hard pebbles.

Svetlana stared up at Katya, stunned by how her sexual attraction to this woman had expanded to overwhelming levels. Svetlana wanted to kiss Katya everywhere, touch her, explore her sex until she knew it intimately. She wanted to hear Katya's cries of fulfilment in her ear as her hands caressed her breasts and brought her to peaks and valleys of pleasure.

She was unaware that every naked emotion was reflected in her blue eyes.

Katya smiled a smile of power. 'You like that, don't you?'

'Yes.'

'You'd like it if I touched you, wouldn't you?'

Oh, yes. Please do. Touch me, kiss me, lick me. 'Yes.'

'Do you want to ask me?' Katya asked.

'What?'

Katya bent forward, brushing her lips over Svetlana's, trailing her fingers down Svetlana's abdomen.

'Ask me,' she whispered. Her breath was hot and honeyed against Svetlana's mouth. 'Ask me to touch you.'

Svetlana flushed with shame. 'I can't.'

Katya rubbed her hands over Svetlana's breasts, pulling at her nipples and creating such pleasure that Svetlana began to moan and writhe underneath her. Her hand found Svetlana's sex, and her fingers began working the heavy bud of her clitoris. Svetlana gasped, her body arching towards the touch of the other woman.

'What do you want?' Katya hissed.

'Touch me, please,' Svetlana choked, her head falling back as whimpers emerged from her throat. She stretched her arms over her head in submission. 'Touch me.'

Katya smiled and climbed on top of Svetlana, straddling her lower body so their sexes brushed together. Svetlana sighed and shifted, pushing her body up towards Katya, loving the weight of the other woman. Katya bent over Svetlana's prone body and gave her a long, deep kiss that sent a fresh burst of fire crackling through Svetlana.

'Say please,' Katya ordered.

'Please,' Svetlana moaned. 'Please. I need you.'

Katya increased the pressure on her clitoris, her fingers stroking rapidly and expertly. Tension tightened in Svetlana's loins as she began to build towards the final, explosive release. She pushed her pelvis up frantically, trying to impale herself on Katya's fingers. She heard the other woman's husky laugh of amusement, but she was beyond caring.

And then, suddenly, Katya stopped.

Svetlana's eyes flew open in confusion and bewilderment. 'What . . .'

Katya gave her a cold look edged with cruelty.

'Be careful, Svetlana. There's no telling what Alexei might discover. But, for now, you and I will be the only ones who know how desperately you crave female companionship.' She smiled. 'Particularly mine.'

Svetlana stared at her in shock, her body aching for the release that had been so abruptly denied. Before she could move, before she could even respond, Katya pulled on her nightshift and dressing gown. She left the room without looking back.

For a long while, Svetlana didn't move. Her body went cold as embarrassment and shame took over where pleasure had been. Unable to bear her nakedness any longer, she climbed off the bed and thrust her arms into her dressing gown. Her sex quivered with unfulfilled desire. She curled up on the floor in front of the fire, trying to warm herself from the chill of rejection, humiliation, and the frozen knowledge that she had deserved this for what she did to Katya.

Too ashamed to give her body the release still throbbing inside her, Svetlana wrapped her arms around herself and closed her eyes. Her self-disgust seemed to be growing by the day as she found herself doing things she would never have thought herself capable of.

She was losing Alexei, if she had ever really had him to begin with. He never came to her at night anymore, and he ignored her during the day as if she had never existed in his life. Katya had taken her place – Katya, who had gone trustingly with her to the camp and then been betrayed after so many hours of sensuality. Katya, who was here through no fault of her own, who was Alexei's lover by circumstance and not because she had seduced him.

Svetlana wanted Katya and she wanted Alexei. She wanted to be loved; she wanted someone to touch her and please her without thinking only of their own pleasure, without some hidden motive. And without making her feel so hideously ashamed afterward.

Ivan found her like that, curled on the floor as if she were trying to hide in herself. He stepped into the room, his forehead creasing with worry as he saw her prone figure.

'Svetlana?' He hurried across the room, panic stirring in his gut. He dropped to his knees beside her, reaching out to touch her shoulder. 'Darling, are you all right?'

She shifted, waving her hand ineffectually in the air.

'I'm fine,' she said, her voice muffled. 'Go away, Ivan.'

'What's the matter?' Ivan persisted. His heart ached at the despondent slump to her body, and he had little doubt that the captain was the cause. Anger stirred inside him like a fire being stoked to life.

'Was it the captain?' he asked, his voice hardening. 'Did he do something to you?'

'No. Please, Ivan, just go away.'

'Not until you tell me what's wrong.' He reached over and pushed her hair away from her face, brushing his fingers over her cheek. She was so delicate, so fragile, like a teacup threaded with dozens of hairline fractures. 'You're sure it wasn't that bastard of a captain?'

Svetlana shook her head. 'No. He has barely spoken to me in days.'

Ivan heard the despair in her voice and it sliced into his heart like a knife. He stroked his fingers through her hair in a soothing, rhythmic movement, silently willing her to realise the truth about the captain she professed to love so deeply.

'All right,' he murmured. 'You don't want to tell me?'

Svetlana shook her head again. Her body was trembling underneath her dressing gown, although from cold or emotion, Ivan could not tell. He gathered her in his arms and pulled her towards him. She didn't protest, and he was gratified when he felt her relax against his chest; her body soft and pliant, and so womanly he could have touched and kissed her for weeks on end.

They sat like that for a very long time. Ivan began to think Svetlana had fallen asleep, but then she turned to look at him. Her blue eyes looked so haunted and lost that his heart cracked.

147

'Oh, Svetlana,' he whispered, touching her face with his fingertips. 'Whatever it is, it can't be that horrible. Whatever it is, I'll help you fix it. I promise.'

He bent his head and brushed his lips against hers, drinking in everything good and gentle about her. He wanted to obliterate the damage Alexei had done, to eradicate all thoughts of the arrogant Cossack. Encouraged by Svetlana's small whimper, Ivan urged her lips apart with his as his hands drifted down to the ribbons on her dressing gown. He pulled them off, sliding his hands underneath to touch her skin.

Her body surged and warmed in his hands. His penis began to strain at the front of his trousers as he lifted her breasts, rubbing his thumbs over her nipples. Svetlana moaned a soft sigh of pleasure, her eyes heavily lidded as she reached up to stroke her hand down his jaw.

'Ivan, I –'

He kissed her to prevent the words, swirling his tongue in the warm crevice of her mouth. He didn't want to hear anything. He only wanted to drown in her scented softness, to make her forget whatever had caused such a terrible, empty look to invade her blue eyes.

Ivan slipped Svetlana's dressing gown off her shoulders, then lowered her to the floor. His gaze roamed heatedly over her large breasts and taut nipples as he stripped off his clothes, sighing with relief when his cock sprung free. He took one of Svetlana's nipples in his mouth, sliding his fingers down to her sex.

His fingers touched the soft, wet lips of her labia. He was surprised by how slick she already was, his finger slipping easily into the tightness of her vagina. She began to pant and gasp, her writhing movements encouraging him to continue. Ivan moved his fingers around her clitoris, rubbing the tight, swollen bud. An orgasm rocked through Svetlana's body with a sudden force that made her buck against him and cry out.

'All right,' Ivan murmured, when he saw her eyes

open and look at him with something resembling shame. He did not want her to ever be ashamed in front of him. Not for anything. He lowered himself over her body, covering her nakedness with his own.

'God, you're beautiful,' he whispered. 'Everything about you is amazingly soft, warm, and perfect. I love watching you spend, your entire being becomes so alive, so totally uninhibited.'

Svetlana flushed, but this time it was a flush of pleasure rather than shame. She even smiled as she rubbed her hand over his cheek, her eyes warming.

'You're a dear, Ivan.'

He wished she wouldn't speak to him as if he were a child. Their age difference was less than six years, and it didn't matter to him anyway. He knew from the bottom of his soul that he could give her much more than the damn captain could.

'Is that all I am?' he asked softly, pressing a series of hot kisses against her neck.

Svetlana closed her eyes. Her legs parted as his cock nudged at her thigh, seeking the hot wetness of her sex. Ivan reached down to urge her legs farther apart as fire slipped through his veins and his heart raced with desire for the woman before him. He sank into her, groaning with ecstasy at the sensation of her inner flesh clenching around him. Hooking his hands underneath her thighs, he spread her apart, driving into her with a force that made her body tremble.

'Is that all I am?' Ivan asked again, his breathing torn by pants and moans of pleasure.

'Oh, God, no,' Svetlana gasped, lifting her arms to pull him back down to her as she wrapped her legs around his thighs. 'No, Ivan, no. You're my perfect, glorious lover. You're my companion, my confidante, my Ivan.'

Her words rang like music in his ears. Burying his face against her breasts, he drove into her again and again. His fingers worked her sexual bud with an aptitude borne of a desire to electrify her, and her body convulsed

149

around his until he could stand it no longer. He spilled himself into her with a groan and a rapture so intense it was almost painful.

Katya walked down the corridor to her bedchamber, irritated by the mild pangs of regret plaguing her over what she had done to Svetlana. She was the one who betrayed me, she told herself in disgust. She deserved everything she got. Probably more. But on the other hand, she thought, Svetlana's lover is suddenly screwing another woman – no doubt without any explanation, knowing the captain – and she has a right to be upset. Of course, she resolved, that doesn't mean she had to take it out on me and contrive to debase me the way she did.

So engrossed were Katya's thoughts that she didn't even hear the commotion until she had almost reached the door of her bedchamber. She stopped. Male voices snapped commands and orders, and other voices rose in protest. Curious, she hurried over to the stairway overlooking the foyer. She paused by the railing, staring down at the two dozen men in shackles who stood on the marble floor.

Katya gasped, her hand going to her chest as she recognised the uniforms of the Tsarist Army. *Prisoners of war.* Her heart hammered wildly in her chest. The sight of the shackled soldiers brought back the crushing reality of what she was doing here and of what was occurring in the country she loved so deeply. Tears filled her eyes.

The Cossack captain emerged from his study and strode into the foyer. The commotion died down at the first glimpse of his powerful presence. He stopped and crossed his arms over his chest, his disdain evident.

'Who is in charge of these prisoners?' he asked.

There was a brief silence before a voice spoke up. 'I am.'

Alexei's gaze went to the speaker.

'You?' he sneered. 'Wearing the uniform of a private?'

150

'Our captain was killed.'

'Since when is a private in charge of a group of prisoners?'

'Since we were taken prisoner.'

A brief amusement lit in Alexei's dark eyes. He motioned with a curt gesture for the speaker to step forward.

Shock reverberated through Katya's entire body. She clamped her hand over her mouth to stop herself from crying out as she recognised the private. Nicholas Fedorov.

'Oh, God,' Katya whispered. Her knees went weak, and she grabbed on to the stair railing to steady herself. 'Nicholas.'

She stared in disbelief at his familiar features, his jaw now darkened with bruises, his uniform torn and ragged. Shadows from the overhead chandelier cut across his face. An ache started in Katya's very soul, expanding outward like the ripples of a pebble tossed into a pool of silent, still water. She couldn't move, couldn't think beyond the fact that her love was standing so close to her, unaware of her presence.

And there was nothing she could do.

With a muffled groan, Katya sank to her knees on the cold, marble floor. She clutched the bars of the stair railing as her heart began to pound recklessly in her chest as though she had run for miles.

Nicholas and Alexei stared at each other for a long minute. Alexei was taller, his figure more powerful and intimidating, but Nicholas carried himself with equal amounts of courage and confidence.

'I am the captain of the Revolutionary Army,' Alexei said. 'What is your name?'

Despite his exhaustion and evident pain, Nicholas drew himself up and looked the older man in the eye without a hint of trepidation. 'Nicholas Fedorov. I've been a soldier in the Tsar's army for eight years.'

A smile quirked at the corner of Alexei's mouth. 'Not

anymore. Now you can call yourself a prisoner of the Revolutionary Army.'

'You bastard. At any minute, the Russian people will demand the reinstatement of the monarchy.'

'Perhaps. But, you might never know whether that happens.' The captain made a sharp gesture with his hand.

Ivan and several other Revolutionary soldiers shoved their rifles at the prisoners and herded them towards the cellars. Katya held her breath as Nicholas passed underneath her. Her entire body felt so weak that it took all her strength simply to breathe.

Nicholas. Here. With her. Also as a prisoner of war.

'You think they will save you, Princess?'

Katya's gaze jerked to Alexei, who was standing with his shoulder against the door-jamb, looking up at her. Her heart lurched in her chest. He was so damned perceptive, and she could only hope that she hadn't given anything away by her expression.

'Not as prisoners of war, they won't,' she replied.

'Do not think you can help them escape, Katya,' Alexei said shortly. 'None of my soldiers will hesitate to kill both you and them if you do. And neither will I.'

He turned to go back into his study, but threw Katya another look. 'The keys, by the way, are kept on a hook just inside the cellar door. I trust you will not have need to use them. Do not defy me again.'

Katya sat trembling on the cold, marble floor for countless minutes as she tried to take in Nicholas's presence in this huge, dilapidated manor. She wrapped her arms around herself and tried to stop shaking, refusing to give into her confusion over the captain's mental games. In a short while, Ivan and the other soldiers came out of the kitchen area. They were laughing and boasting about what they had done to the Tsarist soldiers.

Katya recoiled, her only thought being that she had to get to Nicholas as soon as possible. She waited until the soldiers had disappeared into the workroom. With her heart in her throat, she clutched her dressing gown around her and hurried down the stairs.

She ran through the foyer and kitchens, barely noticing the coldness of the stone underneath her feet. She grabbed a rusty bucket and filled it with water from the pump outside. Her breath came in rapid gasps as she yanked open the cellar door and descended the steps, closing her fist around the keys hanging on a hook. Several male voices spoke through the storage doors to each other. Katya waited, frozen, until she discerned Nicholas's voice from the others. She crept along the corridor until she reached the storage area that was now a prison. A heavy, wooden door with only a small, cut window barred the cell.

Katya waited until the voices had died down, and then she slid the key into the lock of Nicholas's cell. Holding her breath, she turned the key and opened the door. Her hands shook with nervousness as she slipped into the cell and closed the door behind her.

She blinked to let her eyes adjust to the dim, flickering light given off by the campfires glowing through the high window. She made out Nicholas's form sitting against the wall, his legs drawn up to his chest, his forehead resting on his knees in a posture of defeat.

Katya's heart ached. 'Nicholas,' she whispered.

He didn't move. Katya put the bucket of water down near the door and hurried across the expanse of the cell.

'Nicholas.' She knelt next to him and put a trembling hand on his arm.

After a long minute, as if he were absorbing the fact that a physical hand was on his arm, Nicholas lifted his head to look at her. He looked so tired and dispirited that Katya experienced a rush of fury towards the Cossack captain and his damned army.

Nicholas stared at her in disbelief, as if she were an apparition. 'Katya?'

Her hand tightened on his arm.

'Yes,' she whispered. 'I ... I've been here for several weeks. They brought me here before we reached Novocharkassk. Sofia managed to escape.'

Nicholas continued staring at her in silence.

'Nicholas, it's me. I saw them bring you in. I couldn't believe it.' Tears stung the backs of her eyes as she lifted a hand to his bruised jaw. A cut lashed across his cheek, lined with dried blood. 'Did they hurt you very badly?'

He didn't respond. Katya retrieved the bucket of water, then took the belt off her robe and dipped it in the cold water.

'This is cold.' She pressed the damp cloth against his wound and gently cleaned away the blood.

Nicholas's hand suddenly shot up to grasp her wrist and he clutched her almost painfully. 'Katya.'

'Yes,' Katya said in a choked whisper as her entire soul filled with emotion for him, for them. 'It's me, Nicholas. Really. I'm here.'

'Oh, God.'

Katya's tears overflowed when Nicholas brought his hand to her face and cupped her cheek with infinite tenderness. The cloth fell from her grip. Then their arms went around each other and nothing else mattered. Every instance of pain and despair dissolved into oblivion as Katya felt Nicholas's strong arms hold on to her and steady her spinning world. She buried her head in his shoulder and let her tears of relief pour out.

They clutched on to each other forever, slowly absorbing the reality of being in each other's arms again through some divine miracle. Katya cried until she had no tears left, never wanting to let him go again. Even when her sobs died down, she refused to release him, only pulling back slightly to gaze at him.

'Nicholas.' She gave him a watery smile. 'It feels so good to say your name.'

Nicholas reached up to brush her hair away from her forehead, not wanting to stop touching her.

'I can't believe it's you,' he whispered. 'I can't believe

you're here.' His eyes darkened with concern suddenly. 'What have they done to you? Have they hurt you?'

Katya shook her head, desperate to alleviate his concern. 'No, I'm fine. They haven't hurt me. They've just wanted me to work in the kitchens and do laundry.'

Nicholas didn't look convinced. Katya leant forward to brush his mouth with hers, glorying in the familiar feeling of him.

'Truly, Nicholas. I'm not hurt.' She pressed her lips more firmly against his. 'I'm not,' she murmured.

Warmth spread into the pit of her stomach; warmth and love and relief. He felt so good, so familiar, that her throat choked with tears again. Nicholas threaded his hand through her hair in a tender gesture, parting his lips over hers and drinking deeply from her. Katya closed her eyes and blocked out a sudden, unwanted image of Alexei as she gave herself up to the only man she had ever loved. They explored each other's mouths with a leisurely slowness, getting to know each other once again, stirring the embers of desire that had lain dormant for too long.

'Oh, yes,' Katya breathed as she sank into him, her breasts pressing against his hard chest, the coil of love and desire tightening in her belly. 'Kiss me. Touch me.'

'I've thought about you every day,' Nicholas murmured, as his hand slid down to her thigh. He began easing up the cotton of her nightshift. 'Every hour. I swear, Katya, you've haunted my nights.'

She sank into him, positioning herself so she was leaning against his thighs and resting diagonally across his chest. Nicholas supported her back with his left arm as he continued to gently plunder her mouth. The fingers of his right hand brushed against her thigh, and Katya shivered as she bent her knees and parted her legs.

Nicholas's fingers trailed up the soft skin of her inner thigh to the welcoming heat of her sex. His touch was familiar, but slightly hesitant. Distance, time, and experience had made them both a bit uncertain, but neither of them was willing to sacrifice everything they had ever felt for each other.

'Yes,' Katya whispered in encouragement, as Nicholas slipped his finger into the velvety folds of her labia. 'Like that. Just . . . like . . . that . . .'

She felt the growing evidence of his need pressing on her lower back and a thrill went through her. She shifted against him, smiling when a low murmur of pleasure resounded through his chest and into her. Her sex dampened at the touch of his fingers sliding along the crevices of her labia, lingering at the warm passage of her vagina. Her breathing became slow and heavy as she allowed her body to relax against him.

'Tell me if I'm hurting you,' she murmured, conscious of the fact that he was probably bruised in other places.

'Ah, Katya, you could never hurt me.'

His words pierced her like arrows, and Katya closed her eyes tightly, reaching up to run her hand through his thick, dark hair. She drew in a sharp breath when his forefinger slipped into her. She gave in to the familiar sensation of him as lovely memories of their lives together burst forth in her mind.

Easing her hand between them, Katya found the heavy bulge in his trousers and squeezed it lightly. With deft fingers, she undid his trousers and reached into the opening to find his penis. Her fingertips touched his hot, throbbing skin, and Nicholas murmured another sound of pleasure, shifting to give her easier access to his engorged flesh. Katya revelled in the familiar feeling of him. She knew his body as well as she knew her own, and she slid her enclosed hand up and down his shaft in the rhythm she knew he liked. The movement of his fingers in her sex began to increase in pace. Katya reached down with her other hand to stop him.

'Wait,' she whispered, desperately wanting to give him something, anything, to prove to him how much she still loved him. 'Wait, Nicholas.'

'But, you feel so good.'

'Let me –' She eased herself away from him and turned around; her gaze was fixed on his erect cock in the reddish, flickering light.

She grasped the base in her hand and bent her head to slide her lips over the hot tip. Nicholas groaned as the wet cavern of her mouth enclosed him. Loving him with everything in her, Katya inhaled and slackened her throat muscles as she eased her lips over him. Her eyelids drifted closed as she slid down him until she had nearly taken all of his hard, long length in her mouth.

Triumph fluttered in her. She gripped the base of his cock and began to stroke him with her lips and tongue. Nicholas's breathing grew ragged, his hand clutching the back of her neck.

'Katya, I can't –' A hoarse groan rumbled through his chest as his body convulsed into a climax.

Katya swallowed every drop of his seed and continued to stroke him hard, easing the last sensations out of him. She pulled away and sat back on her heels, her hand still wrapped around his cock. Her sex throbbed hotly in response to his arousal, but Nicholas didn't meet her gaze.

'What?' Frowning, Katya reached out and turned his face towards her. 'What's the matter?'

'I'm sorry,' he said. 'It's just been so long that I couldn't –'

'Oh, Nicholas, no.' Katya's chest tightened. 'I wanted you to. I'm glad you did.'

She leant in to kiss him again, stroking her tongue over his lower lip. He opened his mouth to take her in, and his hand slipped between her legs again. He fondled her sex with an expertise borne of familiarity and began tracing his fingers over her labia. Katya was so wet and aroused that an orgasm throbbed through her body the instant his thumb stroked her swollen clitoris. Nicholas's lips muffled her cry of pleasure as she sank against him, her breathing hard on his neck.

Katya clutched at him almost desperately, pressing

her face into his shoulder as his arms went securely around her.

'I can't believe you're here,' Nicholas murmured, his voice rough. 'You're like a dream come to life.'

Katya's arms tightened around him. 'No. Not a dream. Not anymore.'

Chapter Nine

Katya looked surreptitiously at the clock on the wall as she slipped a piece of bread into her apron pocket. Five long hours before she could try and sneak down to see Nicholas again. The mere thought of him warmed her to the bone, and she sent up another silent whisper of thanks to whatever force had brought him back to her.

She finished the supper dishes, then made her usual trips to fill buckets of hot water for a bath. She soaked for over an hour, considering the idea of releasing the prisoners. With access to the keys, she had the ability, but the result would be hopeless. The Tsarists were wounded and weak, and the Cossacks wouldn't hesitate to kill them on sight. As Alexei had clearly warned her. Katya sighed and eased herself out of the bath. She would just have to wait for Lev's signal. She slipped her nightshift on and walked out into the corridor.

'Miss Leskovna, the captain wants to see you.'

Startled at the sudden voice, Katya turned to find Ivan standing in the shadows. 'What?'

'He's in his study,' Ivan said. 'He asked for you.'

Katya frowned, thinking of Nicholas. 'Now?'

'Immediately, miss.'

'All right. Thank you.'

With a sigh, Katya tightened the belt of her dressing gown and padded down the ornate staircase to Alexei's study. She tensed as she passed through the converted drawing room, now filled with soldiers working at desks and tables, poring over maps and battle charts with the aid of lanterns.

Several of them grinned at each other as Katya hurried past. Nausea swirled in her gut at the thought of what they were thinking. She tried the doorknob of Alexei's study, only to find it locked. She knocked impatiently.

The door swung open to reveal the Cossack captain, lit from behind by the flames housed in the huge, stone fireplace against the wall, looking like an other-worldly demon.

A shiver slipped down Katya's spine at the sight of him. Had he discovered that she disobeyed him and went to Nicholas last night?

She read nothing on his inscrutable features.

'Come in.' Alexei stepped aside.

Katya entered the room, blocking out the low laughter emerging from the workroom as the door closed behind her. The click of the lock sliced through the air.

Katya's breathing shortened. If Alexei could shame her to fathomless depths after discovering she had stolen a kitchen knife, then there was no telling what he would do if he discovered that her lover, her Tsarist Army lover, was under the same roof. She slipped her trembling hands into the pockets of her dressing gown to hide them.

'Ivan told me you wanted to see me,' she said.

'Yes.' He leant against the door, crossing his arms over his chest, his gaze sliding over her body. 'Take off your clothes.'

She bristled at the order. Even after so many weeks, she hadn't gotten used to being ordered about. She suspected she never would.

Still, the thought of Nicholas caused her to reach for the belt on her dressing gown. The sooner this was over, the sooner she would be able to sneak down and see him.

She slipped the gown off and started to pull her nightshift over her head. Alexei's cold: 'Wait,' stopped her.

Katya's hands dropped to her sides, and she looked at him in confusion. 'Captain?'

Alexei's gaze slid past her to rest on a corner of the room. Shivers prickled the back of Katya's neck as she became aware of another presence.

Slowly, she turned her head to look at the man sitting in a chair near the fire. His thick, blond hair was brushed away from his forehead, his sharp, arrogant features split into planes of light and darkness from the fire. His cobalt-blue gaze pierced her like an arrow.

Katya's breath caught in her chest. Oh, God. What did the captain have in store for her now?

'This is Victor, my second in command,' Alexei said. 'He was responsible for the capture of the Tsarist prisoners.'

Katya had a sudden urge to grab her dressing gown and run out of the room. Instead, she said, 'Is that so?'

'He's been on the field for nearly a year,' Alexei continued. 'I'm sure you've heard rumours, Katya, that the battlefield is hardly the place to find a respectable woman.'

Nerves tightened her stomach. Surely he didn't expect . . .

Her dark eyes flashed with accusation as she looked at Alexei. 'You said you weren't going to . . . that you wouldn't . . .'

A black eyebrow lifted slightly. 'That I wouldn't what?'

'Turn me over to your soldiers,' Katya said in a rush, her skin crawling at the thought.

'Ah, but Victor is hardly "my soldiers,"' Alexei murmured.

He approached her in three strides, his hand coming

up to brush her hair away from her face. His powerful, potent sensuality slid along Katya's nerves, the warmth of his hand heating her skin.

She stared up at him, her throat tense with the effort of reigning in her emotions. 'Don't –'

She wanted to ask him if this was retribution for having disobeyed his orders about the Tsarist prisoners, but she didn't dare. He might not know anything about it.

'Come, Katya,' Alexei whispered, bending his head to brush a gentle kiss over her lips. 'Do not disappoint me.'

As if Victor were not in the room, he pulled her into his arms, letting her rest her head against his chest. The heat of his body spilled into her, and Katya could not help herself from relaxing against him. He frightened, angered, aroused and compelled her; she could not stop herself from wanting him. Even with Nicholas under the same roof.

Such an acknowledgement sent a whirl of confusion spinning through her. She pressed her face against the captain's shirtfront, squeezing her eyes shut.

'Don't,' she whispered again, hating the plea in her voice even as she knew anger would only exacerbate the situation. 'I can't –'

'You can.' His voice held the implacable, hard note she had come to recognise. It sent a rush of coldness through her entire body. 'You will.'

Begging would get her nowhere. Her pleas would fall on deaf ears. Anger would make the situation worse, and the outcome would be the same.

And, yet, something inside Katya stirred to life. Something that would not let her surrender meekly. She knew instinctively that Alexei would not leave the room. All right, then, Captain, she thought. I'll do as you wish. I will not disappoint you.

Even with her new sense of resolve, she trembled in his arms. 'Why?'

'Victor has never had the opportunity for a delectable

taste of royalty,' Alexei replied in amusement. 'And you, my dear, are a lovely introduction for him.'

He stepped away from her, letting a rush of cold air penetrate the space between them. Katya wrapped her arms around herself, trying to gather her courage in both hands. She could do this. She was not inexperienced. He was just another man, not a monster.

She shot Victor a quick glance. He hadn't moved. He was rather handsome, reminding her a little of the Bolshevik soldier she had met on the train to Novocharkassk. His eyes looked a hundred years old. She could see the evidence of his strength in the sinews of his forearms. Katya took some comfort in the knowledge that her dagger – Alexei's dagger – rested in the pocket of her dressing gown, not far from her reach. If Victor tried to hurt her, she would not hesitate to use it.

She waited. The air thickened with sexual tension and hunger. Alexei moved away, sinking into a chair on the other side of the room.

Victor stood. He wasn't as tall as Alexei, his features finely drawn, his body lean and tautly muscled. Shadows highlighted his face as he walked towards her.

'You are, indeed, quite lovely,' he murmured, his blue eyes glinting with arousal.

Katya forced herself not to move, not to step away from him in fear and apprehension. Without preliminaries, he lifted his hands to cup her face, sliding his fingers through the thick strands of her hair as he brought her mouth to his. Katya jerked backward at the sensation of his lips on hers, every muscle tensing in shock. His lips moved over hers with an utter lack of finesse, his tongue plunging into her mouth with a stab.

Katya suppressed a shudder of distaste over what the captain was making her do, but she strengthened her resolve with the knowledge that she still held at least one card in her favour. Or, she hoped that she did. He could not degrade her if she didn't let him.

Victor's hands slipped over her body, probing and

groping her soft curves with a sudden urgency. Already, Katya felt the hard bulge in his trousers pressing against her belly. She wrapped her arms around his neck, sinking her fingers into his hair as she forced herself to slide her tongue along his lower lip. She moved her lips away from his mouth, pressing them over his cheekbone to his ear.

'Wait,' she whispered. 'Go slowly.'

She took his hands in hers and guided them to the buttons of her nightshift. She closed her eyes and thought of Nicholas, a thought that brought an immediate rush of warmth through her body.

Victor's soldier hands fumbled with the delicate, pearl buttons, and he muttered a sound of impatience. Surprisingly, Katya was rather touched by his clumsy haste. She reached down to help him, slipping the buttons out of the holes and gradually baring her flesh. Victor's gaze rested hungrily on the curve of her breasts, the taut nipples tenting the cotton fabric of her nightshift. Katya glanced up at him through her lashes with what she hoped was an inviting look.

'Take it off,' she murmured.

Victor slipped the gown off her shoulders, drawing in a sharp breath at the sight of her pale nakedness in the firelight. Katya fought the urge to cover herself from the heated gazes of two men, one who still sat silently in the corner, his expression betraying nothing.

Victor's hot gaze roved over Katya with unappeased hunger. His unhidden desire sparked something warm and fluid inside her, curling through her body. When he reached out and palmed her breasts, she let her eyelids drift closed. For Alexei's benefit, she deliberately arched her back, pushing her breasts into Victor's hands.

Victor palmed her breasts, teasing the nipples into hard, jutting peaks and sending quivers of pleasure twining through her body. Her blood warmed in her veins with a swiftness that surprised her. She hadn't expected his touch to be arousing. With hands that shook only slightly, she slipped her fingers over his lean chest, down to the thrusting bulge in his trousers. With a husky murmur of pleasure – loud enough for Alexei to hear across the room – she rubbed her fingers over Victor's groin, feeling it expand even more underneath her touch. Katya made quick work of his trouser buttons and reached in to find the hot flesh of his manhood.

When her hand closed around his erection, Victor groaned. Katya shot him a quick smile, running her hand along the hard length. Longing coursed through her body, settling in her loins, her sex swelling with moisture. Her breathing came rapidly as she tugged Victor's trousers over his hips, and she knelt down in front of him as he stepped out of them.

Without sparing Alexei a glance, Katya leant forward and began laving Victor's erection. She made a point of murmuring plenty of lewd, noisy sounds of pleasure as she stroked her tongue up and down his length, her face flushed, her eyes half-closed. Victor's hands clenched in her hair as he growled low moans of approval.

Katya took a deep breath as she began to slide Victor's cock into her mouth. His shorter length made complete submersion much easier than trying to take in all of the captain, but Katya knew instinctively that her show of acceptance and desire to please Victor would rankle Alexei. Letting her lips slacken, she moved her head back and forth, her hands on Victor's thighs as he slid in and out of her mouth.

Victor's hands tightened on her head.

'Stop,' he said hoarsely.

With a flutter of satisfaction, Katya pulled away. Her chest heaved, her skin blooming a flushed red with desire. Without a word, she laid down on her back, parting her legs in invitation, leaving neither man in any doubt as to the extent of her arousal.

Victor stared at her, his eyes glazed with desire. He dropped to his knees, almost reverently, gazing at her sex as if it were a perfect flower.

Katya shifted impatiently.

'Victor,' she said. 'Now. I want you inside me.'

Victor continued staring at her sex, then bent forward to kiss it. Katya's body twitched in response to the touch of his lips, her lower body lifting off the floor. She spread her legs farther apart and moaned loudly to express her approval, even though Victor began to lap at her as if he were a thirsty dog.

She lifted her hand, reaching down to touch his head. He looked up at her, his breath puffing rapidly against her hot, damp labia.

'Turn around,' Katya said.

Victor did, hitching his legs over her chest and burying his face between her thighs again. Katya took his cock in her mouth once more, making a great show of moaning noisily and writhing about to show Alexei just how much she was enjoying this little game of his.

She gasped in surprise when a small, intense orgasm rocked through her body as Victor rasped his tongue over the swollen nub of her clitoris.

'Oh, yes,' she groaned loudly. 'Yes, Victor, that feels so good.'

He moved around her, adjusting positions to kneel between her thighs. Katya suddenly wanted him inside her for reasons that had nothing to do with proving something to the captain. Her channel felt achingly empty, her nerves humming with sensuality and the need to be filled and satisfied.

'Put it in me,' she gasped.

Victor's chest heaved as he guided himself to the opening of her body. Katya closed her eyes, her entire being anticipating the delicious penetration.

And then, Victor was wrenched away suddenly from between her legs, tossed aside as if he were a rag doll. Katya's eyes flew open, clashing with the dark, heated glare of the Cossack captain, who stood over her like an angry, scowling demon.

Katya drew in a sharp breath, crushing the shimmer

166

of fear in her belly as she realised that her plan might have worked a little too well.

'You little whore,' Alexei snarled. 'You really want it, don't you? You'd milk the prick of any man who has one, wouldn't you?'

Katya was too shocked to move or react. She stared at the captain as he unbuttoned his trousers just enough to free his large, stiff cock. Without another word, he dropped to his knees and plunged into the slick, hot, dampness of her, filling her beyond belief.

Katya cried out with pleasure, her body jerking as she received the full impact of his thrust. He started pounding into her, his teeth grazing her breasts, his hot breath on her skin, his cock moving inside her as if it had a life of its own.

Part of Katya knew she had won, that she had driven him to such irritation that he had halted his own game. And the other part of her revelled in his power and passion, lost to the sensations of him thrusting rock hard and hot, inside her. He pushed her legs up over his shoulders, penetrating her to the fullest extent and lifting her buttocks off the floor.

Sweat broke out on Katya's skin. Her breasts shook with the force of his thrusts, her body ablaze with need and want. Alexei's jaw was clenched tight, his muscles taut with strain as he put his fingers over her clitoris and began rubbing her hard.

An orgasm shattered her within seconds. She nearly screamed her pleasure as violent waves of sensations rolled through her body with the power of a tempest. And then one, final thrust, a deep groan rumbling from Alexei's chest as he slammed into her for the last time.

He collapsed on top of her, his shirt damp with sweat, his body hot and heavy. Katya closed her eyes, relishing the sensation of him, and of the things he could do to her. And of the things she could do to him.

When she finally caught her breath, the memory of Victor penetrated her lust-fogged brain. She opened her eyes and turned her head. He was sitting in a chair nearby, his eyes closed, his head against the back of the chair, and his mouth half-open.

Alexei stirred on top of her, putting his hands on either side of her head as he lifted himself off. He caught sight of Victor. Katya felt his body tense.

'Get out,' he snapped.

Victor's eyes flew open at the tone in the captain's voice. He fumbled for his trousers, tugging them over his legs. 'Y-yes, sir.'

Hastily buttoning up his trousers, he hurried out of the room, closing the door behind him.

Katya looked up at Alexei. His hard features masked any expression of desire or need. Without a word, he pushed himself off her and stood. He pushed her nightshift towards her with his foot.

'Cover yourself,' he said coldly.

His contempt was intended to shame her, but didn't. Katya slipped her nightshift on, buttoned it, and reached for her dressing gown. She stood, running her hands through her hair.

'Well, Captain,' she said lightly. 'I think I'll go back to my bedchamber. Thank you for a most enlightening evening.'

His expression darkened with anger, but Katya darted past him and went out the door. Triumph seized her. She had won this round.

Alexei reached back to rub the tense muscles at the back of his neck. Fatigue cut him to the bone. They were fortunate to have a group of Tsarist soldiers as prisoners, but the Revolutionary Army regiments were not faring well in the surrounding territories. He frowned. Other Tsarist troops had probably received word of their comrades' capture. The Revolutionary Army would have to be on guard for a retaliatory attack.

He looked up at the sound of a knock. 'Come in.'

The door opened to reveal Svetlana, clad in a silky

dressing gown, her spun-honey hair falling loosely around her shoulders. She gave him a tentative smile as she closed the door behind her.

Alexei watched her approach him, his gaze flickering over the heavy weight of her breasts underneath her gown.

'I wanted to know if you were all right,' Svetlana said softly.

'I'm fine.'

'I'm so sorry about that woman and the gypsy,' Svetlana went on. 'You can never trust the gypsies, but I can't imagine Katya Leskovna engaging in such a depraved act. I suppose she really is just a whore underneath her veneer of royalty.'

Alexei didn't respond.

Svetlana stopped by the side of his desk. 'I'm sure you punished her accordingly,' she said.

'You seem to be very interested in the matter.'

'Only because I hate to see you made a fool of,' Svetlana murmured.

Alexei's eyebrows lifted slightly. 'Is that what you think happened?'

'I don't know.'

Alexei studied her for a minute. His prick grew heavy at the sight of her large breasts. His mind flashed back to the previous night, when he had yanked Victor off Katya with a rage like none he had felt before, plunging himself into her body to remind her that she was his.

He frowned. He detested the thought that his actions were sparked by jealousy, but he had hated even more watching Katya writhe underneath Victor with such evident sensual pleasure. And he would pay her back for making him lose control, if only for a brief moment of time. No one did that to him. Especially not an arrogant princess who thought she held some sort of sexual claim over him.

No one did. No one ever would. And Katya Leskovna would regret her actions.

'Come here,' he ordered, pushing himself away from the desk.

Svetlana's lips parted in surprise. She hesitated briefly before she came around the side of the desk to stand in front of him.

'Take off your gown.'

A flush coloured her cheeks, but her hands went to the belt of her gown. She drew her dressing gown over her shoulders, leaving her clad in a flimsy, white cotton shift.

Alexei reached out a booted foot and slid it underneath the hem of Svetlana's gown. Slowly, he traced the inside of her calf upward past her knee to her thighs.

'Spread them,' he commanded softly.

Svetlana's head dropped forward as if she were suddenly regretting what her actions might lead to. Her thighs parted hesitantly. Alexei moved his foot upward, the cold leather of his boot pressing against Svetlana's silky inner thigh.

'Oh!' She gasped, reaching behind her to place both hands flat on the desktop, as the toe of Alexei's boot reached the secret lips of her labia.

With a calculating movement, Alexei rubbed his boot back and forth between Svetlana's thighs, watching her through narrowed eyes as her face grew flushed and her body began to shift against the leather.

'You're a whore at heart, aren't you, Svetlana?' he asked coldly.

Svetlana's eyes flew open as a cloud of shame fell over her.

'No,' she murmured. 'You know I'm not.'

'Then why would you take pleasure from both Katya and the gypsy?' Alexei continued moving his boot between her legs with a harsh kind of satisfaction.

Svetlana gasped in shock. 'Alexei, I d-didn't –' Her voice trailed off.

'Don't lie to me,' Alexei snapped. 'I know what you did. Tell me how it felt.'

The blood drained from Svetlana's face, leaving her white. 'I . . . I told you that Ivan went –'

'Then why did the gypsy know everything about you? Why did she know you have a mole on your back? Why did she know how you scream when you come? Why did she know what you like?'

Svetlana's fingers tightened around the edge of the desk. 'I didn't m-mean to –'

'Ah. But you did.' In truth, Alexei only had suspicions about Svetlana's involvement with the two other women, but Svetlana herself had just confirmed those suspicions.

'She gave me something to drink. Some sort of drug.'

Alexei's mouth twisted derisively as he continued to rub his boot against her. 'That didn't prevent you from enjoying them, did it?'

He smiled without humour when Svetlana didn't respond.

'You're pathetic, Svetlana. What did you expect to gain by telling me about Katya and the gypsy?'

'Nothing!' Svetlana jerked away from him, one hand coming up to clutch her dressing gown together as a wave of anger swept through her body. 'She's the whore, Alexei! She started touching and kissing the gypsy as if she's done it plenty of times before! Whatever you think you're going to do with her, you might as well know right now that she'll never make a suitable wife for you. She will always find ways to take her pleasure elsewhere, no matter what you might do to try and stop her!'

Heart pounding, Svetlana turned and rushed out of the room. Her entire body trembled as she ran up the stairs in a flurry of silken material, blind to the covetous eyes of the soldiers she passed.

Damn him! How dare he accuse her of unfaithfulness when he was spending all his time with his captive princess? Her gut clenched at the thought of the other woman, and she realised with a start that stirrings of jealousy simmered underneath her anger. Not jealousy over Alexei, but over Katya.

The thought disturbed her to such a degree that she didn't even realise she was about to collide into a male body.

'Svetlana?'

He reached out to steady her as she came to a sudden halt. Startled, she looked up at Ivan, her eyes wide, her breathing ragged.

He frowned at the sight of her. 'Darling, what's wrong? You're as white as a ghost.'

'N-nothing.'

'Has someone hurt you?' His entire body tensed. 'I'll kill them if they have.'

'No. No one hurt me.'

'Come here, then.' Ivan put his arms around her and tried to draw her against him. She resisted, her thoughts and emotions whirling around like a hurricane, but Ivan was stronger than she was.

'Tell me what's wrong. Tell me what happened.'

Svetlana's eyes filled with tears. She had used him horribly, this kind, gentle young man who worshipped the ground she walked on. And her only reason for being with him had been to make Alexei jealous.

'Nothing happened.' She tried to pull herself out of his arms. 'Let me go, Ivan.'

He didn't. He bent his head and brushed his lips against hers, his big hands pinioning her against his chest. The heat of his body seeped into her, and she could already feel the hardening member inside his trousers. Shame flooded over her for what she had done to him, how she had deceived him.

'I love you, darling,' he murmured. 'You know that. You have to know.'

Svetlana closed her eyes. Her heart filled with pain.

'Stop it, Ivan.' She forced the words out of her mouth, forced herself to speak past the sudden lump in her throat. 'I don't want to be with you anymore.'

He pulled back with a stunned expression. 'What?'

'You heard me.'

'But –'

'Leave me alone.' She wrenched herself out of his grasp, noticing too late the flare of anger in his eyes.

Before she could move away from him, his hands shot out to grasp her shoulders. In one movement, he pinned her against the wall, holding her in place so there was no possibility of escape.

'You think I'm going to let you walk away from me?' Ivan snapped, his usually placid features dark with rage. 'After what we've done? After I've fallen in love with you?'

Desperate, Svetlana grasped on to the one fact which Ivan could not refute. 'I'm Alexei's woman, Ivan. You know that.'

His fingers dug painfully into her shoulders. 'By the devil you're his! You're *mine*, Svetlana! You've been mine since the night you walked into my tent and stripped off your clothes! What do you want me to do? Do you want me to challenge him to a duel? I'll murder him if I have to, if that's what it takes for you to admit that you no longer love him!'

The romantic expansiveness of his words stirred something underneath Svetlana's despair, even as she knew in her heart that Alexei wouldn't bother fighting a duel for her. Besides she had no intention of allowing Ivan to commit so foolish an act.

Still, his passion could not help but touch her. She leant her head against the wall and closed her eyes.

'Oh, Ivan,' she whispered. 'I've used you terribly. You don't want me.'

'The hell I don't,' he snapped. 'Say it, Svetlana. Say you love me.'

His hands worked the belt on her dressing gown, moving roughly over her body as he began to pull up her nightshift.

'Ivan . . .'

'Say it,' he hissed. His hands grasped her naked thighs, pushing them apart and exposing her to the cold air.

She couldn't say it. She willed everything in herself to believe it, wishing she could love Ivan as she loved Alexei, but the feeling simply wasn't there.

'Stop.' She grasped his wrists, pushing him away, unable to stand anymore. She forced herself to regain the cavalier attitude that gave her the advantage. 'I'm tired of your boyish groping, Ivan. Perhaps when you learn to make love like a man I'll allow you into my bed again.'

Her words stopped him cold. He stared at her as if he had never seen her before.

Svetlana couldn't bring herself to look at him, not wanting to see the deep, hurt expression in his eyes. Knowing she had wounded him made her feel horrid. And the fact that Alexei was the cause infuriated her.

She wrenched away from him and ran down the corridor to her bedchamber. She slammed the door and threw herself on to the bed, shaking with rage at the injustice of it all. She could not stop thinking that Alexei belonged to her – she would never stop thinking that – but it was getting harder and harder to believe. With a muffled groan, she rolled on to her back and stared at the bedraggled canopy over her bed. Never had she imagined she would be caught up in a sexual web that seemed to be consuming her, leaving her defenceless against her own hidden needs and desires.

Her thoughts drifted towards the dark-haired woman who seemed to have invaded both her and Alexei's souls. Well, hers, at least. Svetlana didn't think anything or anyone could nudge past the barrier of Alexei's inner self. She remembered the sensation of Katya's skin under her hands; how their breasts pressed against each other; how their fingers probed, searched and explored one another.

A liquid heat diluted some of the anger in Svetlana's veins. Alexei had no right to call her a whore. He had no right to make her feel ashamed of her own sensual pleasure. Nothing, no ties, vows or promises, bound her to him.

Nothing except her own heart.

Svetlana sat up, swinging her legs to the floor. A new resolve took hold of her with both hands, something that defied Alexei's arrogant domination of everything and everyone around him.

She went to the door and stepped out into the hallway, making her way silently down the stairs towards Katya's bedchamber. Her heart leapt into her throat when the door to the chamber opened. Expecting to see Alexei emerge, Svetlana ducked into the shadows.

Katya came out of the room, her arms tucked underneath her cloak as if she were holding something close to her chest. She glanced furtively down the hallway before hurrying towards the staircase.

Curious, Svetlana followed, her slippers soundless on the cold marble of the corridor. She remained a good distance behind Katya as she made her way through the dining room and into the kitchens. Katya pulled open the door leading down to the cellars and was soon swallowed up into the vast depths of the underground.

Svetlana came to a halt outside the cellar doors. Why on earth, she mused, would Katya want to go down to the dank, freezing cellars? There was nothing down there but supplies and the Tsarist Army prisoners ... of course! Without further thought, Svetlana went down the stairs and followed Katya through a corridor which led to the storage cells where the prisoners were held.

Katya's dark, shadowed figure paused by one of the cell doors. She took a key from her pocket and unlocked the door before opening it just enough to slip inside. The door closed with a quiet click behind her.

Svetlana frowned. She knew that Alexei had instructed several of the Cossack soldiers to make hourly rounds through the cellars, but Katya appeared to have timed her visit perfectly so as not to coincide with the night-watch. Which meant she had done this before.

175

Svetlana hurried back to the main cellar and found a wooden, milking stool. She carried it back to the room into which Katya had disappeared and positioned it by the door. Then she stood on the stool and peered through the door's small, high window.

Firelight from the soldiers' campfires above flickered eerily through the window of the cellar, providing a reddish illumination which danced with distorted shadows. Svetlana's gaze adjusted to the light. She saw Katya seated with a Tsarist soldier in a corner of the stone room, her hand on his thigh as she watched him devour the bread and soup she had smuggled in.

So, considered Svetlana, the princess has defied the captain's orders after all. Svetlana smiled to herself. She had little doubt how Alexei would react to such information.

'Was it enough?' Katya's concerned voice carried through the empty, stone cell. 'It was all I could manage today. I'll try and bring you some stew tomorrow.'

'It was enough,' said the soldier.

'I'll also bring you hot water and soap for another bath. And a razor. I think you need a shave.'

The soldier smiled, reaching out to thread his hand through Katya's dark hair.

Her interest piqued, Svetlana curled a hand around the door-jamb to steady herself. What was going on between Katya and this handsome soldier? Handsome, indeed. Black hair, strong, sharp features marred only by several bruises and a cut across his cheek. He didn't appear to be as tall and strong as Alexei, but his chest was broad underneath his tattered uniform and his muscled legs were evidence of many hours spent on horseback.

'How do they treat you here?' the soldier asked, stroking his hand through Katya's hair and watching the firelight shimmer through the dark strands.

'I told you before,' Katya replied. 'Fine. I work and help in the kitchens. I haven't been mistreated.'

Svetlana almost laughed. Quite the opposite, Princess.

'I worry about you constantly,' the soldier said.

'I know you do.'

'You shouldn't risk coming here.'

'Do you think anything could keep me away?'

The soldier's resolve seemed to falter as he gazed at Katya.

'I hope not,' he finally whispered. 'God, I hope not.'

'Nothing will, Nicholas. Nothing can.'

Nicholas. Svetlana recalled Alexei mentioning the younger man's name.

Nicholas's hand curved around the back of Katya's neck as he drew her towards him. Svetlana watched with a trace of fascination as their lips met in a long, deep kiss that spoke of familiarity and passion. Had they known each other in their distant lives, she wondered, before the revolution created so much upheaval and disaster?

They must have, she mused. People didn't touch each other with such ease unless they had quite a bit of practice. They seemed to melt into each other, their bodies sinking together simultaneously as Nicholas's hands came up to cup Katya's head. They drew closer to each other. Katya eased herself between his thighs, her fingers fumbling with the fastening of her cloak.

'You'll be cold.' Nicholas caught the folds of Katya's cloak before it fell away from her.

'No. Not anymore.' Katya pushed the cloak away impatiently, grasping his wrists as she brought his hands to her breasts. 'Touch me.'

The soldier needed no further invitation. His hands moved with slow gentleness over the outside of her dress, and Katya reached up to first undo the row of small buttons bisecting her bodice and then the laces of her corset. She released her breasts into Nicholas's waiting hands as he murmured over and over how lovely she was, how much he adored her. He bent his head to kiss her breasts, taking her nipples in his mouth and laving them with his tongue. Katya's breathing grew heavy. She slipped her hands to his groin and worked the buttons on his trousers.

Even Svetlana was impressed with the size of the soldier's manhood as Katya stroked her hand over its length. Svetlana clutched the wood of the door and tried to stop herself from imagining what it would be like to make love with this handsome soldier who sparked such obvious pleasure in the princess.

Katya didn't bother to undress. Nicholas slid his hands underneath her skirts and eased her over his lap. With a gasp, Katya guided him into her, sinking down on his erection and wrapping her arms around his neck. Her hands threaded through his thick hair as she pressed kisses over his forehead, each touch of her lips accompanied by loving whispers. Nicholas's arms encircled her waist as she started to move, her body lifting and lowering with an increasingly rapid rhythm stimulated by his throaty murmurs of encouragement. He held her as if he would never let her go, his lips moving urgently over every inch of her breasts, throat, and shoulders.

Svetlana responded to the sight of the couple's love-making as any healthy woman would. Her sex grew heavy and damp, her heart thudding against her chest as if it were a bird trying to escape the confines of a cage. She leant her forehead against the splintered oak of the door and closed her eyes, willing away the ribbons of arousal winding around her body. She refused to succumb to the need to relieve the aching tension, thinking it was perverse to stand on the outside watching an intimate act and taking pleasure from it without the knowledge of the participants.

Svetlana would not debase herself, would not touch herself as if she were some sort of uninhibited sexual creature for whom pleasure was simply physical release and nothing else.

She turned away from the door. Her limbs felt both cumbersome and weak as she made her way silently up to the kitchens. Image after image of Katya and Nicholas fluttered through her mind like clouds sweeping across a dark blue sky. Their touches and caresses spoke volumes of love, compassion and history.

Svetlana flattened a hand against her chest. She felt hollow and sad inside, like an empty husk that had nothing left to offer. Alexei didn't want her; even if he did marry her one day, he would never forget the princess. Her plan to demean Katya had backfired, both with Alexei and Katya. Katya had succeeded in proving that she could manipulate Svetlana to her will, based on nothing except Svetlana's desire for her. And now this discovery that Katya had a lover. A *lover*, under the same roof; a soldier she had known before, a man she obviously adored.

The injustice of it came washing over Svetlana in a second wave, as if it had been made stronger by the currents. Her sadness hardened inside her gut into a tight ball of anger coated with jealousy. This had to be made right. It wasn't supposed to turn out like this; Katya, the prisoner, had everything – Alexei and Nicholas, and love, sex and power. And Svetlana herself.

Pressing a hand against her mouth, Svetlana choked back a sob and ran upstairs to her bedchamber. No, she thought fiercely, Katya won't have everything. She'll lose in the end.

Chapter Ten

Katya woke to the sensation of a rough, male hand sliding up the curve of her naked hip. Even in a twilight sleep, she knew his touch. Her blood shivered as she remembered the scene with Victor, then sneaking down to be with Nicholas and then, on her way back to her room, encountering the Cossack captain in the foyer.

Tall, dark and intimidating; wrapped in darkness and shadows like the devil she knew him to be. She had stammered out an excuse about being hungry – not exactly a lie, she thought, since her entire body craved Nicholas – and hoped to heaven Alexei wouldn't want her tonight, not after she had just been with Nicholas. Somehow, in the very depths of her soul, Katya knew Alexei would know that she had been with another man.

But he hadn't wanted her to be with him. He hadn't raked his gaze over her body; hadn't demanded in a harsh voice that she remove her clothes; hadn't burned with heat and sexuality.

And Katya, feeling an odd, vague disappointment despite the fact that her wish had been granted, slipped past him to return to her bedchamber.

Now he had come, she thought to herself, as the weak, dawn light broke through the ragged curtains to spill into her bedchamber. The crackle of burning wood in the fireplace scented the room with pine and warmed the air. She was facing away from him, her face buried in the pillow, her mind and body still wrapped in the cobwebs of sleep. She had known he wouldn't be able to stay away for long.

An image of Nicholas, trapped alone in the depths of the cellar, flashed in her mind. She fought the sudden wave of pain and guilt that washed over her. The captain had come to her and she would succumb to his touch as she always did, regardless of Nicholas's presence in the manor.

The knowledge rubbed like sandpaper against her soul, even as she knew she could not allow Alexei to have the slightest suspicion that things were not as they seemed. Pleasuring was not the same as loving. What Alexei did to her was not the same as what Nicholas felt for her. But she welcomed both touch and emotion without trying to understand or rationalise them.

A husky murmur of approval emerged from her lips as Alexei's hand slid up to her breast. He cupped it in his hand, his thumb flickering over her soft nipple until it tightened underneath his touch. Katya stretched like a cat, feeling her muscles lengthen gloriously, her body pliant and relaxed after a night's sleep. She turned to face him, her eyelids lifting with dreamy slowness as she focused on his face.

Alexei looked down at her with an inscrutable expression, his jaw darkened with a coating of whiskers, his black hair ruffled. His shirt and trousers were wrinkled, as if he'd slept in them, and a glint in his eyes made him look almost calculating.

Katya started to lift her hand to touch his face, but then she remembered how angry he had been last night after she had made her point with Victor. She wondered if he had forgiven her yet. Instead of touching him, she shifted slightly, pressing her breast into his palm, giving a little sigh of pleasure at the sensation of his callused fingers stroking her skin.

A corner of Alexei's mouth tilted upward, but his eyes remained hard. 'You're a lustful, little princess, aren't you?'

'No more so than you're a lustful captain,' Katya murmured, unperturbed by his words. He couldn't keep away from her anymore than she could resist his touch. Amusement flashed in her eyes as she glanced down at the front of his trousers. 'Although, I would hardly call you "little."'

She lifted her arms above her head to allow him freer access to her body and let the bedcovers slip away from her torso to leave her naked.

'Sleep in the nude now, do you?' Alexei asked dryly, as he began to roll her nipple between his thumb and forefinger.

Katya frowned. She couldn't remember taking off her nightshift. She certainly wouldn't have got into bed without it since it was too cold. She glanced to the side and saw her shift lying rumpled on the floor.

'You took it off while I was sleeping, didn't you?' she said, giving Alexei an accusing look.

'I wouldn't think of such a thing.'

Katya smiled slowly. The hell he wouldn't.

'Well, it's all right,' she murmured. 'Makes things more accessible.'

'That it does,' Alexei agreed.

Katya lifted her hand to stroke it over his thigh, feeling his muscles tense underneath her palm. She slipped her hand towards his groin.

'No.' Alexei's hand shot down so quickly to clamp around her wrist that Katya had no time to react.

Her eyes flew to his in surprise. 'What?'

Alexei's grip softened, but he still had the calculating gleam in his eyes that made her wonder what he was up to.

'This time,' he said, his voice both soft and edged with danger, 'you don't touch me.'

'Don't?' Katya's voice faded as she looked up at him.

A glimmer of excitement started in her belly as she remembered the night in the cellar. Cold, hot, terrifying, shocking, exhilarating, and unbearably, unutterably arousing. A tremble went through her body just remembering it. She had never gone through so many emotions and sensations in such a short period of time.

'Don't.' Alexei reiterated the command as his hand slid down her torso.

His fingers reached the curls of her mons. Katya's legs parted almost of their own volition as she waited for him to touch her intimately. His finger slid into her sex with all the pressure of a feather. Katya made a noise of frustration, pushing herself towards him. Alexei chuckled, trailing his finger through the pleats of her labia.

'You want more, do you?' he asked.

She always wanted more where he was concerned. Not that she would ever tell him so. She reached down to grab his wrist, wanting to guide his hand lower. He shot her a look that warned her to keep her hands to herself.

Sighing, Katya laid back on the bed. She fully expected him to arouse her to the edge, to make her tremble and whimper under his expert caresses. Already, pulses of heat were winding around her nerves, her sex dampening at his light touch, her heartbeat increasing in pace. And she was shocked when Alexei suddenly climbed off the bed and went to the *armoire*.

Katya lifted herself on to her elbows and looked at him in confusion. What in heaven's name was he doing? He looked through her dresses before tossing one on the bed – a deep green, silk dress with a series of pearl buttons up the front and a flowing skirt that brushed her ankles as she walked.

'Get dressed,' Alexei said shortly. 'Don't put on any underclothes or petticoats. No stockings.'

'What?'

'Do it,' he ordered.

She knew that tone in his voice. Grumbling to herself at the injustice of crushed anticipation, she reached for the dress and clambered off the bed.

Alexei stood by the *armoire*, his gaze unmoving as he watched her slip the dress over her hips and start to button the bodice.

'Stop.'

Katya's head jerked up. She had only fastened the pearls to her breasts, which were now cupped by the silky material of her bodice. Her nipples were barely covered and her cleavage exposed indecently.

'I'm not finished,' she protested.

'Yes, you are.'

She stared at him. 'Alexei, I am not walking around this encampment with nothing on under my dress and my breasts practically bare!'

An odd, humourless smile curved his mouth. His eyes looked like chips of black ice, glittering and cold.

'Oh, yes,' he said softly. 'You are.'

'What are you, a sadist?' Katya snapped, indignation and anger rising inside her. 'Do you have any idea what will happen to me if I go out like this? You told me yourself that most of your soldiers haven't had a woman in ages. What do you think they're going to do when they see me prancing around half-naked?'

Alexei sighed. 'I grow tired of your constant arguments, Katya. You will not leave my side for the entire day.'

Katya paled. 'You want me to walk around next to you looking like this?'

The thought shocked her, even more so than the idea of going about her daily chores barely dressed. Alexei's command meant no one at the encampment would have any doubt as to his power and control over her.

'That is the plan, yes,' Alexei said dryly. 'Put on your shoes. I have work to do.'

Nothing in the world could make Katya move. Her heart raced in her chest and her legs started to tremble as she thought of the implications in playing the submissive mistress to the captain's dominance.

'Katya, for heaven's sake, you're not naked,' Alexei snapped impatiently. 'Look at you. You're almost respectable.'

'It's the "almost" that's the problem,' Katya mumbled.

Amusement glinted in his expression. 'My dear, you're far more respectable now than when you're writhing around naked in the throes of passion.'

Colour bloomed in Katya's face. She knew why he was doing this. She knew he was re-establishing his authority in their strange relationship after she had chipped away at it.

But why did he have to do so in front of the entire camp?

She looked down at the floor. She felt betrayed. The captain's authority and control had never been in question among the soldiers and the servants. Only Victor knew of Alexei's sudden rage; of the way his order had backfired and he had succumbed to the force of his physical emotions and needs.

Perhaps Victor's knowing was enough. A man like Alexei would not want a single person to even sense that he was not in complete and total control of himself.

None of that made it any easier. If Alexei had wanted to do something to her sexually, like the night in the cellar, she could have borne it. Heavens, she conceded, she would have ended up gasping and pleading for him if that first scenario was anything to judge by. But to be displayed as his mistress to the entire encampment was something very different in Katya's mind.

'This doesn't seem like you,' she murmured.

'On the contrary, Princess,' Alexei replied. 'This is exactly like me.'

185

Katya knew she would not win. And he might make things worse for her if she resisted. She slipped her feet into a pair of shoes, her heart strumming like an instrument, as she gave her bodice a futile tug and followed Alexei out into the corridor.

The stares started immediately. It wasn't simply the fact that a woman was walking around with her breasts half-bared, but rather the fact that the captain was obviously making her do it. And the fact that the soldiers hadn't had a woman in longer than they cared to remember.

Katya fought the urge to defy Alexei and button her dress to hide her skin from lecherous eyes. She was acutely conscious of her nakedness, her legs and sex bared to any breeze that happened to insinuate itself under her skirt. She followed him down to his study, hoping he might close himself off to work. Instead, he found it necessary to confer with the soldiers in the workroom, all of whom spent most of the conversation staring at Katya's breasts.

At first, it made her hugely uncomfortable and embarrassed. She wanted to run back upstairs and hide in the folds of her cloak. But, after a couple of hours, she began to get used to the stares because she expected them. And then she started to find it rather amusing. Who would have known that two mounds of flesh could inspire such fervour?

She was mulling that idea over in her mind as Alexei examined a chart of battle techniques with one of his men. She stood next to him behind the table, keeping her ears alert for any mention of the Tsarist armies Lev had told her were in Don Cossack territory. Suddenly, she felt Alexei's hand on her bottom.

She reached back to swat him away, but he ignored her. Instead, he grasped her skirt in his fist and began to pull it up with a lazy insolence. Katya nearly choked in surprise. She was standing very close to a wall but that didn't mean no one would notice what he was doing.

Without pausing for a second in his discussion of battle, Alexei lifted Katya's skirt until her bottom was bared to the cold air. She shivered, her pulse beginning to beat like wildfire through her veins as Alexei's callused hand caressed the globes of her buttocks. She looked at him in shock, but he didn't take his eyes from the chart. And then the next thing she knew his fingers were pushing between her thighs to stroke her sex.

Katya had to curl her hand around a nearby chair to steady herself. Alexei's fingers worked magic in her, inducing a shiver of excitement in spite of her shock. He knew exactly where to touch her and how to please her; and he did so now without the slightest hesitation. Katya looked frantically around the room to see if any of the other soldiers noticed what the captain was doing, but they were all either attempting to work, or openly staring at her breasts.

She bit her lip to suppress a gasp of pleasure when Alexei's finger slid inside her. He worked it back and forth before he pulled away from her abruptly, letting her skirts fall back to cover her.

'All right.' Alexei pushed away the chart, gesturing towards the young soldier who sat nearby. 'Let's have a look at the weapons list.'

Katya couldn't believe it. Her entire body throbbed, her sex craving more of Alexei's expert manipulations. Her skin was flushed with arousal, her breathing rapid, and yet he sat there acting as if nothing untoward had happened.

'Bastard,' she muttered under her breath.

He ignored her, but she saw amusement light his eyes.

He kept her on the edge all day long. His hand would sneak under her skirts at the most inopportune times: sometimes to manipulate the folds of her sex, sometimes just to give her a proprietary caress on the bottom, sometimes to slide his fingers into her so that she had to force herself not to work her body up and down as she strove for release. She was constantly warm, her breath coming in small, uneven gasps.

She had to admit that the captain was doing a pretty good job of re-establishing the balance of power in their relationship.

As they sat at the dining table with fifteen of the top soldiers, Alexei's fingers skimmed up her thigh in search of her heat. He smiled when he felt her part her legs to allow him access, but he did not speak to her or look at her. Katya trembled with need when his forefinger travelled slowly around her aching clitoris. She bit her lip, wondering what the soldiers would say if they knew their captain was masturbating her while he calmly ate his supper.

He was busy talking about a skirmish that had recently occurred on the steppe. Katya knew she should be paying attention, but the movements of his fingers were so distracting that she couldn't even focus on her food, let alone his words. He began squeezing and rubbing the wet lips of her labia as his thumb manipulated her clitoris, urging the bud out from beneath its protective hood. One, hard caress as his forefinger slid into her damp channel, and an orgasm shuddered through Katya's body with a force made all the stronger by her perpetual hovering on the precipice.

She gasped, her fork clattering to the plate as her body shook and her thighs clamped around Alexei's hand.

Alexei looked at her quizzically, his black eyebrows lifting. 'Are you all right, my dear?'

Katya coughed to hide her agitation, well aware that all of the soldiers were staring at her. She reached for her water glass with a shaking hand as pulses of arousal continued to course through her body.

'Fine,' she managed, willing her heated colour to return to normal. 'I must have bitten into a hot pepper or something.'

'Hmm,' Alexei murmured.

He slipped his hand out from between her thighs,

swiftly licking his forefinger as if savouring the taste of a delectable morsel. Katya's face flamed.

'One must be careful of those hot peppers,' Alexei continued mildly. 'They have a tendency to bite back.'

Katya shot him an angry glare, embarrassed beyond belief. Touching her was one thing, but making her spend in front of his soldiers! It was too much. She pushed her chair away from the table, smoothing her skirts down at the same time.

'If you'll excuse me, I'm going to my bedchamber.'

'Oh, I don't think you are,' Alexei replied evenly. 'Not yet.'

She gave him a mutinous glower. 'Your soldiers know quite well that you're fucking me, Captain. I hardly think the sight of my breasts is going to indicate something they don't already know.'

This brought a surprised murmur from the soldiers, as well as several chuckles. Alexei crossed his arms and sat back in his chair, his amused gaze never leaving Katya.

'No?' he asked. A gleam lit in his dark eyes that she did not like one bit. She had the sudden thought that she should have kept her mouth closed. 'Well, then, Princess, why don't you show them your breasts?'

Katya heard the shocked mutterings from several of the soldiers, but her ears filled with a roar of humiliated outrage. She started to shake, and not from pleasure.

'They all know what a woman's body looks like,' she snapped.

'Not yours,' Alexei murmured. 'And as you informed me on your first night here, one would be hard pressed to find feminine attributes such as you possess. Perhaps you should show the men what ideal they should be searching for.'

'Oh, you know I wasn't being serious.'

Maybe this was his idea of a joke, she thought frantically. He couldn't possibly make her display herself as if she were some sort of prize horse.

One look at him told her that, indeed, he could. Katya paled.

'Well, Katya?' Alexei prodded. 'We're waiting.'

A thick, heavy silence filled the dining room. Every single, hungry male eye was fixed on Katya as the soldiers waited with heightened anticipation.

She couldn't move. And then her instinct for self-preservation stirred. She took a step towards the door, willing herself to make a mad dash for the stairs, consequences be damned. Before she could force her legs to move, Alexei stood and approached her.

His hands settled on her shoulders, trapping her. Katya felt light-headed, as if she were suddenly swimming underwater in an unreal, parallel world in which rules and dignity meant nothing.

'Alexei, for heaven's sake –'

'Come, my dear. I'm sure the soldiers would love to see breasts as lovely as yours.'

He turned her towards the table so he was standing behind her. Katya tried to think past the embarrassment of the scene and the fact that every soldier was gaping at her. And wishing they had the captain's power.

Alexei's hands moved over her shoulders to the front of her bodice, his fingers brushing the swell of her cleavage as he reached for the first fastened pearl button. Katya's heart thudded in her chest. She tried to tell herself it didn't really make a difference; her breasts were half-exposed anyway and all they would be seeing was her nipples.

She failed to convince herself. This wasn't just about other men seeing her nudity. This was about the captain's control over her. About what else he might do should she try to tip the scales again.

His long fingers worked four buttons on her bodice. Heat radiated from his muscular chest into her back, his pelvis pressed against her bottom, and she could smell the mingled scent of smoke and wine clinging to him. She wanted to sink into a hole in the ground when he

190

tugged apart the halves of her dress and let her bare breasts fall into his hands.

Katya closed her eyes, blocking out the murmurs and increased breathing arising from the seated soldiers. Alexei's lips brushed against her ear as he palmed her breasts, rolling her nipples between his fingers until they hardened with arousal. Until everyone could see what he could do to her. His hands slipped underneath her breasts, lifting and caressing.

His touch felt good. Very good. An emotion stirred inside her that she didn't recognise. The captain's hands moved on her as the soldiers watched, and heat slid in a direct line from Katya's nipples to her sex. She had the sudden thought that Alexei might push the dress to the floor, revealing her complete nudity to his soldiers. A quickening of excitement started in her loins at the possibility. She felt herself arching her back to push her breasts into his hands.

The action horrified her. If he kept touching her would she start to enjoy this exhibition? What kind of depraved person was she?

Several soldiers shifted in their chairs, mumbling words that Katya didn't want to hear. She had little doubt that the scene Alexei was enacting for them had an arousing effect. She turned her head, pressing her temple against his throat, feeling the strong pulse beating heavily under his skin.

'Stop,' she implored him. 'Please, Alexei. Stop.'

'Go and wait in my bedchamber,' Alexei ordered, his voice low and guttural.

He released her. Hot with shame and confusion, Katya drew the halves of her bodice together and stumbled from the room wihout looking at the soldiers. Tears of humiliation stung her eyes. She went up the stairs, clutching her dress together, her mind spinning with the horror of what else Alexei might be capable of. And the knowledge that she might like it.

'My lady?'

Katya lifted her head in surprise. Lev, her only ally, stood in the shadows of the corridor. She stopped.

'Lev.'

'You look upset. Are you all right?'

Katya's hand shook as she reached up to push her hair away from her face. No doubt Lev would hear the entire story by tomorrow. The entire camp would know what the captain had done. Which, she supposed, was probably part of his plan.

'There was just … I had a bit of unpleasantness,' Katya stammered. 'I'm all right.'

Lev's gaze darted down each side of the corridor. 'I can't stay long,' he said. 'I wanted to tell you that the Tsarist regiment knows prisoners are being held here. I've sent word of the encampments weaknesses and they are working on a strategy for attack.'

Relief made Katya's body weak. She couldn't possibly take much more of this. 'Wonderful. When?'

'Within the month, I hope,' Lev said. He stepped away as they heard two voices coming from the far end of the corridor. 'I will try to warn you before it happens.'

He turned and headed in the opposite direction. His long stride took him a good distance in a matter of seconds.

Katya's spirits lifted a little. This wasn't going to last forever. Alexei wouldn't always be able to manipulate and control her. She would have her freedom again.

But not yet. She remembered the captain's command, and she didn't dare defy him. She hurried down the corridor to his bedchamber and let herself in, closing the door behind her.

She thought that he would come soon and that maybe he was as aroused as she had been all day. But it was close to midnight before she finally heard the doorknob turn.

Alexei stepped into the room, closing and locking the door behind him. He stripped off his captain's jerkin and began to unbutton his shirt. Katya watched him from her curled-up position on his bed, her arms wrapped around her legs. He looked dangerous and powerful, his movements edged with impatience as he sat down to remove his boots.

He didn't look at her until he was naked. His cock was already half-erect, projecting from his body as if it had a life of its own. His muscled skin glowed in the moonlight, scar wounds crossing his chest and shoulders, his thighs hard and strong. Katya continued watching him warily. She had no idea what to expect from him.

'Take off your dress.'

She slid off the bed and unfastened the remaining buttons on her bodice. Her dress slipped to the floor around her feet in a puddle of green silk, leaving her naked. Alexei stretched out on the bed, his gaze cold and unwavering in the dim light.

'Come here,' he ordered. 'I want you to fuck yourself on me.'

Katya drew in an unsteady breath at the blunt rawness of his words. A shiver of excitement rained down her spine, her sex surging with anticipation. She eased back on to the bed, kneeling beside him as she reached out to curl her hand around his cock and urge him to a full erection.

This was an odd situation, for the captain had never been passive. He had never lain back while she touched and caressed him. Katya had a momentary feeling of power before the thought occurred to her that he was allowing her to touch him now, just as he had forbidden it this morning. Not allowing, but commanding. She was only following his orders. The scenario could change at any second and he would be the one to dictate the change.

'Now,' he said, after she had taken him in her mouth and his sex was hard with arousal. He watched her through the darkness, one hand behind his head, his dark eyes enigmatic.

Katya straddled his pelvis, her heart pounding as she

grasped the base of his cock in her hand and eased herself down on to him. His sex slid easily into her damp passage, filling her with such glorious hardness that she moaned with pleasure. It wasn't easy to take all of him in this position, and she struggled to relax her muscles so he could possess her completely.

He throbbed inside her, pulsing blood against the inner walls of her channel, sending heat beating along every vein. She pushed down as she tried to accommodate her body to his, wincing when his cock bumped against her cervix. Her breathing came in rapid gasps as she leant forward, bracing her hands flat on his broad chest.

She looked up and met his gaze through a veil of hair that had fallen over her face. His eyes were smoky and satisfied, as if she had done something that he wanted her to do.

'You liked it, didn't you?' he murmured, his husky voice vibrating through his chest and into her hands.

Katya stared at him. He knew so much, saw so much and perceived so much more than she wanted him to.

'You humiliated me,' she gasped.

'It excited you.' He pressed his hand between her breasts. 'Here. In here.'

'No . . .'

'Not humiliation. Being uninhibited. Free.'

How could he know that when she barely knew it herself? Or maybe she just couldn't admit it. The thought shamed her. Her gaze dropped away from his.

He wasn't about to let her hide from him. He began to caress her breast with one hand, while the other hand slid underneath her chin and lifted her head so that she had to look at him again. Fire and heat burned in his expression.

'Move,' he grated. 'Look at me while you fuck yourself.'

A thrill raced through her. She wondered how such crude words and commands could be so unbearably exciting. Her fingers dug into his chest as she started to pump her hips, feeling him sliding in and out of her with powerful strokes made all the more potent by his dark, heated gaze. Her body shook, pleasure mingling with the occasional twinge of pain as his stalk stretched and filled her. Driving her body down on him, Katya didn't try and shift positions for her comfort. She accepted the pain, even revelled in it; she considered it some sort of penance for her incomprehensible desires.

Alexei's hands moved over her breasts and slid down to the curves of her hips, his fingers biting into her skin. He never stopped watching her. Her writhing movements became faster and more frenzied as she impelled them both towards the final, explosive release.

And she couldn't take her eyes from his, not even if she wanted to, because she knew then that she was trapped in a sexual spell that had been incited and stimulated by the Cossack captain, but whose origins were in the depths of her very own soul.

Svetlana stood at the window of her bedchamber, gazing down at the tent where Ivan spent his nights. He was there now. She saw the light of his lantern and imagined he was working at his desk.

In the time that had passed since she told him their relationship was over, she had seen him at least once a day. He almost never spared her a glance, but when he did, his eyes were so remote that she felt as if they had never been lovers.

She hadn't meant to hurt him so badly. Nor had she thought that doing so would make her want to die.

Svetlana turned from the window. She reached for her cloak and tossed it around her shoulders. She had wronged him. And, although he might very well rebuff her, she had to try and make amends. She wouldn't be able to live with herself if she didn't try.

She went down the dark corridor to the stairs. Ignoring the curious glances of the soldiers, she stepped outside and walked to Ivan's tent. Her heart suddenly began to pound with fear that he wouldn't listen to her or accept her apology.

'Ivan?' She put her hand on the tent flap. 'Ivan, it's Svetlana. Please, can I come in?'

'What do you want?'

At least he hadn't said no. She eased the tent flap aside and stepped into the warm interior. As she had thought, Ivan was working at his desk. He looked unbearably handsome, his brown hair glowing in the lantern-light, his shirt sleeves pushed up to reveal his forearms. His expression was marred by coldness and suspicion.

Svetlana clutched her hands together to stop them from shaking with nervousness. 'I thought you might be here.'

'As you can see, I am,' Ivan replied dryly. 'What do you want?'

Svetlana took a deep breath, her words coming out in a rush. 'I wanted to apologise, Ivan. For what I said to you. I didn't mean it. I'm not – I'm not like that.'

His eyes remained cold. 'Aren't you? What's the matter, Svetlana? You haven't had a prick inside you for a while, so you thought you'd come back here and see if you could still work yourself on mine?'

The crudity of his words stung, echoing Alexei's remark that she was the whore. Tears filled her eyes, and she blinked them away fiercely.

'No,' she whispered. 'That's not it at all. I know I acted like I've seduced many men, but I haven't. I only did with you because I knew you had been watching me. I'm sorry, Ivan. I used you to get back at Alexei, and it didn't work. I didn't mean for you to fall in love with me. I didn't want to hurt you.'

'Then what in the hell did you want?' Ivan shouted, a wash of anger flushing over his face. 'What did you want from me besides my prick? Did you think the captain would come after me with a sabre to defend your honour? Has he ever told you he loves you? Has he

196

ever promised to marry you? Has he given you the slightest hint of affection beyond fucking you? He doesn't love you, Svetlana! He's incapable of it! And yet you cling to him as if somehow you can make him love you! Well, I'm telling you that you can't.'

He turned back to his desk, his shoulders slumping as he dragged a hand through his hair.

'He doesn't deserve you, Svetlana,' Ivan said wearily. 'He never has.'

He was right. The clarity of the realisation shocked her. Svetlana pressed her hand against her lips, struggling to fight back tears. She didn't succeed. They spilled down her cheeks in salty rivers.

'Ivan.'

He looked at her, appearing older than he ever had before. 'Don't, Svetlana. You'll never get over him. Even I know that.'

'Maybe that's only because I've never thought I could be with anyone else,' Svetlana whispered. 'Ever since I was a little girl, I thought there was no one else for me except Alexei.'

'Well, then, you have some things to figure out, don't you?' Ivan replied. He looked down at his desk, not meeting her gaze. 'Love isn't supposed to hurt, Svetlana,' he said, his voice low. 'It's not supposed to make you miserable. It's not about fucking every now and then and hoping that will somehow turn into love. It's not about the way the captain treats you. If that's what you want from love, then it's too twisted for someone like me to give you.'

'Ivan, please –'

He shook his head, stopping her words in her throat. 'I can't play this game with you anymore. And I won't compete with him. Not in your heart.' He sat back down, rubbing a hand over his face. 'You'd better go.'

Svetlana swallowed hard, tears streaming down her face. She wanted desperately to go to him, to comfort him and stroke his hair, to ease the tension from his shoulders, but she knew he would reject her.

'I'll go,' she choked. 'But tell me one thing before I do.'

'What?'

'What do you want from love?'

Ivan gave her a sad, crooked smile. 'That's simple. I want the same thing in return.'

Chapter Eleven

'*A* lexei.'

Alexei looked up from the map he was working on. Svetlana stood in the doorway, her hands on her hips, her blonde hair twisted into a knot at the back of her neck. She wore an immaculate, blue dress that matched the colour of her eyes and made her look more like royalty than Katya. Alexei's first thought was that she looked different. More certain of herself; more confident.

'Yes?' he asked.

'I've come to tell you something,' Svetlana said as she stepped into the room. 'You can take it as you like.'

Alexei's eyes narrowed. 'What?'

'It's about Katya Leskovna.'

'Yes, I figured as much,' Alexei said dryly. 'You're determined to disgrace her, aren't you?'

Svetlana lifted her chin and gave him an icy glare. 'I'm not doing anything,' she said. 'She's the one with the Tsarist lover.'

'What in the hell are you talking about now?'

'I saw her down in the cellars,' Svetlana explained. 'Nicholas is his name. She brings him food and comforts him with her body when she's not with you. You're being mocked, Alexei. I tried to warn you earlier, but you refused to listen.'

A shaft of anger speared through Alexei like a lightning bolt. He stalked around the table towards Svetlana, reaching out to grab the front of her dress in his fist. He yanked her towards him until her face was inches from his.

There had been a time when she would have cowered; when she would have lowered her eyes and stammered out an apology. This time, she met his angry gaze unflinchingly, her blue eyes cool and remote.

'Don't direct your anger towards me, Alexei. I'm simply telling you what I know.'

His fist tightened on her dress. He gave her a hard shake. 'You're a lying, little bitch.'

'Am I? Maybe that's what you want to believe. Meanwhile, your princess is screwing a Tsarist soldier. It doesn't take a genius to figure out why.'

'You've had a vendetta against her since the day she arrived,' Alexei snapped. 'Suddenly, I was fucking another woman, and you couldn't bear it.'

'If you're telling me I was jealous of her, you're correct,' Svetlana said. 'However, she's now fucking, as you so delicately put it, another man. What are you going to do about that?'

Alexei thrust her away from him with such force that Svetlana stumbled backward. She grasped the back of a chair to retain her balance.

'Get out,' Alexei said coldly.

'With pleasure.' Svetlana drew herself up, turned, and swept out of the room.

Alexei forced away a hot wave of jealous rage at the thought of Katya with a Tsarist soldier. Not any Tsarist soldier, but the private, the one who claimed confidently to be the head of their pathetic regiment. Alexei knew, of course, that Svetlana could very well be lying, but somehow he doubted it. He remembered the night when he had encountered Katya in the foyer. She had mumbled an excuse about having gone to the kitchens to get something to eat.

Alexei scowled darkly. The princess wouldn't defy him again. Not after the episode with the gypsy woman. Not after his assertion of control. Not after he'd forced her to expose herself to the soldiers. She wouldn't dare test the limits of his tolerance.

Would she?

That very night he waited for her at the foot of the stairs, hating the jealousy simmering like acid in his gut, hating the knowledge that she had driven him to this. He had never prowled around, never tried to conceal himself, never lurked in the shadows as he was doing now. It was not in his nature to hide; not from the enemy or from himself. And especially not from a woman.

Anger tightened every muscle in his body. When the old clock in the hallway struck quarter past midnight, he heard the soft shuffle of Katya's slippers on the marble floor. She came down the stairs, as lightly as a ghost, her hands wrapped around an object underneath her cloak.

Alexei waited for some time, absorbing the evidence of Katya's betrayal before going down to the cellar. He knew what he would see. He did not know how much the sight would enrage him.

'Oh, I love you.'

Katya's pale hands stroked and caressed the soldier's hair as she lay naked before him. Her legs were spread, her knees drawn up to allow him access to her innermost core. Her throat arched in the shifting, reddish light, her breath coming in ragged gasps.

And there, lying between Katya's legs as if he were devoted only to giving her pleasure, was the Tsarist soldier. His hands reached underneath her to cup her bottom as he lifted her sex towards his mouth. With an ardent tenderness, he stroked his tongue through the glistening folds of her labia, swirling it around her clitoris before moving down to the quivering flesh of her vagina.

Katya's hands tightened on the soldier's hair. Her body trembled with urgency and need.

'Nicholas.' She gasped his name in a throaty whisper, pushing her lower body up in an uninhibited offering. 'Oh, please . . .'

The soldier's hands slid over the soft skin of Katya's belly until they reached her breasts. He palmed her breasts, his fingers teasing and pulling at the tight peaks as his mouth continued to work the flower of her sexuality. His tongue darted into her tight channel, making her cry out brokenly. He was totally absorbed in her, his single-minded pleasuring designed for her unending rapture. His hands continued to stroke her breasts as her body shook with spasms under him. Katya cried out again, her moans echoing off the stone walls.

The soldier did not stop. He steadied her as her orgasm rocked through her and then he slid a finger into her vagina as his tongue continued to stroke the swollen nub.

'I can't,' Katya choked, making Alexei wonder just how many times the soldier had already brought her to orgasm. 'I –'

'Oh, you can,' the soldier murmured against her sex, his finger stroking in and out of her passage until Katya's body arched and tensed underneath him.

She whimpered. 'Please, Nicholas –'

The Tsarist soldier did not need to force Katya to beg him.

Alexei's wrath felt as if it would split him in two; it pounded against his insides with the rhythmic throb of his heartbeat and scorched his gut like a white-hot pool of lava. He fought the urge to break into the room and tear the lovers apart. That would be too easy.

The soldier pulled himself up over Katya's body. Her arms lifted to accept him, twining around his neck as she drew him down to her. Their lips met in a hard, urgent kiss, their tongues licking and dancing together. The soldier reached down to release his cock from his trousers and plunge it into the woman writhing underneath him. He thrust into her as she pushed her pelvis up, and they drove into a rhythm with all the harmony and passion of music. Their moaning and panting reverberated through the cell as they spiralled towards the release of their pleasure.

Even as he stalked away from the cells, fists clenched with rage, Alexei could still hear the sound of their lovemaking as if it were a mocking laugh that had come to haunt him.

Alexei did not enter Katya's bedchamber the following night, nor the next, although he told her both times to expect him. He knew she wouldn't risk his anger by not being there when he arrived, but she had surprised him enough times that he found it necessary to station a soldier at the end of the corridor to confirm that she didn't leave.

The soldier reported that Katya didn't leave either night. And on the third night, Alexei walked through the corridor and entered Katya's bedchamber.

She was curled up on a chair in front of the fire, reading a book. Her legs were tucked underneath her, and she wore a white nightshift that buttoned to her neck and fell in soft, sweeping folds over her body. She looked natural and innocent with the glow of the firelight dancing in her dark hair.

For a moment Alexei stood there and looked at her while his mind worked out her incongruous nature. She infuriated, enraged, inflamed, and stimulated him like no other woman had before. This seemed an odd conclusion given that she looked, at present, rather sweet.

Her gaze lifted from the pages of her book to look at him. Wariness clouded her eyes. 'Captain.'

'Katya.' He closed the door behind him and locked it.

'I expected you last night,' she said. 'And the night before.'

Alexei frowned. 'Are you making some sort of demand on me?'

'No, of course not, but I –'

'I come to you when I want to, Princess,' Alexei interrupted coldly. 'Not when you want me to. I thought I had made that quite clear.'

'Yes. You did.'

'Good.' He stopped halfway across the room and rested his hands on his hips, his eyes narrowing as an image of Katya opening herself for the Tsarist soldier flashed in his mind.

She recognised the change in him because her hand trembled slightly as she reached up to brush a lock of hair away from her face. 'Would you like some tea?' She gestured to the chipped, brown pot resting on a nearby table. 'I brewed it not fifteen minutes ago.'

'No.' His mouth curved into a slight smile. 'How domestic you've suddenly become. What might the reason be behind your sudden desire to please me?'

'Nothing. You've treated me well enough. I'm grateful to you. This situation could have been much worse.'

'Yes,' Alexei mused thoughtfully. 'It could have, couldn't it?'

He crossed the room and stopped behind her chair, reaching out to lift several strands of her shiny, dark hair. He examined carefully the way the firelight caressed their length and created reddish highlights glowing in the darkness.

'Much worse,' he continued, twisting one strand around his forefinger. 'For instance, if you'd found it necessary to take pleasure with one of my soldiers ... well, that would be unforgivable, wouldn't it?'

'Of course.'

'The gypsy situation, that was excusable in the end,' Alexei went on. He slid his hand over the back of her head and down to her neck. 'I suppose I can understand a woman of your sensual nature wanting to be with

204

another woman. Mind, I still dislike the knowledge that you betrayed me.'

His hand slipped around her neck until his fingers rested on the pulse at the base of her throat.

'And be warned, Katya. My understanding does not extend to your fucking another soldier.'

Her pulse fluttered against his fingertips. He pressed on it.

She swallowed hard. 'I-I wouldn't . . .'

'Wouldn't you?' Alexei queried softly. 'I wonder.'

'I'm not stupid, Alexei. I wouldn't be fucking one of your soldiers under the same roof.'

Hard amusement glinted in Alexei's expression as he considered her careful choice of words. *No, not one of my soldiers, Princess,* he thought to himself. *One of yours.*

'I should certainly hope not,' he murmured.

Katya pulled herself away from his touch. Alexei noticed that her hands continued to tremble as she closed her book.

'Should we get into bed?' she asked.

'Bed? Sleep isn't what I had in mind.' Alexei moved around to stand in front of her, his heavy boots soundless against the plush carpet.

Katya's hand went to her throat. 'Alexei, for heaven's sake, stop stalking around me like a wolf. You're making me nervous.'

'I'm making you nervous? You mean I don't already?'

'Well, of course you do, but only because I never know what to expect from you.'

Alexei reached out and slid his forefinger underneath Katya's chin, applying enough pressure to ease her to look up at him. A feral gleam lit in the depths of his eyes.

'That, my dear,' he said softly, dangerously, 'is part of the game.'

Her throat worked as she swallowed. 'That's all this is to you?'

His eyebrows lifted. 'It's something else to you?'

'No.' She paused, her arms coming up to cross over her chest in a self-protective gesture. 'I understand. You're the hungry wolf, and I'm your prey.'

Alexei laughed. The sound rumbled through the room, deep and rich with true amusement. 'My prey? My defenceless prey? That's how you think of yourself?' He shook his head, his eyes still twinkling with humour. 'You disappoint me, Princess. I would place you much higher on the scale of species.'

'And lower yourself?' Katya retorted.

Alexei chuckled again. 'In the end, I suppose, we really are all animals, aren't we? We eat, sleep, drink, and fuck like animals. And humans would probably be a great deal happier if that's all we had to do.'

Katya shook her head, her dark hair shifting against her neck like a thick curtain. 'No. We wouldn't be happier if we didn't know what it felt like to love,' she said.

Alexei's mouth twisted cynically. 'Then you're a romantic. Animals do quite well without emotions getting in the way. Instinct keeps them alive. Those that are slower or weaker simply don't survive. And yet they all indulge in the most basic physical needs.'

'What about pleasure?' Katya countered. 'Animals don't have sex for pleasure. They do it to procreate, because their instinct tells them to. It has nothing to do with attraction. Nothing to do with want.'

'Doesn't it?' His gaze moved down to the curve of her neck to consider the v of skin disappearing into the depths of her cotton nightshift. Something flared inside him suddenly, something primal and intense. 'Animals possess. They have mating calls and dances. They have markings and feathers designed to attract the opposite sex.'

'Not like us,' Katya said. Her voice dropped a note, taking on a husky quality. 'Not like humans. They don't know why they're attracted to each other. All they know is that nature makes them do it. They don't take the time to . . . to please each other; they don't do it out of love or emotion.'

'Or anger.'

Her eyes widened slightly in surprise. 'Well, of course. Not anger.'

'And you don't think there is something primitive about human sexual relations?'

'Primitive, yes, but only because we've been doing it since the beginning of time.'

'But there is no pleasure in the primitive?'

'There is pleasure in emotion.'

'Ah.' Alexei mulled that thought over in his mind before he grasped Katya's arms and pulled her out of the chair towards him. 'You don't think I give you pleasure?'

She flushed, her hands spreading over his chest to prevent herself from getting too close. 'Yes. You do.'

'Then what is this "emotion" that you feel towards me?'

Katya stared at him. Her flush deepened as confusion marred her expression, exposing her soul to him as he knew she always would whether she wanted to or not.

'I don't know,' she finally confessed.

The burn of jealous anger seared through Alexei's gut again. He detested it. His features hardened into stone as he gazed down at her and his fingers bit into the soft flesh of her upper arms.

'No?' he asked, his voice barely above a whisper and yet so menacing that she began to tremble again. 'Then tell me, Katya, what is the emotion you feel towards your Tsarist lover?'

She went white. She stared at him in utter shock as her lips parted to try and form a denial, an excuse or an explanation. But the words refused to come and, instead, terror flared in her eyes.

'Alexei –'

His hand clutched the back of her head, immobilising her.

'I told you that the gypsy was excusable,' he whispered, his breath brushing across her lips. 'I would not have been so kind had it happened a second time. A Tsarist prisoner, however –' his voice trailed off, leaving her in no doubt as to the depth of his rage.

'I didn't . . . he's not . . .' she stammered.

'Don't insult us both by trying to deny it.'

She closed her eyes. Her hands came up to cover her face as her body shook.

'Don't hurt him,' she said. Her voice was barely audible. 'Do whatever you want to me, but don't hurt him. It's not his fault. He didn't –'

'How very touching of you to sacrifice yourself for him,' Alexei drawled caustically. 'And what a lucky man he is to be taken prisoner, only to have a woman bring him food and then spread her legs for him. Perhaps I would do well to be taken prisoner myself.'

Katya's hands dropped away from her face. Anger suddenly simmered from her skin.

'Don't you dare corrupt what Nicholas and I have,' she snapped. 'This is exactly what I was talking about. I know I betrayed you; I know I defied your orders again; I know I wronged you; but I did it because I love him! I've loved him for years! This is what separates us from animals, Alexei, this ability to love and care for someone so much that you're willing to risk anything, *anything* – even the wrath of the most vicious wolf on the planet – to be together!'

'You think you're so different?' Alexei grated. He pulled her body fully against his, pressing her into his groin to make her feel the growing hardness of his erection. 'You think you fucked your soldier for no other reason than love? You think you didn't writhe around on the floor because you want to feel an orgasm rock through your body? Because you liked the way it felt when he stuck his tongue in you and then when he stuck his prick in you?'

Her body went rigid with anger and humiliation at

the realisation that he must have seen what she and Nicholas did. Her hand flew up and slapped Alexei hard across the face, her eyes spitting fire at him. The blow barely moved him, but it stung. Rage uncoiled in his gut like a snake.

'Don't talk like that about us!' Katya shouted. 'You know nothing about us, nothing about what we feel for each other! You don't even know how to feel!'

'Oh, I know how to feel,' Alexei murmured coldly, then grabbed the front of her nightshift and ripped it off her body with one, brutal tug.

She gasped and fought to escape his grip, but he cleaved her to him with a strength made all the more powerful by anger. He stroked his hands roughly over her body, knowing every spot that gave her the most pleasure; rubbing his thumbs over her nipples until they hardened, sliding his fingers between her legs into the cleft of her bottom, pressing his erection against her belly until he felt her start to give way underneath his hands.

'Feeling,' Alexei hissed, 'is only a matter of knowing what another person likes.'

His finger slid into her vagina, the heel of his hand rotating slowly over her clitoris.

'Do you like it?' he whispered harshly, watching her with a calculated callousness as her legs parted further.

She was trying to fight it, he could see her struggle, but then her eyelids drifted closed and her hands tightened on the front of his shirt.

'Do you?' he asked again. His cock throbbed inside his trousers, making him ache.

'I . . . yes,' Katya breathed brokenly. 'Yes, I do.'

'Well, then, that proves my point,' Alexei said, his anger and satisfaction both solidifying as he watched her capitulate. 'This isn't love, Katya. This isn't emotion. This is primitive. And this is pleasure.'

He released her as he pulled off his belt and unbuttoned his shirt. He sat down on a chair to take off his boots. Katya watched him with a heavy-lidded, almost resigned gaze, as if she had known all along what was going to happen. As if she had known that she would not only surrender to him but would revel in her surrender.

She knelt in front of him to work the buttons on his trousers and pull them over his legs. She gave a ragged, little sigh at the sight of his long, thick cock, taking him in her hand before she bent her head and slid her mouth over his shaft. Alexei's body instantly registered the sensation of her hot wetness enclosing him, even though he thought she was trying to appease him so he wouldn't do anything to the Tsarist prisoner.

Alexei smiled grimly. If that was what Katya was thinking then she had underestimated him.

As it was, there was nothing calculating about the way she was licking and sucking on his cock, her face flushed with arousal and her hands slipping between his thighs to caress him. He watched her for a moment, remembering what she and the private had done to each other and he wondered suddenly if she was thinking about the other man now.

The thought enraged him and sent fury scorching through his veins. He grabbed her hair and pushed her away from him. Katya stumbled backward, her gaze going to his in surprise.

'Alexei?'

'Are you thinking about him?' Alexei snapped, coming to his feet in one movement. 'Imagining him? Wanting him? Loving him?'

She looked stunned. 'No! No, Alexei, I –'

'You what?' he snarled, his expression dark with rage.

'I don't think of anyone else when I'm with you!' Katya gasped. 'I never have. I think about you: the way you feel, the way you taste and smell, the way your hands touch me and how much I want you inside me.'

'Do you? You're thinking about pleasure, then?' He grabbed the back of her neck, forcing her to look up at him. His voice lowered to a guttural whisper. 'Do you want pleasure, Katya? Is that what your instinct is telling you?'

Her tongue darted out to lick her dry lips. 'Y-yes. I want you. You know I do. You've known it since the day you brought me here.'

Alexei's mouth twisted. 'And what is that, then? Nature? The primal urge that has no explanation or excuse? The utter lack of emotion?'

Katya closed her eyes. 'I don't know,' she said.

'Get on your hands and knees.'

'What?'

'Do it.'

She obeyed.

He took her from behind, plunging into her so hard that her body jerked forward. She gave a strangled cry of pleasure as he began to thrust into her, slamming against her buttocks. He wrapped his arm around her waist to hold her steady. His knees kept her thighs splayed apart so his prick could slide effortlessly into her as her inner walls gripped his engorged flesh with a strength that made him want to stay buried inside her forever.

Katya's head fell forward causing her hair to veil her face as she pushed back against him to increase the strength of their union. Her hands clawed at the faded, Oriental carpet, sinking into the soft material as whimpers came from her throat.

Blood pounded in Alexei's head. He took her like the vicious, dominant wolf she had accused him of being, staking his claim on her with a vengeance she would not easily forget. He pressed down on her damp, lower back with the palm of his hand, feeling her body sway and jerk with every movement. He raked his hand up her back and tracked his fingers along the bumps on her spine, burning every part of her into his mind. Sweat glistened on his chest as he leant over her, his breathing rasping against her naked skin. He reached to pull the length of her hair away from her face, gathering it in his fist. He yanked her head up so suddenly that she gasped.

'Alexei –'

'Look,' he hissed fiercely, pulling on her hair, and forcing her to look into the full-length mirror resting against the opposite wall. 'Look at yourself getting fucked like an animal. And liking it – no, loving it – and wanting more.'

She could no longer shield her face with her hair. Her eyes closed as a hot flush of shame burned spots of colour into her cheeks. Then, as Alexei had known would happen – for he knew the darkest parts of Katya's heart and soul better than she – her eyelids lifted with slow hesitation. A glimmer of astonished excitement flared in the depths of her brown eyes as she stared at the reflection in the mirror.

She saw herself splayed naked on her hands and knees, her white skin shiny with perspiration, her breasts swaying; and behind her Alexei's muscular body drove into her as he held her head up by her hair and leant over her back. They were like rutting animals, moans and pants issuing forth in low rumbles, drenched in a sexual fog that blocked out everything but throbbing sensations, heartbeats and fire.

Alexei released Katya's hair but Katya did not lower her head to shield herself from their reflected image or Alexei's piercing gaze. His mouth twisted into a cruel smile. His princess would not disappoint him. Her carnal nature thrilled her. He knew that no one else existed with whom she could discover the dark, hidden sides of herself with such uninhibited fascination. She knew it, too.

'Tell me what you want,' he growled, as his other hand reached underneath her to stroke through the curls of her vulva.

'You ... I want ... can't ... please, Alexei, I –' The words spilled in a torrent from her lips.

Her body continued to receive and accept the full force

of him, her back arching. Her skin was hot where he touched her and scorching between her legs. She cried out when his hand delved into her wetness, stroking roughly around the nub of her sensuality, feeling her secret walls pulsing against his fingers. Alexei gritted his teeth against the pressure building in his cock in an effort to stall to his own release.

He thrust into her completely with one, hard shove. When her bottom hit the hard planes of his lower belly, he clenched her hips in his hands to stop her writhing against him.

'Captain,' Katya gasped, her eyes glazed with need and desperation as they met his in the reflection of the mirror. 'Alexei –'

His fingers dug into her hips. Every muscle, every bone, every vein inside him fought to retain control over himself. He took a deep, ragged breath, almost wincing when he felt Katya's inner muscles tighten around his prick. His fingers slipped underneath her again as he began to manipulate her very core.

'Tell me who you belong to,' Alexei grated from between clenched teeth, his jaw tight with effort, his muscles straining.

'I . . . I . . .' She moaned, struggling to move against him.

He clamped his arm around her waist like a steel band.

'*Who?*' he hissed furiously. 'Who do you belong to?'

'Oh, God. You, Alexei. You.'

His arm released her. He drove into her with the power she craved, his fingers working until her body shook with convulsions of rapture as she squirmed and writhed and cried out. And then Alexei went over the edge with her and he thought that this must be what it was like to die.

Chapter Twelve

*S*vetlana secured a fresh bandage on the Tsarist soldier's arm and sat back on her heels. She had been tending the wounds of the prisoners with Alexei's knowledge but not his outright consent. She knew that Alexei had no plans to kill the soldiers, and she did not want them to suffer the horrors of death by gangrene or infections. She had seen such deaths amidst their own Cossack soldiers. The agony was unbearable.

'Has the doctor come to see you again?' she asked the grizzled, old soldier who sat before her on an empty barrel.

The soldier shook his head.

Svetlana frowned. Alexei had allowed the Cossack doctor to examine the prisoners when they first arrived and he had promised Svetlana that the doctor would make regular visits.

'I'll speak to him,' she said. She stood, brushing off her skirts. 'Perhaps he can give you medication of some kind.'

She doubted that the doctor would want to waste sparse medication on a prisoner, but it wouldn't hurt to ask.

The Tsarist soldier looked at her, his expression

touched with respect and appreciation. 'Thank you,' he said. 'You're a good woman.'

Svetlana tried to smile, but couldn't. He had no idea what kind of woman she was.

She picked up her basket of supplies and turned towards the door, where a big, burly Cossack guard stood waiting for her. The guards didn't leave her alone with the prisoners, a service for which Svetlana was grateful. She did not fear the Tsarists, but nor did she want to be alone in an enclosed cell with them.

She stepped out of the cell as the guard closed and locked the door.

'That's the last of them then, miss?' he asked.

'Yes.' Svetlana hesitated, glancing down the corridor. 'No, wait. I want to see someone else.'

The guard followed her to the cell of Nicholas Fedorov.

'This one's not hurt at all,' the guard said. 'Couple of scrapes and bruises, but nothing life-threatening.'

'I know. I wish to speak with him alone.'

The guard shook his head. 'I can't leave you alone with him.'

'You can,' Svetlana said firmly. 'You will. Return to your post. If I need your assistance, I'll call you.'

The guard opened his mouth to protest but Svetlana had already unlocked the door. She stepped inside and closed it behind her, her gaze sweeping through the small cell and coming to rest on the figure leaning against the wall.

'Who are you?' Nicholas looked at her suspiciously while reaching up to push his hair away from his face.

'My name is Svetlana,' Svetlana replied, approaching him with caution. 'I've been tending to the injuries of several prisoners.'

'I'm not injured.'

'Your face is cut.' She put the basket on the floor and knelt down a short distance away from him. 'If you don't tend it properly, infection can set in.'

'I'm fine.'

Svetlana looked at him for a moment. Images of Katya flashed in her mind: Katya cleaning his laceration, Katya bringing him hot water so he could bathe and shave, Katya putting her hand on his thigh as if it were the most natural thing in the world to do; Katya kissing him gently, her hands cupping his face.

A shuddering sigh eased out of her lungs. She missed Ivan. She hadn't thought she would, but she did. Not just physically – he had always been so good to her. He had simply always accepted her.

Nicholas watched her as if he were trying to determine her motives. 'You're a Cossack,' he said.

'Yes.'

'Another woman used to bring us food,' he said carefully. 'She hasn't been here in over a week.'

Svetlana nodded. 'Katya.'

'Do you know where she is?'

'She's still here.' Svetlana wondered what Alexei had done with the information she had given him about the princess and the Tsarist soldier. She had told him out of jealousy and anger, but also because she hated knowing that Alexei was being deceived.

Svetlana's heart softened a little at Nicholas's evident concern. 'She's terribly busy. There is a great deal of work to do.'

Relief flashed in his eyes like a firefly. 'She's all right, then?'

'I believe so.'

Svetlana could tell he wanted to ask more, but wasn't certain if that would be wise.

'May I ask you a question?' she said.

'What kind of question?'

'If a woman did something to you,' Svetlana said. 'I mean, if she used you without thinking about the consequences and without realising that she would hurt you, would you ever be able to forgive her?'

Nicholas looked at her, appearing somewhat puzzled.

216

Svetlana almost smiled. She supposed prisoners of war didn't often have women asking them questions about male and female relationships.

'I guess it would depend on what she did,' Nicholas finally said. 'I don't think I could forgive being used.'

Svetlana bit her lip. 'No, that would be difficult, wouldn't it?'

Nicholas continued watching her with curiosity flickering in his dark eyes. 'Of course, if I really loved her and if I could understand why she did it, then I might be able to forgive.'

Svetlana gave him a wry smile. 'What if the reason was another man?'

A startled expression crossed his face. 'I don't think anyone would be able to forgive that.'

They fell silent. Svetlana wondered what Nicholas would say if she told him about Katya and Alexei. Of course, Katya hadn't used either one of them, but another man was still another man. And knowing Alexei, Katya was deriving a great deal of pleasure from him. Even with Nicholas imprisoned in the same manor.

The thought irritated Svetlana. She, of all people, knew how compelling Alexei could be, but Katya's alleged true love was sitting in a dank, stone room with torn clothes and barely a blanket to keep him warm. The whole situation seemed unjust.

'I'm sorry you're here,' Svetlana murmured. 'You must miss her, whoever she is.'

He looked surprised. 'Why do you say that?'

'You must have a woman in your heart,' Svetlana said. She smiled. 'All soldiers are supposed to cling to the memory of a long-lost woman. I believe that's rule number twelve in the soldier's handbook.'

To her pleasure, Nicholas chuckled. It was a rusty sound, as if he hadn't laughed in ages, and it warmed Svetlana's heart.

'Then I suppose I have to confess,' he said, still amused. 'I do miss her.'

'You love each other?' she asked.

'Yes.'

'Would you forgive her for deceiving you?'

'I could probably forgive her anything.'

'Have you ever deceived her?' Svetlana asked.

'No,' he answered.

'Never with another woman?'

His head jerked up suddenly, his eyes narrowing, but not before Svetlana caught the glimpse of guilt in his expression. He looked away.

'Well, that's not exactly deception,' Svetlana said soothingly. 'After all, a man like you can't be expected to be celibate when you're out travelling and fighting. Of course you need release.'

His gaze darted to her. 'That's all it was.'

'I know. That's all it has to be.' She edged closer to him, reaching out to put her hand on his leg. She began to stroke him.

'You didn't deceive her,' she said softly. 'You won't.'

Nicholas watched her with a hint of wariness. She slipped her cloak off her shoulders and let it fall to the floor. A surge of satisfaction coursed through her as Nicholas's gaze went to her breasts which strained against the bodice of her dress. Svetlana knew he was battling his conscience. She would have to ease it for him.

Her hand slid further up his leg until she was caressing his hard thigh. Without taking her eyes from his face she brushed her fingers over his groin. An unmistakable, growing hardness met her fingertips.

'Do you want to kiss me?' she breathed, her gaze going hungrily to his mouth. Yes, she had imagined this, wanted it, since the day she saw him and Katya together.

Nicholas didn't reply, but his hand came around to the back of her neck. He drew her towards him, touching her lips with his in a caress so gentle it nearly brought tears to her eyes. She moved closer, her hand massaging the bulge in his trousers as she pressed her breasts against his chest.

A low murmur emerged from his throat. She parted her lips, allowing him to sink into her, to explore her mouth with his tongue. His lips and tongue moved with glorious heat over hers, warming her all the way to her sex. A shudder of urgency ran through Nicholas's body, sparking a responding need inside Svetlana. Her nipples hardened and pressed against her bodice, urging his touch.

Nicholas withdrew slightly, leaning his forehead against hers.

'Don't tell me you do this with all the prisoners,' he murmured.

Svetlana shook her head, her breathing rapid. 'God, no. I said I tended their injuries, not caused them.'

They looked at each other, then they both laughed. Svetlana's entire soul warmed. She had never known how nice it was to laugh and be intimate at the same time. Nicholas pulled her closer and kissed her again. One of his hands tangled in her blonde hair and the other began to work the buttons of her bodice.

Svetlana helped him ease her dress over her shoulders, closing her eyes when he exhaled sharply and bent to kiss her breasts. He cupped them in his hands, swirling his thumbs around the hard peaks. Moisture dampened Svetlana's sex. She grasped his shoulders and tried to tug him down on top of her, her entire being craving everything he had to give her and more.

'Wait.' Nicholas reached for her cloak and spread it on the stone floor before helping her lie back.

He pulled Svetlana's dress slowly over her hips and down her legs, touching his lips against her bare skin as it was revealed to him. It was like being kissed by a warm butterfly: light, teasing, and so delicious that her skin tingled when he lifted his head.

When she was naked, he came over her, his dark hair tickling her as he pressed her breasts together and took one nipple, then the other in his mouth, sliding his tongue around the areolas. Svetlana gasped, her fingers clutching his hair. Ribbons of fervour wrapped around her body, tightening in her loins. She parted her legs, giving a little moan of anticipation as his erection pushed against her. She slid her arms over his shoulders, helping him take off his jacket and shirt. His chest was magnificent: hard, muscular, and covered with a layer of dark hair and without any of the ugly scars that marred Alexei's.

Annoyed by the intrusive, unbidden thought of the Cossack captain, Svetlana put herself to the lovely task of exploring Nicholas's body. She stroked her hands over his skin, memorising every muscle and sinew, kissing the hot hollow of his throat as her fingertips skimmed down his back. She felt his erection pulsing against her through his trousers, sending heat directly into her sex.

'Nicholas, aren't you forgetting something?' she whispered in his ear.

She took the opportune moment to trace her tongue around the shell of his ear and nibble on his earlobe. She nudged her vulva against him in case he hadn't got the message.

'Right,' Nicholas said, his voice breathless and hoarse. He lifted himself off her with his forearms, his eyes smoky with desire. 'He's twitching around like a snake.'

Svetlana giggled. 'Does he need help?'

'He always appreciates a woman's touch.'

Smiling, she made quick work of the buttons on his trousers. She pushed them down and her fingers closed around his cock as it sprung free from confinement. Svetlana stared down at his erection, stroking her hand over the long length, feeling the blood pulsing through him.

'You're beautiful, Nicholas,' she said as she looked up at him.

Her blue eyes met his black eyes. A crackle of electricity lit the air between them. With a groan, Nicholas lowered his head and pressed his mouth against hers, sliding his tongue into her.

'So are you,' he whispered heatedly against her lips. 'Beautiful.'

He reached down to push her legs further apart. Svetlana gasped when she felt his cock nudging at the lips of her sex, her body arching up to meet him. He thrust into her with a guttural moan of pleasure, his body sinking down on to her again as he began to pump inside her.

Svetlana wrapped her arms around his shoulders and her legs around his hips. She felt so warm, sizzling with desire from inside and out, the very air around them heavy with heat. Nicholas buried his face against her breasts. His hands slid underneath her thighs as he opened her for his strong thrusts. He was hard and powerful in her, on her and over her; Svetlana surrendered to the swirling tides of sensation that overwhelmed them both.

She gasped his name when a climax ripped through her body, shuddering along her nerves with a power that made her cry out with pleasure. Nicholas drank the cry from her lips, silencing their passion from the outside world. Svetlana dug her fingernails into his back, unable to stand the glorious sensations as he slid in and out of her with increasing frenzy, his breath hot on her skin, his fingers clutching her flesh. He moaned hoarsely against her breasts as he slammed into her one last time, his own body shaking with release.

Nicholas collapsed on top of her, his face against her neck. Svetlana held him tightly as their harsh breathing began to calm and the final pulses ebbed away. After what seemed like an eternity, Nicholas lifted himself on to his hands and looked down at her. His eyes were dark with lust and satisfaction.

'You're amazing,' he murmured. 'Who the hell are you?'

Svetlana laughed. 'Your fairy godmother?' she suggested.

'I think you're more of a sorceress than a godmother.'

Svetlana smiled, tracing his lower lip with her forefinger.

'How about just your friend?' she whispered.

He bent his head to kiss her, murmuring his agreement against her lips. Svetlana would have loved to indulge in another few hours with him, but reality nudged at the back of her mind.

'I have to go,' she said, her voice heavy with reluctance. 'They'll come looking for me if I don't return soon. The guards seem to think I'm going to end up copulating with one of the prisoners if they leave me alone.'

Nicholas chuckled, easing himself off her. 'Well, we can't let that happen.'

'Heaven forbid.'

Their amused gazes kept returning to each other as they shook out their clothes and began to dress. Svetlana buttoned up her bodice, feeling Nicholas approach her from behind. He pushed aside the swath of blonde hair and kissed her neck. A shiver of warmth slid down her spine.

Svetlana knew she had to leave now or she was in danger of melting into his embrace. She turned, placing her hand against his jaw, memorising every detail of his handsome face.

'I'll think of you,' she murmured.

She pulled her cloak around her shoulders and hurried from the room without looking back.

'Miss?' At the end of the corridor, the Cossack guard stood from his chair. 'You're all right?'

'I'm fine.' Svetlana pressed the cell keys into his hand. 'I forgot to lock the last cell. Would you do it, please?'

The guard nodded and took the keys. He started down the corridor towards Nicholas's cell.

Svetlana went back up into the kitchens. If there was

anything she could not have borne, it was locking Nicholas in his cell.

Pausing outside the cellar door, Svetlana absorbed the warm, tingling feelings that made her entire being alive and whole. She felt good. Better than she had in a long, long while. She wrapped her arms around herself and smiled.

Katya had no way of warning Nicholas. She didn't dare even approach the cellar doors for fear that somehow Alexei would find out. With a muffled groan, she pushed her book to the floor and pressed the palms of her hands against her eyes as she tried to sort out her emotions.

She no longer knew what to feel. Alexei had touched something dark and primal inside her and Katya wondered if she would ever be the same again. And she wondered if Nicholas would still love her if he discovered the truth about the savage and cryptic urges that so aroused her.

She wanted to cry, her throat ached with need, but her eyes remained dry. Hollowness and shame filled her. Over a week had passed since Alexei had taken her on the floor and she hadn't seen him since. Although she despised herself for thinking it, she couldn't help but wonder if that had been the end, if his overwhelming display of possession had been his final act. If he was now finished with her.

Well, if he was, she told herself, then that was a good thing, wasn't it? That was what she wanted.

Wasn't it?

Katya made a sound of frustration as she rose and went to the window. The cold, clear night was little solace for her chaotic thoughts. Soldiers slept inside their tents, surrounded by dying fires. Gusts of smoke rose from the crimson embers and ashes.

Without thinking about what she was going to do, Katya went into the corridor. In the darkest hour of night, an ominous, weighty silence filled the manor.

Unstable shadows appropriated the occupancy of the rooms and corridors, sliding against the walls and floors like lost souls.

Katya hurried down the corridor, her shoes clicking loudly against the marble. Her breathing came in short gasps as she came to a halt in front of the door to the captain's bedchamber. She didn't dare knock, for fear of losing her courage, but put her trembling hand on the doorknob and twisted it open.

'Captain?' Her low whisper was swallowed up by the vastness of the room.

Tentatively, she stepped inside and closed the door behind her. The flames in the fireplace burned low, but had not completely died. Katya's gaze scanned the room until they came to rest on Alexei's fully-dressed figure seated in an upholstered chair by the fire. He wasn't reading, he didn't have a drink in his hand, and he wasn't writing anything or reviewing reports. He was simply sitting there. Waiting.

Katya shivered, wishing suddenly that she hadn't followed her reckless instinct. Alexei's dark eyes fixed on her.

'Ah,' he murmured. 'The princess has arrived.'

Katya hugged her arms around herself, trying to hold in all her inner turmoil. The words came out of her mouth almost of their own volition.

'Have you done anything to him?' she whispered.

One black eyebrow lifted enquiringly. 'Him?'

'Nicholas.'

'You really are devoted to him, aren't you?' Alexei turned his attention to the vanishing fire. 'I'd advise you not to be, Princess. Such attachments can be devastating in the end.'

Katya had nothing to lose. She walked across the room to him, pausing a short distance away. 'Alexei, I'm asking you because I think you're an inherently honourable man.'

That got his attention again. He looked up. Amusement flickered in his eyes. 'Honourable? I've been called many things, but never that.'

'Please, Alexei. Tell me the truth. Have you done anything to him?'

'If I have, what difference would it make to you? You won't see him again, not if I have anything to say about it.'

'I need –' Her voice caught. She took a deep breath and clenched her hands into fists so that her fingernails dug into her palms. 'I need to know.'

Alexei fell silent for so long that Katya thought he wasn't going to reply at all. Then, finally, he shook his head. 'No. I haven't done anything to him.'

Relief eased away Katya's apprehension. She didn't know what to think about the captain – she never had – but she did know he was not an untruthful man. She almost thanked him, but stopped the words just in time. She had displayed enough of her feelings for Nicholas.

'All right,' she murmured. 'I'll leave you alone, then.'

He didn't respond, his gaze fixed again on the low flames. Katya turned and walked towards the door before his voice halted her.

'Come back here,' he demanded.

It was a command, but he didn't dictate it in the imperious tone he usually used with her. Katya looked at him, expecting to see the gleam of impending desire in his eyes, but it wasn't there. She returned to stand in front of him, feeling confused and slightly unnerved.

'Sit down,' he said.

Katya sank to her knees and settled her hands on his thighs. He made a sudden noise of irritation that surprised her.

She glanced up at him, her eyebrows drawn together. 'Captain?'

'I said "sit down," not "suck my prick,"' Alexei said shortly.

'Oh.' Katya's face flamed at her misunderstanding.

She eased herself away, settling back on to the floor

and wrapping her arms around her legs. A cold shiver slipped down her spine. Had she been right in her speculation that the captain was now finished with her? She remembered how she had given herself over to him so completely that she couldn't have done anything else; how scorching heat and savageness had dissolved her senses and thoughts, leaving her submerged in the rough sensuality of their union.

She lowered her forehead to her knees to hide her flush. She felt Alexei's gaze on her as if he could see right into her soul.

'Look at me,' he ordered.

Katya lifted her head. Her eyes met his without the crackle of sexuality that always sparked between them. She was both surprised and dismayed by the weariness buried in the depths of Alexei's dark eyes.

'Are you all right, Captain?' she whispered.

A corner of his mouth turned up in a humourless smile. 'I suppose that depends of your definition of the word.'

'You look very tired.'

'I suppose war has drained the strength of millions of men.'

'And women,' Katya added.

The other corner of his mouth lifted, and he inclined his head slightly in an acknowledgement of her words. 'And women,' he agreed.

Katya studied him for a moment. The lost-soul shadows of midnight softened his hard, austere features, making him look more approachable than she had ever seen him before. His long legs were stretched out towards the flames and crossed at the ankle, the lines of his body still not at ease.

'What is it?' Katya asked quietly. 'Not just the war.'

When he didn't reply, she inched closer to him.

'Alexei? You've given your family estate over to the army. You've given yourself over to the revolution. You

226

once told me that you're fighting for Cossack land and freedom, but you no longer have either one for yourself.'

Alexei looked at her for a very long time.

'We all give ourselves over to something, don't we?' he finally said, then added, 'Or someone.'

Heat rose in Katya's face again at the reminder of her desperate surrender, but she didn't take her eyes from him. 'Most people don't trap themselves into doing so.'

She risked moving across the floor to his side, resting her shoulder against the chair next to his legs. She didn't know why, but she wanted to ease the horrible, weary look from his expression. It wasn't the look of the autocratic, Cossack captain she knew him to be.

'You capture other people,' she murmured. 'But you don't know that you've trapped yourself.'

'And what do you suggest I do about that, my perceptive one?' Alexei asked, a thread of amusement running through his deep voice.

His hand slipped down to stroke through her hair, sending a warm tingle down her spine. She closed her eyes, disliking the truth of her broken words, her own admission that she was irrevocably his.

'I don't know,' she confessed, tilting her head forward so he could slide his long fingers over the back of her neck. 'You have so much power, Alexei. So much authority. You know that. People always do what you tell them.'

'So I need to relinquish my authority?' He shook his head, his mouth tightening. 'Never.'

'Maybe you just need someone to tell you what to do every so often,' Katya suggested.

'Oh, is that what I need? You wouldn't hope that someone might be you, would you?'

Katya's mouth curved into a smile. 'Maybe.'

Alexei chuckled. 'All right, then. You tell me what to do.'

'And you'll do it?' She turned to look at him in surprise.

'Maybe,' he replied, noncommittally.

Katya sighed and shook her head at him. She should have known he wouldn't accede to such a request. She decided to test him.

'Take off your clothes,' she ordered in the same, dictatorial tone he always used with her.

To her complete shock, Alexei rose from the chair and began to unfasten the buttons of his shirt. Katya stared up at him, unable to believe that he had obeyed.

Alexei's eyes glinted with humour as he looked at her. 'Don't look so stunned, Princess. Hasn't anyone ever listened to you before?'

Katya swallowed hard. 'Well, yes, but I never expected you to.'

'Then enjoy it while you can because there's no telling how long it will last.'

He slipped off his shirt to reveal his muscular chest and shoulders. The shirt dropped to the floor and his hands went to the buttons on his trousers.

Katya's mouth went dry as she watched him undress in movements edged with masculine grace. He bent to unbuckle his boots and take them off, then slid his trousers over his hips. Katya's eyes followed his hands with growing hunger.

'Anything else?' Alexei stood in front of her, unselfconscious in his nakedness, his hands resting on his hips.

Katya rose, steadying herself on the arm of the chair.

'Yes,' she said. 'I want you to undress me and kiss me everywhere.'

A slight smile tugged at the corners of his mouth as he moved towards her. He unfastened the buttons of her dress, his fingers brushing casually over her bare skin. He eased the dress over her hips and then set to work on the ties of her petticoats. Katya had long ago given up wearing constricting corsets and her skin shivered with awareness as he touched her.

She stepped out of the folds of her dress, her heart hammering with the excitement of their momentary exchange of roles. A slow burn struck in Alexei's eyes as he looked at her, his hands going to her waist.

'Kiss you all over, you said?' he asked, his voice dropping a note.

Katya drew herself up and looked him in the eye.

'Everywhere,' she commanded.

He lowered his head to her neck. His lips touched her lightly as his tongue flickered out to lick a trail of fire over her skin. Katya's breathing grew unsteady as he pulled her closer to him. His hands splayed across her lower back, drawing her body against his. Katya's pulse raced as she encountered the growing hardness of his erection, and she fought the urge to touch him.

His thick, dark hair brushed across her neck. His mouth moved to her shoulders, sliding down to her breast, closing over the hard peak of her nipple as his tongue swirled around the areola. Katya's eyes drifted closed as pleasure washed over her, her limbs relaxing and loosening in response to him. He continued to hold her against him, his fingers rhythmically stroking the sensitive spot at the base of her spine.

Then, to Katya's further shock, the captain went down on his knees in front of her, his lips never breaking contact with her skin. Katya opened her eyes and looked at him in surprise. His hands slipped to her bottom, and he dug his fingers gently into her flesh as he pressed kisses across her belly. Katya's hands sank into his hair, stroking the thick strands away from his forehead and steadying herself at the same time.

Alexei's mouth moved lower. His hands went to the backs of her thighs, applying enough pressure so that she opened them to his ministrations. Her body began to tremble as his teeth closed lightly around the skin of her inner thigh. Without a pause, he moved to the juncture of her legs, his hands slipping between them from behind to push her farther apart.

Katya nearly collapsed when she felt his tongue flicker over the sensitive tissue of her labia. Her fingers tightened in his hair. Warmth spread through her groin. The exquisite combination of Alexei's lips and tongue, his hot breath against her moist folds, created an inferno of desire that twisted in her lower body.

'Wait,' she gasped. 'Stop.'

He pulled away immediately, his hands still holding her thighs. His eyes smouldered as he looked at her.

'I haven't kissed you everywhere yet,' he pointed out huskily.

'Everywhere,' Katya murmured, her breathing rapid. 'Except there. Not yet.'

'Whatever you say.' He moved around behind her – still on his knees – and began to press kisses over her back, tracing her spine with his tongue and biting down on the flesh of her bottom.

Katya let out another gasp of surprise when she felt his tongue start to trail down the crevice of her buttocks. An unearthly bolt of stimulation shot through her, even as colour bloomed in her face from the unexpected caress. She reached for the chair again to steady herself, stunned by how terribly good his erotic stroking felt.

Alexei avoided the heat between her legs, but didn't hesitate to move his lips over the backs of her thighs and calves, even down to her feet. By the time he was finished, the entire surface of Katya's body tingled with electricity. The tension in her loins had tightened to intense proportions and her skin glowed the deep reddish colour of passion.

'And now?' Alexei asked, his own breathing ragged, his manhood almost fully engorged.

Katya could barely think past her haze of desire, but she wasn't about to miss the opportunity to dictate orders to him. She lowered her shaking body into the chair and sank into the velvety upholstery. She closed her eyes to block out the sight of Alexei, his skin glistening in the dying firelight, his every muscle tensed with arousal, his dark eyes scorching her.

'I want –' She could hardly get the words out. She wet

her lips with her tongue and tried again. 'I want you to tell me something.'

'Tell you what?' He sounded closer now.

'Tell me ... tell me about the first time you ever had sex with a woman,' Katya ordered. Her heart pulsed wildly in her chest.

A moment of silence lingered in the air between them. Katya sensed Alexei move closer, right in front of her, but he didn't touch her. She opened her eyes, locking her gaze on to his. He eased his body between her legs, put his hands on the arms of the chair and his hard thighs brushed against hers. Katya thought for a moment that the game was finished and that the captain would take over, but he merely continued looking at her. She fought the urge to push forward and impale herself on his stiff penis.

'Go on,' Katya said, injecting a note of irritation into her command. 'Tell me. In detail.'

He leant towards her. His body was so close that she could feel the heat emanating from his skin, his breath against her lips and even his cock trembling between her legs. And yet, still, he did not touch her.

'Shall I kiss you first?' he whispered.

A surge of satisfaction rose in Katya.

'Yes,' she breathed.

Alexei pressed his lips against hers. As his tongue swirled into the damp cavern of her mouth she experienced an intense eroticism that made her blood flame. Then he pulled away from her, but only to the distance of her thighs. His gaze never left hers.

He told her of his first woman in a voice husky with the echo of remembered passion and youth. He was sixteen; she was twenty-one: a Cossack woman of dark beauty with curling hair and a rounded figure. She moved with voluptuous grace, her full breasts swaying, her hips rocking with every step. She saw him one warm, twilight evening in late summer when he was riding in the woods, collecting logs for the approaching autumn months.

'Or, rather,' Alexei murmured, 'I saw her. She had been out picking mushrooms, and she'd fallen asleep in a small clearing. I stopped to look at her – for she was quite lovely – and then she shifted and reached down to pull up her skirts. She slipped her hand inside her drawers and started to pleasure herself. Being sixteen, I was utterly captivated by the sight.'

'And she opened her eyes and saw you?'

A smile tugged at the corner of his mouth. 'No. I approached her as she started to writhe and whimper. I knew she was nearing her climax, but for some reason, I didn't want it to happen without her knowing I was there. I put my hand right over hers – between her legs. Her eyes flew open and gasped with surprise at the realisation that I'd been watching her. My prick was already as hard as a rock.

'I wanted her badly. I put my hand on her breast, kneading her flesh with my fingers, and I felt her nipple tighten. Without thinking, I grasped the neckline of her blouse and pulled it over her breasts, baring them to the forest air. She broke through her shock and tried to swat me away, but the heat between her legs fairly burnt against my hand. I knew she wouldn't force me to leave. I bent my head to kiss her nipples, sucking on them until I heard her raspy breathing. I had kissed women and girls before – felt their bodies – but what I really wanted was to sink my prick into her.'

'Did she touch you?' Katya whispered, her body hot with arousal over the thought of Alexei and the Cossack woman. She could well imagine him as a strong, handsome youth with all the defiance and rebelliousness that would ultimately evolve into his dominating authority.

His eyes darkened. 'Yes. I unfastened my trousers, and she took me in her hand, and then her mouth. I thought I was going to spend before I'd experienced the rapture of penetrating her. She was more skilled than her initial resistance had led me to believe. She pushed down her drawers and opened herself, already stimulated by her own hand. I eased my prick into her cunt with torturous slowness, wanting to experience every second of feeling her tight heat close around my flesh. When I was –'

'Stop,' Katya interrupted. She was in flames. Her chest heaved as she pushed herself towards him, her sex surging at the sensation of his cock brushing against her outer labia.

'Do it to me now,' she ordered. 'What you did to her.'

Alexei's hands gripped her hips. His shaft slid into her with the unhurried slowness he had just described, and Katya's entire body craved his complete immersion. She felt him stretching her, filling her, and then his hips nudged against her and he could go no farther. Katya's head fell against the back of the chair, her eyelids closing in ecstasy as the hard length of him throbbed into her inner walls. Her throat worked as she swallowed.

'And then what did you do?' she whispered.

'Then I started thrusting inside her,' Alexei said, his voice gravelly, his fingers digging into her hips. 'Working my prick back and forth, sliding into her heat as if nothing else existed in the world. And it didn't, not then, not when she gripped me like a vice. I fell over her, licking and biting her breasts, craving the moment when I'd explode inside her and yet wanting the sensations to go on and on –'

'Do it,' Katya gasped. 'Now!'

He dragged her off the chair and on to the floor, coming over her like a firestorm, his hands on either side of her head as he began thrusting. In some dim part of her mind, Katya knew that Alexei had just recaptured control with one movement but she no longer cared.

The feelings he evoked in her as he did to her what he'd done to the Cossack woman flared inside her like shooting stars, brilliant with light and speed. He lowered his mouth to her breasts, nibbling and sucking them, his body pounding into hers until she climaxed with a moan and a series of intense shudders. He followed, his hoarse groan hot against her breasts as his own release tore through him.

Alexei's body sank down on to hers, his breathing harsh on her neck. Katya closed her eyes, fighting another wave of confusion over this enigmatic man who awakened such carnality in her. He pushed himself off her, rolling to the side, his arm slung across his face.

'God's blood,' he muttered roughly. 'I'll never let you go.'

His words pierced through Katya's pleasure-fogged brain. Yes, she conceded, he was still the one with the power. And aside from driving her admission of captivity from her, Alexei had never spoken of their tenuous connection.

She turned her head to stare at him, but his eyes were closed and his arm blocked his expression. Within minutes, his body shifted into the deep rhythm of sleep. Katya watched him for a long while before a cold breeze touched the back of her neck. She shivered. The fire had gone out, leaving burnt embers.

Katya sat up, reaching for Alexei's shirt. She slipped it over her shoulders and buttoned it. The fabric smelt like him and was still warm from his body heat. The thought of staying with him stirred something deep and unexplainable inside of her. And yet, if the captain meant what he said, that he would never let her go, then Katya knew she would have to relinquish her very soul to him.

That she could never do.

She hugged her arms around herself, tucked her body against his and settled down to sleep.

Chapter Thirteen

*D*awn broke through the curtains when Alexei awoke. He felt Katya's warm body pressing against his back, her knees tucked behind his legs, her arm wrapped loosely around his waist. He remained still for a moment, absorbing the sensation of her before easing away. Katya murmured a protest, but continued to sleep.

Alexei stood, stretching his muscles like a jungle cat as he walked to the adjoining bathchamber. A servant had already brought up hot water and Alexei bathed and shaved. He dressed in a clean uniform and went back into the bedroom just as Katya stirred.

Her eyelids fluttered open as she sat up slowly. She was wearing his shirt, which was far too big and made her appear somewhat lost.

'What time is it?' she asked.

'Five.' He sat down to put on his boots. Sensing that Katya was still watching him, he looked at her. 'There's hot water left if you want to have a bath.'

Katya smoothed his shirt over her thighs.

'Did you mean it?' she asked quietly.

'Did I mean what?'

'That you would never let me go.'

Alexei frowned. 'What are you talking about?'

'Last night,' Katya replied. 'Right before you fell asleep you said you were never going to let me go.'

Alexei forced his mind back to the previous night. He'd been so sated that he figured he could have said just about anything. And, yes, he did remember the words escaping his lips as he hovered on the edge of unconsciousness.

He sat back in the chair and fixed his gaze on Katya.

'And what did you think of that statement?' he asked.

'I don't know.'

'What would you do if I did make you stay?'

'I don't know.'

'You admitted that you belong to me.'

Katya looked down at her hands, her fingers clenching on the fabric of the shirt. 'You couldn't have meant it. You're too independent to attach yourself to anyone.'

'Suppose I did mean what I said,' Alexei murmured. 'How would you feel?'

Her hands started to tremble. She didn't meet his gaze.

'I can't, Alexei,' she whispered. 'I can't.'

Something dark and unpleasant clenched in Alexei's gut.

'I didn't ask if you would agree,' he said. 'This isn't a question of choice. I asked how you would feel.'

She lifted her eyes to him, her expression stunned, as if she had just realised that it was not, indeed, a question of choice for her.

'I would be afraid,' she finally admitted in a low voice.

'Of me?'

'Yes. And myself.'

Alexei smiled without humour. 'But, you would revel in it, wouldn't you?'

A flush heated her face. She didn't respond.

'You would surrender completely,' Alexei continued, watching with satisfaction as the implications of his words took root in Katya's mind. 'You would give yourself over to me without a second thought. Your entire existence, everything you are, would become submerged in the exploration of your hidden desires.'

Katya fell silent for a long while.

'You would do this,' she said huskily. 'You would do this knowing all the while that I was in love with another man?'

'Your "other man" will be driven from your thoughts if I have to fuck you twenty-four hours a day to do it,' Alexei snapped, his blood hardening in his veins at the reminder.

'No!' The sudden vehemence of the word rang through the room as Katya's hands clenched. Her head came up and she gave Alexei a hostile glare. 'No. You still don't understand, do you? You can do anything you want with me, Alexei, you can force me to stay with you, you can turn me into your personal slave, you can fuck me all you want, but nothing can ever drive Nicholas from my thoughts! Nothing. Not even you. And that will always be the one part of me over which you will never have control!'

Anger sunk deep claws into Alexei's skin. 'Those are quite strong words from a woman who keeps reiterating the evidence of her betrayal.'

'What are you going to do about it, Alexei?' Katya snapped. 'Remove the sections of my heart that are reserved for him? Fine, then, take out the whole damn thing! I could stay with you for an eternity and never forget him, never stop loving him. Parts of me will never belong to you.'

Alexei rose from his chair and stepped towards her. Fury seethed within him, coating a red mist over the world and clenching his every muscle.

Katya recoiled, as if realising she had pushed him too far. Alexei reached down and grabbed the front of her – his – shirt in his fist, yanking her to her feet. Katya gasped and grabbed his arm to retain her balance.

'I asked you once who you belong to,' Alexei grated, his voice very low. 'And I'm asking you again.'

Fear lit deep in Katya's eyes, but she didn't try and fight him.

'Belonging,' she whispered, 'is not the same as loving.'

Alexei hauled her against him, his wrath spilling over like a volcano.

'You little bitch,' he hissed. 'You're all morals and romance when you're not lying on the floor naked with your legs spread, aren't you?' His fist tightened on the shirt as he fought the urge to shake her. 'I also asked you if you think about him when my prick is in you. Why don't we make a bargain? If you tell me you do, if you admit you think about him, then maybe, just maybe, I'll be gracious enough to concede defeat.'

He pulled her so close that her body heat burnt through his uniform.

'Well?' he snarled. 'Don't lie to me, Katya. Do you think about him?'

Katya closed her eyes. Her inner struggle made her body tremble. The word, when it passed her lips, was so quiet as to be nearly inaudible. And yet, they both heard it as if it were a loud cry. 'No.'

Alexei released her, pushing her away. Katya turned, wrapping her arms around her torso. Her expression was tortured.

'You see, Katya,' Alexei said coldly, his gaze raking over her. 'Once you surrender, there is no turning back.'

Alexei walked down the steps to the cellar, his boots reverberating against the stone floor. He removed his keys from his pocket and stopped in front of the wooden door of Nicholas's cell. He twisted the key and stepped inside, closing the door behind him.

Nicholas was seated against the wall with his legs drawn up. He was still clad in the trousers and torn, wrinkled shirt, of his uniform. His gaze went cautiously to Alexei.

'Your name is Nicholas, is it not?' Alexei asked.

The soldier nodded.

'I hope you consider that you have been treated well here,' Alexei said. 'I don't think you would have been so lucky had you found yourself at the hands of the Bolsheviks. They are, of course, our allies, but I do find them rather barbaric.'

Nicholas didn't respond.

Alexei crouched in front of the younger soldier, resting his weight on the balls of his feet. He reached out to brush the hair away from Nicholas's forehead in a gesture that was almost a caress. The Tsarist private watched him; his dark eyes wary and touched with the slightest hint of fear.

'What is it you think about when you're locked up here all alone?' Alexei asked, his voice a low whisper.

Whatever question the private had been expecting, it wasn't that. Nicholas stared at Alexei for a moment before his gaze dropped away.

'Do you think about ways to escape?' Alexei asked. 'Do you think about how you got here? About the enemy? Or war? The Bolsheviks? Do you think about your life before the revolution? Do you think about women?'

Alexei slid his hand underneath Nicholas's chin, forcing the younger man to look at him. 'Women, Nicholas? Is that what you think about? Do they occupy your thoughts when you're here alone? Do you fantasise about them while you jerk your flesh in the pathetic substitute of your fist? Come, now,' he urged gently, 'you can tell me. Do you imagine kissing their breasts, sliding your prick into their wet cunts while they writhe and moan underneath you –'

Alexei chuckled when Nicholas broke away from him, a dull flush covering his handsome features. Alexei stood and stepped a few feet away from the Tsarist soldier, his gaze unwavering and cold.

'Yes, I imagine you would think about women,' he mused. 'We can rip Russia apart with our bare hands, but at night we will always want a willing woman to sink into.' He paused, his eyes scanning the length of Nicholas's body. 'Like your friend Katya.'

Nicholas drew in a sharp breath. His gaze flew to Alexei in shock.

Alexei smiled. 'She's quite lovely, isn't she? She proved to be much more entertaining than I originally anticipated.'

His voice lowered to a level of dangerous softness as he watched Nicholas struggle to understand.

'Don't worry, my friend. I never took her against her will. Quite the contrary, in fact. She has a lustful streak that one wouldn't expect from a well-bred member of royalty. And she doesn't hesitate to enjoy her sexuality, does she? She tells you in a thousand ways how much she likes it without uttering a word. Those little noises she makes at the back of her throat right before she comes apart underneath you, the way she wraps her legs around your thighs in a silent plea for you to fill her deeper, harder, the way her breasts swell in your hands, the way she moans with approval when you rub her with just the right amount of pressure, the way she reaches down to touch your cock as you're sliding in and out of her incredibly tight, little cunt –'

A mask of murderous rage crashed down over Nicholas's features.

'You bastard!' Clutching the rough, stone wall to steady himself, Nicholas heaved himself off the ground and lunged at Alexei with a swiftness that belied his weakened, physical state.

He clipped Alexei's jaw with his fist before Alexei grabbed his arm and slammed him face-first up against the wall, pinning him on the cold stone. Alexei's thighs pressed on the backs of Nicholas's to hold him in place, his pelvis pushing against the younger man's buttocks. He twisted Nicholas's arm behind his back. Nicholas grunted and tried to recoil out of his trapped position between the wall and the Cossack captain. Alexei's clutch was inescapable.

'Well,' Alexei said softly. 'This is an interesting turn of events.'

He was several inches taller than the private, and he bent his head to put his mouth close to Nicholas's ear. 'You move quickly for someone who has been a prisoner for so long. I don't doubt that Katya's nightly visits have had something to do with your strength.'

Alexei felt the younger man's rush of despair as he realised that the Cossack captain knew his and Katya's secret.

'Know this now, my friend,' Alexei continued softly, his grip iron-strong on his prisoner's arm. 'Your princess has been anything but faithful to you during her stay here. She loves having a stiff prick thrusting into her, and it doesn't matter who the prick belongs to. And she has a dark streak, too. You didn't know that, did you? If you blindfold her and tie her hands together, she trembles and moans like a cat in heat. And sometimes she doesn't even need a prick, not when she's with a woman. But then that idea probably excites you, doesn't it?' He shoved his pelvis against the other man with a rough thrust. 'Doesn't it?'

Nicholas's breath came in ragged, wretched gasps. 'I'll fucking kill you –'

Alexei chuckled. 'Will you, now? Tell me, have you ever taken Katya from behind?' He twisted Nicholas's arm with a cruel wrench, eliciting a groan of pain from the Tsarist soldier.

Nicholas closed his eyes and turned his face to the wall, but he could not escape the relentless onslaught of Alexei's words.

'No?' Alexei murmured. 'Pity. She likes it rough when you're pounding into her so hard that her entire body shakes with the force of your thrusts. She comes so violently that she convulses around your prick as if she's trying to suck you dry. And she very nearly does.'

Alexei released Nicholas's arm, shoving him away so suddenly that Nicholas had to grab at the wall to stop himself from falling. His hand closed around the edge of a stone as he fought waves of humiliation and anger that made his body tremble.

'I've warned her before of the consequences of her defiance,' Alexei said coldly. 'She knows quite well what kind of situation she has put herself in. However, I don't think she has ever imagined that you might be punished for her indiscretion. Should she return here again, I suggest you warn her.'

Nicholas huddled in a corner of the cell, staring blankly at the ground. The horrifying thought had struck him like a blow. The Cossack knew that Katya had been coming to see him. What in the love of God would he do to her?

He couldn't think about it, couldn't imagine what kind of risk she had put herself in for him. But, if he didn't think about that, then his mind was filled with other unbearable thoughts. He could not rid himself of the images. They seared his brain every time he closed his eyes, burning behind his eyelids, twisting into nightmares. Katya on her knees in front of that fucking Cossack captain; Katya naked, her legs spread, the captain thrusting inside her like a goddamn animal; Katya moaning with pleasure.

Nicholas groaned, pressing the heels of his hands against his eyes. He knew the Cossack wasn't lying to him. His words rang with stark, brutal honesty. He had pleasured Katya in ways Nicholas had never even imagined.

And she had liked it.

'Oh, Christ,' he whispered, his gut clenching as pain gripped him.

She wouldn't have come to the cellar to make love with him if she had been abused at the hands of the captain. Nicholas knew Katya too well. He knew that she would not tolerate the utter degradation of herself. She was intelligent and clever, and she would have found some way to manipulate the Cossack into thinking that nothing he could do would hurt her.

Maybe that was it. Maybe she had just been pretending. Even as he willed himself to believe it, Nicholas knew it wasn't the truth. If it had been, Katya would have told him. She had never lied to him. And the Cossack hadn't taken her against her will. She hadn't pretended.

This was his own fault, Nicholas thought, he should have gone with her. He should have left the damn army to make certain she got safely to Istanbul. It would have been terribly risky for both of them, but at least they would have been together.

He had to see her and talk to her. She was his heart and soul, his motive for enduring when he had thought so many times in battle that it was the end. She was everything; his reason for living. He couldn't do anything, couldn't move, could barely form a coherent thought until he saw for himself that she was unharmed.

And his chances of seeing her grew more distant and unreachable with every passing second.

Svetlana filled the brass samovar in the workroom with water and lit the flame at the bottom of the urn. She picked up the dirty tea glasses piled on a table nearby and placed them in a wooden bucket. After wiping the table with a damp cloth she picked up the bucket and turned towards the kitchen.

'Can I carry that for you?' A young soldier appeared at Svetlana's side, reaching for the bucket.

'Thank you.' Glad to be relieved of the burden, Svetlana handed him the bucket, and they started through the foyer.

'I hope they don't make you work too hard,' the soldier said.

Svetlana smiled. 'They don't "make" me do anything,' she said. 'I'm here because I want to be here.'

'Because of the captain, I assume.'

Svetlana didn't reply. Her gaze fixed on the young man heading towards them, his attention concentrated on a report in his hands. He looked up when he heard them approach. His eyes narrowed at the sight of Svetlana with another soldier.

All three of them stopped when they reached the centre of the foyer.

'Ivan.'

'Svetlana,' said Ivan, as he shot the other soldier a pointedly hostile glare.

A little thrill went through Svetlana at the knowledge that he was jealous. That meant his feelings for her hadn't died.

'You can leave that in the kitchen, please,' she told the other soldier. 'I'll take care of it later.'

The soldier shrugged and headed towards the kitchen.

'He's your new conquest, is he?' Ivan asked, his voice edged with jealousy.

'Not unless carrying a bucket of dirty glasses constitutes a conquest,' Svetlana replied dryly. She shook her head. 'You really think I'm capable of turning to another man so quickly?'

'I don't know what you're capable of anymore. You turned to me without having left the captain.'

Svetlana flushed at the reminder of her manipulative tactics. 'I've apologised, Ivan. You have to understand how horrible I felt. He'd turned all of his attentions to another woman – to a prisoner – without giving me a second glance. I admit, I had no right to involve you, but I wasn't being consciously malicious.'

Ivan's expression softened a little. 'No. I know you're not malicious.'

'Please. Come with me.' She took his hand and started to lead him down a narrow corridor.

'I don't –'

Svetlana cut off his feeble attempt at a protest with another shake of her head. 'It's over between Alexei and me, Ivan. It's been over for a long time. I just didn't realise it.'

'You're telling me you've suddenly fallen out of love with him?' said Ivan, his voice cool. He followed her into a storage closet.

Svetlana closed the door. 'No, that's not what I'm telling you. I was used to loving Alexei. I'd loved him since I was a little girl. When you're so accustomed to something, it can get to the point where you aren't even aware that other things exist.'

Ivan looked at her guardedly. 'Like what?'

'Like what you told me. Being loved in return.' Her gaze slipped down to the hollow of his throat. 'He never loved me, Ivan. I know that. I wanted him to, but no longer. I don't want to be with a man who can dismiss me so easily.'

'And I don't want to be with you just to soothe your damaged ego,' Ivan replied.

Svetlana leant forward and pressed her lips against the warm hollow, before flicking her tongue out to taste his salty skin.

'You don't have to be,' she murmured. 'I know I hurt you. And I know what that feels like.'

His pulse began to beat more rapidly underneath her lips. Svetlana hitched herself up on to a nearby table and put her hands on Ivan's hips. She drew him to her, parting her legs to bring him closer. Her eyelids drifted closed as she pressed a series of kisses up the side of his neck, adoring the familiar scent and taste of him.

'Then what do you want from me?' Ivan asked, his voice sounding slightly thick.

'I want you to love me,' Svetlana murmured, nipping his earlobe between her teeth before sliding her lips over his jaw. Her lips touched his. 'I know you do. I won't hurt you again, Ivan. I might even love you.'

'Might?'

'I don't know,' Svetlana said honestly, her breath brushing his mouth as she slid her tongue over his lower lip. 'I don't know what it feels like to love anyone besides Alexei. And I don't even know if that was love. Maybe it was obsession or infatuation.'

Ivan's breathing grew ragged as he allowed himself to respond to her soft kisses. 'I don't want to be an experiment for you, Svetlana.'

Svetlana spoke between a series of gentle, heart-wrenching ministrations, as her hands slid around his waist.

'No. Not my Ivan.' She slipped her tongue between his teeth, slowly exploring the damp cavern of his mouth. 'I've missed you so much.' Desire broke inside her as she stroked her hands through his hair, tightening her legs around his hips. 'I do want to be with you. I do want to love you.'

Ivan started to return her kisses, putting his hands on her lower back to tug her body against his.

'This has nothing to do with Alexei or anyone else,' Svetlana breathed, guiding Ivan's hands to her breasts as arousal awoke in her body. 'I admit I can't promise you anything, but please take what I'm offering you now.'

'Christ, Svetlana,' Ivan murmured, his final barriers crumbling like a broken sandcastle. 'I love you so much. Just promise me you don't think of him or want him.'

She lifted her head to look into his eyes, determined to leave him in no doubt as to the honesty of her words.

'I do think of him, but it's always in contrast to you. I think about how much kinder you are, how much more caring and intimate. I think about you telling me you love me. I think about his cruel nature and ruthlessness, how he's never said an affectionate word to me, how he has to overpower everyone around him. I don't want him, Ivan. I want you.'

A groan escaped Ivan's lips as he pulled her against him, his mouth coming down hard on hers. Warmth blossomed through Svetlana like a spring bud coming to life. She parted her lips, letting her head fall back as he swept his tongue through her mouth and tangled his fingers in her hair. He pushed his hips closer, his hard bulge nudging against the spreading heat between her legs.

With a gasp, Svetlana pulled away so she could unfasten the buttons of her bodice. Her fingers shook as she pulled down the cups of her brassiere, baring her breasts to Ivan's heated gaze.

'You're so perfect,' Ivan whispered.

He lowered his head to press his lips against her flesh, trailing his mouth down to swirl his tongue around her nipple.

A lightning bolt of desire burned through Svetlana, centring in the growing ache of her sex. Her thighs clenched around his hips, her nerves tightening, body trembling. She rested the back of her head against the wall, but did not close her eyes. She wanted to see everything Ivan did to her and everything she did to him. And she wanted him to know she was watching.

His hands began to push up the folds of her skirt, his palms stroking her thighs as they moved towards her damp heat.

'Lift your hips,' he said, licking the delicate curve of her neck.

She did, and he slid her stockings and drawers down her legs with infinite, reverent care. His eyes blazed with hungry need as he gazed at the spread lips of her sex, his hands urging her thighs further apart. The delicious pain in Svetlana's loins augmented to intense proportions.

'Ivan,' she gasped.

She reached for the buttons on his trousers, her fingers clumsy in her haste. His cock sprung free, and Svetlana enclosed him in the warmth of her hand, rubbing her fingers over the surging length of his erection.

Ivan's chest heaved with the force of his breathing as he positioned himself between her legs. With a groan, he sank into her. Svetlana's muscles clenched around him as they both luxuriated in the ecstasy of their union.

'Now, Ivan,' Svetlana whispered brokenly. 'Now.'

He grasped her hips, pulling her towards him as he began thrusting inside her. He rained kisses over her breasts, circled her nipples with his tongue, and created such a shower of pleasure that Svetlana wanted to cry out her rapture. The tension was unbearable as it coiled around her like a rope and yet she wanted the feeling of Ivan inside her to last forever.

She murmured his name over and over, burning into him the fact that she knew she was with him and that she wanted to be with no one else. She cupped his face in her hands and lifted his eyes to meet hers; she wanted him to see the haze of desire in her blue eyes and know that he was the cause. She pressed her lips against his and as she breathed his name into his mouth the word became a rhythmic incantation timed with the intensity of his thrusts.

And when spasms of rapture shuddered through her as she convulsed around his cock, she clutched him to her and cried out his name, her mouth open against his neck. Ivan's arms went around her tightly, his body embedded in hers, shaking with a climax so potent that she forgot where she left off and he began.

Chapter Fourteen

'Quickly.' Lev motioned for Katya to follow him, reaching behind him to take hold of her wrist.

The cold dawn air bit through the wool of Katya's cloak. Her heart pounded like a drum, her blood hot with adrenaline despite the freezing air. She and Lev hastened around the side of the manor, gathering the shadows against them and hoping their darkened forms would go unnoticed by the other soldiers. Katya knew that Lev was risking himself for her and she was eternally grateful for his assistance.

'Here,' Lev whispered, pushing Katya towards a clump of bushes lining the side of the manor. 'The window is to the right.'

Before she could thank him, he turned and disappeared, his boots almost soundless on the hard-packed dirt. Katya ducked behind the bushes, reaching out to find the window. Small, dirty, edged between the ground and the wall, the window was her only link to her love. Her fingers touched cold glass and iron bars. She slid her fingers along the edge, touching the metal latch. At first, she thought it wouldn't give way. It had probably never been opened and she struggled with it for a heart-stopping minute. Then, finally, the latch twisted underneath her fingers.

Katya pushed open the window with a rush of relief. The cellar room was below, under the manor.

'Nicholas?' She didn't dare speak above a whisper. 'Nicholas?'

She knelt in the dirt and tried to peer down into the cell. Her pulse throbbed so violently she could hear the beat inside her head. Please, please, please, she prayed, let him be all right.

'Nicholas, answer me,' she implored. 'I'm here by the window. Please.'

Her spirits surged when she saw his shadowed figure detach from the opposite wall and move towards the window.

'Katya?'

Tears filled her eyes. She put her hand through the opening and reached down into the darkness. She needed to touch him. 'Yes. Take my hand.'

The instant his strong fingers closed around hers, Katya thought nothing could possibly happen that would ever keep them apart. Not if they held on to each other tightly enough. Lust was one thing. Love was something else altogether. For a long moment, they simply clasped each other's hands.

Then Nicholas's voice drifted up to her. 'Are you all right?'

'Yes. Are you?'

'Yes. I thought he might have hurt you.'

Katya closed her eyes. A lump rose in her throat, and she could barely speak past it.

'No,' she whispered. 'He didn't hurt me.'

'I imagine he didn't,' replied Nicholas.

It was an odd statement and Katya didn't know how to respond. She tightened her fingers around his. 'Nicholas, there's a soldier here who is a Tsarist spy. His name is Lev. He told me the Tsarist soldiers have heard of this encampment and they don't like the idea of an anti-monarchist, Cossack army. They've been planning an attack. I didn't want to tell you until it was certain.'

'They know we're here?'

'Yes. They know there are at least twenty prisoners.'

'Including you?'

Katya frowned. 'Of course, including me. What do you think I am?'

'I don't know. Does the Cossack captain consider you a prisoner?'

Katya went cold inside. Dear God, she thought, what had Alexei told him? 'Nicholas, is there something you're trying to tell me?' she asked.

'No, but is there something you want to tell me? Something you might have omitted?'

She shivered. The coldness from the frozen ground seeped through her skirts and stockings into her very bones.

'Nothing that you want to know,' she whispered.

'On the contrary. I think I do.' His voice was flat but he hadn't let go of her hand.

Katya closed her eyes, leaning her forehead against the windowpane. What could she possibly tell him? How could she explain? 'I didn't have a choice,' she said.

'He told me he didn't rape you.'

A hot flush coloured Katya's cheeks. God, no, she thought. Alexei had done anything but rape her. 'No. He didn't.'

'He seduced you, then?'

'Yes,' she murmured.

Her skin grew warm at the simple reminder of her first night in Alexei's bedchamber, and then self-disgust rose to choke her throat. Nicholas had been the furthest thing from her mind.

'You would go from me to him?' Nicholas's words hardened with jealousy and bitterness. 'Or from him to me?'

'Please don't do this. He could have made my life hell, but he didn't. He could have given me to any number of

251

his soldiers, and there would have been nothing I could do. He could have beaten me, raped me, tortured me. He could have killed me. But, he didn't.'

Nicholas was silent, and then he sounded so pained that Katya felt something break inside her. 'Do you have feelings for him?'

She didn't know what to say, nor would she lie to him, so she told him the truth as best she could. 'Not like what I feel for you.'

'That's not a "no".'

'He saved my life, Nicholas. I was being attacked by a gang of drunken Bolsheviks. If he hadn't stopped, I would be dead.'

'He's a cruel bastard,' Nicholas muttered. 'I can see that. You can't tell me that he has treated you with gentle care for the past months.'

'No. He is difficult. Rough. But, he never hurt me.'

'And you liked it.' His voice was thick with betrayal.

Katya didn't reply. She couldn't.

'Lev says the Tsarist forces should be here within two weeks,' she murmured. 'They're waiting for several of the Revolutionary regiments to return before they attack. I'll try and come back if I hear anything else.'

She squeezed his hand and slipped her fingers out of his, then she hurried back to the manor. She went through the early-morning bustle of the kitchens, ignoring the cook's irritated comment that she had better get to work. Katya swerved around the cook's bulky form and went into the foyer.

She stopped. Something was wrong. The air in the soldiers' workroom crackled with energy; voices rose about the din caused by papers shuffling and people rushing in and out.

Katya caught sight of Ivan. She hurried over to him.

'Ivan, what's happening?'

He gave her a distracted look while he folded communiqués that were to be delivered to Revolutionary and Bolshevik armies. 'You haven't heard? The Tsar and his family have been exiled to Siberia. There is word that they are going to be assassinated.'

Colour drained from Katya's face as she struggled to absorb the words. Exiled? Assassinated? 'But they were supposed to go to London.'

'The British Government withdrew its offer of asylum,' Ivan said, cold satisfaction glinting in his expression. 'They know the revolutionary factions will retain power, and they don't want to risk relations at this stage.'

Stunned, Katya turned away. Her eyes met Lev's from across the room. She desperately wanted to ask him what this meant for the approaching Tsarist armies, but she didn't dare. Instead, she ran upstairs to her bedchamber to prevent herself from going to Alexei and demanding to know what he would now do with her, Nicholas, and the other Tsarist prisoners.

Her body trembled as she sank down on to the bed, covering her face with her hands. It was over. The Tsarist armies couldn't possibly stage an attack on the encampment now. The monarchy would never return to power, and the Communists would rule the country. And she would have to live under such a regime should Alexei refuse to release her.

Katya didn't dare try and go to Nicholas with so much activity amongst the soldiers. The furore in the encampment waned as night fell, but did not die completely. Several late hours slipped past before Katya could work up the courage to approach the Cossack captain. He held her fate in her hands, as he had since the day she arrived. She washed in a tub of cold water before dressing with care in a torn but clean blouse and skirt.

Before she even made her way across the room, the door swung open with a presumption that could only come from one person. Alexei stepped into the room, closing the door behind him. He was wearing his captain's uniform, his tall, imposing frame leaving no person in doubt as to the extent of his authority.

Katya put her hand on a tabletop to steady herself.

Her heart pounded hard. She wanted to confront Alexei about what he had told Nicholas, but that was impossible. The last thing she needed was for the captain to know that she had tried to see Nicholas again.

'It's true, isn't it?' she managed. 'The Romanovs are in exile?'

'That's correct,' Alexei said. He walked into the room as if it were his lair, his fingers working the buttons of his jerkin. 'The monarchy was finished the day the Tsar abdicated the throne. What do you think has been happening all these months? The Russian people no longer want the monarchy to rule Russia.'

Katya fought a wave of despair.

'What are you going to do?' she whispered.

Alexei shot her an amused look. 'Don't you mean "what am I going to do with you?"'

'That, too.'

'I haven't decided yet.' He sprawled out in a chair, stretching his legs out in front of him. 'Go and see if there's any fresh tea, will you? And bring up the bottle of vodka from the study.'

Katya suppressed an urge to tell him to get it himself. She knew she had to avoid angering him. She hurried out the door, down the stairs and past the few soldiers who were still working at the long, scarred tables. After retrieving the vodka from the study she went to the kitchens and started to brew a fresh pot of tea. A few servants continued to cook and clean at one end of the room.

The cellar door was so close. Katya cast it a furtive glance as she stood by the stove, her fingers tapping restlessly on the counter.

'Katya,' whispered a voice in the vast, quiet space.

She whirled around in surprise at the sound of her name. 'Lev!' she exlaimed.

He stood in the shadows of the doorway, obscured from the eyes of the servants. He held a finger to his lips and motioned Katya towards him.

'What?' she whispered frantically. 'What's going to happen now?'

Lev's expression was contained; his eyes were hard and his lips tight.

'They're not going to waste any more time now,' he said, his voice low. 'They'll be here by dawn.'

Katya stared at him in shock. 'They'll attack by dawn?' she gasped.

Lev nodded. 'Stay in your bedchamber. They know you're here, and they know where the prisoners are. Keep away from the windows.'

'But –'

Lev cut her off with a quick shake of his head.

'There is no time left,' he said shortly. 'The Tsarist Army must attack before the Bolsheviks take over. With the Romanovs exiled, we have very few options left. Be prepared. They'll attack now, when the Revolutionary Army least expects it.' He turned and left.

Stunned, Katya absorbed the implications of his words. It was too soon, she felt. As many months as she had been here, and as much as she wanted to be free, she couldn't stop herself from thinking that it was too soon. She had to get to Nicholas again; she had to figure out what she was going to do and where she would go. She had to warn Alexei – Oh, God. Her thoughts skidded to a halt. Warn Alexei?

Alexei. What on earth could she say to him? Her feelings were completely incomprehensible, but the idea of the Cossack captain under siege from Tsarist forces – in danger of being killed – made her feel ill.

With shaking hands, she poured boiling water into a teapot and picked up two tea glasses. She returned to her bedchamber and busied herself with pouring tea, unable to look at Alexei for fear of what she might do.

Finally, when she could stand it no longer, she sat down on the sofa near him. She couldn't tell him the absolute truth. If she did, he would send his soldiers into massive preparation for a defensive attack.

Katya's thoughts and emotions were in such turmoil that she didn't know how to sort them out.

'Alexei, you don't want me with you,' she murmured. 'We both know you're too independent.'

His eyebrows lifted slightly as he drank some tea. 'Oh?'

'Why don't you leave?' Katya asked desperately, her fingers clutching her skirt. 'This army has taken away that which is most important to you. You need to leave.'

His eyes narrowed. 'You're telling me to desert my own army?'

'I'm telling you that you're killing yourself,' Katya said. 'You can go, Alexei. Now. There's no longer any need for a Revolutionary Army, not when there's no hope of the monarchy returning.'

Alexei frowned. 'What's the matter with you?'

Katya stared at him. Tears filled her eyes so suddenly that they shocked her. She didn't know what was the matter with her. She had hated and resented him for so long, and now all she wanted was for him to be free and unharmed.

'Alexei –' She swallowed hard, trying to force away the tears. 'Please listen to me. Please leave. Right now. I'll – I'll go with you, if you want me to.'

Katya couldn't believe the words had come out of her mouth. Confusion gripped her with sharp talons, making her breathing rapid. She went to the *armoire* and opened it, grabbing her valise from the lower shelf.

'We won't need much.' She began tossing items of clothing into the valise, ignoring the tears spilling over on to her cheeks. 'Take some clothing, Alexei, and we'll need food and water. If you know of a place where –'

Suddenly, he was beside her, his strong hands reaching out to grip her shoulders and turn her towards him. His frown deepened as he looked at her anguished expression.

'Stop it,' he commanded.

Katya was shaking so hard that her teeth chattered.

She reached for him blindly, wrapping her arms around his waist as she buried her face against his shirt front. Her twisted, misplaced sense of loyalty terrified her.

'Oh, God, Alexei, I'm so scared.'

His arms went around her, pulling her body against the length of his. The hard warmth of him eased into Katya's shattered nerves, soothing them somewhat. His hand rested on the back of her head, his fingers sliding down to stroke her neck.

'I d-don't know what to do,' Katya stammered, her voice muffled and choked with tears. 'Everything is h-happening all at once, and then you said you weren't going to let me g-go, and I still want you to be f-free, even though you've forced me t-to stay –'

'All right,' Alexei murmured, halting her rambling words. His deep voice reverberated through his chest, sounding unbearably comforting. 'Calm down. I know you're afraid.'

'You don't understand.'

'Come here.' He cupped his hand underneath her chin, lifting her face. His lips brushed across hers lightly, his thumb stroking away the tears on her cheek.

A familiar tingle quivered through Katya. Her hands clutched the front of his shirt. 'Alexei, please. Please let's go. I said I would go with you.'

'You're not going anywhere,' Alexei muttered, his breath warm against her skin as his mouth moved to her cheek. 'And neither am I.'

His tongue flicked out to capture another spilled rivulet of tears. His hands slid up and down her back in reassurance; his soothing murmurs were a solace to her despair.

His tenderness was her undoing. Never had he treated her with such care, as if he were afraid she might break. Her arms tightened around his waist and for a moment she never wanted to let go of him.

'Alexei –' She shivered as his lips brushed hers again. The tactility, sound, taste, and scent of him conspired against her rationalism, and she began to descend into the fathomless waters of their desire.

'It's all right, Katyusha.'

The endearment nearly broke her heart. She slid her hands to the back of his neck, threading her fingers through his hair as she opened her mouth to him. His tongue stroked hers, sensuously exploring the crevices of her mouth, and sent heat pulsing into her. One last time, Katya thought hazily. One last time and then we'll leave.

Alexei clutched Katya's buttocks, his fingers pulling up the folds of her skirt until he could slide his hands around the backs of her thighs. His mouth continued to make love to hers, his husky murmurs easing away her lingering anxiety. He lifted her against him in one movement.

Katya wrapped her legs around his hips, her head sinking into his shoulder as her body cleaved to his. She tightened her thighs around him, feeling his growing hardness pressing between her legs. Turning her head, she touched her mouth to the side of his neck. She shifted and kissed his throat, the hot hollow where his pulse beat rapidly against her lips. Alexei took several long strides to the bed, lowering Katya on to her back as he came over her.

He began to undress her, pressing kisses against her skin as he revealed it, her blouse, skirt, and petticoats falling to the floor like clouds. Alexei continued murmuring low in his throat, but Katya no longer heeded his words. She was conscious only of his tone: a deep, calming rhythm that caressed her with the pattern of his hands, bathing her in the warm light of reassurance.

His body was heavy and hard on hers, his mouth sliding over the slope of her breast to caress the taut peak. Katya gasped, arching her back in offering when he captured her nipple between his teeth. Heat swirled in her loins, draining her of everything except sensation and need. Alexei's touch, the weight of his body, the feel of his lips on her naked skin, ruthlessly drove away all other thoughts.

She revelled in the strength and power of him. Her hands slid up his hard forearms, memorising the sensation of his sinews and muscles under her fingertips. She unfastened the buttons of his shirt and pushed it off, gazing hungrily at his naked chest.

'Lie back,' she whispered, placing her hands on his shoulders.

To her surprise, he complied. His dark eyes were filled with smoky heat as he watched her sit up beside him. For a long moment, Katya simply looked at him, mapping in her mind his scarred torso and the rough planes of his face. She trailed her finger over a scar leading from his shoulder to his breastbone, then bent to follow the line with her lips. Shivers of electric warmth travelled up her arms as she stroked his chest, her fingers tracing every muscle and every bone, sliding down over his ribcage to his flat, hard belly and under the waistband of his trousers.

Her fingers crept lower and brushed against the hot skin of his groin. Alexei muttered a sound of frustration that made Katya's lips curve upward. She quickly rid him of his trousers and underclothes, then wrapped her hand around his erection. As she took him in her hand, she felt the blood pulsing through his engorged cock. She traced the sinuous veins on his shaft, touching the glans with her fingertip. Her other hand slipped down to caress the tight sacs of his testicles. Part of her knew she was burning everything about him in her memory for the day she would leave him forever, while another part of her never wanted that day to dawn.

She looked up at his face, her breathing ragged with desire. Alexei's jaw was rigid, his eyes half-closed, the light in them intense and primitive as he watched her touch him.

Without a word, Katya tugged on his forearms to make him sit up as she settled on her back, her legs parting to accommodate him. Urgency flooded her veins, urgency and desperation. She put her arms around him to draw him to her, her fingernails digging into his skin. His cock throbbed hotly against the moist heat of her sex, barely nudging past the lips of her outer labia. Katya's heart pounded a firestorm through her as her arousal tightened like a strained cord and perspiration dampened her skin.

'Alexei –' She closed her eyes, his name escaping her on a gasp.

Alexei held his upper body off her with his strong arms, his dark gaze scorching her with heat. The head of his cock slipped into her velvety folds, brushing against the aching nub of her clitoris. Katya pushed her body upward, her nerves sensitised to breaking point by the delicious feeling of Alexei's hard knob teasing the pleats of her sex. But then, she could stand it no longer; she was desperate to be filled by him and lost to their passion. She reached down and grasped the base of his cock in her hand, before guiding him to the opening of her body.

He plunged into her with one thrust, immersing his body in hers with a force that made Katya cry out his name. She clutched his shoulders, pulling him down to her so his chest pressed against her breasts. Alexei's hot breath rasped against her skin as he began to move inside her, his shaft pulsating against her inner walls. Katya accepted all of him, craving everything he had to offer her, revelling in the pleasure of their intense union. Her sex swelled with moisture, easing the path of his constant penetration.

She did not know how long their coupling lasted, but it felt like a frenzied eternity. Their bodies damp with sweat, were in constant motion: their chests heaving with ragged breaths as they shifted from position to position. Katya turned so Alexei could thrust into her from behind, or from the side; his cock either sinking into her or being engulfed by her with a fierce, intense rhythm of their own making. Climaxes swept over Katya in unending waves. She pushed Alexei back on the bed and rode him until he clutched her hips and rolled her aside, thrusting into her with powerful strokes, his hands grasping her breasts. Tears of need and arousal coursed down Katya's cheeks, where the salty trails were kissed, licked, and stroked away by the Cossack captain.

Katya was drowning. Her mind only registered various levels of pleasure from extreme to gentle, each level shuddering through her and demanding the attention of her senses. Her entire body became one with Alexei, their legs and arms tangling together, their lips everywhere, their fingers gripping and caressing, their skin creating friction of heat, their breath mingling. Their voices consisted of moans and gasps, Katya choking out the captain's name when the intensity became overpowering.

Finally, after their pleasure had been exhausted to the final surges of rapture, they collapsed on to the bed. Katya fell heavily on top of Alexei's body, her hands burying in his hair as her leg slid between his and her forehead pressed against his chest.

'Oh, God,' she gasped, feeling Alexei's heart beating hard. 'How could this happen? I hated you, Alexei, I didn't want –'

He put his hands on either side of her head, lifting her tear-streaked face from his chest.

'You don't have to like someone to be aroused by him,' he murmured. 'As I told you, pleasure is not necessarily emotion.'

'Don't say that,' Katya whispered. 'Not to me.'

Something flickered in the depths of his eyes that Katya didn't recognise or understand. She eased her body off his, fatigue and satiation nudging her into sleep. As she started to slip into darkness, a nagging thought tickled the back of her mind, leave, yes, we have to leave before they arrive. Before she could grasp on to the urgency of their departure, sleep stole over her.

* * *

Only an hour later, the barrage of gunfire broke through Katya's dreamless slumber. She sat up in confusion as the sharp cracks split through the last threads of sleep. Footsteps rang on the marble corridor, the shouts of soldiers starting to fill the manor. Katya put out her hand automatically for Alexei, but he was already pulling on his trousers, his expression dark.

'What in the hell,' he muttered, stalking towards the window. He looked out the window at the blasts of fire slicing through the encampment.

'Alexei –'

He swore violently, his body tightening with tension as he yanked on his boots.

'Captain!' The bedchamber door flung open, and a frantic young soldier burst into the room. 'Captain, they're attacking! The Tsarists, they broke through the entrances and enclosures, and they've even cut through a –'

Alexei grabbed his shirt and captain's jerkin, storming out the door behind the soldier. The door slammed shut behind him, sounding like a gunshot.

Katya wanted desperately to follow him, but she didn't dare. Heart thudding, she pulled on her dressing gown and went cautiously to the window. The eerie, dawn light cast a reddish glow over the vast encampment, as the roused Cossack soldiers mobilised in defence.

Alexei's Revolutionary soldiers had been extremely well-trained, and the advent of a surprise attack galvanised them into instantaneous action. Volleys of retaliatory gunfire hindered the crushing advance of the Tsarist forces, who lined the boundaries of the encampment both on foot and horseback.

A sickening feeling of nausea mingled with relief swirled in Katya's gut. She moved away from the window and sank down on the floor, hugging her knees to her chest. She didn't know what to do. She wanted to take action, to do something, but she didn't know what. Fear and confusion made her body tremble.

She rested her forehead on her knees, wanting to disappear into herself as the shouts and gunfire continued; the dreaded, choked grunts of dying men, the frantic noises of horses trapped in battle. When Katya could stand it no longer she forced herself to dress and left the room with shallow breath.

Katya slipped into the chaotic corridor, staying close to the wall as she made her way to the stairs. Soldiers thundered past.

'You'd better stay in your bedchamber, miss,' one of the soldiers shouted at her.

Katya ignored him and went downstairs, stunned by the frantic activity in the manor. Soldiers loaded guns and pistols as they rushed outside, the steel blades of sabres flashing in the light.

Careful to stay out of the way, Katya went into the kitchens, where tense, frightened servants boiled pots of water. Katya caught sight of Svetlana. The blonde woman looked terrified, her lips pressed together as she made herb poultices.

'Can I help?' Katya asked.

Svetlana stared at her. 'What?'

'I want to help.'

'I . . . yes. They're trying to bring the wounded men to the area behind the kitchens.' Svetlana waved her hand distractedly towards the door. 'There are dozens of them already. The doctor is desperate.'

Katya picked up a bucket of hot water, a pair of scissors, some rags, and poultices. She hurried outside, her heart lurching at the sight of bleeding, groaning Revolutionary soldiers scattered over the grass like burnt, autumn leaves.

Blocking out her own turmoil, she dropped to her knees next to a Cossack soldier, touching his forehead. His eyelids fluttered open, his eyes dilated and glazed with pain.

'Hang on,' Katya whispered. 'I'm going to help you.'

Blood seeped from a wound on the soldier's thigh. Katya cut away the material of his trousers until she could examine the bullet hole. The wound was violent and ugly, and burnt deep into his muscle.

'You have to remove the bullet.'

Katya looked up at the doctor, who stopped next to her. Deep lines of tension grooved his face. He handed her an instrument that looked like a pair of long tweezers with a scissors handle.

'Me?' Katya choked. 'I can't –'

'You have to,' the doctor said shortly. 'We have too many dying men here. I can't take care of them all. If you're going to help, you have to be prepared to do unpleasant work.' He turned and headed towards another soldier.

Katya stared at her soldier, who returned her look painfully but steadily.

'Go ahead,' he whispered, his voice hoarse and weak. 'I know you're helping me.'

Katya's chest tightened. 'I'm going to hurt you.'

'I know.'

Katya took a deep breath, forcing her hands to remain steady as she probed at his wound with her fingers. She couldn't see the bullet. She picked up the instrument and inserted it carefully into the wound, wincing when the soldier's body jerked in pain. Sweat broke out on her forehead.

'Make it fast,' the soldier hissed. 'Not slow.'

'I'll hold him,' a woman's voice said.

Svetlana knelt on the other side of the soldier, placing her hands flat on his abdomen. Her eyes met Katya's. A strange, inexplicable understanding passed between the two women, as if they realised that their similarities counted for more than their differences.

'I can't see the bullet,' Katya said.

'You'll have to search for it. Hurry. I'm holding him.'

Katya grasped the handle, her muscles tightening as

she pushed the point deep into the wound. The soldier screamed. The sound wrenched Katya's heart. Svetlana held the man down when he tried to recoil from the pain. Palms sweating, Katya concentrated on finding the bullet. Her teeth sank into her lower lip so hard she tasted blood. Finally, the instrument hit something hard. Katya fumbled as she grasped it, feeling a rush of relief as she pulled the bullet from his body.

She tossed the bloody thing aside in disgust and looked at the soldier.

'He's passed out,' Svetlana murmured. 'That's a blessing.'

They cleaned and dressed the man's wound. Katya wrapped a bandage around his thigh, and Svetlana washed his sweaty face. After checking him for other wounds, they moved to the next mutilated man.

Hours passed. Katya and Svetlana tended to soldier after soldier. Katya's hands became steadier, her nervousness abating as she dressed wounds, removed bullets and stitched sabre lacerations. The blasts of gunfire continued to resound in the background like thunder, shouts and yells falling like rain.

The number of maimed Cossacks grew. Eight of them died as Katya attempted to tend to their severe wounds; others begged her to fix them so they could return to the battle. Dusk fell over the encampment before she realised the noise had abated.

'What happened?' she asked.

Svetlana looked up from another wounded soldier. 'I don't know.'

The question was answered by a group of half-a-dozen Tsarist soldiers who came around the side of the manor, their rifles ready for firing.

'Oh, no,' Svetlana whispered. 'No.'

The Tsarists wasted no time in herding the less severely wounded Cossacks to their feet. One of the Tsarists approached Katya and Svetlana.

He looked at Katya. 'You're the prisoner?'

Stunned, Katya nodded.

'Have these bastards hurt you?'

She shook her head.

'You might want to check on your belongings, if you have any,' he said, nodding towards another soldier. 'Yuri will escort you.' He directed his rifle at Svetlana. 'You'll have to come with me.'

Katya and Svetlana exchanged shocked looks.

'Wait.' Katya got to her feet, clenching her trembling hands together. 'There's no reason to imprison her. She had nothing to do with this.'

The Tsarist soldier's eyes narrowed. 'She's a Cossack, isn't she?'

'Yes, but –'

'That's reason enough, then.' With a prod of his gun barrel, the soldier herded Svetlana towards the dilapidated Cossacks.

'Come on, miss,' said the Tsarist called Yuri as he appeared at Katya's side. 'I'll go with you.'

'All right.' Katya felt light-headed and numb as they walked through the manor.

Tsarist soldiers milled about, examining the damage caused by several skirmishes. Paintings and tapestries were slashed by sabre blades, bullet holes embedded in the walls and blood stained the marble floors. Several Cossacks sprawled on the floor and stairs, either in shock or unmoving as they waited for the Tsarists to imprison them.

'What happened to the Cossack captain?' Katya asked Yuri as they walked to her bedchamber.

'Oh, he's chained up in a stable with his own personal guards,' Yuri replied with a grin. 'They've squeezed as many Cossacks as possible into the cellar, and the rest are being transported.'

Katya turned away so he wouldn't see the rush of despair that coursed through her.

'Katya?'

Startled at the sound of her name, she looked up at the

man coming down the corridor towards her. 'Oh, God. Nicholas.'

The sight of him ripped her heart in half. Tears choked Katya's throat. She ran to him as if terrified he would disappear into thin air; then she was in his strong arms. She had come home.

Nicholas tightened his hold on her, lifting her against him. Katya felt a tremor run through his body.

'Are you all right?' he whispered. 'Tell me you are.'

'Yes. I am.' The tears spilled over. She clutched his shoulders and buried her face in his neck. 'Are you?'

'Yes.'

'If you two will stay for the night, we'll help you get to Kostov tomorrow,' Yuri said. 'We want to take care of the prisoners first.'

Nicholas nodded, lowering Katya to the floor. 'Of course. You can leave her with me.'

'That's all right with you, miss?' Yuri asked Katya.

'Yes. Thank you.' Katya took Nicholas's hand tightly in hers, guiding him towards her bedchamber.

She closed the door behind them, so drained and exhausted that she didn't know what to do. Relief swirled in her as she drank in the sight of Nicholas.

'Have you eaten?' she asked.

'Yes. They brought us some food from the kitchens.' Nicholas sank down into a chair by the fireplace, glancing around at the torn, decrepit furnishings. 'This is where you stayed?'

Katya nodded, embarrassed and feeling an odd twinge of guilt that she had her own bedchamber when he was trapped in the cellar. The bed linens were still rumpled and twisted from her powerful coupling with Alexei.

She bit her lip as she thought of the Cossack prisoners.

'Do you want to sleep?' she asked. 'You must be exhausted.'

Nicholas shrugged, reaching for the vodka bottle that still rested on the side table. 'Too much adrenaline, I think.'

'I'll go and make some tea.' Katya picked up the teapot and headed for the door before he could protest.

She hurried downstairs, pausing to stop a Tsarist soldier. 'Please, can you tell me where your captain is?'

'Captain Gordov should be in the library, miss.'

'Thank you.' Katya put the teapot down and went into Alexei's library. A streak of indignation swept through her at the sight of the Tsarist captain seated at Alexei's desk.

'Captain Gordov?'

He looked up. He was a rugged, older man, his dark hair liberally streaked with grey.

'Yes?'

'My name is Katya Leskovna,' Katya said, taking a deep breath as she approached him.

'Ah, yes. We were told of you. I hope you have not been badly treated by these barbarians.'

'On the contrary,' Katya said. 'They treated me quite well.' She paused, then plunged on, knowing she had only one chance. 'Captain Gordov, I have a favour to ask of you.'

'Certainly.'

'I would like to request the release of fifty Cossack prisoners.'

Gordov's head jerked up in shock. 'What?'

Katya repeated her request, much to Gordov's stunned amazement.

'Why on earth would you make such a request?'

'They've been kind to me when they could have killed me,' Katya explained. 'They're a mercenary army, Captain. All they want is to hold on to their land, which isn't an unreasonable objective. Please, you can't –'

'That's the most ridiculous thing I've ever heard,' Gordov snapped, his expression darkening. 'What have they done to you? Release the prisoners! Ha!' He shook his head in disgust.

Katya leant forward over the desk. Her heart was palpitating, but she would do anything at this point. She

268

had come to a deep understanding of her own power over the past months.

'Please, Captain Gordov. I'll do anything.'

'Then you're a foolish woman. Our forces lost lives to these Cossacks.'

'And how many have you killed and captured?' Katya retorted. 'You have hundreds of prisoners. I'm asking that you release fifty.'

She moved around to him. She reached out to push his chair away from the desk and then straddled his thighs. Gordov stared at her in surprise, but Katya saw the dark gleam in his eyes. She almost laughed. Men could be so easily persuaded.

'Please, Captain,' she murmured, pushing her sex down on the crotch of his trousers. 'Only fifty.'

'You're a sneaky, little witch, aren't you?'

'But you want me,' Katya rocked back and forth so he could feel the heat of her sex through his trousers. 'Don't you?'

He didn't respond, and she knew she had him. Smiling, she reached down and rubbed her fingers over his growing bulge.

'How long has it been since you've had a woman, Captain Gordov?'

'Too long,' he growled.

'Well, then, let's not make you wait.' Katya unfastened his trousers, slipping her hand inside to find his prick. Her fingers spread over his length, making him draw in a breath.

'My,' Katya murmured. 'A man like you shouldn't be so long without a woman.'

She stroked his penis until it grew hard in her hand, then pushed Gordov's knees apart and knelt between them. She took his cock in her mouth, sliding her tongue over the shaft, her fingers caressing his testicles as his breathing grew heavy with excitement.

'God,' he gasped. 'You are a witch.'

Katya's lips curved. She flicked her tongue into the

little hole at the head of his cock, moving her hand up and down as his blood started to throb. Gordov began gyrating his hips to work his cock against her hand. When Katya felt him start to tense, she drew back and pressed the tip of his cock together to prevent him from spending.

'Fifty prisoners, Captain.'

'Twenty-five,' he panted. His face was red, his mouth open.

'Fifty,' Katya insisted.

She started on his cock again, taking his testicles into her mouth and rubbing her finger over the secret area underneath his genitals.

'Take off your blouse,' Gordov ordered, his hips still working.

Katya gave him a pointed look. 'Fifty prisoners.'

'Oh, all right, you little slut! Fifty prisoners!'

Katya smiled and began to unfasten her blouse. 'Write it down, please.'

'The hell I –' Gordov's words stopped in his throat when Katya began to refasten her buttons.

'All right!' he snapped, grabbing a pencil from the desk. He scrawled the promise on a piece of paper and handed it to Katya.

She examined the rather violent, but legible handwriting and gave Gordov another smile. 'Thank you, Captain.'

She tucked the paper into her pocket, then resumed removing her blouse. She supposed she could have left him, but that wouldn't be fair.

Gordov's hungry eyes followed every movement as she took off her blouse and brassiere, baring her breasts to him. He reached out to touch them, his fingers moving over the taut peaks of her nipples as Katya returned her attention to his penis. She stroked him and slid him into her mouth as he continued caressing her breasts in fascination. Katya stopped his imminent spending twice more before she let him loose. Gordov groaned loudly, his entire body jerking as his semen spurted out on to Katya's breasts. She stroked him until the final waves ebbed away; then she cleaned herself with the sleeve of his jerkin, which hung on the back of his chair.

'Christ,' Gordov grunted, his head falling back as he recovered. 'Where did you learn that?'

'It's an innate talent, I think,' Katya replied. She buttoned her blouse and smiled at him. 'Shall we choose the prisoners now or later?'

Gordov opened his eyes to frown at her. 'You move fast, don't you?'

'I've discovered it's the only way to get things done,' Katya replied dryly.

She shuffled through the papers on his desk until she found the list of the Cossack prisoners. 'Wounded men, of course, must leave, in addition to a woman named Svetlana and a soldier called Ivan. We must release both older and younger men, as well as servants. The Cossack captain is really of no use to anyone, and I'd also like the release of –'

'No!' Gordov thundered suddenly, as her words penetrated his sated mind. 'Not the captain.'

Katya's heart sank, even though she knew it was a slim possibility. 'Captain Gordov, the Cossack isn't –'

'No,' Gordov interrupted. 'Absolutely not. Anyone but him and his top men. We have too much information to get from them.'

Katya sighed and tried to argue, but Gordov was adamant. In the end, Katya had to be content with a list of fifty prisoners that included neither Alexei nor his immediate officers.

All in all, it wasn't a bad outcome to her efforts. She grinned to herself as she went upstairs. Her power as a woman never ceased to amaze her.

'What's he talking about "gesture of goodwill"?' Nicholas snapped, stalking beside Katya as they went through the corridor. 'Goodwill towards whom? Releasing prisoners is an act of cowardice!'

'Nicholas, calm down,' Katya said. 'There are hundreds of Cossack prisoners.'

She took his arm as they walked out the front door. The sight that greeted them saddened Katya somewhat. The encampment grounds were utterly destroyed: ripped tents, scattered firewood and ash, papers that littered the grass, all mingled with the acrid smell of gunsmoke still lingering in the night air. Horses and Tsarist soldiers roamed about the grounds.

In front of the gate, fifty Cossack prisoners waited for release, shifting and murmuring impatiently. Katya's eyes roamed over them, fixing on a familiar figure.

Svetlana saw her, too. The two women moved towards each other.

'I know it was you.' Svetlana looked haunted. Her face was red from crying and her eyes were lined with dark circles. 'I know you had something to do with this.'

'I hope you'll be all right,' Katya murmured.

Svetlana tried to smile, gesturing to the soldier who stood a short distance away. 'Ivan and I are going to try and go to Petrograd. He should find work there, either with the police or another regiment.'

Her gaze went to Nicholas, eyes widening with recognition. Nicholas gave her a slight smile.

'You're not hurt?' he asked, his voice oddly gentle.

Svetlana shook her head as her expression softened. Something passed between them that Katya didn't like. A sudden rustle of jealousy stirred in her gut.

'Thank you.' Svetlana tore her gaze away from Nicholas and returned it to Katya. 'Ivan thanks you.'

Katya wished her luck. She and Nicholas watched as the gates opened, and the Cossacks streamed out towards the roads and freedom. When they had all been released, Katya and Nicholas turned back towards the manor.

'You know Svetlana, do you?' Katya asked, casting Nicholas a sideways glance.

A dull flush covered his handsome features as he came to a sudden halt. 'No – I mean, not really –' he stammered.

Katya reached out and put her hand on his jaw.

'Stop,' she said softly. 'Don't tell me. I don't want to know.'

Nicholas pulled her into his arms, holding her body against his.

'I love you,' he said. 'I've always loved you, only you. You know that, don't you?'

Katya wrapped her arms around his neck, buried her face in his shoulder, and nodded.

Chapter Fifteen

Katya found the keys in a guard's pocket. At three o'clock in the morning she crept outside with a bottle of vodka in her hand. She made her way across the ruined grounds to the stables, clutching her cloak around her. Several horses lingered among the rubble. Katya grasped the reins of a strong, grey stallion and urged him forward. Right before she reached the stables she tied the reins to the branch of a tree.

The two guards were sprawled at the entrance, busy playing cards. They looked up suspiciously as she approached.

'I've brought you some vodka,' Katya told them, knowing her features were obscured by the hood of her cloak. 'I thought you might need it to warm you.'

'Who are you?'

'Just a friend.' She handed the bottle to one of the guards.

He took it and greedily drank the potent alcohol. When both guards returned their attention to drinking and cards, Katya crept a short distance away to wait.

The wait was longer than she expected, but eventually one guard fell into an alcoholic sleep and the other went off to relieve himself. Her heart in her throat, Katya ran forward and knelt next to the drunk guard. Terrified that she would wake him, she began to feel his pockets for the keys. After what felt like an eternity, she located one in his shirt pocket. Katya held her breath, eased her hand carefully into his jacket, and removed the key. The shuffling noise of the returning guard broke through her caution; she scrambled to her feet and yanked open the stable doors just enough to slip inside.

She stopped and tried to let her eyes adjust to the darkness. The musky smell of horses and hay filled her nostrils. She made out the shapes of horse stalls, but all were empty.

'Alexei?' Katya whispered. Her voice sounded like an echo against the wooden structure. She walked into the stable, hearing her own breathing. She peered into the stalls, passing three before she finally saw his shadowed frame sitting on the ground, leaning against a stall partition.

'Alexei.' With a muffled murmur of relief, Katya entered the stall and dropped to her knees next to the captain. 'Thank heavens I found you.'

He looked at her, his dark eyes glittering. 'I thought you'd gone,' he said.

'No. I'm leaving tomorrow.'

Alexei shifted. The dim light glinted on the heavy chains that linked him to the wall. Manacles were clamped cruelly around his wrists. Katya's heart wrenched violently.

'I'm sorry,' she whispered. 'I'm so sorry they've done this to you.'

'I had to surrender.' His voice was heavy with self-disgust. 'We'd lost too many men. They outnumbered us.'

'Quick.' Katya grasped his arm, her fingers feeling for the lock on the cold, metal manacle. 'I have the key, Alexei, but we don't have much time. One of the guards is asleep. I hope the other one followed.'

'How many of my men are prisoners?'

'I don't know,' Katya replied. 'Fifty men and women were released. Most of the soldiers have already been transported elsewhere, and the rest are locked up in the cellar and the other stable. You can't save them, and you can't try and form a counter-attack. Don't even think about that.'

She fumbled to fit the key into the lock, praying it was the correct one. The lock gave after several frantic twists. Katya hurried to unlock his other wrist, then clutched his hand in hers.

'At the far end of the estate, there's an opening in the enclosure,' Katya whispered. 'The Tsarists cut through the bars. You can escape from there.'

She led him to the stable doors, peeking around the corner at the guards. Dismay filled her when she saw that one of them was still awake.

Alexei put his hands on Katya's hips, urging her to the side. He pushed open the door.

'What —' said the startled guard.

Alexei's fist shot out and slammed into the man's temple. The guard let out a choked moan before he collapsed. They stepped outside, and Katya replaced the key in the sleeping guard's pocket.

'This way,' she whispered.

She ran to the tree and untied the horse, swinging into the saddle before Alexei could stop her. He vaulted up behind her and reached around to take the reins.

'The opening is on the south side,' Katya said. 'Near the cluster of juniper bushes. One of the soldiers explained the mechanics of their attack to me.'

Alexei nudged the horse forward with a minute shift of his legs. The animal plodded along quietly as they moved away from the manor. Katya's blood pounded through her veins, her nerves taut with adrenaline and the fear of what would happen if they were caught. She settled her back against Alexei's chest. The strange irony of the situation hit her then: how she had come to this place in the same manner. Only then, Alexei had captured her. And now, she was helping him escape.

Katya shook her head to clear her disconcerted thoughts and pointed south. Alexei urged the horse into a slow trot the further they went, and then they started to gallop.

Cold wind whipped against their faces as they stormed over the hills of the estate. Trees passed in a blur, coating the world in a series of dark shadows. The far reaches of the grounds were deserted save for grass, trees, and the occasional wild animal. Alexei's hand slipped around Katya's waist to hold her against him as they neared the estate's enclosure.

Reining the horse to a halt, Alexei jumped off and went to the fence. The Tsarists had sliced a portion off and pulled it aside as if it were a gate – leaving room for horses and riders to invade the Cossack territory.

Alexei swore, his muscles tensing as he saw evidence of the ease of the attack. While he was turned away from her, Katya reached into her pocket and removed an emerald and diamond necklace that had been part of her royal jewellery. She dropped the necklace into the saddlebag and slipped off the saddle.

She walked to Alexei and put her hands on his back.

'Alexei, it's over. There's nothing more you could have done.' Her chest constricted. 'You have to save yourself.'

He turned, his features hard and uncompromising even in the soft moonlight. 'You knew, didn't you?'

'Don't ask me that,' Katya whispered.

'Why did you want me to leave?'

She stared at him, her entire soul aching. She wanted to cry, but the tears choked her throat. How could she explain? What could she possibly say to make him – to make herself – understand why she was reacting this way?

'I don't know,' she murmured. 'I want to be free. And I want you to be free.'

'Come here.' He grasped her shoulders and pulled her

towards him, lowering his head to press a fierce kiss on her lips.

Arousal sparked in Katya's body as if the captain had struck a match. She parted her lips desperately and her hands tightened on the material of his shirt. She drank in the taste and feel of him as their tongues danced together and electric currents rippled through her body. Her sex dampened at the sensation of Alexei's body pressing against hers, her mind spinning with the knowledge of the pleasure they could bring each other.

'Quick,' she gasped, unable to stop herself from indulging in their powerful desire one last time. 'Alexei –'

'Yes,' he murmured against her lips. 'I'm here.'

'I want –'

'I know. And I want you.'

He had never said that to her before. Katya melted into his embrace as he lowered her to the ground. Her arms came around his back to hold him tightly. Alexei pushed his hands underneath Katya's skirt. His fingers clutched the fabric of her drawers as he pulled them down her legs. His breath was hot on her neck; his muscles tense with urgency.

Katya tugged frantically on the buttons of his trousers, her pulse pounding violent blood through her veins as she became submerged by the need to have him inside her again. His cock was already hard and throbbing; the skin hot underneath her hand. She ran her fingers over his shaft to the tip, searing the sensation of him into her mind. Alexei drew in a sharp breath as she touched him. Her hand tightened on his length in a silent and unmistakable entreaty.

She opened herself to him completely as he slid into her, stretching and exposing her beyond the boundaries of pleasure. A moan escaped Katya's lips. Alexei's body thrust into hers again and again, stimulating a swirl of desire that tightened her every muscle. Alexei slid his hands underneath her, clutching her bottom as she lifted her hips to meet his forceful thrusts. A delicious kind of pain began to wind in Katya's lower body, building pressure that threatened to overflow at any second. Her hands grasped Alexei's forearms. Her consciousness of his body, of the way he felt inside her, heightened to unbearable proportions.

Alexei moved his hand to the sensitive nerves of her clitoris, stroking his fingers around the nub before touching it directly. The one touch ignited a path of firey convulsions through Katya's body, making her cry out his name as rapture shuddered along her nerves. Alexei's cock slammed into her again and again before his hoarse groan was followed by a climax so powerful that it sent another wave of pleasure into Katya.

Breathing hard, Alexei lowered his mouth to Katya's as she fought a sudden onslaught of tears.

'I don't understand this,' she whispered hoarsely. 'I don't know if I ever will.'

The corners of Alexei's mouth turned upward as he gazed at her, stroking a finger down her cheek.

'Oh, you will, my Katya,' he murmured. 'You will.'

Katya stared at him for a moment, pained at the thought that she would never see him again. She trailed her fingertips over the austere lines of his face, running her forefinger over his eyebrows, touching his lower lip with the pad of her thumb.

'You have to go,' Katya murmured. 'Once the guards discover that you've escaped, they'll raise hell to find you.'

They parted, straightening their clothes. Alexei grasped Katya's hand to help her to her feet, then he turned and took the reins of the horse.

He swung into the saddle in a motion of pure, masculine grace. Katya looked up at him. She had first encountered him this way: him astride a stallion as if he and the animal were one being, shadows shifting over his figure, his expression inscrutable, black eyes gleaming as he watched her. Like a dark lord from the depths of Hades.

'Goodbye, Alexei,' Katya said, her throat closing over the words.

Alexei reached down suddenly and clasped his arm around her waist. In one movement, he lifted her off the ground and crushed her against his chest so hard that she could feel his heart beating. His mouth came down fiercely on hers, his tongue plunging into her mouth as if, by some savage instinct, he was claiming her, possessing her.

For a heart-stopping instant, Katya thought he was going to carry her off with him. And, at that instant, she didn't care. Her hands clutched at his arms as the universe spun around them, leaving nothing but overwhelming heat and desire. Alexei scorched her with his final kiss and it was then that Katya knew the Cossack captain would always remain in a dark, cryptic part of her soul.

He lowered her to the ground as suddenly as he had lifted her from it. And then he turned, digging his heels into the stallion's flanks as he guided the animal through the enclosure opening and into the beyond. Within seconds, he urged the horse into a gallop, and then he was gone.

Alexei's departure was not discovered until early the next morning. Katya was in her bedchamber, packing her few belongings when Nicholas strode into the room.

'He's gone,' he said. 'The Cossack captain. He escaped last night.'

'Did he?' Katya folded her ragged skirts, aware that Nicholas was watching her. 'How?'

'They don't know. The guard still has the key.'

'Are they looking for him?'

'Yes, but he's probably long gone by now.'

Katya placed her skirts into her valise and reached into the *armoire* for her remaining clothes. 'Well, that's none of our concern anymore. Once we get to the Kostov train station, we'll be on our way.'

Even if they did discover that she had planned the

280

captain's escape, there was little they could do about it. She looked up and met Nicholas's gaze. His eyes were narrow with suspicion.

'Katya, did you –,' His voice broke off and he shook his head, a hint of despondency glinting in his expression. 'Never mind. I don't really want to know.'

Tenderness and adoration filled Katya's heart. She walked across the room to him and wrapped her arms around his waist. Her feelings for him were so pure and uncomplicated. After months spent in a sexual labyrinth of darkness, confusion, and turmoil, she welcomed the resurgence of love for her soldier.

'None of it matters,' she whispered. 'I do love you. Please believe me.'

'I will.' Nicholas brushed his lips across hers. 'One of the Tsarists gave me contacts to help us get to Istanbul.'

Katya nodded. She knew they would be fine. She still had most of her jewellery, the sale of which would keep them comfortable for years. All they had to do was leave the country safely.

'Several people might be able to help locate your relatives,' Nicholas said. He stroked his hand through her hair. 'You don't regret anything, do you?'

Katya considered his question. 'Only that we were ever apart.'

'What about him?' His voice tightened.

'I was his captive,' Katya said. She wondered if she could ever fully explain it, but she wasn't certain she even wanted to. 'It was like being trapped in a thunderstorm. Terrifying and brilliant all at once. And then, when it's over, the darkness lifts and you realise you couldn't possibly live in such turmoil forever. You don't want to. You want light and clarity. You want love.'

Nicholas looked at her for a moment. 'You know you have mine.'

'Yes.' She smiled at him. 'You'll always have mine.'

His mouth came down on hers in a kiss that spoke of trust and devotion. They held each other tightly, each one knowing that the strength of their emotions would never fail to submerge any hidden uncertainties.

'I'll meet you in the foyer,' Nicholas said, lifting his head with reluctance. 'There's a motor car outside that will take us to the station.'

He kissed her again and left the bedchamber.

With a lighter heart, Katya turned back to her packing. She shook out one of her dresses and winced when something sharp sliced painfully into her forefinger. Blood oozed out of a small cut. Frowning, she felt carefully in the pocket of the dress. Her hand closed around the handle of a dagger.

Alexei's dagger. Katya pulled it out and stared down at the blade; sunlight glinted off the metal. She touched the Cyrillic engraving on the handle: Alexei's initials. The silver letters mirrored the light and Katya's eyes. Understanding broke through her remaining defences as she stood there looking at the dagger.

In some strange, enigmatic way, Alexei had freed her. This was what he had meant so long ago, when in the depths of the cellar, he had whispered prophetic words to her. *One day, Katya, you will realise that the exploration of your sensuality requires honesty. Only then will you know what so many others have failed to discover.*

The Cossack captain had taken Katya's mysteries and forced her to confront them, to confront herself, in ways that had changed her forever. She had revealed the darkest secrets of her soul to him, and Katya knew now that such release could only be followed by liberation. For what better way to revel in the power of freedom than by obtaining a deep awareness of oneself?

An odd peace stole over her, alleviating her lingering anxiety and confusion. She located the dagger sheath in her night table and slipped it over the blade; then she put the weapon in her valise. Taking a deep, calming breath, Katya looked around the bedchamber for the last time. And then she left to find her love.

* * *

A tall Cossack sat astride a stallion on an embankment opposite the crowded platform of the Kostov train station. His gaze was fixed on a woman who stood alone, holding a single valise. Her hair shifted loosely around her shoulders and she reached up to run her fingers through the black strands.

The Cossack's dark eyes shifted briefly to the approaching train. Billows of steam rose like great phantoms as the waiting passengers stirred. The Cossack returned his gaze to the woman. She turned to look behind her just as a man slipped through the crowd to her side and reached out to carry her valise. The Cossack watched as the woman spoke to the man and then placed her hand on his arm. She gave him a smile as they prepared to board.

The train settled to a halt in front of the platform, blocking the Cossack's view of the woman. After several minutes, the engines came to life again and eased back into motion like an awakening beast. The platform was now deserted. The Cossack watched the train move away until only a spiral of steam hung suspended against the sky.

And then the Cossack turned, urging the stallion forward with greater and greater speed. Within minutes, they were soaring over the grassy embankments until both horse and rider had vanished into the immense expanse of Russian land.

Visit the Black Lace website at
www.black-lace-books.com

**FIND OUT THE LATEST INFORMATION AND TAKE
ADVANTAGE OF OUR FANTASTIC FREE BOOK OFFER!
ALSO VISIT THE SITE FOR . . .**

- All Black Lace titles currently available
  and how to order online
- Great new offers
- Writers' guidelines
- Author interviews
- An erotica newsletter
- Features
- Cool links

BLACK LACE — THE LEADING IMPRINT OF WOMEN'S SEXY FICTION

TAKING YOUR EROTIC READING PLEASURE TO NEW HORIZONS

LOOK OUT FOR THE ALL-NEW BLACK LACE BOOKS – AVAILABLE NOW!

All books priced £7.99 in the UK. Please note publication dates apply to the UK only. For other territories, please contact your retailer.

THE SILVER COLLAR
Mathilde Madden
ISBN 978 0 352 34141 9

Eleven years ago a powerful ancient werewolf ripped Iris's life apart. One full moon night it attacked the two people she loved most in the world, killing her twin brother Matthew and leaving her boyfriend Alfie changed forever. Iris and Alfie vowed revenge on the Beast, but when Alfie began to show a twisted loyalty to the creature who had made him, Iris lost him too.

Now, Alfie is back in Oxford where Iris - still haunted by her dead brother - is heading up the Vix, a shadowy organisation dedicated to killing his kind. But Alfie needs Iris's help or what the Beast did to him that night may yet prove fatal. His body is fragmenting - the rules that govern his transformations into a wolf are changing. His only hope of keeping his deadly beast under control is the Silver Collar - an ancient artifact currently owned by the Vix. But Iris isn't prepared to help Alfie secure it until he agrees to defy the rules of his kind and help her avenge Matthew's death.

Alfie and Iris both think that what happened between them eleven years ago has destroyed the love and trust they had for each other forever. The Silver Collar shows them that they're both wrong.

SPLIT
Kristina Lloyd
ISBN 978 0 352 34154 9

A visit to Heddlestone, a remote village in the Yorkshire moors, changes librarian, Kate Carter's life. The place has an eerie yet erotic charge and when Kate is later offered a job in its puppet museum, she flees London and her boyfriend in order to take it.

Jake, the strange and beautiful curator and puppeteer, draws her into his secluded sensual world, and before long she's sharing his bed, going deeper into new and at times frightening explorations of love and lust. But Kate is also seduced by Eddie, Jake's brother, and his wild Ukrainian wife, and she becomes tangled in a second dark relationship. Split between the two men, Kate moves closer to uncovering the truth behind the secrets of Heddlestone, ever sensing danger but not knowing whether the greatest threat comes from ghosts or reality.

WILD KINGDOM
Deanna Ashford
ISBN 978 0 352 33549 4

Salacious cruelties abound as war rages in the mythical kingdom of Kabra. Prince Tarn is struggling to drive out the invading army while his bethrothed - the beautiful Rianna - has fled the fighting with the mysterious Baroness Crissana.

But the baroness is a fearsome and depraved woman, and once they're out of the danger zone she takes Rianna prisoner. Her plan is to present her as a plaything to her warlord half-brother, Ragnor. In order to rescue his sweetheart, Prince Tarn needs to join forces with his old enemy, Sarin, whose capacity for perverse delights knows no civilised bounds.

Coming in December 2007

THE SILVER CROWN
Mathilde Madden
ISBN 978 0 352 34157 0

Every full moon, Iris kills werewolves. It's what she's good at. What she's trained for. She's never imagined doing anything else . . . until she falls in love with one. And being a professional werewolf hunter and dating a werewolf poses a serious conflict of interests. To add to her problems, a group of witches decides she is the chosen one - destined to save humanity from the wolves at the door - while her new boss, Blake, who just happens to be her ex-husband, is hell-bent on sabotaging her new reltionship. All Iris wants is to snuggle up with her alpha wolf and be left alone. He might turn into a monster once a month, but in a lot of ways Iris does too.

MINX
Megan Blythe
ISBN 978 0 352 33638 5

Miss Amy Pringle is pert, spoilt and spirited when she arrives at Lancaster Hall to pursue her engagement to Lord Fitzroy, eldest son of the Earl and heir to a fortune. The Earl is not impressed with this young upstart and sets out to break her spirit through a series of painful and humiliating ordeals.

The trouble for him is that she enjoys every one of his 'punishments' and creates havoc at the Hall, provoking and infuriating the stuffy Earl at every opportunity while indulging in all manner of naughtiness below the stairs. The young Lord remains aloof, however, and, in order to win his affections, Amy sets about seducing his well-endowed but dim brother, Bubb. When she is discovered in bed with Bubb and one of the servant girls, how will father and son react?

Black Lace Booklist

Information is correct at time of printing. To avoid disappointment, check availability before ordering. Go to www.black-lace-books.com. All books are priced £7.99 unless another price is given.

BLACK LACE BOOKS WITH A CONTEMPORARY SETTING

BLACK LACE BOOKS WITH AN HISTORICAL SETTING

BLACK LACE BOOKS WITH A PARANORMAL THEME

BLACK LACE ANTHOLOGIES

BLACK LACE NON-FICTION

To find out the latest information about Black Lace titles, check out the website: www.black-lace-books.com or send for a booklist with complete synopses by writing to:

Black Lace Booklist, Virgin Books Ltd
Thames Wharf Studios
Rainville Road
London W6 9HA

Please include an SAE of decent size. Please note only British stamps are valid.

Our privacy policy
We will not disclose information you supply us to any other parties.
We will not disclose any information which identifies you personally to any person without your express consent.

From time to time we may send out information about Black Lace books and special offers. Please tick here if you do <u>not</u> wish to receive Black Lace information. ❏

Please send me the books I have ticked above.

Name ....

Address ....

....

....

....

Post Code ....

Send to: Virgin Books Cash Sales, Thames Wharf Studios, Rainville Road, London W6 9HA.

US customers: for prices and details of how to order books for delivery by mail, call 888-330-8477.

Please enclose a cheque or postal order, made payable to Virgin Books Ltd, to the value of the books you have ordered plus postage and packing costs as follows:

UK and BFPO – £1.00 for the first book, 50p for each subsequent book.

Overseas (including Republic of Ireland) – £2.00 for the first book, £1.00 for each subsequent book.

If you would prefer to pay by VISA, ACCESS/MASTERCARD, DINERS CLUB, AMEX or SWITCH, please write your card number and expiry date here:

....

Signature ....

Please allow up to 28 days for delivery.